...to my daughters

who sometimes put up with me...

The Divine Masquerade Series

The Gods Among Us

Whom the Gods Destroy

The City of God

Lords and Ladies of the Zoo

House	Office	City	Children	Ships
			WATER	
<u>Uncial</u>	*Chancellor*	Greenstone	Uncial IV, Eunice	
<u>Catagen</u>	*Commodore*	Catagen City	William, Dewey, Tiberius	*The Three*
Duma	*W. Northern Sea*	McFarland		*Hood*
Med		Navarre	Mark, Maureen	
Cannes		Calabria	Anthony, Amelia	
Joculo		Kelly Tree	Joculo IV, Janice	
			FIRE	
<u>Excelsior</u>	*Defender of Titan*	Turner Hill	Alexander, Adriana	
<u>Quid</u>	*Treasurer*	Greenstone		
Corsair	*W. Southern Sea*	Arcadia		*Yamato*
Hyperius		Hadrianus		
Arien		Alicante		
Salamandro		Sunna	Corona	
			AIR	
<u>Gemello</u>	*Defender of Twins*	Geminus	Borelo	
<u>Miser</u>	*Judiciary*	Greenstone		
Tel	*W. Eastern Sea*	Coldwell	Telmar	*Argo*
Djincar		Misty Dale	Djincar IV	
Liberion		Astraea		
Ganyme		Ganymii		
			EARTH	
<u>Gauntle</u>	*Master of the Pass*	Quartz	Oliver, Genevieve	
<u>Jingo</u>	*Marshall*	Greenstone		
Rance	*W. Western Sea*	Harper		*Bismarck*
Zeliox		Pythe	Clovis	
Oxymid		Capro Bay	Ophelia	
Virgon		Anatolia	Vigo	
			DEME	
<u>Tzu</u>	*Master of the Lone One*	Shangri-La		

How many Ages hence
Shall this our lofty scene be acted over
In states unborn and accents yet unknown!

William Shakespeare
English playwright
circa 1600: Earth Standard

Prologue

Tartarus

"How could they end up at the wrong planet?" Head of the marine biology department, Dr. Lily Tidewater achieved her life's ambition by being a perfectionist. She hated incompetence of any sort. She hated the military even more. "Those ignorant fly-boys! How could they make such a huge mistake?"

"Ah," soothed Dr. Aquilo Stromboli. Born among the Aeolian Islands of Sicily, the good-looking Italian was a renowned expert in aeronautical physics. "There was always a risk – we knew that from the beginning."

But Lily Tidewater bristled with rage. *Forty years in space,* she riled. *Forty years! And they couldn't find the right planet?* The squeaking of her shoes on the cold, steel deck made her yearn for the balmy waters of her Carolina home. "Is your Environment Pod ready to go?" she demanded of the Russian geologist.

"Yes," said Dr. Ferris Terraspol in his trademark monotone. As he never fully mastered the English language, he spoke slowly and deliberately, carefully considering every word. "All…are ready. You…know that."

"What…do…you have…in mind?" teased Stromboli, casting a gleeful frown at the geologist. His deprecating portrayals of the disliked Russian were quite popular.

"You know what I have in mind," said Tidewater, hating the necessities that led her to this place. "We're scientists, not soldiers. Our goal is to colonize a world, any world. The one below us looks just fine."

"The planet is ideal," said Dr. Yingqui Vitalis. A native of Hong Kong, she was a medical doctor who specialized in biogenetics. Her father was a British surgeon; her mother, a famous acupuncturist from the Guangdong province of China. "Class 'M.' Unpopulated. We couldn't hope for much better."

"You heard the Captain," said Dr. Kendal Blaine. She was a geothermal engineer. A beautiful redhead from Mount St. Helens, she had a fiery temper and a brat for a son. "He's determined to continue the military objectives."

"Jump to another system?" scolded Tidewater. "We don't have enough fuel for that."

"I know a helluva lot more about fuel than you do."

"Do you really?" growled Tidewater. She cowed her rival with a dismissive glare before turning on the others. "This mission is a failure. Any fool can see that. It's best we salvage what we can…"

But she was interrupted by a disaster far worse than a navigational error.

The floor jumped, then dove; their celestial ark shuddering from the meteor that just hit it. Lily Tidewater knew a rare moment of panic as she was thrown upon the ceiling. Splayed aloft against the cold hard steel, she felt the hum of the engines whirr into action – in a valiant effort to keep *Tartarus* suspended in high orbit.

Yet nothing could stop the listing that spun her towards her doom.

"What happened!?!" cried Vitalis as she tumbled upon the wall.

"We're all going to die!" screamed Stromboli.

Sirens blared their unneeded warning – a wailing, pitiless lament. The shrieks of children haunted the hallways – ode to a dying ship.

"This is the Captain," said a voice through wounded *Tartarus*. "General Quarters! General Quarters! All hands, man your duty stations!"

"That doesn't tell us much."

"Maybe it wasn't too bad."

Decompression explosions rumbled below them, spilling life-giving oxygen into the empty void of space. Stumbling along her spiraling universe – heedless of the thunder – the biologist reached an access port to the central computer. The floor was briefly the floor again as she typed "DAMAGE REPORT" on the tiny keyboard. A schematic of the ship appeared, angry red blotches decorating the screen.

"Di' a` mio!" muttered Stromboli. "The port bow has been completely obliterated."

Lily Tidewater calculated how many people just died. *At least three hundred, possibly four.* Grateful her quarters were on the starboard side, she called her twenty-year-old daughter. "Teresa!" she demanded of her Comm Unit. "Where are you?"

"In the Aqua-Environmental Pod – been listening to the military channels. Meteor strike – caught in the gravity well – they're going to try a forced landing – large continent – southern hemisphere."

My God! thought Tidewater. *Everyone on this ship is going to die!* "Prepare to jettison the Pods."

2

"Already started the countdown sequence. Just waiting for you and Dad."

"Your father!" she swore. *That man! He'll probably insist on staying with the ship.* "Input landing coordinates to all four Pods."

"Done. Selected suitable landing sites – a small archipelago – three point seven hundred miles east-northeast of the predicted landing coordinates."

"You mean crash coordinates," griped Blaine.

"Input the coordinates. Continue the countdown. Tidewater out." Snapping her Comm Unit closed, she glared at her startled colleagues. "Any more discussion about mission objectives?"

Before they could answer, their whirling world went black – plunging them into total darkness. A moment later, the dull red glow of the emergency lights cast a pall upon their ghost-like faces.

Tidewater decided for the rest of them. "Into your Environment Pods! All of you. Teresa's laid in the landing coordinates. Use the discreet frequency to contact each other once you're on the planet surface. Collect what personnel you absolutely need, but do *not* alert the crew. I want every pod jettisoned in ten minutes."

"What about my people?" said the doctor. "Sickbay doesn't have a Pod."

"You can come in mine," offered Stromboli.

"Ten minutes," barked Tidewater, "not a moment longer."

"What about the rest of the crew?" asked Blaine.

"They'll have to take their chances with the ship."

"Who died and made you God?"

Tidewater balled her fists at Blaine. "We can't save everyone! You know that! If you want to stay with the ship, fine. Otherwise, you'll do as I say."

The redhead glowered, retreated a step, then donned an angry scowl.

The others nodded their humble heads, acquiescing to Tidewater's demands.

They'd do what she ordered; she'd always been their leader…

…I wonder where I'm leading them now?

"See you on the surface."

Chapter One

Greenstone

Born upon the Egg,
Alone, among the fishes of the Sea
And Her name was Diandre
Yet She knew it not...

"Lay of the Deluge"

Proteus V

Pallas was an ordinary girl – though no one knew it. She came from an ordinary fishing village, which lay upon the gentle shores of the Eastern Sea...

Yet my ordinary days were far behind me. Six months ago I rode a dolphin, outwitted a lady of the *Zoo*, and escaped an army of soldiers. A week ago I beat up a prince and tamed a shrew...

...and just last night I escaped the fabled fury of the Lord God Mulciber.

Why did a God want me dead? Even I didn't know. I was just a slave, after all, unlearned in the ways of heaven. But I knew someone who did.

Othello!

My fluffy mentor had been the evil God's pet. *Didn't my kidnappers mention a spy? Isn't it logical that he's the mole?*

But that didn't make sense. *Othello taught me how to read,* a talent forbidden by the mighty Gods. If the cat truly wanted to kill me, he unwittingly orchestrated my miraculous escape.

Because reading's the only thing that's kept me alive!

So I wondered. Was Othello a friend...

...or a conniving little spy?

5

The trip to the quay was filled with whispers, a fleet of sailors leading my way. The ride on the gig was hushed and muted. Even the Commodore had nothing to say.

I felt imprisoned. Not by the loyal mariners, but by my own irreverent fame. I gulped with relief when we reached the *Yorktown*.

The coxswain blew a horn pipe. Sailors lined the prow. Curious and eager, they stood and saluted.

"Mistress of the Sea, arriving!" shouted Mr. Rees.

I feebly boarded the flagship. Mariners ogled and stared. Their mood was ominous, sacred. I wished that someone would break the stillness when the Twins embraced me with an earnest hug.

"Pallas!" popped Lucy. "You gave me such a fright!"

"Honestly," pouted Casey. "Why couldn't we come along?"

I bit my lip, willing myself not to cry.

Buoyed by the Twin's excitement – emboldened by their friendly embrace – the sailors peppered me with their many questions…

"What happened, Mistress?" asked Mr. Rees.

"Were those chariots from Volcano?" asked Mr. Gridley.

"There was Fire in the forest…"

"Rain on a cloudless night…"

"Was it really the Lord God Mulciber?!"

Oliver silenced them with a wave of his hand, with surprising authority for such a young midshipman. Yet he, too, entered a plea. "Can you tell us, brave Mistress?"

The fervent sailors tightened their ring, as if desperate for their Goddess to speak. But I was too emotional for anything but tears. Grimacing my face, I fought my craven fears.

"Oh, bosh!" burst Lucy, as gay as a sprite. Hiding my face in a protective hug, she whispered, "Can't have you blubbing."

Casey answered in a worried hush, "Not in front of the crew." Marring her face into a vicious scowl, she rounded on the midshipman. "Honestly, Oliver! Can't you tell the poor thing's tired?"

"I…I didn't mean," he stammered.

"She's going to our cabin to freshen up," said Lucy. "Straightaway, without all of your bothersome questions."

"And do tell Cook to prepare a meal."

"Something scrumptious and light."

"Of course," he muttered. "Only the Commodore," he motioned to the soundless lord, "ordered me not to leave her alone, under any circumstances."

"She won't be alone," riled Casey.

"She'll be with *us* girls."

"You know what I mean," he said.

"Oliver!" said Lucy. "The child just battled the Volcano God. She did it on her own."

Casey flashed an impish smile. "Do you honestly believe she needs a git like you to protect her after she just got the better of a God?"

Oliver looked to the Old Man. The Commodore nodded his wordless approval.

"Very well," said Oliver. "If you will escort the Mistress to her cabin, I shall arrange for her supper."

"And don't forget ice cream," said Lucy, "She's especially fond of chocolate."

"Yes, your majesty," he said with a bow.

They dragged me to the safety of their splendid cabin.

"Please Pallas, tell us what happened!"

"And don't skimp on the slightest detail!"

But I did not heed their giddy pleas. Instead, I glowered at the vicious cat. Perched on the windowsill like a merciless predator, he gouged his claws into the supple wood.

"Disappointed, are you?" I said aloud.

"Why should we be disappointed?" said Casey.

"Honestly," gulped Lucy. "We're just glad you're alive."

I studied the terror on their cherubic faces. I knew they had had a terrible night. *What have I done to House Catagen — to the Commodore — to the Twins?*

Before I could answer, the hatch swung open, revealing the most beautiful girl I'd ever seen. Sapphire eyes filled with reproach, she carefully toured our guilty faces. "Think you were clever; sneaking off the ship? Think it's funny, now that she's alive? Never mind the entire fleet has been looking for her! Never mind I've spent the entire night crying! Never mind that Grandfather has been absolutely mad with worry..."

"Please, Elena," I muttered. "It was my fault..."

"Of course!" she tittered with a vindictive laugh. "Because it's just a jolly game, isn't it? Grandfather nearly died rescuing you. He's lost his allies *and* his friends, shielding you from the Volcano God. Yet you steal away like a common urchin?"

I hung my head in shame. "I'm sorry. I didn't mean..."

The princess pursed her ruby lips. "Come, Pallas. I want to hear all about your...your little jaunt."

I sighed at the Twins and reluctantly obeyed. For even though I'd ridden a dolphin – even though I'd bested a God – I didn't have the courage to quarrel with Elena.

∞

That night I was wakened by a searing pair of claws. It was two in the morning, yet I wasn't surprised. I knew this would happen – knew it would happen at his very favorite hour. Wrapping a shawl around my shoulders, I obediently followed him to the secluded bow.

The cat was fierce and angry. "I thought I told you to stay on the ship!"

"I thought I could trust you!"

"What?" he said, taken aback.

"You're a spy, aren't you? A spy for that wicked Fire God!"

"A spy?" he huffed. "Of all the impertinent things to say."

"Admit it. You knew I was going to shore and set the whole thing up to get me kidnapped!"

"You told me you weren't going! You promised me, in fact."

"You *knew* I was lying. You tricked me into lying..."

"Tricked you?"

"Yeah," I snarled. "So that the Fire prince could capture me and take me to Mulciber."

For a moment, the cat was at a rare loss for words. But he quickly recovered, with a vindictiveness which gave my heart a lurch. "Don't flatter yourself. Believe me…if I was working for Mulciber, you'd be begging for death."

Faltering at his vicious rebuke, I opened my mouth in an attempt to reply.

"What did Mulciber look like?" he spat. "Was he an older man or a young blond?"

"You should know," I sulked. "You were his pet."

"Just answer the question," he scolded, his tinny voice dripping with venom.

I shrugged. "He looked around twenty…blond, with striking dark eyebrows."

"What *exactly* did he say?"

I told him everything. Though the cat kept up a withering commentary, even he was startled at how close the God had been.

"He called me a Water Witch," I complained. "As if!"

"Water Witch?" he purred. "Now there's a clever idea."

"What do you mean? I'm not a Witch!"

"You're not exactly a drone, either," he said, apparently enjoying my ire. "Ah…but you wouldn't understand."

"You are so mean."

"The wretched creature has a point. A Water Witch indeed! Perhaps I should buy you a pointy hat and teach you to fly a broom."

"Whatever," I said, having no idea what he meant. "But what about that owl?"

"Owl? What owl?"

"The one that gave me this knife?" I said, revealing the dolphin-shaped blade. "I mean…it looked like an owl. Only it had three wings…and they twirled around in a neat little circle."

He raised his brow in answer, evidently impressed. "Though it's rather hard for me to believe, it appears you've somehow made a good impression on Poseida." He took a moment to chortle aloud, as if enjoying some ridiculous joke. "On the other hand, no one wants a new Token – especially one as entertaining as you – dying off too soon. Any decent mouser will tell you…the excitement is in the chase."

"What are you talking about?"

"You'll learn," he smarmed, "or you'll die. In the meantime, you'll remember who gave you that knife: Poseida, Queen of the Unquenchable Sea. And in remembering, you shall be grateful. *Eternally* grateful."

He continued his interrogation far into the night, determined to hear the smallest detail. Yet he refused to offer me the same courtesy.

I asked why Mulciber wanted me dead. I asked about the knife.

But all he offered was a handful of lies, cherishing his many secrets to himself.

Inwardly, I saw the knife as a secret source of hope. For it meant that someone, *Poseida…I suppose,* was watching over me. Help would come when I needed it the most, almost as if…

Was I really praying to the welter of the waves, bowing my head in a penitent request? *When did I become so devout?*

But I had something else to consider. *I fired the summoning box, learned how to use the compass, and moved the raft by learning how to read.*

The tools of the Gods were enchanted, with deep and powerful magic, *yet they can be wielded by an ordinary slave…a mortal who can read.*

Mulciber called me a Witch. Could he be right? If I conjured the marvels of those holy artifacts, *does that really make me a sorcerer?* Othello taught me how to read. *Did he also make me a magician?*

Was the road I followed narrow and straight, or were my epic deeds wicked and depraved?

∞

We arrived at Greenstone the very next day, *Yorktown's* banners in regal display. Sailors and fishermen stopped to stare as *the Fighting Lady* made her entrance.

The port was littered with thousands of masts, weirdly reminding me of a dead, leafless forest. The horde of boats was loud and vast, yet I didn't linger on ships when I had a kaleidoscope of colors to savor.

Before me lay the capital of my tiny world. Merry streets of cobblestone rose above the quay as the terrain climbed away from the bustling harbor. Myriads of chimneys dappled the rise, continuing the forest-in-winter theme.

I could hardly believe the monstrous size. Twenty times, forty times the breadth of Kelly Tree, the city sprawled as it scaled the growing mount.

My eyes reached the very top to behold the most fantastic structure man had ever created. On the highest pinnacle stood the God-like *Zoo*. Like an ageless crown adorning a mighty monarch, it thrust its spire high into the Sky. Towering over the tiny inhabitants, its bronze roof aging to a mottled shade of sage, it reminded me of the letter "A." *Though no one else, except that stupid cat, would ever think to describe it that way.*

"Impressive, isn't it?" said Lucy.

"Unbelievable."

"Though nothing compared to Atlantis," Casey jibbed.

I smiled. "No, nothing like that at all."

The Twins smirked, enjoying their little game. After my brilliant battle with the Fire God they, like everyone else, were certain I was a denizen of Atlantis. Thus, they kept tricking me into revealing the secrets of heaven.

But as I'd never been to Atlantis, it wasn't a difficult secret to keep.

Yorktown pulled alongside the dock. To the right were the admiring stares of *Argo*. To the left, *Yamato* looked angry and resentful. Her motley sailors actually spit in the Water as *Yorktown* moored to the narrow pier.

Once the ship was fully stopped, Elena emerged from her lonely hermitage. Pale from a fresh bout of Seasickness, she ordered me to her cabin.

"I thought we were going ashore?" I said as I entered her stateroom. It was the largest, of course, a more opulent version of Dewey's cabin aboard *Hornet*.

"Not dressed like that, you aren't. Those dungarees are fine on a ship," she said, though unconvincingly, "but you're part of House Catagen now. As such, you're expected to make an appropriate entrance."

"Why?"

"Why?" she tittered. "Is that a question? You are about to be presented to the whole of Greenstone…for everyone to see! You *must* look the part."

I smiled, pondering the Fates that brought me to this happy place. *A few months ago I was a lowly slave from a smelly fishing village.* Now I was an honored princess of the Sea. I'd be attending the best school in the world and have the chance to compete in the University Games.

Yet whom did I have to thank? *Certainly not the Old Man.* He wanted to sequester me to the safety of the Isle. No. It was Lady Uncial, Chancellor of the *Zoo*, who came to my unasked-for aid, *ordering* me to attend University.

I wonder why?

But I couldn't be bothered with trivialities when faced with a thousand delights. Elena bragged about Greenstone while Abbey prepared our hair.

Dressed and groomed to Elena's exacting standards, we finally returned to the deck.

The wharf was crammed with eager onlookers – tens of thousands, more people than I ever thought existed – keen to watch House Catagen bravely disembark.

I studied their curious faces, noticing something odd. The slaves of Kelly Tree tended to have high foreheads, while those on the Isle of Catagen had ruddy cheeks. Here in Greenstone, they were weak shouldered with sallow skin. Yet they all shared the same blank looks, the same glassy stares.

I'd heard the Bull brag that the nobility were more intelligent than the rabble.

They're more educated, there's no denying that. But are they really smarter?

But I didn't have time to ponder the question. A band started a triumphant march, raising cheers from the eager onlookers. In a choreographed procession worthy of a king, House Catagen filed ceremoniously ashore.

First came a retinue of Marines, dressed in martial blue. Then an army of servants, followed by a contingent of naval officers. Finally came the family members themselves. The Twins reached the wharf when the music was interrupted by a low, mournful horn.

Thundering their way through the gathered crowd shoved a grim parade of sallow knights. The brown-clad horsemen, resplendent in heavy mail, surrounded a carriage encrusted with gems.

"Triton's Waves!" scowled the Old Man. "That man likes to show off."

"Who is he?" I asked, watching a balding lord lumber out of the carriage. He was so stout, several servants had to help him.

"Lord Gauntle," Elena said with a frown.

"Oh." I was about to ask if the Catagens and the Gauntles were friends, when something quite unexpected stole my breath.

Oliver appeared on the deck: not wearing a sharp naval uniform, but a chocolate cape with thick, black boots. A golden breastplate adorned his chest, stark contrast to his charcoal pants and shirt. Whisking towards me in a militant march, he froze to a stiff attention. Loudly, with unexpected violence, he stomped his heel on the wooden deck. Then he knelt and kissed my hand, cradling it with simple, gentle reverence. "Please, Mistress. Forgive me."

Elena raised her chin in her arrogant pose. "Forgive you? Of course she forgives you."

But the mariner ignored her, gazing in my eyes. His face was a grimaced frown – as if he were apologizing to the Mistress – as if he'd betrayed me somehow.

Clamping his teeth into a stubborn smile, he stood and strode across the narrow gangplank. Stomping his foot like he had before, he faced the lumbering lord. Their greeting was forced and oddly formal.

"But...I thought." But I hadn't thought at all. *It never occurred to me that he was anything but a midshipman being groomed to become an officer.* "Oliver's related to Lord Gauntle?"

"Didn't you know?" quipped Elena. "Lord Gauntle is his father; Captain William is his grandfather. His mother is Clyme, my older cousin. Ah, there she is now," she waved.

Father? Grandfather? Cousin?!? All at once, I felt desperate and afraid.

I don't know anything about the great Houses, anything at all! Sure, I fooled the Catagens. But Othello's right, they want to believe my fictitious account. What will the other Houses think, the ones who don't like the Water?

I didn't hear the roar of the crowd as the Commodore took my nervous arm. Nor did I witness the banners that welcomed their mythic princess. Instead, I felt the crushing weight of my delicate tiara.

What am I doing? Why am I here? I'm just a slave! A stupid girl who got lost in a raft.

It was a wonder I didn't fall off the narrow gangplank as I entered this dangerous arena. Before I realized I was on the wharf, the Commodore was introducing me to the fat lord.

"What?" I flushed. "Pleased...uh, pleased to meet you." And though Elena spent hours teaching my how to curtsy, I completely forgot.

"I...should think so!" boomed Lord Gauntle. "Not everyday...you meet...the Lord Master...of the Pass!"

"Now, now, Gauntle," said the Old Man. "There'll be plenty of time for titles."

"It's about time...she learned...don't you think?"

"That's why she's here," said the Commodore, with a growl that made the onlookers wince.

Gauntle huffed. The Commodore scowled. There was a very awkward moment, the two lords glaring at each other, when Oliver broke the brutal silence.

"Mother, this is the hallowed Mistress, Pallas."

"I know who she is," came her hollow reply. The only child of Captain William, unfortunately favored of her father. Tall and overbearing, Clyme had dark hair and large, mannish hands. I could see very little of Elena or the Twins in this older cousin.

The greetings came to another embarrassing halt, the in-laws glowering at each other.

They're family, I thought. *Yet they hate each other.*

The uneasiness seemed eternal when a pretty, lithe girl appeared. Her glowing face, a rapturous smile, she embraced me in a heartfelt hug.

"Mistress," said Oliver, with a tenderness quite unexpected from the salty mariner. "Please...allow me the honor of introducing my fair sister, Genevieve."

"I've been waiting all summer to meet you," said Genevieve, affectionately holding both my hands. "Oliver's told me all about your adventures. I'm so jealous of you, dear brother, as you've spent so much time with her already."

I couldn't help but gawk. *She's their daughter?* It was hard to believe this graceful girl was the progeny of these considerable hulks. Genevieve looked nothing like any of them, their overlarge features replaced with thin, delicate lines. Oliver never smiled, and his parents looked like they didn't know how, yet Genevieve seemed illuminated with happiness.

I instantly liked her.

"But Oliver didn't tell me how beautiful you are. Really, brother, you couldn't help but notice."

"Oh, he noticed all right," shot Elena.

I gaped with mounting surprise. *Where did that come from!?*

"Elena." Genevieve floated to the tall beauty, kissing both her cheeks.

The contrast was bold and palpable. *Elena's more beautiful.* Yet the smile that decorated Genevieve's face was more attractive in my mind.

"You should have visited us on the Isle, poor dear," said Elena. "Then you too could have met our rising star."

"You're too kind," said Genevieve, with a charm so innocent it seemed impossible to contrive. "What a lovely invitation. I promise to travel to the Isle next summer."

"Perfect," said Elena, raising her chin in her signature pose.

Another awkward moment arose, the two great Houses flaunting their enormous egos.

Once again, it was Oliver who broke the stagnant silence. "Come here," he said as he pressed Genevieve's feathery frame into a bear-like embrace, "and give me a hug."

"I have missed you, brother," she blithely cried.

Clyme scolded the loving pair. "Genevieve, please. Oliver, you're making a scene."

But the two ignored her, as if they hadn't heard.

π

The ride into the city was practically a parade. Elena had never seen so many spectators. Thousands of slaves crowded the streets, hoping to glimpse the dolphin rider.

Only a few months ago, Elena thought to herself, *they would have been shouting for me, the crown-jewel of House Catagen.* Instead, shouts of "Mistress of the Sea!" and "Daughter of Triton!" filled her jealous ears.

Back straight, head high, chin up – she assumed a regal pose. Right next to the careless, slouching God.

She's so silly, so inane, so completely unaware. She glanced at the divinity's blushing face, desperate to know her parentage. Was she a bastard child of an Aquarian God – perhaps even Triton himself? *I hinted at the prospect a hundred times. She didn't even know what I was talking about!*

She graced the Goddess with a welcoming smile, careful to hide her heretical musings. *She knows nothing about civilized behavior, nothing about politics. She doesn't even know how to wear makeup!*

Were the Gods born, fully grown? *Did she really hatch from that Egg?*

She hated her envy, but she simply couldn't help it. Elena had been the queen of her universe, the undisputed lioness of House Catagen, the most beautiful woman in the world. *Now I'm playing second fiddle to a girl who doesn't know the difference between eye-liner and blush?*

Still…the Goddess saved her from Borelo, tamed a dolphin, and escaped the wrath of Mulciber. *If she's not an Atlantian, I can't imagine what she is.*

Yet deep down, she fought a growing anger. For Pallas' light was growing ever brighter, *while mine is surely fading.*

They finally reached the citadel near the very top of the city. Passing beneath the heavy gates, the carriage pulled into the walled enclosure.

"This is the Water Quarter," she patiently explained. "These six manors are where the six Aquarian Houses reside."

"What about the Air and Earth?" came her ignorant reply.

It's like talking to a child! Didn't they teach her anything in heaven? "They have Quarters of their own, dear Pallas. Air to the left, Earth to the right. Fire is opposite Water on the other side of University."

The Atlantian gazed at the largest of the manors. She rudely pointed at its flag: a Sea of white emblazoned with a blue cup. It was a flag of storied might, with a long history of influence and power.

"That flag has the shape of a ewe on it," said the God.

"A female sheep? Of course, it doesn't."

"Who lives in that manor, the one with that flag?"

"The Lady Uncial, of course."

Chapter Two

Bored

Tell me muse, how it all began...

Aeneid
Virgil, Roman author
circa 10 BC: Earth Standard

"I'm bored," said the Goddess, "I'm tired of being perfect."

"Humph," muttered her friend. "It certainly beats the alternative."

"I suppose," she said as minions pampered her platinum hair. "But just look at me. I'm absolutely ravishing – a perfect, scrumptious, dish. And no one even cares."

"Plenty of people care. Poseida, Rhodes, Bonnie..."

"No *men* care."

"Oh."

"I'm five foot ten with dazzling hair. Sapphire eyes, luscious lips, ballerina's legs, a tiny waist. Yet I'll never turn a single head."

"Whose head do you want to turn?" said Tess. "I mean...what's the point? You have all the time in the world – to expand your mind, to learn and be learned, to right the injustices of the world. What more do you want?"

"Passion. Romance. Deep, churning love."

"Like the ones you read about in books?"

"Yes," said Cypris, "like the ones you read about in your silly books."

Tess sighed, a touch of introspection on her sensible face.

"I want to *know* love," said Cypris. "I want to *be* loved. Not because I'm a God, but...for who I truly am."

"What? A self-centered, narcissist shrew?"

"Uh?!" she flourished, "You are *so* unkind."

17

"Bother," tittered her friend. "If you want to be loved, what about Zephyr? He's quite fond of you…"

The Goddess rolled her eyes as she sipped the *ambrosia*. "That dirty old man? You know how he carries on through Aeolia."

Tess did know. The King of the Sky was famous for his many liaisons. "What about one of the younger Gods? Helios is quite the charmer."

"He's nothing but a dandy. All the men in Aeolia are. I want a man. A real man."

"There are plenty of men in Erebus. The Earth is full of…"

"They're ever so dull. And they never look quite clean, do they? Like they've got dirt under their fingernails or something."

"What about Triton?"

"Been there, done that…and Poseida absolutely was furious. Thought I'd never hear the end of it."

"Then you'll just have to settle for one of the Taurans. The marriage of Earth and Water, you know…"

"One of those maggot men? I'd just as soon have a drone."

"Why don't you? There are dozens of interesting specimens."

"Please."

"I've been studying them. They're really quite fascinating."

"Everyone knows your infatuated with the drones."

"I'm not infatuated."

"No one shares your love for the ignorant breed."

"Teresa does."

Cypris immediately swallowed her contempt. "Teresa's different."

Chapter Three

School Days

HOUSE UNCIAL – The most influential great House, House Uncial resided in the capital of Greenstone. A Water House, it held the office of Chancellor of the Lords, and Voting Member of the Zoo. House Uncial was constantly barraged by numerous plots to unseat its leadership over the Zoo. The political infighting and intrigue reached a peak during the tenure of Uncial III, in which the embattled Lady did everything she could to prevent an outbreak of open war...

"Rise and Fall of the Pentathanon Gods"

Herodotus III

Greenstone was everything I hoped it would be. The week flew by in a glorious haze as I explored the bustling city. As Elena was a very late riser, I spent mornings with the Twins. Afternoons were devoted to the teenage matron, usually going shopping.

My ecstasy came to an abrupt halt, however, the day I met the other sophomore girls in Aquarian Academy. As we would be taking classes together, Uncial IV and Eunice IV – princesses of House Uncial – invited Elena and me to tea. As the Chancellor wanted to speak to the Old Man, the three of us visited the Uncials together.

Uncial Manor had a feeling of power, boasting a history of magnificence and might. Easily dwarfing the others, the building dominated the Water Quarter like a lion lords over his pride. Yet the structure itself was graceless and gray, sitting upon the square like an enormous box.

I still wondered at the "U" on the Uncialian flag. I worked out (all by myself) that the word "Uncial" must begin with the letter "U."

But how do the Uncials know that?

I asked Elena what the symbol meant, but she had no idea.

"There isn't a ewe upon any flag. Honestly, Pallas, where do you come up with such silly ideas?"

Othello was no help either. "Never you mind about that. Probably just a coincidence."

But it's not a coincidence! There's something important there...something about reading.

We were invited into the ostentatious foyer, rivers of marble lining the ceiling, walls, and floor. A pair of imposing statues, long-dead matriarchs of House Uncial, guarded the tomb-like hall. Larger than life, they looked down at us with an Air of manipulative triumph.

Uncial III appeared with her daughter and niece. The lady was short and thin, sporting the confidence of someone who has so much power she doesn't need to flaunt it. As Chancellor, she presided over the *Zoo*, the ruling body of our tiny world. Never having a civics lesson in my entire life, I didn't really know what a Chancellor was. I only knew that the tiny woman was the most important mortal on the planet.

After our uncomfortable meeting with the Gauntles, I was surprised that the Commodore embraced the Chancellor like an old friend. "And this, my Lady," he gestured with pride, "is our fair Mistress, come from the Sea."

The lady did not speak. Instead, she studied my grey eyes, as if searching for some hidden secret.

I stared right back, just as I'd done with Lady Oxymid. But keeping eye-contact with the Chancellor was more difficult than the ruler of Capro Bay.

Ensnared by her penetrating stare, I was again reminded that this was the lady who brought me to Greenstone. *At the time, I thought it was a gift.* Yet pierced by her domineering gaze, I was forced to reconsider.

Just when I thought I could stand it no longer, Uncial took both of my hands, smoothing them in the traditional Aquarian greeting. "Welcome, child. I pray the Commodore has kept you well?"

"Yes...yes, Ma'am. He's...been wonderful, really."

"I expect he has," she said with a smile. "That's the kind of man he is."

"Blimey, Lady Chancellor," he chuckled. "You make an old man blush."

"Old Man?" she tittered. "Not according to Lady Oxymid. She described you as a demon-possessed sewer rat."

"Did she now? Best compliment I've had in years."

"And more than you deserve," she laughed before finally turning to the beauty. "Elena, dear. What a joy to see you again."

"Thank you, my Lady," she said with a curtsy.

Oh my Gods! I completely forgot! Glancing over at my new best friend, I knew she'd be slighted at being addressed last.

"Of your courtesy," said Elena, "Father bids Lady Uncial glad tidings, and sends his compliments to your most excellent Lady."

"I expect he does." Uncial smirked. "How is the old Sea dog?"

Elena flushed. I knew she was trying her best to impress the Chancellor and was annoyed by the lady's bawdy tone. But Elena was nothing if not a politician and found within her the perfect response. "To be perfectly honest, my Lady, he's in a right state. You know how he gets when he's surrounded by landlubbers for more than a day at a time."

Uncial laughed. "Well! You tell the good Captain that I'm still waiting for that cruise he promised me."

"I'd be absolutely delighted," she said with another curtsy, pleased at making a good impression.

Smarmy little suck-up.

"And where is that case of Catagen brandy?" Uncial teased the Old Man. "I've been out ever since..."

The pretentious banter irritated me. Eunice's snarky look goaded me even more. Surrendering to a nasty fit of pique, I loudly interrupted...

"That symbol on your flag...why is it a 'U'?"

The Uncial teens cast reproving stares.

The lady silenced me with a deadly glare.

Elena looked mortified.

Uh....not good.

The Commodore opened his mouth as if coming to my rescue, when the lady recomposed her mirthful face...though the menace in her eyes remained. "How marvelously observant, Pallas. But I'm sure I have no idea what you mean. I'm afraid you'll have to ask my grandmother," she laughed, theatrically waving to the older of the two statues, "as it was her design."

The Uncialian girls shared a nervous giggle, adding to the tension in the chilly Air.

Elena forced a weak smile.

Oh my Gods! I'm in so much trouble.

"Commodore," said the Chancellor, "if you will attend to my office; there are matters of state I wish to discuss."

"Aye, my Lady," he said with a sigh.

"Perfect," she said, turning sharply to proceed up the flight of steps. The Commodore doggedly followed, a glum expression on his weathered face. Half-way up the spiral stairs Uncial stopped, towering over us teenage girls. "I'm afraid I must be off. Do have fun, my ladies; and tell Pallas all about…" and here she marked Elena with a reproachful stare, "…what is *expected* of her at University."

"I shall, my Lady," Elena said with a curtsy.

I could tell she was absolutely furious.

The tea party was little better. Uncial IV was a short nervous girl who rarely spoke. Eunice IV, on other hand, spent the entire time gibbering about her stupid boyfriend, Keleron, the nephew of Lord Joculo. Her colorless life was completely consumed by the day she'd marry the prince from Lady Smith.

We exchanged small gifts and forced conversation. I received a delicate silver mirror from the noble pair. Its frame was surrounded with silver dolphins, their eyes encrusted with tiny emeralds.

"The Lady Uncial designed it herself," mumbled Uncial IV.

"Why, it's the most beautiful thing I've ever seen," said Elena. "What a perfectly charming gift!"

"Yeah," I said. I actually liked the mirror, as the dolphins reminded me of happier, less complicated times. But I was too embarrassed to say so. Instead I thought about the dolphin knife and the hopeless terror of that fearsome night.

"Did you notice the dolphins, Pallas?" said Elena, valiantly trying to get me to speak. "It was made in honor of your adventure in Capro Bay. Uncial, Eunice; would you like to hear her thrilling account?"

"We've already heard it," said Uncial.

"Keleron's told me a hundred times," said Eunice.

"Indeed?" said Elena with a falsely cheery voice. "Oh, Pallas…do look. It's a Paulista creation."

"A what?"

"Paulista. The Paul family are the very best silversmiths in the entire world. Uncial dear, won't you please tell the lady that Pallas simply adores her gift."

"Of course," huffed Uncial IV.

"Why can't she tell her herself?" Eunice sniped.

But I wasn't listening. Instead, I studied my reflection in the mirror, remembering what Othello had said…

"I see a princess pretending to be a peasant."

Well, I didn't see anything of the sort, glad the mirror didn't reveal me for who I truly was – an uneducated urchin, masquerading as nobility.

After an obnoxious, miserable, grueling hour, we made our welcome retreat, back to the solace of Catagen Manor.

"I don't think they liked me."

"Honestly," shot Elena, "what was your first clue?"

"If they'd only talked about something interesting, like sports. But all they wanted to talk about was boys."

"Don't be so jolly clever. You know very well why they acted like that."

"I'm sorry," I said. And I meant it. "I know they thought I was stupid."

"You are *so* unkind!" she nearly cried. "It was simply frightful the way you interrupted the lady."

I shrugged.

"They were only trying to be sweet. Who cares what kind of flag they fly?"

I didn't argue. *They weren't sweet. They were snobbish and rude.* I was still wondering why the lady acted so venomously to my simple question when we ran into another Aquarian princess.

"Oh, my Gods!" squealed a happy brunette, surprising the beauty with a rapturous hug. "Elena!"

The teenage matron rolled her eyes, grudgingly returning the fond embrace. "Darling, this is Janice, daughter of Lord Joculo."

A feeling of horror pitted my gut. I knew exactly who Janice was, as I'd seen the princess about a hundred times in Kelly Tree.

Stupid twit! Of course Joculo's children attend University!

Janice was the same age as I. A plain girl, she was a kind person who shared her father's love for the slaves. There wasn't a soul in Kelly Tree who didn't recognize Princess Janice.

I hope the same can't be said about me!

Janice trapped me in a caring hug. "Pallas! I'm like, so happy to meet you."

Afraid to meet her joyous eyes, I garbled an incoherent reply.

"Of your courtesy, noble friend," said Elena. "Let's do sit in the courtyard so the two of you can become better acquainted."

I was absolutely mortified.

But Janice was delighted. "That'd be great!" said the tittering jailer, dragging me to the courtyard, imprisoning me with her happy smile. A square of sycamores completely surrounded us, caging me completely in their arborous cell. The leaves of the trees had turned with the season, ablaze with red and yellow and gold.

"Daddy's told us all about your adventures," said Janice. "He's a real fan of yours. Goes on and on about your stories. I'm like, so jealous."

Afraid she'd recognize me for who I was, I was too frightened to speak.

Elena forced a weak smile.

"It's so unlucky you ended up in Capro Bay. If only you'd come ashore in Kelly Tree, Daddy would have given you a royal welcome."

Yeah, I thought, *I wish I'd washed ashore in Kelly Tree too.* But words completely escaped me.

A couple of young men walked lazily past.

"Mark and Anthony," whispered Elena. "You remember. Princes of House Med and Cannes. Pay no attention."

The two sauntered wordlessly past, pretending not to notice us girls. But Mark betrayed his interest when he peeked behind his shoulder.

"DG!" Janice giggled. "That Mark is *such* a dreamer."

"What?" said Elena, annoyed.

"What!?!" I gasped, so shocked, I dropped the delicate mirror. It shattered on the cobblestones, falling into ruin.

"Look what you've done!" said Elena. "You've broken it."

But Elena's scorn was nothing compared to my own internal horror. The fragile dolphins were mangled and torn, their jeweled eyes lost amongst the Fiery leaves.

What a terrible omen!

"I'm sorry," said Janice, picking up the shards. "Was it something I said?"

I knew I shouldn't press the matter. *Othello would be absolutely furious!* But I had to hear it again. "What did you say?"

"DG," she whimsically replied. "Daddy says it's a 'Definite Glance.' He's so silly."

"But...how does he know that?" I knew what a "D" and a "G" were. *But how did Lord Joculo know that sacred secret?*

"Oh, I don't know. Daddy's always holed up in that office of his, absolutely surrounded with parchment." She giggled till she noticed my startled face. "You *do* know what parchment is, don't you?"

I knew all to well, having copied *Mr. Mistoffelees* on a roll of it last night. "It's used to make charts, I've heard."

"I suppose. Anyway, nobody has any idea what he does in there. Not even Mother."

I wondered as well when Janice said something to make my blood freeze.

"Say...haven't I seen you before?"

"No."

She narrowed her hazel eyes. "You look really familiar. Ever been to Kelly Tree?"

"Where?" I said, blanching with fright.

Elena furrowed her brow.

"Kelly Tree," said Janice. "On the Eastern Shore."

"I...uh...came from the Egg," I stammered. "The Egg has never been to...uh...Jelly Tree."

"Kelly," she said. "Kelly Tree."

"Whatever," I said with a flippant wave.

But inside, my heart was churning. *She's going to figure out who I am!*

I turned away from my adopted sister, closing my eyes with shame. *What will they do when they discover I'm a slave? Beat me, hang me, drown me?*

But Elena was far too irritated to be inquisitive. Instead she stood, mercifully ending the interrogation. "Janice, it's so lovely to see you again. You simply *must* come for tea tomorrow."

"I'm sorry," said Janice, rising as well. "Tomorrow's bad for me. Daddy's taking us shopping."

"Some other time," Elena said as she kissed her cheek.

"Until then," said Janice, returning the favor. Then she turned on me. "I know I've seen you before. I never forget a face."

∞

Othello was in a festive spirit, feasting on tuna and cream. "My, but you made a fine impression on the Uncials! I can't wait till you to meet the other princesses."

"Shut up! And quit spying on me."

"I can't help myself! You are ever so entertaining. You should join a troupe and perform a comedy."

I was about to throw a shoe at him when I heard a knock at the door.

"Come in."

Elena floated into the room, the poise she always exhibited in regal display.

I cringed, anticipating another angry lecture.

"Darling," she sighed, "I…I regret that I was short with you this afternoon. But honestly…you had me in a right state, and I don't mind saying it."

"Sorry," I said, dutifully lowering my head. I knew she was making a huge effort. *Elena never apologizes to anyone.*

"You're very kind," purred the princess. "Thank you for understanding. Yet I'm rather concerned about the reception you'll receive at University. The Leos are mad as hornets about Fort Isolaverde."

"The who?"

26

"The Fire Houses!" she said, exasperated again; raising her eyebrow just a tick. It was a trick she'd recently mastered, one of the many ways she used to make others feel inferior. "Really, Pallas! When are you ever going to learn about House politics?"

"I'm sorry." And I truly was. Safe upon the Isle, comfortable in my cocoon, I was elated about going to University. Now the idea seemed daunting and dangerous.

Seeing the desired effect, Elena put her eyebrow back in place and smiled – a genuine smile. She'd been practicing that too. "There are five Academies, representing the five Pentathanon Gods. Yet we dare not name them after the denizens of heaven."

"OK."

"So we name them after the stars. The Earth Houses are the Taurans, the Air the Geminis, and the Fire are the Leos."

"What about Deme, the healing God?"

"They're the Sagittarians. Only you won't see them until the University Games, as they study at the House of Wonders on the lonely island of Solüt."

"Then…what are we called? Water Houses, I mean."

"Honestly?" she huffed. "The games you make me play? *We* are the Aquarians!"

"Oh…yeah."

Unbidden and unwanted, the loathsome prophecy floated through my head…

> *Born of the Sea, hatched from the Egg,*
> *Child of Atlantis, God with us.*
> *For she shall herald a glorious Age,*
> *and they shall call it – Aquarius.*

I scowled at the wicked, napping cat – author of the stupid poem. *You are so mean! How could I be the beginning of a glorious age? I'm faking my age right now to be in classes with Elena.*

But the cat ignored my heinous heresy, safe within his solemn slumber.

∞

She stood at the edge of a precipice, gazing into a ring of Fire. Flames licked furiously at her naked feet, scalding the hair that blew up and over her shoulders.

Hovering over the tortured child was the Lord God Mulciber. He raised his finger. He shot his ray…

…she fell…like a limp, rag doll…

…into the hell below.

π

She woke with sudden fright, her sheets soaked with sweat. Her teenage heart pounded within her chest – as if seeking a way to escape – as if searching for the solace of another soul, one that didn't harbor so much turmoil and pain.

Rising from her bed, she guzzled down a pitcher of Water – attempting to quench the burning horror.

Snake-like pupils studied the sad, sordid affair. They offered no comfort or cheer. Instead, they watched…and they waited.

π

I spent the entire weekend learning everything I could about my future classmates. It was all too much for me to remember as Elena's repertoire of gossip was nearly limitless. Still, the princess was a patient teacher.

At least more patient than that cat!

As for Othello, he spent my midnight hours dictating stories for me to write. They were always about cats, I discovered, as cats were his favorite subject. At present, he was recounting the epic account of *Puss 'n Boots*. An obnoxious tale in my opinion, the hero was a cat that saved his witless master.

"This is the most ridiculous story I've ever heard!" I said, exasperated at the helplessness of the miller's son. "Nobody's that stupid."

"Look in the mirror and tell me that. Only…try not to break it this time."

28

"Shut up."

Finally, the long-awaited morning arrived, my very first day of University. At the appointed hour the students in the Water Quarter arranged themselves in a column, the oldest in front and the youngest to the rear. The Aquarians wore uniforms of light blue tunics with dark blue pants and skirts. I was both nervous and excited.

I can't believe it's really happening!

I expected a great deal of fanfare and noise. To my surprise, it was a silent affair. At exactly nine o'clock the column of Aquarians proceeded towards University. I wordlessly walked next to Elena, Casey and Lucy following a row behind. Not a word was spoken as we trooped through the marbled gates, leaving the Water Quarter.

The walled enclosure was huge and square, housing fields and stables for each Academy. Situated in the middle was a huge round building – the hallowed halls of University.

We marched through an archway that cut through the building to enter a circular lawn. This was the "Center Lawn," the second most sacred place on the planet. It was forbidden to enter except during the morning procession, and then only on the path that cut the grass into quarters.

My nervousness rose as a phalanx of yellow marched towards us from the left. Borelo, a senior, was in the first rank of Geminis heading towards the converging point – the very center of the Lawn. On my right was a mass of brown and black. I could see Oliver and Genevieve among these Taurans. In front of me, on the opposite side, was a column of crimson and coal.

Along the inner wall were four small shrines. The Aquarian shrine was a fountain of babbling Water. To my right was a massive boulder, gift of the Good Earth. To my left was a glass globe filled with Air. Most dramatic, however, was the Eternal Fire which marked the Leon side of University.

∞

"Water," Proteus declared to the classroom of Aquarians. "It is in every living thing. There is magic in Water. For alone amongst the elements, Water creates Life in its carnival of forms. Water fills the empty places on the Earth and clings to it. Water seeks to unite with Water – flowing together through both rulers and slaves – symbolizing that all men are subject to the same

29

Pentathanon laws. Water is in the Air you breathe, yes, even though you do not see it. It is in the blood in your veins, the food you eat. Water is in the Earth you stand upon – indeed, it is only by the mercy of the Sea that we *have* Earth to stand upon. For the Ocean is mighty, and the Sea mightier still. Water displaces the Air we breathe and destroys the Earth. It drowns the Fire, that which only knows destruction, and indeed drowns any creature who does not heed her eclectic warnings. For there is none more powerful, more awesome, more gentle…than that which is Water."

I've never heard anyone speak with such authority! I thought, the words of the Water Professor stirring my heart. *It's as if I've always known these things, but – never heard them put into words.*

"Boring," said a boy to a round full of snickers. Half a dozen upperclassmen were huddled round a hidden bottle. "Same old thing, year after year."

"Ignore him," whispered Elena. "He's that ill-mannered lord I told you about."

"Uh…Duma? Was that it?" I said too loudly.

"*Lord* Duma," said the plump boy. "My friends call me Dusan, as that is my given name. You, on the other hand, may call me, *my Lord.*"

His friends rewarded him with their gleeful guffaws. Sporting a posh but frumpy velvet suit, he didn't wear a uniform like the others. A mat of messy hair sat askew a face only a mother could love.

"See what I mean?" said Elena.

"Yeah," I agreed, annoyed. *I've never heard it before, and I want to listen.*

That night, I told Othello all about my first day at University. "It was wonderful! Professor Proteus was great. I've learned so much already."

"Really?" he drolled. "What sort of prattle did that old kook tell you?"

But his lack of charm couldn't curb my enthusiasm. "Everything!"

"Everything? It must have been a long lesson, indeed."

"No, silly! Not everything. It just…seemed that way. I learned about Water. You know, how it's the most important of all the Elements."

"Told you that, did he? I wonder if Professor Kindle would agree?"

"Kindle. Whose he?"

"The Fire Professor. Do you think he taught his students about the virtues of Water?"

"I guess."

"Surely you're not that thick? If you'd been listening to Professor Kindle, he would have told you how powerful Fire was, now wouldn't he?"

"Oh, no," I assured him. "You didn't hear Proteus speak. He was quite convincing."

"I see," he said, rolling his eyes.

But if my first day of school was perfect, my second was an absolute disaster. It started well enough; I stood in the very same place in the blue column as it marched to the Center Lawn. But unlike yesterday when I was sequestered with friendly Aquarians, today I'd meet the Tauran, Gemini, and Leon sophomores.

I followed Elena to my very first Etiquette class. The entrance to the classroom was a beautiful crystal door depicting a delicate rose. Inside was a spacious, elegant ballroom.

"Come, come!" barked the teacher, swatting a fan into her chubby hand. Dressed in the most elaborate gown I'd ever seen, Miss Polish was a short, squat woman. "Please be seated."

Nervous, I instantly obeyed.

Unfortunately, Miss Polish saw me. "Uncouth brat!" She pitter-pattered towards me in a breathless huff, yapping like a toy poodle. "Have I taught you nothing, you stupid little girl?"

My classmates snickered their pitiless chuckles.

"Well?"

"I…uh…" *What did I do?*

Curious classmates surrounded me, adding to my sense of disaster – when I locked stares with a black-haired boy sporting cruel, dark eyes.

I've seen him before! In the forest of Fort Isolaverde! It was the boy who tried to kidnap me, the boy who felt Mulciber's angry ray of pain.

He's in my classes?!?

"A lady never sits at a table," screeched the pudgy woman, "without a gentleman first offering her a chair! How many times must I tell you?"

31

Elena distanced herself from the ugly scene as the crowd inched ever closer. Panicked, I darted my eyes upon another familiar face. It was the girl I met in Capro Bay, the daughter of Lady Oxymid, the one who wanted me sacrificed to the Flame.

Oh my Gods! She's here too? It never occurred to me that attending a school for nobility meant *all* of the nobility – even Catagen's enemies. Wondering if he'd been right all along, I suddenly understood the Commodore's fears.

Hounded by the vicious stares, I was ecstatic when a burly Tauran bullied through the throng.

"Miss Polish," growled Oliver, wearing the ugly brown on black, "you are speaking to the hallowed Mistress, come from the Sea. She does not know all of our…customs."

"Is she?" said the professor, narrowing her demanding eyes. Cruelly probing me with those discerning orbs, she studied me for an entire minute. As if deciding I couldn't possibly be I who claimed I was, she let her students know what she thought of the Commodore's story. "Have the Gods taught you no manners?"

"No, Ma'am," I croaked.

"Humph!" scowled the teacher, smugness glittering her chubby face. "Come, come!" she boomed. "Into your seats, all of you!"

The students scattered to the many tables, leaving me alone to my silence and shame. The Aquarians gathered around Elena; the Leos around the black-haired boy. The Taurans congregated around Oxymid's daughter while the Geminis dispersed themselves among several different tables. Oliver was immovable, guarding over me like an angry wolverine.

A gazelle-like girl approached me. Her legs were lean and muscled, a simple ponytail gracing a stoic face. Adorned in Gemini yellow, she looked fiercely into Oliver's eyes.

I thought this was supposed to be an etiquette class? Yet the prejudices of the nobility were firmly in play. As Earth and Air were opposites, it was unheard of for a Tauran to show courtesy to a Gemini.

Oliver ground his teeth into a silent snarl. But the wordless girl insisted; her doe-like eyes, a tapestry of conviction.

The Tauran frowned – his loyalties torn between his family and the Mistress. Letting out a guttural growl, he pulled out a seat for the athletic girl. A wave of whispers thundered across the room as the Gemini took the offered chair.

Oh my Gods! That was so sweet.

Something of his father scorned his brow as he stamped to the opposite side of the table. Plunking himself into the farthest chair, he glowered at the rest of the class. Without a word of comment, Miss Polish lectured about the art of handling silverware.

I whispered to the yellow-clad girl. "Thanks."

She cocked her head in a curious stare, considered me, and said, "You are welcome."

I studied the girl, wondering if Elena had mentioned her. "Gotta name?"

"A name?" she asked.

"Yeah…what is it?"

"A name is a sound that people know you by."

"Yeah," I huffed. "I know what a name *is*. Ya got one?"

She thought for a long moment. "Yes, I do."

Why is she being so difficult? Trying a different tack, I said, "My name is Pallas."

The girl just stared. "Everyone knows that."

If this was meant to reassure me – it did not. My nerves were torn and mangled, my gut a tangled knot. I looked furtively at the busy Aquarians, fawning over their magnificent queen bee.

The Twins were right about her! She's nothing but a two-faced brat. I swear! I'll never speak to her again!

∞

Elena caught up to me on our way to lunch. "Darling, how could you sit next to *her*?"

"Me?!" I flustered, unable to keep my vow. "You're the one who ran away!"

"Oh, what nonsense. I thought you were right behind me."

But I'd seen firsthand the little white lies Elena employed. "Don't lie to me, you know very well…"

"You shouldn't associate yourself with that girl!"

33

"What girl?"

"Atlanta," she accused. "I told you. No one likes her – not even the Gemini's. She's...odd."

I couldn't deny this. The girl said the strangest things. But an hour ago she'd been a better friend than Elena. "At least she didn't run away...like a stinking coward!"

This was too much for the tall beauty. "Fine! If that's the way you want it." Raising her elegant nose, she huffed away to be surrounded by friends.

Blindly turning around, I walked in the opposite direction. As University was a circle, I'd eventually get back to Aquarian Academy. Besides, I wanted time alone to mull over my injured feelings.

"I hate that girl!" I ranted, feeling lonely and betrayed. *Why can't I have a normal friend? Someone like...like Cindy?*

But thinking about Cindy made me pine for my father. *I really miss him,* I thought, fading into long-forgotten memories...

"Strayed a bit far from home, haven't we?"

I looked up, aghast. Obstructing my way was the boy from Isolaverde, flanked by a host of crimson and coal. The black-haired boy was obviously their leader, a crimson key hanging from a golden necklace.

"So..." he said with a vicious sneer. "This is the Water Witch." Arrogantly grabbing my chin, he punctuated his daring with an evil chuckle. "I pictured you a good bit taller. Aren't the Gods supposed to be tall?"

I slapped the offending hand away.

The hoard of red surrounded me.

The prince smiled. "What were you mumbling, foul little Witch? Conjuring another evil spell?"

His audience laughed, a mirthless crow that sent shivers up my spine.

I took a moment to size him up. *I've seen his kind before. Not too strong, not too smart; he's just a stupid bully. Used to getting his way, he's careful to surround himself with people who help him do just that.*

"You should try one that makes you disappear," he said. "Only...don't bother coming back. I don't think anyone would miss you if you simply...ceased to exist."

"Ah," I said. "That spell *is* a favorite. Only the sorcery I was planning is a bit more…diabolical. It turns jerks like you into slimy frogs."

The crowd growled their angry dissent.

The prince looked mildly impressed. "Good luck with that," he smiled, running his fingers through my long blond hair. "But first, let me introduce myself…"

"We've already met." Gone was my misery – gone were my regrets – replaced with a daring recklessness.

He halted his hateful preening. A query spoiled his lurid face. "Where?"

Summoning all the malice I could muster, I wounded him with savage dislike. "Let me see. You were on a cliff. The Sea raged beneath you. There were three Fiery chariots…and one…very…angry…God."

His hand fell limp in my hair. "You! You…saw that?"

"Oh, yeah." Thumping his chest, hard with my knuckles, I added, "By the way, how's the old ticker? Still beating…I hope. Or maybe…not."

The prince recoiled in horror, agony disfiguring his wicked face. Withdrawing his offending hand, he placed it over his stricken heart. Capitalizing on his momentary silence, I drove the hurt even deeper. "A bit twitchy for a crown prince, don't cha think?"

He stole a glance at his trembling hand, reliving the terror of that savage ray. For a moment, I actually felt sorry for him.

But the moment passed as he remembered his rage. "I don't know what devilry you possess," he seethed. "But I promise…you shall rue the day you crossed paths with Alexander, crown prince of House Excelsior."

"Regretting it already," I smarmed in reply.

The Leos grumbled – angry and confused. Growing more aggressive, they pressed ever closer, muttering words of challenge.

"Get her, Alexander!"

"Teach her a lesson."

"Filthy Witch."

"Slimy scum."

I played my best card, I thought to myself. *But it's no use. And I can't fight all of them…* Hopelessly outnumbered – feeling the noose gather round me – I resolved to go down swinging when someone grabbed my shoulder. Pivoting upon my attacker, I raised my fist to strike…

Genevieve?!?

"Alexander!" said the lithe little girl. "How very nice of you to find my darling…*cousin.*" She placed special weight on the word *cousin*, a defiant warning in her soft, hazel eyes. "Lost, I'm afraid. It shall be several days before she gets to know her way around."

"She's not your cousin," said the bully.

"Isn't she? Maybe you should discuss that with…my *father.*"

"Your father…"

But then he paused to think.

Genevieve seized the moment. Aggressively grabbing my hand, she boldly threaded me through the Fire and black. Bewildered, the crimson horde followed a few angry steps. But their reluctant prince called them back.

I gaped in wonder. "I can't believe you got away with that!"

Genevieve giggled. "Oliver was right. You *do* love adventures!"

"I didn't mean… It was an accident."

"I know, love."

"But…" *I barely know this girl. Why did she just rescue me?* "I don't know how to thank you. I mean…that was really brave."

"Not at all, Pallas, darling. Excelsior's been courting my father far too dearly to risk a fight between their dear little cherubs."

"Uh…yeah." I had no idea what she meant, but was grateful all the same.

Soon, we ran into a frantic Oliver. "Mistress!" he demanded. "Where have you been? I've been looking everywhere!"

"I have her well in hand, dear brother," said Genevieve. "Pallas merely…took a stroll."

Comprehension fluttered across his face. "Mistress! Tell me you weren't on the Leon side…"

"Oliver," admonished his sister, "I hope you weren't hounding the darling all summer long. I should love you the less to know that you had played the prude. She was just having a spot of fun."

I shrugged a lame apology.

36

Oliver bit his worried tongue.

In a moment we arrived at Aquarius Academy.

"Here we are," said Genevieve.

"Thanks again," I said to my rescuer.

She lovingly kissed my cheeks. "Don't be too hard on Elena."

∞

"What were ye thinking!?!" stormed the Commodore, pounding the oaken dinner table. "'Er very first class! Caught by those camp-Fire fools! And it was Gauntle's lassie 'at saved her and all!"

A glass of wine spilled upon the linen, its merciless crimson tide rolling towards the tall beauty. Everyone was desperate to leave the ugly scene. Everyone, it seemed, except the Twins.

I didn't know who told the Commodore. *I certainly didn't.* But the smugness on Casey's face told me all I needed to know.

"Where were ye?!?" he demanded of Elena. "Where were ye, lass?"

"I...I thought she was right behind me," she mumbled.

"Oliver and that dainty of a sister looked after 'er more than me own kin! Do ye think nothing of 'ouse Catagen? Do ye care if the whole family falls to ruin?"

"Of course I care!"

"D'ye realize what would befall us if something were to 'appen? Are ye deaf as well as blind? 'Ave ye noticed naught all summer, when She came to us from the salt and the brine?"

Elena whimpered.

"Commodore," I said. "It wasn't her fault."

"I'll decide whose fault it is!" But his eyes grew large as saucers when he remembered whom he was addressing.

I didn't know why I was defending the girl I vowed never to speak to again. But the Commodore's words hurt me, far more than my classmate's vicious jeers.

I thought he defends me because he wants to. Because he loves me. "It wasn't her fault!" I shouted, rising to my feet. "It's not her place to protect me! It's none of yours!"

I violently capsized the heavy chair before storming wildly up the marble stairs.

I flew into my watching bedroom, burying my head into a silken pillow.

"Quite a day you've had!" laughed the evil cat.

But my mind was a tempest I could not tame. "Shut up!" I sobbed, pelting him with an expensive vase. He just scampered away as it smashed into the bureau.

"Mistress?" came a voice at the door.

"Go away!"

"Mistress, I'm…I'm coming in."

"Go away!" I pleaded.

But the door opened anyway.

Before me stood the Old Man. *He is an old man!* I realized for the very first time. Time-worn and weather-beaten, he wore a lifetime of labors on his ancient, furrowed brow.

For a moment, I felt an enormous pang of gratitude. *This man, this sweet old man. He's done so much for me.*

But then I remembered my many woes.

"I thought you loved me!"

The Old Man hesitated, as if summoning a lifetime of experience before uttering a word. Then he said as kindly as he could, "I do love ye, Mistress."

"I'm not a Mistress!" I shrieked through my tears. I knew I was being horrible; knew I wasn't being fair. But chemical imbalances and raw emotion made reason beyond my control. "I don't even know what that means!"

"It means you're…dear to us."

"Dear?" I savaged, the day's events completely uncaging me. "You mean precious! A frail little bauble you can't afford to lose. And you don't even know why, do you? I'm only 'Dear' because some stupid God said I was!"

The sailor recoiled, taking a hesitant step backwards.

"You don't even know who I am! What if I told you? Told you everything?!?"

Othello pounced. But I was far too angry to let him interfere. In one violent motion, I flung him aside. He landed on my bed, hissing.

"You're a blessing to us, lass," rallied the Old Man, "a blessing indeed."

"I'm nothing but a curse! My whole life's been cursed, one miserable disaster after another!" Wickedness sped through my evil veins, a spiteful smile spoiling my face. "And I know what haunts you, old man. I know all about that *stupid* prophecy!"

This, at last, cowed Lord Catagen. Shrinking back with horror, he placed a shaking hand over his pious heart. The wall behind him impeded his retreat.

He's scared of me! Scared of the ruin I could bring! Triton told him nothing about who I was, or why I was here. *He only told him to find me…and protect me.*

"Mistress, I…" But the ancient relic fell silent. Whom – or what – was he talking to? The Sea master did not know.

The anguish on his face made me instantly sorry. Realizing how hateful I'd been, my cresting emotions crashing over me like a deep Ocean wave, I broke down and cried.

I cried about the hateful Raft: the thief that stole me from the Eastern shore. I cried about my father: alone and friendless with his anguish and his doubts. But most of all…I cried about my mother: the mother I would never know.

Shielding myself from the world around me, I coiled my frame into a frightened ball. Through blurry eyes I gazed at the two, *the two who control my future!*

The cat merely scoffed. Shaking his head with bitter disgust, he circled the mantle and curled up his tail. But the Commodore met my teary eyes. Aghast with wonder, lost and confused, he seemed wholly unable to fathom a weeping deity.

Yet something softened his Sea-blue eyes. Steeling himself with a melancholy frown, he took a brave step forward. For though he didn't know how to console a Goddess – having raised four granddaughters – he did know how to comfort a teenage girl. "There now, lass," he said, hugging me with his callused hands. "It'll be all right. You'll see."

"I'm sorry," I lamented, "I'm so sorry."

"There's nothing to be sorry about," he hushed, in a voice so mellow it soothed my rage.

"But," I blubbered, "I've been…so…so awful."

The Commodore didn't answer. Instead, he held me in a noble embrace. Only after a very long while, after my sobs melted into quiet sniffles, did he finally speak. "There now," he said, cradling my chin with leathered hands. Lifting my face to meet his own, he dried my tears with a silken handkerchief. "There's a lass. 'Tis no good fer a sailor to cry."

"I'm no sailor," I whimpered.

"Pallas," he whispered. "Ye are a Catagen. And in *this* family, everyone's a sailor; whither she wills it or no."

It was the first time he'd spoken my name, and it startled me. Searching beyond my emotional flood, gazing into his aged face, I found love in his gentle eyes.

"Yes…yes, sir."

"There now. Thas the spirit. Tomorrow's another day. I'll tell Elena…"

"Oh, please don't," I begged. "Really, it wasn't her fault."

The sailor grinned, a happy twinkle in his Watery eyes. "I'll tell her to keep a better eye out for you, that's all. Triton's Waves! I'm not as bad as all that…am I?"

Chapter Four

The Sixth Column

Much has been written about the Sixth Column. Should they have contacted the Mistress earlier, or should they have remained secret longer than they did? It is a difficult matter, concerning the plots and machinations of so many lords and ladies, of which we still know only the most obvious intrigues. But considering the tragedy that unfolded, it is difficult to defend the actions of…

Still – who can say, even at this latter date, what course might have been best? Even with the advantage of time and experience, it is impossible to truly understand the events that surrounded the coming of the New Age. Many argue that whatever course Lady Uncial took, it was certainly the wrong one, as evidenced by the calamity that followed. But others say that Uncial III walked a tightrope so delicately thin that the path she followed was the only one available, even if it led to her destruction.

"Rise and Fall of the Pentathanon Gods"

Herodotus III

Tomorrow came, just as the Old Man promised. And with the dawn, a new beginning. Breakfast was unusually pleasant as Elena and the Twins forgot their usual bickering. The Commodore was in high spirits, delighted "his little lassies" were getting along. After breakfast, we left the manor, joining the column of princes and princesses.

"Chin up," said Elena. "Head high. Remember, you're a Catagen."

I cringed, wondering how much Elena overheard.

Never miss a trick, does she?

Determined not to let the Old Man down, I did what I was told.

Professor Pythagoras was cross and impatient. Enjoying a vindictive smile, the mathematician started the year with a pop quiz.

I received my tablet with a grunt of dismay. *Such numbers!* I knew how to add and subtract, *but these problems are five rows high!* The multiplication was unbelievable, and as for the last three equations, *I can't make them out at all!* I'd never seen long division before.

I glanced nervously at my classmates to find them working on their tablets. Panic welled inside me as I was again reminded of how ignorant I was. Ten minutes passed and I'd only finished two problems.

Professor Pythagoras took my tablet with a derisive, "Tut, tut."

Then came the ordeal at blackboard, beginning with addition. I wished I could have a crack at one of those, but Alexander was called first, completing the problem with ease. A Gemini breezed through subtraction and Oliver tackled some multiplication before Pythagoras called on me.

The Leos guffawed as I faced the lonely chalkboard. The Professor wrote two long numbers together separated by a half circle and a bar over the second number.

I don't have a clue!

"Well?" said the beady-eyed professor. "Let's have it, Miss …"

"Pallas," I answered, remembering to keep my chin up.

"Ah!" he said with malicious delight. "Yes, I see…the Mistress of the Sea." He paused for effect, allowing his students to laugh at his stupid pun. But then his face turned cold. "Unfortunately, Miss Pallas, this is a class of higher mathematics. No amount of divinity or hallowed birth can make the numbers obey. For mathematics is a science which transcends even the Gods."

The confident laughter of my classmates died to a hush. Students squirmed in their seats, not sure they'd heard correctly.

The professor smiled, enjoying their discomfort. "In any case, you must pass my class, Miss Pallas, divine birth or no. I suggest the next time you enter my class, you come prepared."

I bit my lip, ignobly retreating back to my chair. I watched in gloomy silence as Eunice did the problem I could not.

Elena reached out her hand. I took it.

If this is what they teach, this is what I'll learn. I'll beat this frail wizard! I'll learn the math!

The class ended hours later, leaving me humbled and drained.

"Sorry," said Elena. "Spot of rough luck, I guess."

"Rough luck? I don't know the first thing about that division."

"Honestly," she guiltily replied. "What *did* they teach you in Atlantis?"

∞

The next day brought two surprises. The first was the answer to a dilemma I'd totally forgotten about. The second was a boy.

Though I didn't know it, the *Zoo* had been debating the past few weeks whether I could continue University. Lord Excelsior, the most important Fire Lord, demanded that I immediately return to the Isle of Catagen. But the Old Man won enough support to keep me in Greenstone. When Elena told me about it I was rather confused – last summer the Commodore told me he didn't want me at University because it was too dangerous.

"Lady Uncial changed his mind," said Elena.

"Why?" I asked as we entered the crystal-rose glass door of Etiquette.

"Isn't it obvious? This 'Age of Aquarius' prophecy is a magnificent boon to all the Aquarians."

"That's silly," I scoffed. "No one believes that stupid stuff."

"Of course they believe," sang her minstrel voice. "And the Houses who don't are besides themselves with jealousy…which is even better."

I didn't know how either situation could be good and was about to say so when Liam entered the room. "Hey there, Bright-Eyes."

"Oh my Gods," I muttered, dropping my jaw towards the floor.

"There's no need to pray," he said. "The Gods have already bestowed me upon you."

Embarrassed, I surrendered to a snarky jeer. "How merciful of the them to lay this…gift…before me."

"Well, you know," he chortled, "all good gifts come from heaven."

"Which heaven?" smarmed Alexander. "There are Five, you know."

Liam looked derisively at the shorter boy. "But only one that really matters." Taking a moment to mock him with a grin, he crossed the room and sat next to Oliver.

I grabbed Elena's hand and dragged her to the far corner. "What's Liam doing here? I thought he was a servant? But then I mentally scolded myself for my unworthy words. *Isn't that exactly what I am?*

Elena evaded me with a turn of her head. "Servant was…perhaps…an inaccurate term. A more precise description is that Liam is an ambassador…of sorts, who did for a time serve aboard *Enterprise.*"

Why is everyone being so evasive? But that, it seemed, was the least of my worries. I looked across the crowded room to see him flash that smile at me. "Which House is he in?"

"He's a guest of House Catagen," said Elena. "An honored guest. But he doesn't actually belong to a House, so he can't compete in the University Games."

"That's…sad," I said, gawking at his chiseled biceps.

"Don't get any ideas," warned Elena. "And don't ask him to explain. He won't tell you a thing. Consider him a friend…and nothing else."

But I couldn't – not after gazing into that face, not after hearing that voice, not what he told me that night aboard *Yorktown…*

"There's a plan. A plan to seat you at the right hand of the Creator."

Why does everything have to be so complicated? But my anxiety died as I looked into his eyes, transfixed by the glory that dwelled there.

∞

I spent the evening in Elena's room, safe within her web of charms. We talked like schoolgirls about simple things, boys being the simplest thing we could think of. She prattled endlessly about the princely array, cataloguing each with her complicated equations. Lineage and prestige figured prominently in her many-layered calculations.

"You really miss your mother," she said abruptly. She often made these shrewd statements, usually out of nowhere. Her understanding of people's emotions, especially mine, never ceased to amaze me.

I paused, thinking about my answer. "I guess. Only...I don't really remember her. How can I miss someone I barely knew?"

"You miss her smile, her touch, the sound of her voice. The way she comforted you, the female kinship you felt for one other."

I glimmered in the warmth of wistful reverie. Elena could be so kind, so lovely, so beautifully poetic. "What was your mother like?" I asked.

"She was sweet. And fun. She loved to tell stories."

"What kind of stories?"

"Silly stories," she sighed. "Stories about flying. Isn't that odd?"

It *was* odd. For I'd been raised on the same, foolish tales...

I wandered back to yesteryear, a time when my mother was still alive. Yet, for some reason she was gone, she'd "flown" away, my father told me.

Of course, he told such fantastic yarns – stories too impossible to be believed. He always acted serious in the telling, then laughed at the end as if it were all a big joke.

Only this story was different. He'd made a toy for me; he called it a kite. It was large and frail, thin leather stretched across a feeble frame of birch and twine. I remembered how I begged to paint it, how I colored the canvas with a beloved face...

Triumphant, the toddler carried the totem like a barbarian queen with a stolen prize. Streaks of blond topped eyes of grey, large and proud as the rising sun. The child had painted a thin red smile. But the image looked more like a dour sentinel.

The child, of course, didn't know or care. She was proud of the picture of her mother.

She followed her father to the happy shore. Lively and fun, she loved the ceaseless swarming of the warm, welcoming beach. The roar of the waves, the rippling of the sand, the hide-and-seek creatures who darted near at hand.

"My dearest baby girl," said her father. "Ready to test your kite against the Wind?"

The toddler stuck out her defiant chin, reluctant to surrender her trophy.

Her father laughed. "You can have it back. I promise."

"Daddy," said the child. "My kite!"

"Don't you want to see it fly?!"

"Fly?!" asked the toddler. "Like...like birds in the Sky?"

The old man laughed again. "Exactly! Now...hold the string in your hand."

The toddler loosed her iron grip. Clutching the ball of twine, she watched as her father held the kite above his head. Feigning a look of shocked surprise, he released it on a gust of Wind.

It soared high into the happy heavens, gay and sprite upon the bubbly Sky. She marveled how it danced and climbed, imbibed with such wonderful magic. Higher and higher until...

The brilliance of the sun gobbled up her prize! "Daddy!" she cried. "My kite!"

Her father smiled. "The kite's not gone, Pallas. It's still in your hands."

The toddler looked at the unraveling ball. Spinning relentlessly – tugging into the thieving Air – it seemed to have a mind of its own.

He bent down behind her, snuggling her in his arms. "Can you feel the string pulling in your hand?"

"Yes, Daddy."

"That's the kite, my dearest baby girl. Here," he said, stopping the spinning and winding it in. "It'll come back if you pull it."

It took longer than the anxious child would have liked. But sure enough, the faithful kite reappeared. The garish face peered from the firmament – imperious, noble, and sad.

"She's looking down on us," he said, "from way up high. Just like...just like your mother's love. Though you may not always see her, Pallas, she's always watching over you. Always."

Her mother's face was nestled in the heavens. It was strangely comforting to the trusting child.

"Only, like the string, you must hold on tight," he told her. "Hold on tight, and never let go. Never let go of your mother's love."

"Tell me, love," asked Elena. What was your mother like?"

I turned away, sweeping a tear from my eye. "She was like a kite."

∞

I ran with the Twins during practice next day, enjoying their playful jibes. But the fear of inadequacy gnawed at me. *If I want to get on the team, I need to train as hard as I can.* Picking up my pace, I waved goodbye to my sisters. "See ya, slow pokes!"

"Slow pokes?" Casey snarled. "Just wait till I get on a horse!"

"You'll need a horse to catch her!" Lucy laughed.

The autumn Wind felt brisk in my hair, the joy of running…fresh in my veins. But I grimaced a scowl as a young man raced to join me.

"Hi," said Liam.

"What are you doing here?"

"Same as you. Running."

I don't know why, but his unexpected reappearance made me extremely uneasy. "Elena said you can't compete."

"Bid me run," he replied, "and I will strive for things impossible."

"Huh," I huffed, surrendering to a smile. "Sounds like something my father would say."

"Doesn't surprise me," he laughed. "It's a quote from a famous poet."

"Whatever," I snorted. After the storyteller's grossly exaggerated account of my rescue from Capro Bay and the annoying prophecies that hounded me ever after, I wasn't keen on poets these days. "You didn't answer my question."

"Need to stay fit," he said. "Besides, I can help you train."

"Or maybe you like spending time with me."

"Maybe," he smiled.

∞

47

Othello was just waking when I climbed into bed that night.

"My, you're up early," I griped. Elena was already asleep, she got a lot of "beauty rest" as she liked to call it. The Twins were out prowling. I would have loved to tag along, but the weight of my daytime classes and my midnight lessons were taking their toll.

"I know," yawned the cat, gouging his claws into the bedpost. "I don't know what's wrong with me. Can't seem to sleep more than eighteen hours a day."

"That's terrible," I mocked. "Listen. Do you mind if we don't read tonight? Tomorrow's a big day, and…"

"What happens tomorrow?"

"I'm going to my first practice…to compete in the University Games! I'm trying out for Mounted Javelin and the Circus."

"Horses! Yeach! I can't understand what anyone sees in the big, ugly brutes."

"Well…they're very sweet, and they're very strong."

"Overgrown monstrosities. What a nightmare! Any civilized creature would learn to use a litter box, but no, they just…"

"I get the picture. Still, they're very smart."

"Have you ever met a horse who could talk?"

"No."

"I rest my case."

I settled beneath my blanket. "I'm going to race."

"Well, I wouldn't. It sounds so dreadful and dirty and noisy," he said, scrunching up his nose, "around all those…animals."

After school the next day, I followed the Twins to the Aquarian fields. Elena, of course, had nothing to do with sports – *she might break a nail or something*. But the Twins were quite athletic. As Casey was an excellent horseman, she'd be trying out for Mounted Javelin. Lucy wanted to box. Considering the size of the older boys, I thought the idea hilarious, but I didn't want to hurt my sister's feelings.

Mounted Javelin was my best event. I also hoped to run the 24 Stad, the longest of the footraces. But what I really wanted was to drive a chariot in the

Circus. The winner of the Circus had the unbelievable honor of driving a golden chariot during the closing ceremonies.

I wanted that golden chariot.

But am I good enough? I was one of the best athletes back in Kelly Tree. And that was when I'd had no time to practice because of my work in the fields. But the competitors at University would be nothing less than superb. The children of the nobility might be better than me.

A tall, lanky senior whistled the Aquarians for silence.

"That's Joculo," said Lucy. "He's the new team captain."

But I already knew the boyish face. Joculo IV, crown prince of House Joculo, was a favorite topic among the pretty girls of Kelly Tree. The fawning slaves adored him, going on and on about how handsome he was.

The only reason they think he's good looking is because he's the only prince they've ever seen.

As Joculo had always been at University at the time, he'd never been to the Games in Kelly Tree. Thus, he never saw me compete, and didn't share his sister's suspicion that he'd seen me before.

Because he never mingled with us peasants like Janice and Lord Joculo. How many times had I seen Janice and her father walk among his subjects, spreading empathy and cheer...and sometimes even money!

Young Joculo, on the other hand, was said to be his mother's son, keeping to his noble set of peers. Because of this, I felt much more comfortable with young Joculo than I did with his sister Janice.

"Quiet!" he called. "Quiet. I have something to say before we begin." Gazing about the eager faces, he formed a ruddy scowl. "Last year was a complete disaster; finished last place."

The Aquarians grew instantly glum. They didn't need reminding of the drubbing they'd received.

"As the new team captain, I've decided we're going to have tryouts for every position...including the Circus."

Gales of complaints greeted this announcement.

"But I've ridden in the Circus since I was fourteen!" said Lord Duma.

"Yes, and you've lost every single time!"

I giggled with the gale of laughter.

Dusan looked absolutely furious.

"We're going to train harder and longer than we ever have before," said Joculo. "Every night, four to seven, rain or shine."

The tawny athletes mewled like kittens.

"It'll be dark…" Anthony complained.

"What about our studies?" said Mark.

"I'm not training in the rain," said Urban.

"You will if want to be on the team," said Joculo.

"It'll be cold," whined Dusan, "We might catch a flu."

"What a sissy!" I retorted. "No wonder you got clobbered last year."

Lord Duma rounded on me and glared. "What did you say?"

Stop, I told myself; *be nice to people!* "I only meant…if we're not willing to train hard, we can't expect to win, now can we?"

"Who asked you, anyway?" said Mark. "Think you can try that God-stuff out here?"

"The Commodore gonna put you on the team?" said Anthony.

Lucy stepped in. "That's not fair, and you jolly well know it!"

"I'll decide what's fair!" shouted Dusan. "*I* am a lord!"

Joculo jostled himself betwixt the angry pack. "She's trying out, my Lord, just like everyone else."

"Yeah? Well she's gonna lose," said Urban. "And then she can sit on the sidelines and pout."

"If you beat her, you can drive, just like you did before."

"I am a lord of the *Zoo*," said Dusan. "Why should I have to prove myself against a stinking girl?"

"That girl," said Joculo, "is a dolphin rider, or hadn't you heard? Besides, if she's just a girl, she shouldn't be hard to beat, now should she?"

"Of course not," he blustered. "It's just not right. I am a lord."

"I'll be a lord some day," Joculo growled.

"I'm a lord *now*."

"Only because your old man was chasing wenches when he should have been producing an heir."

"How dare you?!"

"How dare I what?" Joculo pulled himself to his lanky height, peering down at the pudgy boy.

Dusan took a hesitant step backwards.

Turning from the obnoxious boy, Joculo addressed his team again. "I'm team captain. And I say *everyone* is trying out. Now," he spoke directly at Dusan, "I want fifty laps from all of you! Then the *real* fun begins."

The princes and princesses huddled away, lamenting their horrible lot. The Twins and I raced ahead of the others, distancing ourselves from Dusan and his friends.

"That was weird," I said.

"No kidding," said Lucy. "Honestly! I've never seen Joculo in such a huff."

"Wants to set an example," Casey mused. "Put Dusan in his place."

"Put him in his place?" I asked.

"Well, you know…Dusan is lord of House Duma."

"And a real idiot," said Lucy.

"Well, yes, of course," said Casey, "That's why Joculo has to prove that he's in charge."

"Who made Joculo team captain?" I asked.

"Uncial," said Lucy.

"Dusan wanted the position, of course," said Casey.

"But Uncial gave it to Joculo instead," said Lucy.

"Why?"

"Uncial's furious with House Duma," said Casey.

"Has been for a really long time," said Lucy.

"Really. Why?"

"Bother," laughed Lucy. "Who cares? I can't believe you told him off like that!"

"Absolutely brilliant!" Casey agreed.

"Your very first day, and you've already made a name for yourself."

Yeah…you're on the team for five minutes, and they already hate you.

I gloomily surveyed my homework that night. Fifty mind-boggling problems, all multiplication and division.

I reluctantly asked the cat for help, but Othello didn't know how to divide any more than I did.

"Why would I concern myself with that obnoxious drivel?"

"It's called math."

"I don't care what it's called. It looks so…depressing."

Next, I tried Elena, who knew perfectly well how to multiply and divide. But whereas the princess could talk all day about politics, she had little patience for numbers. She petulantly tried to help me when an unexpected visitor arrived.

"Genevieve! What a smashing surprise!"

"I wanted to visit my favorite cousin." Genevieve kissed Elena's cheeks and smoothed over her hands. "And the Mistress of the Sea," she said as she kissed me as well.

The three of us sat down. Elena told Abbey to prepare a tea. After a few minutes of small-talk, Genevieve picked up my homework.

"Working on long division?"

"Yeah."

"I just adore math, don't you?"

"Uh…yeah. Well…no, not really."

"Genevieve!" piped Elena, a stroke of brilliance on her opaline face. "You are ever so clever at numbers and facts and…things. Be a dear and help me explain…"

"Why, I'd be delighted. Only, we'll need better light."

"There's a lamp in my room," I offered. I used it at night to do my writing.

"Perfect," said Genevieve as she followed me to my bedroom. "You don't mind, do you Elena?"

"Of course not, darling. In fact, I'll be right along," she lied as she scampered down the stairs.

"Oliver told me about Pythagoras," Genevieve explained. "I'm quite good at math. I can help, if you like."

"But…you're a year younger than us."

"That doesn't matter. I have private tutors at home. Pythagoras' class is just a review for me."

"Wow. That'd be, uh…great."

I walked her to my bedroom and lit my lamp. A big white bird fluttered from the windowsill.

"Do you mind if I close the window, love?" asked Genevieve. "There's a bit of a breeze."

"Good idea," I said as Othello pattered into the room. "It will keep my cat from caterwauling all night."

Othello stuck out his lurid tongue before pouncing on my bed. Gouging my pillow with his vicious claws, he lay down and waited.

Genevieve wasn't bragging; she was good at math. Patient and thorough, without a hint of conceit, she taught me how to work the many problems.

"I like math," she said. "Have a problem, get an answer. I find that…satisfying. Don't you?"

"Uh…sure."

First we started on the gargantuan multiplication. I thought I was pretty good at multiplication, but compared to Genevieve, I was quite slow.

The tiny Tauran produced hand-written flash cards she'd made from strips of wood. "When I was learning, I reviewed these a few times a day. Here, you have them."

"Oh, no. I couldn't."

"You can give them back if you'd like. Try them. You'll find they make a big difference."

"Thanks."

Next, we tackled long division. "It's really just multiplication in reverse, with a little estimation."

I found this was true, delighted to decipher the mystery of the quotient.

We worked late into the night, giggling softly by the soft lamplight.

"Look at the time," said Genevieve. "Father will be worried."

"Yeah," I said, finding myself unexpectedly sad. *Genevieve's a beautiful princess who will see her father in a few moments. I'm just a slave who may never see my father again.*

"I'm sorry, love. Was it something I said?"

"No...it wasn't you."

"Yes it was," she soothed. "It must be hard. Away from your family, away from your kin."

"Listen. You've been really great. I can't tell you how much I appreciate..."

"Same time tomorrow, then?"

"You sure? You've done so much already."

"Of course, love. Anything to help a friend. Only, why don't we meet in the Aquarian library instead?"

"The what?"

"Library. It's a place to study."

"OK," I said as I led her down the stairs. Once inside the foyer, a marine opened the heavy door.

A gust of Wind billowed inside, catching the Tauran by surprise. Panic calloused her gentle face. "I hate the Wind," she savagely declared, clutching her cloak against the breeze.

"Really? Why?"

"I...I don't know why. I can't explain it. I just have an intolerable loathing of the Wind."

"I'm sorry. Would you like me to go with you?"

"No, love, of course not. I'll be fine once I'm inside my carriage. Goodnight." She kissed both my cheeks.

"Thanks."

"You're late!" hissed the cat.

"I was working."

"You were wasting my valuable time…time I could have been sleeping."

"So sleep!" I said, exasperated. "Nothing's stopping you."

"And leave you alone with Gauntle's daughter? Not on your life."

"I *like* Genny. You saying I can't trust her?"

"I'm saying she's a Tauran. And just for the record…I don't trust *anyone*."

"She's helping me with my math!"

"Which is the most pathetic ruse I've ever heard. As if anyone 'liked' that numerical nonsense."

"I have to pass my classes, don't I?"

"I suppose. It's just so droll, the trivialities you humans invent to make things complicated."

"Maybe you should learn to divide," I said. "You know, expand your horizons."

"Don't be ridiculous. I'm much too important to be bothered with that servile nonsense."

"And why is that?"

"Because I'm a cat, and you're not."

"So."

"Cats are superior in every single way. The fact that I condescend to talking to you…"

"Don't give me that rubbish," I testily replied, when I noticed something lying on my dresser. It was a tiny silver pendent.

"It's a box," I said, dangling it by its chain. Candlelight shimmered off its glimmering sides, speckling the room with a rainbow of color.

"Cube," he said, gawking at the charm. "Where did you get that?"

"It was just sitting here."

A blue crystal was encrusted on one of its six sides. On the opposite, an identical one of red. I quickly inspected the other sides. Brown opposite yellow, green opposite…but the opposite side was blank.

"That's odd. This side doesn't have a jewel."

"Column," he mumbled, deep in furrowed thought.

"Column?"

"Uh…what? I meant…" But he didn't finish his sentence. Instead, he started pacing.

"You said column," I said, studying the cube. *They are columns!* Each gem had a minuscule pedestal with an ionic capital on the top. I returned to the side that was blank.

"Don't touch that."

I deliberately disobeyed him.

"Stop!" he hissed.

I heard a muffled click. The jewel-less side was a tiny door.

"Meow!" he wailed, reverting to his native tongue.

I peered inside. *There's something small in there.* I shook the charm until it fell into my hand.

"Please stop," he begged. "Put it back, before…"

I gazed at the jewel. It was a column, the same as the columns on the sides of the cube. Only it wasn't a jewel, but a black little chip.

"What is it?"

He paused, fabricating the best lie he could on such short notice. "I…I don't know."

"Yes you do."

"If you don't put it back…"

"What? The Sky's going to fall?"

"It might."

"I know you know what it is. Why don't you just tell me?"

But Othello started pacing again. "Who could have? Was it that Tauran? It must be a sign. Orders perhaps, or…"

"What are you talking about?"

He suddenly stopped his feline march. "You must wear the necklace. Yes, that's it. Wear the necklace at all times…after you put the Sixth Column back where you found it."

"Sixth column?" I said, examining the splinter.

"Oh!" he gasped. "I didn't say that!"

"Yes you did. You called it a sixth column."

"She shouldn't know that! She mustn't be told!"

"What shouldn't I be told?"

The cat was agitated, far more than I'd ever seen him before. He seemed troubled, guilty – on the verge of making a spectacular confession – when he suddenly mastered himself. "Put the column back in the cube and *never* take it out."

"What is it?"

"Put it back."

"Not until you tell me what it is."

"I'll tell you once it's back inside the cube."

I paused, knowing for the very first time I had him backed into a corner. "It's a secret, isn't it? A gift from the Gods?"

"The Gods?" he chortled. "Not exactly."

I surveyed the tiny cube. Its metallic sheen reminded me of the magic summoning box, the one that contained the dreaded Fire. But it was far too small to be a weapon.

It must be something wonderful, something nice and sweet and frail!

But then I remembered the silver mirror. The emerald eyes of the dolphins, lost amongst the Fiery leaves. "It reminds me of the silver mirror Uncial gave me. The jeweled eyes, the delicate silver, the…"

"Uncial?" he accused. "Uncial gave you a mirror?"

"Yeah. Got it from her brat of a daughter. Only I dropped it and…"

Othello rolled his eyes. "*Uncial* gave you that mirror!?"

"That's what I said. Janice said something funny. She said "DG" and I dropped it in surprise because those are letters of the alphabet and…"

"Janice? The daughter of Lord Joculo?

"Yeah. She said her father told her this funny joke and…"

"Lord Joculo knows the alphabet?!"

"Uh…I guess?"

57

The cat looked mortified. "Joculo knows the alphabet, and you thought you'd keep it to yourself?"

"I forgot."

"Uncial gave you a silver mirror, and you didn't tell me?"

"I thought you knew."

"Please!" he said with a longsuffering wail. "Even you, with your exceedingly limited intelligence, must realize how dangerous your life has become. I need to *know* these things if I'm to protect you."

"From what? The three blind mice?"

"There are people out there who want to kill you, or hadn't you noticed?"

"Yeah…because of you."

"Me?" said the cat. "Don't be dense."

"Admit it. None of this God-stuff would've ever happened if it hadn't been for you."

"I'll do nothing of the sort," he snapped. "Shepherding you through this brutish labyrinth has been its own hellish reward. I'll not burden myself with further insult by granting you an ecclesiastical confession."

I almost retorted, but stopped myself short. His complicated words always frightened me.

"Now," he said with forced patience, "I want you to put the black column back into the box."

"If I do, will you tell me what it is?"

"Yes," he said. "I promise."

I placed the column back in the cube, closing its miniature door.

I looked up, ready to hear his rare explanation.

The cat was gone.

I jumped from my bed, swearing a curse.

If I ever got a hold of that cat!

Chapter Five

Romancing a Drone

*An animal may be ferocious and cunning,
but it takes a man to tell a lie.*

> *The Island of Dr. Moreau*
> H. G. Wells, English author
> circa 1900: Earth Standard

"I know I'm bored," mused the Goddess, "but…do I really want to do this?"

It wasn't the fact that he was an animal. He was, after all, an Alpha drone; statistically 8.6 times more intelligent than a Gamma moron. Nearly human in every way, his genetic deficiencies were internal, and thus…hidden.

No, it was her own recklessness that gave her pause. *The witless creature could do anything, say anything.* The beast could even harm her. The danger was palatable, real…

…and ever so exciting!

The Goddess lived for excitement. Heaven was a tedious chore. Even *ambrosia* had lost its savor. *My happiest days were with Teresa, escaping the bleakness of Atlantis, on our secret, gallant adventures.* Besides, she'd done so much to help the drones. *Why can't I have a little fun?*

Teresa, of course, wouldn't approve. She'd say she was abusing the witless creature, or cite her own "prime directive" of non-interference, or something queer like that.

Cypris sighed. She studied Teresa, loved Teresa, owed her life to Teresa. Yet…she didn't understand Teresa at all. Her mentor had everything – beauty, intelligence, power and lineage. All she had to do was appease Poseida, and Atlantis would some day be hers.

But Teresa refused to obey. She quarreled with Poseida instead.

Well, she thought, *what Teresa doesn't know won't hurt her.* Besides, why should she, a Goddess, follow the rules of the biggest rule-breaker on the planet?

He was tending cattle upon the gentle steeps of McFarland. Tall and handsome, his noble face betrayed his superior breeding. Why Duma III, the crown prince of House Duma, heir designate of a Voting Member of the *Zoo*, was shepherding a herd of cows, Cypris didn't know. She only knew she wanted him, he was alone, and she was ready for a bit of fun.

She loved animals, of course. The kind that walk on four legs, especially. So she stole a vial of pheromones Teresa recently developed. Hiding her chariot on the Seaward side of the mountain, she laced the Air with its powerful scent. Designed to make friends with predatory mammals, the pheromones gathered a remarkable brood. The fawning wolves delighted her, as did the following bear.

What a splendid joke! To meet my prince with this carnivorous clan?!

The prince was not amused. Indeed, he seemed aghast. He dropped his crook and notched an arrow…

"Why do you greet me thus?" she laughed, enjoying the terror on his frightened face. "We've only come to play!"

Wide-eyed and trembling, the prince just stared. Then – all at once – his emotions changed: from vapid fear to vivid inspiration. He flung himself upon penitent knees. "Hail, your blessed holiness! Wither you come from Atlantis, or Aeolia, or even the depths of Erebus. Are you high-born Tess of the lovely hair, or perhaps even Rhodes? Let me build you an altar upon the highest peak."

"Why do you liken me to the deathless ones?" she blushed. "Nay, my prince, I am but a mortal, and a woman was the mother that bore me. Uncial is her famous name." She enjoyed the contrivance of the clever lie. She pretended not to be a God, but a noble-born mortal. After all, she wanted a lover, not a pet.

"Forgive me, my Lady. But…I know the only daughter of the Lady Uncial. She is not as comely as you. Nor does she wear a gown with the brightness of Fire, nor a splendid robe of gold. Her necklace does not dazzle in the sun, nor do hungry beasts flock to her side."

"Oh?" she tittered. She hadn't thought to change her attire into something more…pastoral. And why should she? She loved wearing gold, loved the perfumes that floated in her hair. *Though the wolves are rather hairy,* she thought as they nuzzled against her legs. The nervous cows brayed their dismay. *I wonder? Is it going to be a problem if the wolves eat the cows?*

Her little adventure was going awry. This aggravated Cypris, who was used to having everything exactly her way. *Why can't I plan an escapade as easily as my mentor?* she pouted. *Teresa made it look so easy.* She briefly regarded, then disregarded Teresa's careful preparations, wondering why she hadn't made her own.

She decided on boldness to salvage her lie. "Take me, young prince. Take me now."

"Take you, my Lady?"

She couldn't hide the crossness in her perfect eyes of blue. *He's so dim-witted!* she thought. *Or is his innocence adorable?* Cypris couldn't decide. She moved enticingly closer. "Take me in your arms, stainless and unproved in love."

"You want to marry?"

The term was only vaguely familiar to the Atlantian: an ancient ritual that had something to do with sex, but full of pagan promises and outdated loyalties.

"Of course," she cooed, "if that is what you call it."

Handsome desire filled his face. "Oh, my Lady, beautiful as the Gods – if you are indeed mortal, and Uncial is your mother, then neither God nor mortal shall restrain me till I have lain with you in love right now. Prepare the sweet marriage that is honorable in the eyes of men."

His poetic words melted her heart, even as she mocked him. She giggled, wondering at the naivety of the eloquent animal.

She rose from the skins of the deep-roaring lions which the drone had slain and made for his bed. The waning passion of the afternoon spent, she recoiled from the filth that surrounded her.

She gazed upon the magnificent view of the Sea below. A drone might consider the cottage comfortable, even charming. But the Goddess had eyes for the specks of dirt on the handsome flagstone floor.

She felt a bit guilty, and perhaps even afraid. What would the Demes think of her little liaison? What antiseptic horrors would she undergo to rid herself of the filth of men?

I won't go to the Demes. I'll go straight to Teresa. Teresa would move heaven and Earth to protect her favorite creation. She considered for a moment which was worse, disappointing her faithful mentor or undergoing the cruelty of the Demes. Deciding on her creature comforts, she decided on Teresa.

She popped a pill of *ambrosia,* instantly feeling its soothing power. Feeling braver, she turned to go. But…what to do with the sleeping drone? For she suddenly had a horrible thought, one that *ambrosia* was powerless to quell. *What if he realizes who I am? What if he brags about what he's done?* Acting on impulse, she decided to end this dangerous threat.

She donned her heavenly garments and left the humble hovel. The Sky below was streaked with pink, climaxed with Fiery orange and red. The wolves were gone, as were the cattle. The carcass of a half-eaten cow was all that remained. She wondered if the lost herd would cause him any trouble.

"Up, son of Duma!!!" The hovering chariot, shining silver upon the dying sun, magnified her voice to epic proportions. "Why do you sleep so heavily!?"

Her clothing was no different, nor the twisted brooches or golden earrings, nor the sparkling necklace in the guise of laughing flowers. But now she stood on a golden chariot, a covey of doves circling around her. Summoned by another sweetly crafted vial, their high-pitched songs were lively and gay. The lights of the chariot dazzled her diamonds, speckling the brilliance of the rose colored sunset.

Naked, Duma stumbled from the hovel. Frightened, he fell upon his knees. He hid his face in praying hands. "As soon as I saw you, I knew you were divine! But…you did not tell me truly. Mighty Poseida, have pity!"

His pathetic pleading pleased her. *I like being a God!* With the Air of smug superiority, she spoke to the craven drone. "Take courage, and be not afraid. You need not fear harm from me, nor from the blessed ones."

He raised his fallen head. She saw the love he had for her in his handsome eyes: fresh and genuine, so different from the cynicism of her plastic world. For a moment, she almost loved him…

But he shattered the moment with a pathetic request. "Oh my holiness, take me to Atlantis, where I can be your husband. Take me to heaven, and I shall rule by your side."

She laughed. *What can he be thinking, the stupid, ignorant fool?* What she said was slightly kinder, even if it was a lie. "Would that you could live deathless amongst the hallowed Gods. But old age will enshroud you – ruthless, wearying; dreaded even by the Gods."

"Then stay here, your holiness. Stay and spend your days with me. Bear me strong sons, and live as a wife of a Voting Member of the *Zoo*."

Her laughter lilted like a song. *How funny?! Really! He's just too much!* But her words were carefully measured. "Would that I could, dear prince. But Fate claims us all, and my Fate is to abide in Atlantis. Peace and long life be upon you, and may your progeny prosper and grow."

She touched the control panel and turned the reverb two levels higher. "But be warned!" she said in a deadly growl. "If you foolishly boast that you lay with an Atlantian, Poseida will smite you in her unquenchable anger. Take heed, name me not, but have regard to the anger of the Gods."

The anguish in his eyes was real, the loss he felt…palatable.

Satisfied, she tossed her head and jetted into the firmament.

Chapter Six

Steeple Chase

Men trust their ears less than their eyes.

The Histories of Herodotus
Herodotus, Greek author
circa 450BC: Earth Standard

Herodotus III was one of my favorite professors. The Twins thought history was boring. "Just a bunch of old-dead-guys." But I was fascinated by his many tales, stories about people, and not the stupid Gods.

"Poseida selected Uncial to be the first House in the year zero," said the professor. "That is the start of our calendar, and our history."

I paused. It was now the year 100. *The whole world started a hundred years ago? That doesn't seem right!*

I thought about all the things mankind had built: ships, houses, castles. Yet in my own short life, nothing had ever been invented. In fact, I'd never even heard the word "invented" until Othello made me copy it as part of my Vocabulary.

How could we have learned so much a hundred years ago, and nothing ever since?

"Professor," I asked, "what happened before the year zero? Before Uncial formed the first House?"

Herodotus looked perplexed. "Nothing happened."

"Something had to happen. Who were Uncial's parents? What were they like?"

Elena gave me an angry glare. Classmates murmured to themselves. Herodotus changed his expression to interested curiosity. I couldn't tell if he was amused or annoyed.

"It is something I only teach to seniors – the origin of the world. It's a secret the slaves must never be told: knowledge for the nobility alone. For it is a solemn thing to know the genesis of man."

Eager to hear more, the sophomores sat up in their seats.

"In the beginning, the sacred Gods hurled themselves upon the Good Earth in a hollowed bolt of Fire."

Alexander and the Leos shared superior grins.

"A fragment of that Fire landed on the very top of the tallest hill of this city. There, it cooled into a luminescent green stone. Thus the name...Greenstone."

Cool! I was always fascinated by names.

"The nobility memorialized the holy artifact by building the *Zoo* atop that hill. You'll see this splendid wonder when you visit the *Zoo* later this year."

Awesome! I couldn't wait.

"Many Gods settled our world, living in peace and harmony. Yet one God tried to enslave the others. His name was Tigh. Such was his arrogance that he gathered an immortal army."

There are more than five Gods? An entire army? I've never heard that before!

"Tigh forced his army to construct an unholy Tower, a monstrous colossus of metal and steel. A tower so tall it might reach the stars. Yet there were five brave Gods who resisted. These we worship today: Poseida, Vulcana, Terra, Zephyr, and Deme. They fought the despotic ruler."

"Thus started a cataclysmic war, one that shook the Earth and the Sky. Yet neither side could prevail. For who can best immortals? After ten years of devastation – pestilence and famine; war and pain – one of the Tighs saw the wickedness of their ways and helped the Pentathanon Five. Shiva we call her, the Destroyer. Sower of kindness...and desperate despair. Using dark magic, unearthed from the bowels of some fathomless crypt, she released the Automatons from the depths of Tartarus. Vile, three-legged creatures – spreading death and destruction ere they went – the Automatons crushed the cursed Tighs, casting them deep into the bottomless abyss."

The silent class was mortified, grateful the Pentathanons triumphed over the Tighs.

"Then...how did we get here?" a Tauran asked. "People, I mean."

"Deme created the slaves who serve us. But Shiva – the Destroyer whom we do not speak of – was not satisfied. She felt that man could rule himself, that men and women should have wanton autonomy. She used her deep and mysterious magic to create a new breed of man...a man in the image of the Gods."

65

The classroom listened with wide-eyed wonder.

"It was she who created the *Zoo* nobility, empowering us with wisdom to rule the slaves. Not only that, but she gave us the skills man needed to survive. She taught us how to lay bricks, construct bridges, build ships, wrought steel…"

For the first time in my life, I actually admired a God, this Shiva who ended the endless war. *And that explains how we learned so much so quickly; she taught us everything we know!*

Yet something troubled me. "Why have we never heard of this Shiva before?" I asked.

"After the war, Shiva thought herself equal to the Pentathanon Five and committed an act of treachery. Defying the will of the Heavens, she sought to endow a terrible knowledge upon the nobility, a secret that would surely doom him. For with such knowledge, man would think himself a God…and die."

An iceberg plummeted through my fearful soul. *This terrible knowledge, could it be reading!?* Othello made me swear to keep reading a secret. Never tell anyone, for any reason. *In fact, he acts like reading is more sacred than the Gods!* Had the demon tainted me with a horrible sacrilege?

"What happened to Shiva?" asked Alexander, sporting a knowing grin.

"Mulciber imprisoned her in a timeless cell, of smokeless Fire that never shall fail. There, she suffers eternal damnation. For such is the fate of those who defy, the holy and sacrosanct Pentathanon Five."

My classmates nodded their righteous agreement.

I merely scoffed. *The history lesson sounds like a deity lesson; the deity lessons sound like science.* Pythagoras alone dared to call his field, "a science which transcends even the Gods."

"They just chucked her?" I brandished. "She saved the world, so they gave her the boot?"

Confident in their ignorance, my classmates hissed and jeered.

Herodotus regarded me with a look of introspection. His expression was quizzical, yet cautious. "If you wish to divine the morality of the Gods, I suggest you speak to Professor Hesiod…"

Ophelia confronted me in the hallway after class. "You really have a death wish, don't you?"

"What?" I said, having no idea what she meant.

Elena charged the Tauran princess. "What did you say?!"

Ophelia retreated a startled step. "I'd keep a muzzle on that pet of yours, Elena. Before it bites off more than it can chew."

"Why don't you crawl back beneath that rock you've been hiding under?" snarled Elena.

Ophelia quavered, confused by the princess' belligerence. "I...uh..."

"Shut up, you stupid prat! And keep your ugly nose where it belongs."

I marveled at Elena's ferociousness. *I've never seen her so hostile!*

Evidently, Ophelia hadn't either as she fled to her knot of Taurans.

"I hate that girl and I always have!" shrilled Elena. "And to think her mother sits in the *Zoo*! Perhaps it's time for Father to visit Capro Bay again."

I was about to wholeheartedly agree when she huffed away, barreling rudely through a group of children.

I didn't understand Elena's resentment until practice that afternoon. First thing were laps, endless laps. Urban IV, a minor Uncialian prince, was an excellent runner, but he was also quite lazy. He held back with Mark and Anthony, the waddling Lord Duma bringing up a distant rear.

Liam and I were becoming good friends. It was easy to like the handsome boy as he was incredibly intelligent and surprisingly kind. Better yet, he even stopped that "harbor of disaster" nonsense, or whatever it was called. I was convinced the Twins put him up to it as one of their silly jokes.

We normally talked about the coming Games. But today I thought about my sister. "I wonder why Elena is so jealous of Ophelia?" I didn't expect him to answer. *After all...what could he possibly know about House politics?* So I was surprised when he actually did.

"Lots of reasons. Her mother nearly killed the Commodore."

"Yeah..." *Like, how could I forget?* But I thought there was more to it than that. "She said something about Ophelia's mother sitting in the *Zoo*."

"Come on, Bright-Eyes. Think about it."

"Think about what?"

"Elena is unbelievably beautiful. But to her, it's actually a curse."

"What do you mean?"

"The Commodore's a schemer. He won't miss an opportunity with the most beautiful girl in the world."

"What kind of opportunity?" I said, a wave of warmth sweeping over my sweaty body. Somehow, I didn't think it had anything to do with running.

"The Commodore became powerful by making shrewd alliances with potential enemies. Backroom deals...you know."

"So?"

"Every prince wants to marry Elena."

I didn't like where this was going. "So...she gets married? It's not the end of the world."

Liam sighed. "Who will succeed the Commodore after he dies?"

I paused. I'd never thought about it, and never heard Elena talk about it either. That seemed odd. She was always talking about lines of succession. The obvious answer both surprised and annoyed me. "William, I guess."

"Exactly. Now...who comes after him?"

I didn't know. William's only daughter was married to Gauntle, the most powerful Earth lord. They had two children, Oliver and Genevieve.

"See? The Water gets pretty muddy."

"But surely Oliver wouldn't become Lord Catagen? He's the son of Gauntle."

"Yeah, but Gauntle has a younger brother, Fletcher, who's Oliver's uncle. He could take the reign for Gauntle and leave Catagen to Oliver."

I quickly became dizzied with the complications of the Catagen succession. Anger made me pick up the pace. "So where does that leave Elena?"

"Nowhere. The beautiful wife of an influential lord."

I thought about Borelo, the Air prince who could cement a new alliance for House Catagen. I thought about the muddy stream.

"What's that got to do with Ophelia?"

"Think about it. Ophelia's an only child; she's guaranteed a spot on the *Zoo*. Even though she's a mindless idiot, whoever marries her will become the husband of Lady Oxymid. On the other hand, there's Elena – a politician if ever there was one."

My eyes betrayed my surprise. *Most men compliment Elena for her beauty, not her mind.*

"I know what you're thinking, but I'm serious. There's more to Elena than her pretty eyes. I've seen how she influences people. She's a natural born leader. But she'll never sit in the *Zoo*, because anyone important enough to marry her will already be powerful enough to have a Voting chair."

I started becoming annoyed again. "How do you know all this stuff?"

Liam laughed. "I pay attention."

We finished the laps, slowing to an aching walk. I knew I'd run too hard when a cramp hobbled me to the ground.

"You OK?" he asked.

"Cramp," I said though gritted teeth.

"Where?" he said, bending down to massage both my calves – kneading them with strong, tender hands.

"Thanks."

"No worries."

∞

The Twins and I headed back to Catagen Manor after practice. I wanted to talk to Elena, but her bedroom door was closed. I knew not to disturb her, so I went to my bedroom instead. Strangely, Othello wasn't there.

Probably out chasing mice…

Oh, I forgot…he's way too lazy.

Back in Kelly Tree, I spent most of my time alone. Here in the busy Manor, it seemed impossible to get a moment by myself. I had a separate bedroom, of course, but was forced to share it with that ridiculous cat. Having the room to myself was like a treat.

I looked around, thinking what I would do with my momentary privacy.

Of course! I thought, opening the trunk to retrieve the magic harness. "I haven't seen you in ages," I said as I strapped it on.

Even after all this time, there were many wonders the harness refused to share. Most intriguing were the handles on the side of the frame. AERO-FOIL was written on each.

I wonder what they are?

Othello ordered me not to touch them, but curiosity got the better of me. I pulled the handles…

"Fool!" he spat, flying from beneath the bed. "Put them back this instant!"

I jumped with alarm. A silky canvas stretched across my back, like the giant fins of a manta ray.

"What if you're seen!? Put them back!"

I pulled the handles again. The fins retreated into the harness.

"Cool."

"You are such an imbecile! There's no telling what that harness might do."

"What's an AERO-FOIL?"

"I don't know."

"Do they help you swim? I've seen manta rays with fins like these. I mean it makes sense, doesn't it? The harness helps you swim; that's why they put it on a raft that floats in the Water."

"Yes, yes. I suppose."

I took off the harness and buried it in the trunk. "Is reading a sacrilege?"

"What makes you say that?"

"Professor Herodotus told us the story about Shiva the Destroyer, about how she tried to teach us mortals a terrible knowledge, knowledge that would doom mankind."

"So."

"Well…this knowledge. Could it be reading?"

"Ridiculous!" he chortled in a high-pitched din. "That, my dear, is the most preposterous thing you've ever come up with…"

Disbelief was painted on my scowl. "I know you're lying. Why can't you just tell me?"

He narrowed his eyes, unable or unwilling to fabricate a convincing rebuttal. Flitting his tail with annoyance, he gazed at me with his evil stare.

Yes! I thought. *Reading is a sacrilege! That's why he keeps my lessons a secret!*

"So…" I said. "Did you find out if Lord Joculo can read?"

"Joculo is a dunce."

"Then how does he know the letters of the alphabet?"

"Which letters does he know?"

"I told you. 'D' and 'G.'"

"'D' and 'G!'" he said with alarm. "Why, with those two letters, he can spell as well as you!"

"Ha, ha."

Othello pounced upon the bureau. "Just because a drone happens to stumble upon a letter or two doesn't mean he can read."

"The point is – if he knows those two letters, maybe he knows even more. I think Uncial does too."

"*I'll* do the thinking, thank you very much. As for Joculo and Uncial, *you* shall stay far away from the both of them."

"Why?"

"Because I said so. Because it's dangerous. Because if I ever catch you…"

"Why does everything have to be such a big secret?"

Othello furrowed his brow. I could tell he was angry, but trying to control himself. "Sometimes the Gods aren't as careful as they should be. Sometimes they let things slip."

"Like you did with that sixth column thing?"

He narrowed his dangerous eyes. "Whereas the Gods are allowed to make mistakes, you would do well to remember your peril."

"Come off it. That's what you always say."

"Then let me make myself perfectly clear. You shall never mention the cube or the column or reading or anything else…"

"Or else what – you'll meow or something?"

He flicked his whiskers in a gesture of supremacy. "I'm going to take a nap."

"Fine!"

∞

The next few weeks, I focused on qualifying for the team. As expected, the competition was much stronger than in Kelly Tree. Though I was a good runner and competed well in the races back home, I had no chance against Keleron, Urban, and Anthony. Instead, I concentrated on Mounted Javelin and the Circus.

Casey and I were a shoo-in for Mounted Javelin. The Circus, however, was another matter. The boys didn't want me racing.

"Women drivers!" snickered Lord Duma. "What's next?"

But the Aquarians had more surprises than women charioteers. Over the last few weeks, Dio, the University weapons master, had been training Lucy to box. Dio swore her to secrecy, a vow that extended even to her twin.

"I can't believe you're not going to tell your own sister!" Casey complained. The three of us were running laps together – Joculo's penchant for punishment, firmly in place.

"Honestly," Lucy huffed. "I would if I could. But Dio made me promise."

"I'm your better half! It's like keeping secrets from your self. It's not healthy!"

"Listen!" Lucy bristled. "Call it Pax, or you'll learn firsthand all about my boxing!"

"Great!" said Casey, throwing her hands in the Air. "Who needs family anyway?"

I giggled at the warring pair when I heard following footsteps. Stealing a glance behind me, I saw Liam sprinting into view. He raised his eyebrows in a flaunting display as he started to pass around us.

Feeling impish, I leapt into his path.

Liam dodged chivalrously clear, splaying his arms to find his balance. I muscled aggressively into the teetering boy, cleaving my shoulder into his sweaty chest.

He spun about in a mad pirouette, theatrically collapsing on the cold, hard clay. The Aquarian athletes crowed with delight, clapping aloud at his theatrical display.

Liam leapt to his feet. The grin on his face was sheepish, yet pleased.

"Watcha do that for?" asked Casey.

"Just 'cause."

"You fancy him!" said Lucy.

"Shut up."

Casey laughed. "Liar. You like him! Admit it."

I shrugged in silence with a girlish grin. But when Liam caught up again, I sprinted to join him, leaving the Twins with their answer.

∞

"You've got to settle on a team," Casey said as we entered the stables.

Dusan and Uncial were back in a corner, quarreling over a pair of geldings. Both were fifteen hands tall.

Casey frowned at the two. "Joculo's had his team a week now."

"I know," I said as I searched through the leavings.

Casey petted Callisto, her three-year old mare. The Arabian welcomed her with loving affection. The two had a bond I frankly admired.

After feeding Callisto a carrot, Casey moved to another mare. "Anona would be a perfect anchor. Not too big…but patient and smart. Aquata and Adrena make a good pair for the middle. They don't mind being harnessed together and have excellent endurance."

I was impressed. "Why don't you race in the Circus?"

"I don't like the cars."

"But racing's so much fun!" I'd never raced in Kelly Tree, but practiced every day on the Isle during the summer. *And that was with horses that had seen better days.* Now I was surrounded by strong young Arabians, all of them over fourteen hands tall!

"We jolly well better sort out a team for you before worrying about me," snorted Casey.

"OK," I said. "How 'bout the post?"

The post was the horse on the far right position. Because the cars raced left, the post had to cover the most distance. She also had to be strong enough to pull the chariot around the turns.

"There's always Arista," said Casey, "but she's getting kinda old."

"Excuse me, Miss," said a young lad.

"Yes?"

"I've a 'orse for ya," said the stable boy, crumpling his hat as he spoke to the ground. "A fine 'orse…if he'll 'ave ya." Leading us through the huge barn doors, he guided us to an isolated paddock.

A huge white stallion stamped furiously about the ring. A tempest sworn to anger – a steed too proud to tame.

"Calypso!" said the boy.

I'd never seen a horse that big. The mammoth tossed his chiseled head, bristling his massive snow-white mane. "Where did he come from?"

"Been out to pasture," said the cherry-cheeked boy, ringing his cap as if it were full of Water. "They's brought 'im from McFarland, just this morning. Fer stud…you know."

"How big is he?" I asked with awe.

"'vry bit of eighteen hands, 'nd not one jot less."

The stallion arched his muscled neck. Easily the most beautiful horse I'd ever seen, he was also the most dangerous.

"Why doesn't anyone want him?"

"Got a temper, miss," explained the boy, tracing the ground with his foot. "Used to be Lord Duma's. But 'e don't like the whip. No, not at all."

"Stupid git," Casey swore. "Duma's an idiot, lord or no. Tries to make up for his lack of ability with the crack of a whip." She gazed at the stamping fury, frowning with regret. "He's a trained warhorse. You can tell by the way he carries his head. Note his watchful eyes."

I gnawed on my lip with a thrill of excitement. The stallion was powerful and fantastically large.

He'd be perfect!

Casey seemed to know what I was thinking. "Pallas…I don't know."

"What's your name?" I asked the lad.

"Phillip, m' lady," he said with a tip of his cap.

"What makes you think I can tame him, Phillip?"

"Please, miss. I've watched ya, I 'ave. You've a way with the 'orses, just like Miss Casey. Gentle like."

I stole a look at Casey.

She frowned at the stormy giant.

"Well, Phillip," I said. "Let's try him out."

"Right you are," he said with a tip of his cap. "Right you are, indeed!"

Casey shook her doleful head, as if the stallion was beyond repair.

I ignored her. Waiting till the stallion had circled round the far side of the corral, I gently crept over the railing.

The mammoth was not to be fooled. Rounding sharply, he aggressively charged, the Good Earth quaking as he came.

"Pallas!" yelled Casey. "Get out of there!"

Panicked, I almost obeyed. But I checked my courage and stood my ground, staring directly into his infinite eyes.

The colossus stopped mere inches from my head. *Eighteen hands!* I gasped. Cowering beneath the tower, I realized how big eighteen hands really was.

Yet even more terrible than his mountainous size was the ire that stormed in his dark black eyes: obsidian orbs that spoke of maelstroms and war.

"Just back up," Casey advised, "slow and steady."

"No!" I said. "I'm going to train him." Turning to Casey, I was about to say...

"Don't break eye contact!" she hissed. "You're lucky he hasn't trampled you already. Now get outta there, before he really gets angry."

"I can get that kind of advice from Elena," I said, staring boldly into his beautiful, terrible face. "You gonna help or not?"

Casey cringed. "That was way below the belt, sister. Still," she said with a hearty smile, as if recklessness was license for any hazard, "you *do* love adventures!"

I spent the entire morning courting my reluctant beau. Calypso was perfect in every detail, except for the many scars left by Dusan's whip. Together, with Casey's patient guidance and my gentle whispers, we calmed the savage beast.

Urban and Dusan drove aggressively past, each riding a handsome blue chariot. They'd spent the last hour arguing over the one with the golden trim.

"That monster will be the death of you!" Dusan shouted with glee.

"He'll be harder to tame than those dolphins!" said Urban.

I ignored them, continuing to coo.

But Calypso had seen the young lord. Pinning back his ears, he reared high into the Air, thrusting his hooves at his former master.

I backed away from the stormy terror, swearing loudly at the ignorant lord. "I'm going to ride him! And he's going to be my post!"

"Fine by me," laughed Dusan. "Only don't say I didn't warn you!" He whipped his team with a brutal blow, jolting them forward in a panicked rush.

"Don't mind him, miss," said Phillip. "If ye can get this 'orse to handle the yoke, ye'll be driving them cars."

"We'll see."

A soft touch, tons of patience, and a pail full of carrots were the keys to Calypso's heart. Casey and I spent the entire day with him. The livery master griped loudly that it was a waste of time, but I knew better.

If can tame this giant, I'll have a team to rival any in the world!

By the time Dusan and Urban drove back to the stable, I was riding bareback. My long hair flying in the autumn breeze, I posted in harmony with the mighty steed.

Dusan wasn't happy. "That's my horse!"

Calypso reared high into the frightened Air. Flashing his massive teeth, he kicked at the chubby boy.

I hung on for dear life. *Please, oh please, don't buck me off!*

"Think you can handle him, my Lord?" chided Casey.

Dusan smiled as I struggled. "She can't; that's for sure."

I clung on to the vengeful neck, whispering sweetly in the tyrant's ears. But Calypso would not forget his anger, stamping thunderously at the young lord.

"That thing's a monster," said Dusan. "He should be put down."

"Looks likes she's mellowed your monster," said Joculo as he strode to the paddock. "Takes a woman's touch, they say."

Mellow? This is mellow?

"That's my horse," demanded Dusan.

"*Used* to be your horse," said Joculo. You sold him for stud, remember?"

"Yeah, but I was the one who brought him here. I should get first dibs."

"If you want him, my Lord," said Joculo, "go in there and get him. If not, he's for Pallas to ride."

Calypso reached high into the Air again, flaring his dangerous nostrils.

I hung on and prayed.

Dusan seemed frightened by the horse's eyes. "Fine!" he said. "Take the beast. But he'll throw you, I know he will." With that he retreated to the stables, Urban and Joculo trailing along.

It took forever to calm the colossus. His rage, it seemed, would never cease. But I was patient and Casey was skilled.

Joculo returned with the setting sun to check on our progress. "Listen, Pallas," he said. "Dusan beat that horse pretty bad last year. Poor thing's ruined. The livery master says he's only good for stud now."

"I'm riding him, Joculo. And he's going to be my post."

"The horse is a fighter; I can spare no doubt 'bout that. Still, he's not exactly tame…and dangerous for a girl…"

"A girl to what?" I scowled.

"The animal's a rebel, that's all. I don't want you to get hurt."

But I loved a rebel. *I am a rebel!*

"Don't tell me what to do!" I spat. And in a fit of adolescent pique, I kicked the latch of the gate.

Calypso catapulted in a feral burst for freedom, knocking poor Phillip right to the ground.

"Hiiiyah, Calypso!" the little boy cheered. The grin on his face was wild with joy.

Oh my Gods! I yelped. *What have I done?* I'd never felt such power, such raw, incredible strength. Calypso wasn't trying to throw me. If he was, I'd be flat on the ground. He was just running, running for the pleasure of feeling the Wind across his face.

He took me on a tour of University. First, he ran through the gate that led to the Gemini fields. They were empty except for Atlanta. The lonely girl was running laps. The rest of her team had all gone home.

The stallion raced across the supple turf, his feeble rider clinging to his sides. Without missing a stride, he barreled over the wall, vaulting into the Leon fields.

Alexander and Corona were perched on black geldings.

"Look! The Water Witch!" said Alexander.

"Maybe she's up for a little fun!" yelled Corona.

They followed in hot pursuit.

Oh, no! I thought. *What am I gonna do?*

"Hope you rode those dolphins better than that horse!" jeered Corona.

"Trouble staying on, Water Weird?" shouted Alexander.

In truth, I was petrified…completely out of control. But their wicked taunts quickened my anger. "Not as much trouble as you had with Mulciber!"

It was a mistake.

Alexander fetched a whip from his saddle. "You're gonna regret that!"

Then he hit Calypso.

The stallion didn't like being chased. He liked whips even less. Halting short, nearly throwing me, he bristled as the Leos flew thunderously past. Then he charged, pinning his ears, biting at the gelding's hindquarters.

The hunters were now the hunted.

The magnificent blacks veered sharply away, fleeing towards the safety of the Leon stables.

Alexander turned and screamed. "Get off!"

But the Mistress of the Sea adorned a wicked smile. The roar of the hooves made me feel invincible! Besides, Casey was right behind me on Callisto, racing to catch up.

Once inside the stable doors, the Leos tried to slow their geldings. But Calypso charged with savage career. Awash with panic, the blacks fled deeper inside.

The geldings sped through the opposite door connecting the stable to the rest of University. An alert groomsman slammed it shut, barring Calypso's way.

The stallion didn't miss a beat. Rearing to his full height, he crashed the door into splinters.

I was aghast. Too frightened to jump, too weak to stop him – a captive bystander in a reckless crusade.

The hall of stone echoed like thunder as Calypso barreled through the frightened throng. Scurrying to dodge the stormy tempest, Leon students panicked and fled.

I stole a look behind me. Casey wore a jolly grin.

"Get off!" cried Alexander. "Get off!"

"Never!" I merrily replied.

The horses skidded on the slick, marbled floors – a gaggle of Geminis plastered against the walls. Yet they found their voices as the stampede passed…

"Go, Pallas! Go!"

"You can take 'em!"

"Daughter of Triton!"

"Mistress of the Sea!"

The joyous rampage stole my reason. The whistling chorus cheered me along. I chased the prince with wild abandon.

We thundered down the hallowed halls, sharply rounding a narrow bend. Across the passage, directly in our way, was Miss Polish's jeweled door. The turn was too tight for the horses to make, their iron hooves slipping on the cold, stone floor. Alexander's gelding crashed into the glass, shattering the rose in a crystal cacophony.

The frightened geldings bullied through the ballroom, smashing tables and chairs alike. Reaching the far end, Alexander seized a seven-foot-high candelabrum. Brandishing it like a lance, circling his steed on the velvety carpet, he finally faced his pursuer.

I scooped up a candelabrum of my own, pointing its Flames at the arrogant boy.

Students poured into the ornamental arena.

"Teach her a lesson!"

"Go get 'em, Pallas!"

"Prince of Fire!"

"Mistress of the Sea!"

Amidst the gales of cheers and jeers, Alexander finally found his courage. "Hiyaah!" he screamed, pointing his Fiery lance directly at me.

Calypso snorted and lowered his head, vaulting forward in wild career.

I had no idea what I was doing. The lance was awkward and heavy. I leveled it the best I could...

But Calypso was a trained warhorse. Picking just the right moment, he thrust at his nemesis like a dread avenger.

The candles collided in a horrible jolt, erupting in a torrent of wax and Flame. My arm went numb, my hand was stinging...

But Alexander got the worst of it, falling backwards off his horse...right into an ancient china cabinet. Priceless china splattered into the Air, grinding themselves into porcelain dust.

"Aaeeeeeeeh!" screamed a Siren that curdled my blood. Resplendent in a pink bathrobe and matching slippers, Miss Polish scampered through the shattered doorway. Yipping and yapping like wind-up toys, two white poodles scurried behind her. "What have you done?!?"

"Uh..." I said. "Is that a trick question?"

Her face was plastered with green goop. Her hair was tied up in rollers. Her chubby hand held a silver spoon, mangled by an errant horseshoe. "My beautiful china! My masterpiece door! Ruined! Ruined!"

Calypso reared high into the Air – tall and triumphant upon the field of battle.

I closed my eyes and prayed.

"You!" howled Miss Polish. "You're a disgrace! A bane on your family, a blight on this school!"

Chapter Seven

Mathematicians

There are men, gods, and mathematicians.

Pythagoras
Greek philosopher
circa 500 BC: Earth Standard

"What did I tell you?" demanded the Bull, thudding his fist against the oaken desk. "It's high time someone's taken the child in hand!"

"None of that, William," mumbled Grandfather.

A shrill Wind buffeted the windows, filling the office with the bleakness of winter. Elena sat in her Grandfather's office...

...right next to the divine creature.

The senseless Atlantian was huddled on the sofa, cradling her knees close to her chest. A shawl was draped upon her sunken shoulders, making the Goddess-she-shared-a-bathroom-with look pathetic and sad.

Elena bit her ruby lips, trying with difficulty to hide her contempt. Slave to a system of careful etiquette, she couldn't help but be furious.

She's wild, mad, completely out of control!!!

It was already impossible to pacify her friends. The many excuses she used for Pallas' behavior had become tired and strained. Still...she smoothed over her societal sins as best as she could, defending her catalogue of stupid outbursts.

The guilty Atlantian closed her eyes.

Why can't you just behave? thought Elena. How could a God be so foolish, so brash, so...untamed?

I love her, Elena prayed. *I swear...I do. It's just, she's so very...reckless.*

"I told you this would happen!" raged the Bull. "She's a menace – not only to herself, but the entirety of House Catagen!"

"That will be enough, Captain," said Grandfather.

An uncomfortable haze permeated the room as the old lord studied the man who would replace him. The look of disappointment was obvious, though the Bull didn't seem to notice.

What that man doesn't notice could fill an Ocean!

A ball of fur leapt into the room, gently alighting upon her silken lap.

The Bull jumped with surprise. "What's that?"

"It's her cat," said Elena, stroking the pet.

"It shouldn't be here."

"Think he's a spy?" she smarted. The cat was something of a favorite of hers. She didn't know why, but he had a funny way of showing up when interesting things were happening.

"You'll keep a civil tongue in your mouth, young lady."

"Enough!" said Grandfather.

But the Bull was quite un-caged. "You've given her free reign far too long. I'd have the Witch in irons! Chained to her bed!"

Careful, uncle, thought Elena. *That was most unwise…*

"Captain!" It was Lord Catagen who pummeled his fist this time, the wooden desk jumping at the blow. "You'll apologize to the Mistress! This…very…instant!"

The crown prince scowled with fury. "I shan't stand by and countenance your indiscretion, dooming this House by your wanton folly!"

Grandfather answered with a poisonous whisper "You *will* apologize."

"I won't!"

Uh! gasped Elena. *You dare defy the Commodore of the Three?*

Grandfather took a deep breath, glaring at his son. "Captain, prepare *Yorktown* for immediate departure. You sail with the first tide."

William's face grew hot and red. "You shan't send me off…like a school boy to my room."

"Those are my orders, Sir. Are you capable of carrying them out? Or shall I find someone who can?"

The Bull stuck out the barrel of his massive chest. Elena allowed herself a silent giggle. *Honestly! That never worked. When will you ever learn?*

The captain continued to huff and puff, but the Commodore would not be blown down. Finally, as if realizing his peril, he gruffly obeyed. "No, Sir," he mumbled.

"You're dismissed," growled Grandfather.

William rounded on the Atlantian as if he were going to hit her. He gave both us girls a threatening glare before retreating from the room.

Sinking ruefully into his leather chair, the Commodore watched him go. "Forgive me, Mistress. I'm…I'm sorry you had to see that."

A calculating glint sparkled in the princess' sapphire eyes. "Grandfather," Elena cooed, "I…I worry about you."

"Don't worry about me, lass," he said, sagging his iron shoulders.

"You've made House Catagen strong," she said, moving behind him to knead his back. It was her favorite way of buttering him up, a trick she learned at the tender age of six. "You've taken House Catagen from a backwater fishing people to a Voting Member of the exalted *Zoo*."

The mariner furrowed his brow, frowning.

Careful, she said to herself. *We mustn't be too direct.*

She considered for months the sort of lever she'd use. Her own personal happiness? No. Grandfather was much too clever for that. The future of House Catagen? *Even that is not enough!* She picked something even better…something he couldn't ignore. "But now, noble Sire, you must think about what's best for the Mistress. Poseida trusted you to keep her safe."

"I know that," cracked his bitter voice.

She nearly stopped. There was quiet dread in his ancient voice.

But I must be ambitious! For the sake of my family, for the sake of House Catagen!

"Who will take care of Pallas – my darling sister and the love of my life – after you've…" She paused for effect, lilting her voice in a canticle of regret, "…after you've…finally left us?"

Silence. She could feel the tension growing in his shoulders – a searing, iron knot.

"Traditions change," she soothed. "Prudence dictates decisive action. A wise man does what ever is necessary…for the good of his family. For the good of his House."

"What is your point, child?"

Triumph coursed through her noble veins. She'd been waiting for that question, dreaming about it for a year. Months of patient planning, complicated schemes, clever conversations, just so she could say...

"Isn't it a shame...Dewey...wasn't born first?"

She held her breath but continued her kneading, the fragrance of her perfume wafting about his shoulders...

"Aye, mi lass...it is, indeed."

Bliss swept through her with silent acclaim...as Grandfather softened his iron frame.

∞

She stood at the edge of a precipice, gazing into a ring of Fire. Flames licked furiously at her naked feet, scalding the hair that blew up and over her shoulders.

Hovering over the tortured child was the Lord God Mulciber. He raised his finger. He shot his ray...

...she fell...like a limp, rag doll...

...into the hell below.

I woke from my nightmare, hot and damp and panting. They seemed to be happening more often. I didn't know why.

The Aquarians were abuzz with excitement. I fervently wished my steeple chase would just go away. But the story of the dolphin rider besting the Excelsior prince was simply too rich not to tell. The Aquarians repeated it over and over, brazenly gloating over Alexander's defeat.

The Taurans and Geminis added to his shame, enjoying their revenge over last year's Circus champion. Casey, bragging about her part in the epic race, was delighted.

To my amazement, I never got in trouble.

"Mother doesn't want you punished," explained Uncial IV. Her voice was thin and reedy, a brooding look about her jealous face. "She wants your little jaunt swept under the carpet."

"Why?" demanded Eunice. "If it had been anyone else, they'd be expelled straight away."

"I'm quite sure we're all exceedingly glad Pallas is not going to be punished," threatened Elena.

"Of course," Uncial pouted. Casting me a baneful look, she added, "She must really like you...for some very odd reason."

Elena looked absolutely furious.

I, on the other hand, could care less what that Uncial brat thinks. Yet I was grateful for her mother's unlikely reprieve. Once again, the Chancellor had come to my unasked-for aid.

Why?

I sat down in Pythagoras' class, dreading the coming quiz. Last week, I'd gotten six out of ten problems right. It was three times better than my first attempt, but still not even a passing grade.

Saving me his most sarcastic smile, the teacher handed out his chalkboard tablets. "Will you be needing that prayer rug, Miss Pallas?"

I didn't answer, gazing instead at the blizzard of numbers. OK, I did say a prayer. But then I braved the flurry of chalk.

For the very first time the numbers did my bidding. I easily finished the first problem, and then the second. It wasn't too hard. These figures held no secrets I could not decipher.

Have a problem; find an answer – just like Genevieve said.

When the professor called for the chalkboards, he made a point of taking mine first. He studied it with scorn. "Humph! Ten out of ten. Perhaps you should pray more often."

I wiggled happily in my seat. Elena looked annoyed. I expected more problems on the blackboard when Pythagoras took us in a new direction.

"Today we shall review the basic forms of geometry."

Groans from the class told me this was not their favorite subject.

The professor was undeterred, producing blocks of wood in various shapes and sizes. "Who can tell me what this is?"

No one answered. Flush with my success, I raised my hand.

"Yes, Miss Pallas?"

"Please, professor. It's a box."

The sophomores howled. I melted in my seat.

"A box!" cried Alexander. "Brilliant!"

"Did they teach you that in Atlantis?" Ophelia scowled.

Pythagoras looked upon the class with contempt. "Yes, it's a box, Master Alexander. What kind of box?"

"A…a wooden box."

My classmates giggled.

"An urchin might call it a box. But a mathematician would call it a cube. Now…who can tell me the characteristics of the cube?"

Oliver raised his hand. "It has six equal sides."

"Indeed," he agreed, caressing the cube like a lover. "Six equal sides, eight equal corners, twelve equal lengths, twenty-four equal angles. In the entire universe, there is not a single form more perfect than the cube."

"Not this again," whispered Alexander.

"The same every year," said Obsid, a lumbering Tauran.

"Perhaps you can tell the class what the six surfaces of the cube are called, Master Obsid?"

But Obsid couldn't remember. No one could. Their ignorance made Pythagoras ill-tempered. "Year after year I teach you the secrets of the universe!" he carped in a quick staccato voice. "And year after year you forget! Very well, we shall discuss the mysteries of the square."

He ranted like this for hours and hours, focusing on five particular polygons – three of which I could never have imagined. But he kept his emphasis squarely on the cube, placing reverent importance on its faultless symmetry. "And that is why the cube is the most balanced object in the universe, the very perfection of thought. For it transforms the perfect square into a three dimensional form, the classic culmination of ten – the number of the universe."

The heat from the fireplace made the class sleepy, the growl in our stomachs, eager for lunch. Dusan snored. Elena filed her nails. Oliver tried to look interested while Alexander flirted with a Gemini. When the bell mercifully rang, they all rushed to the door.

"Remember your homework," called the professor, annoyed.

I stayed behind, toying with the silver cube around my neck. A sudden thought struck me.

"What do you mean?" I blurted to the professor. "Ten is the number of the universe?"

Pythagoras gave me a dismissive look. "You wouldn't understand."

"Try me."

"Very well," he said, pacing to the blackboard. "One," he said, drawing a single point on the board. "The generator of the dimensions."

"What's a...buy pensions?"

"Two." He drew another point without answering my question. "Length, we'll say, just for argument's sake." He drew a line from the first point to the second. "Dimension One."

I kept my mouth shut, challenging myself to understand.

"Three." He drew another point, connecting this point to the first line with two additional lines. "Now what do we have?"

"A triangle?"

"Two dimensions," he corrected.

I frowned. *He doesn't want me to understand! He's just showing off.* This irritated me, making me concentrate all the more. I hated not being able to understand something.

"Length and width." He drew another point, connecting it to each of the three points of the triangle. "Four," he said. "Now what do we have?"

I thought hard, following the pattern to its logical conclusion. "Three...by-mensions?"

The arrogant scholar considered me for a moment, not sure what to make of my guess. All at once he seemed to completely change his mind about me. "Exactly! And can you tell me what the third dimension is?"

I thought again. Length, width... I looked at the tall chair he lectured from. It wasn't too wide, or too long, but it was pretty high.

"Height?"

"Precisely! Now, what do we get when we add the four points together?"

I was now completely lost. Luckily, the professor answered his own question.

"One plus two plus three plus four equals ten, the same number we base our entire numerical system on. The same number of toes and fingers we have. The number that describes the universe we live in."

I didn't understand how the number of toes I had could possibly describe the universe. But I nodded just the same.

"And that is why the cube is the perfect model of the cosmos, for it transforms the number ten into a symmetrical three-dimensional object…"

The Aquarians performed wonderfully in practice that day. The Twins and I always trained hard. But after my notorious steeple chase, the entire team had a special bounce. Even Urban ran well. Besides, practice was a lot more fun now that I was spending most of it with Liam.

Elena told me to avoid him. But talking to him was like talking to an old friend – a handsome, muscular friend. My heart warmed every time he smiled.

The sun set low, dripping over the mountains that separated me from my home. I chatted happily with the attentive boy, stretching my legs with the rest of my teammates. Warm sweat glistened on my face. I loved the wetness on my brow, the ache of my muscles, the taste of the cold, crisp Air.

Eunice arrived to collect her boyfriend, Keleron. She flashed me a jealous sneer before dragging him away. I didn't know or care why.

"You looked really good out there today," said Liam.

"I bet you say that to all the girls," I said.

"I would," he teased, "except the only other girls on the team are even more cantankerous than you. Casey's amazing on a horse. And Lucy, you know, is a world-class boxer. It'd crazy to mess with her."

I giggled. Casey and I were both competing for the Mounted Javelin. Casey was the better horseman, but I could throw farther. For now, Casey had the upper hand. But Lucy was still mum about her boxing lessons. No one knew what she was doing except for Dio and Liam, her sparring partner.

It drove Casey absolutely mad. But no amount of pleading would make Lucy reveal her secret. Privately, I didn't know what Dio was thinking. Lucy was as quick as a fish, but she was no boxer. One punch would knock her out.

I gazed at the pink-on-purple glow over the Quartz Mountains. *Father is just beyond those mountains…*

Suddenly, I felt ashamed. Long ago, I promised myself that once I got to Greenstone, I'd try to find a way back home. Yet I hadn't given it a second thought.

Why?

The truth was, I was having too much fun. University was an opportunity I'd always dreamed about. The Twins were like soul-mates; Elena, the big sister I never had. The Old Man was like a loveable...

No! I scolded myself. *I already have a father!*

"Thinking about your home again, Bright-Eyes?" asked Liam.

"Yeah," I admitted. "How did you know? And don't give me any of that "catastrophe" nonsense."

Liam smiled. "Your grey eyes wilt when you look at those mountains."

I looked at him, amazed. *Just a lucky guess...or does he really know me that well?* I was about to come up with a sarcastic reply when someone ran into me, nearly knocking me down. "Casey!"

"Oh!" she laughed. "Is that you, Pallas? Didn't see you in the dark."

"Why don't you use your God-like powers and give us a light?" chided Lucy.

"Sorry," I smiled. "Left my halo at home."

"What about that wand you used at Capro Bay?" said Liam.

"I, uh...gotta go," I said, surrendering to the tugs of the Twins. They both pulled me away, giggling with ferocious delight.

Lucy tickled my ribs. "Honestly, Pallas! What were you doing, talking to Liam?"

"Nothing," I shrugged.

"Didn't look like nothing," scolded Casey.

"Don't tell me your jealous...Elena!"

Casey's mouth flew open in mock outrage. Then she charged me, knocking me to the ground. Lucy joined the fray, her laughter punctuating the coolness of the night.

"Uncle, uncle!" I cried.

The Twins celebrated their heroic victory with a hooting, impish dance. Then they too collapsed upon the ground.

We lay there panting on the grass. The sun had finally set, a last splash of color blanketing the mountains until it too, succumbed to grey. We gazed at the inky blackness. Tiny pinpricks of light appeared.

"Do you ever fancy what's up there?" Lucy asked. "I mean...I've heard the Gods came from the stars."

"I've heard they still live there," said Casey. "When they're not harassing us mortals. Do tell us, Pallas, dear. Does Poseida have a bungalow in the stars, for when she goes away on holiday?"

"Oh, yes, please," said Lucy. "It's horrid the way you carry on with that dreadful secret."

I paused. I didn't *think* the Gods lived in the stars. Then I remembered what my father had said in our little "Planetarium."

"There are worlds up there, my dearest baby girl! Worlds full of people!" he'd said, stretching his arms out like an enormous bird. *"The universe is a very big place! Bigger than you can possibly imagine."*

I giggled at the childhood memory. The bird had made me laugh. Quite unexpectedly – surprising even myself – I said, "There's not much difference between ourselves and the Gods."

I expected them to pepper me with questions. I expected them to knead and pry. They didn't. They just looked at me and stared.

"You really think so," said Lucy.

"Yeah. I really do."

We lay quite still for long silent moments. All of a sudden, the once warm sweat became an icy bath. We got up and hurried to the Manor.

I went to the library with Genevieve that evening, delighted that Liam was there as well. He'd said he was having trouble with geometry...

Genevieve treated me with a pair of kisses and a shrewd smile. "Pallas, love."

"Hi, Genny," I said kissing both her cheeks.

"Hi, Pallas," said a nervous Liam. "You...uh, invited me to come...remember?"

"I did?" In truth, I had difficulty thinking about anything else.

A nervous lull descended. We stared at each other with sheepish grins, when all at once we started talking about my steeple chase.

"Of course, Alexander deserved it," said Genevieve. "But it does set a bad precedent."

Frankly, I agreed. People kept seeing Alexander's humiliation as another victory for the Aquarians, another confirmation of that stupid prophecy. Talk of a "New Age" sprouted like weeds, making me tense and wary.

"You're really driving your chariot well," said Genevieve. "You've been training really hard."

"You've been spying on us?" I asked.

"Never," she denied. "Though Oliver has. Says he has to check up on the competition."

"Humph!"

∞

"The universe is composed of five Elements: Earth, Air, Water, and Fire – bound together by the spark of Life."

Science was my favorite subject. Professor Archimedes' eccentric experiments were absolutely fascinating. Last week he lit a candle and placed it under a jar. I was delighted when the lack of Air caused the Fire to die.

But there was another reason I loved science. All of my other professors talked about the past, ideas formed generations ago. Archimedes talked about the future. He strived to understand, and then shape his world.

I found this exciting.

I was alone. The children of the nobility were perfectly happy with their comfortable status quo. After all, the Gods had given them sovereignty over the slaves. The great Houses didn't want to change a thing.

The scientist stoked the Fire beneath the cauldron of boiling Water. "Watch how the steam rises from the Water. Put your hand out. Feel the Water rise."

"But which rises, the Water or the Air?" said Alexander, showing off to a black-haired Leo. She was a pretty girl, except for her crooked nose.

"Those things can't be fixed," whispered Elena.

"Both and neither, Master Excelsior. For there is Water in the Air, and Air in the Water."

"How can that be?" asked a Tauran girl.

"When you wake up in the morning and feel the dew upon the grass, do you wonder where it came from? Water creates cathedrals in the Sky, soaring on vapors into thunderous clouds. It travels great distances with the power of the Wind, striking as lightening with the destructiveness of Flame. I have climbed the mountains and touched the clouds. And I tell you…they are wet with Water."

"But…how can there be Air in the Water?" asked Lord Duma, annoyed.

"Behold the fishes of the Sea. They do not breathe like you and I. Yet breathe they must, as all creatures do. If you take a fish out of Water, you see its gills search for Air it must find in the Water."

I surveyed my classmates. Their disinterest didn't deter the energetic scientist. "The Water *rises* into the Air; you can feel it. Here, one of you try."

The class was as still as stone.

"Come now, don't be bashful. Hurry, before the Water boils away."

I was rooted to my seat. Every time I asked a question, someone ridiculed me. In the beginning of the year it was always Alexander. But lately, he had to be quick with his insults before Ophelia chimed in.

Luckily, someone volunteered me.

"Pallas will do it," said Eunice. "She's not afraid."

"Excellent! Come now, Miss Catagen, to the front of the class."

I looked back at Eunice. The Aquarian wore a malicious smile.

Where did that come from?

"Reach out your hands. Yes, yes, that's it."

I obeyed, feeling the hot moist Air rise around my fingers. I'd seen steam before, of course, as I did most of the cooking back in Kelly Tree. Still, I never considered that it was made of Water, or why it went up instead of down.

"There, you see!" croaked the merry professor. "Heat can even make things fly." He produced a large goose feather, dropping it over the cauldron. To my amazement, it hovered for a second before floating away. "A hawk can soar endlessly over a rise of warm Air without ever beating his wings."

The heat wafted my hair above my shoulders. I was fascinated.

I was alone. Pretending not to be asleep, Obsid propped his head on his hands. Alexander whispered to the black-haired girl. Elena painted her nails.

"Here you witness an important relationship between Fire and Water and Air. The Fire causes the Water and Air to intermingle. They are together, yet separate."

"Yet Fire masters them all," said Alexander. "Look, the Water's gone. The Fire burnt it."

"A fine observation, Master Excelsior. But a flawed analysis, I'm afraid. The cauldron is indeed empty. But the Water is not destroyed; it has melted into the Air. Remember, matter is never created or destroyed. It is re-mastered, reformed, reshaped."

"That's not what Professor Kindle told us. He says Fire destroys everything."

"Of course, given enough heat, even Earth can burn, Water evaporates, Air can be sucked away. Fire alters the shape of things, but it does not destroy them." He lifted a stick from the embers. One end was aflame. "Behold the wood. It is burning, yet it is not destroyed." He scraped the embers into a crucible. "See now the ashes. That is what's left of the wood, that which was Life. The Fire transformed the Life into dust, the living into Earth."

I looked at the blackboard. Drawn on the corner was the familiar square that depicted the five Pentathanon Elements. The symbols for Fire and Water were opposite, as were Air and Earth. In the middle was Life. Like the geometry of the four Academies – like the shape of University – like the morning procession of the four columns of students, the diagram was symmetric in every way.

And yet …

I fingered the silver cube that hung from my neck, thinking about Pythagoras. He called the cube the perfect model of the universe.

What did he mean?

"Put that away," hissed Elena. "You'll get us in trouble."

I looked at her nail polish and ignored her. For I'd just stumbled on something – something important…

"Why aren't there *six* Pentathanon Gods?"

Horrified gasps punctuated the room. Heads turned in righteous indignation. It was the most dangerous thing I'd ever said.

And yet…

It took a moment for the professor to respond. He seemed both intrigued and dismayed. But when he finally answered, he did so with cold logic. "Because, Miss Catagen, Penta means five and not six."

The class murmured nervously, glaring at me with reproachful stares.

"Well, I don't know about the name," I said. "It just seems something is missing."

"What could be missing? You see the diagram. Water is opposite Fire, Earth is opposite Air."

"But what is opposite Life?"

A pall fell over the mortified class. The professor narrowed his gleaming eyes. "Life stands alone. It has no opposite."

"Everything has an opposite. You said so yourself."

"Everything…except for Life."

"But…look at this cube," I said, boldly revealing my treasure. "Professor Pythagoras said it transforms the perfect square into a three dimensional form. He said that was important. Everything has height, and length, and width…like a house or a desk. Your diagram shouldn't be a square. It should be a cube."

"Like your head," crowed Ophelia to the relief of the class.

"Just what is your hypothesis, Miss Catagen? Are you saying there is a God we have not accounted for? One we don't know about?"

I still didn't know what to think of the Gods; didn't know why I brought them up in the middle of a science class. Before the raft, I'd have sworn they didn't exist. But my near-fatal brush with Mulciber made me re-evaluate that assumption…

But if he's really all-powerful, why am I alive? If he's really all-knowing, why didn't he spot me – barely ten feet away?

"You're wrong about the Gods," I answered. "Something is missing. I know it."

Elena whispered a plea for silence as my classmates murmured and glared.

Oliver stared at me with pained interest.

Ophelia hissed and jeered.

Atlanta looked intrigued.

Alexander looked cavalier.

"An interesting theory," said the professor, carefully measuring his words. "Yet this is a lesson in science. The scientific method bids you create an experiment to prove or disprove your theory."

The class bell rang. I followed my classmates into the hall.

"What was that about?" Eunice accused.

"What are you trying to pull?" said Lord Duma.

"Can you really be that stupid?" sniped Ophelia.

"Questioning the Pentathanon Gods?" said Corona.

"It was just a question," I said.

"It was sacrilege!" said Eunice.

"Sacrilege?" I said. "What do you mean?"

"My Gods!" crowed Alexander. "Can you really be that dense? There are *five* Pentathanon Gods! Everyone knows that."

"Maybe everyone's wrong…"

"Shut up!" said Eunice.

"D'ya want Poseida to curse your House?" asked Lord Duma.

"As if you cared about our House!" spat Elena. She raised herself to her splendid height, towering over the frumpish lord. "Holy Poseida has blessed our House. Pallas is an Atlantian!"

"An Atlantian!?!" Alexander howled. "What rot?! The child's a Witch, a demon in disguise! A Witch who mounts beasts she can't control. A couple of lucky twists, and you think she's divine?"

"Watch your tongue!" warned Oliver.

"No! You watch yours." Cruel enjoyment splayed upon his face, he moved to the center of the gathered crowd. "The girl's a Witch; a sacrilegious blight…"

"She's a dolphin rider," growled Oliver, "and the Mistress of the Sea."

"Stop pretending," Alexander said with a gleam. "What kind of God speaks blasphemy? What sort of deity mocks the divine?"

Oliver looked confused. Even Elena seemed flustered.

Unable to refute a single of his claims, I bit my guilty lip.

"Mark my words," said Alexander, "the Witch will bring woe upon the Water Wierds. The smart Aquarians know it."

"I'm an Aquarian," hissed Elena, "and I think you're full of..."

Alexander arrogantly grabbed her chin. "But what do the other wet-ones think? Maybe you should find out...dear."

I slapped the offending prince. "Don't you dare touch her!"

Alexander reeled in surprise, a bright red mark upon his torrid face. Fury in his eyes, he moved aggressively to strike me...

Oliver's chest got there first.

The princes glared at each other – nearly at blows – when the aged professor ambled through the door.

Cowed, the sophomores divided into their colored clusters.

"This isn't finished!" snarled the Leo. Then he turned and skulked away.

∞

After practice, Liam caught up to me and the Twins. "Good one, Pallas! You looked great out there today."

"Thanks," I blushed.

"Listen. Same time tonight...in the library?"

"Yeah. Only, we don't have University tomorrow, so Genny won't be there..."

"That's OK. Maybe I'll see you there anyways? You can help me with my...uh...polygons."

"Yeah." A strange warmth swelled within my chest, my heart pattering with reckless abandon.

"See ya," he said, flashing a winning smile.

For some reason, we never got around to polygons that night...

"Dusan doesn't stand a chance in the Circus," he said. "The reason he's so angry is he knows you're going to win."

I blushed. I found I did a lot of that when Liam was around.

I felt nervous and wonderful being alone with him. Time passed magically as we talked about the Games. The Taurans were the ones to beat, he told me. Clovis, son of Lord Zeliox, won four events last year and placed second in the Circus. But Alexander won the Circus, hoisting the Leos to the narrowest victory in the Leo's five-year dominance of the University Games. The Geminis, on the other hand, looked pathetic. The only one who seemed to be training was that odd Atlanta girl, and it was easy to see that she had no formal training to speak of. As for the Sagittarians, they won Bronze last year and were returning several seniors.

"Oh my Gods," I gasped, "look at the time! He's gonna kill me."

"No, he won't," said Liam. The smile on his face seemed permanently attached. "When it comes to you, the Commodore's nothing but a pussy cat."

In truth, it was my pussy cat I was worried about. *This is two nights in a row I'm late!*

Reluctantly, we packed our things and left the library. Liam escorted me back to Catagen Manor.

"I'm freezing," I said to the biting Wind. In answer, Liam wrapped his arm around me, huddling me close. A warm sensation stirred within my heart...

"So," he asked with a nervous lilt, "you...uh...going to the Ball?"

"Ball?"

"You know," he smiled, "the one before the Games."

I rolled my eyes in disgust. *If I'd spent more time with Elena, I'd have known about the Ball.* But the tall beauty rarely spoke to me these days.

We reached the steps of Catagen Manor. A squad of Marines stood their guard, shivering in the cold. Liam gazed at me with bashful eyes. A muffled silence swallowed us amidst the howling of the Wind.

Why are we standing out in the cold...when it's warm inside that door?

"Who are you going with?" I stupidly asked; awash with fright, not daring to hope...

His shoulders sagged into a guilty shrug. "I...uh...ought to go."

My heart turned ice – my moment of happiness, lost to ruin. "Thanks for...walking me home."

"Yeah," he gloomily replied.

Chapter Eight

Eternal Flame

"Our ordered world is teetering on the brink of destruction. You cannot ignore it any longer!"

"Ordered world," scoffed Terra. "When have you...ever cared...for order? Your entire life...has been spent...on a fool's errand...to increase your own...personal power. You're only angry...the balance of power...is not being altered...in your favor."

"This New Age nonsense will ruin us all. You cannot ignore the prophecy."

He took a sip of his merry ambrosia. "I can ignore it...if I like. It's high time...you swallowed...your own medicine.

The Lord God Mulciber smiled. "Did you know she reads?"

The Earth God glowered, thinking in long stretches as he often did. But when he was quite finished with his formidable thought he said, "What is it...that you propose?"

I wandered into the foyer, absentmindedly thinking about a certain young man, when someone bumped into me.

"Oh!" crowed Casey. "Pallas has a boyfriend."

"I do not!"

"Honestly," Lucy laughed. "You might have told us."

My growl melted into a playful giggle. "There's nothing to tell. We're...friends. That's all. Study partners."

"What are you studying?"

"The birds and the bees?"

"Shut up!"

"Wait till Eunice finds out."

"Why should she care? Besides, nothing's going on."

"Right," said Casey.

"Mums the word!" Lucy laughed.

"Shut up," I said, "I'm serious."

"Why?" Casey nagged. "You afraid?"

"Afraid of what?"

"See what I told you?" said Casey to her twin.

"It is rather sad," said Lucy.

"Sad?" said Casey. "It's pathetic! The effect our prig of a sister has had on the poor child."

"Poor child?" I said, confused.

"Can't anything be done?" Lucy asked.

"Now, now," said Casey, imitating Hebe with surprising accuracy, "I'm afraid it's a rather difficult case...when such an ailment lobotomizes the young..."

"What are you talking about?"

"The Pallas I know is daring."

"Adventurous!"

"Not about to let a challenge go unanswered."

I huffed in dismay, stealing a glimpse into the parlor. Elena was chatting with the Old Man. I led the Twins into the kitchen so we wouldn't be overheard.

"What challenge?"

"We heard about Alexander."

"In the hall, after Archimedes."

"Oh..." I admitted, "...that."

"We *must* pay him back!" said Casey.

"He can't call you a Witch."

"We can't have him touching our sister!"

"But you hate Elena. Both of you."

"Bother," sighed Lucy. "The child is dense."

"Just because we spend our entire life thinking of ways to humiliate our sister, doesn't mean we want some filthy Leon encroaching on our turf."

"It's a matter of the highest pride and deepest honor," said Lucy.

Not wanting any more trouble, I inwardly retreated. The fight between the Old Man and the Bull still unnerved me. "Haven't we already gotten him back? I mean, I knocked him off his horse and everything. And I slapped him today."

"Oh, bosh!" said Lucy.

"Merely the tip of the iceberg."

"Honestly!" said Lucy. "Isn't it obvious that Alexander *hasn't* learned his lesson?"

"We have to show those Leos whose boss."

"We need something even better."

"Like what?" I said.

"We haven't thought that part thru," said Casey.

"It has to be really good."

"And it has to be big, so everyone will know who did it."

"Only we can't leave any evidence so they'll *know* who did it."

"Right," said Casey.

"We could flood the Leon side of University," said Lucy.

"Did that last year," grumbled Casey.

"Right," she giggled. "Honestly, I quite forgot."

"What about clogging up their toilets?" I said.

"That was the year before."

"No, no. It has to be impressive," Lucy said. "Something they'll never forget."

"Something that people will notice straightaway."

I knew I shouldn't, knew that Elena would kill me. But I was unexpectedly ensnared by their giddy excitement. "I have the most excellent idea!"

"What?" they chorused.

"The Eternal Flame!"

"What about it?" said Casey.

"We could put it out!"

"Put it out?" said Lucy.

"You can't put out the Eternal Flame," Casey argued. "It's…eternal."

"Any Fire can be smothered. It's just a matter of figuring out how."

"You know, she's right," said Lucy.

"We can snuff out the Fire…"

"…and paint the gold panels blue."

"That'll show those camp-Fire fools!"

"Capital idea!" Casey exclaimed. "Let's do it! Tonight!"

It was a testament to how much I loved them that I foolishly agreed. After a few frazzled minutes of gathering things we'd need, we ventured into the misty night.

We kept to the shadows, creeping over the wall that separated the Water Quarter from the University grounds. Sneaking under the Aquarian archway, we entered the sacred Center Lawn.

Even in our wild abandon, we dared not walk on the forbidden grass. Instead, we made our silent way down the gravel path.

We cautiously approached the marbled shrine, its walls and ceiling, gilded with gold. The Eternal Flame danced like a demon, casting its eerie light upon the gloom and the fog. Smiling fitfully at the Twins, I placed a fishbowl over the Fire.

"How long will it take?" whispered Lucy.

"Don't know."

The glass got warm to the touch; then hot. The Fire burned as brightly as before.

"Hurry!" hissed Casey. "We don't want to get caught."

"It's no good pulling it off too soon. It'll light back up in a second."

"What keeps it lit in the first place?" Lucy asked.

"No idea." Fire needed Air and fuel to burn. I knew where the Air came from, but had no idea about the fuel. I supposed it came from the tiny brass tube that protruded from the pedestal.

"Come on," I begged.

The demon shrank a tiny bit smaller.

"It's working!" Lucy cried, bouncing on the balls of her feet.

"Shh!" said Casey. "I heard something."

I heard it too. A voice, just beyond the Leon breezeway.

"I don't care what those Water Wierds think!"

"But we must follow the *Forms*. No girl is worth upsetting the status quo."

"It's already upset! All this 'Age of Aquarius' nonsense! It makes me ill just thinking about it."

The Fire became erratic, a dizzy dervish after a drunken whirl. All at once, it sputtered and died.

We froze in terror, stunned at our success.

A door opened and closed. The voices grew louder. Panicked, I led the Twins in a desperate dash.

The voices rounded the corner. "Who is burning with us?"

We dived upon the forbidden grass. The mist surrounded us, concealing us from view.

"The usual," said Alexander. "All the Leos, Rance, Oxymid…and someone you'd never guess."

I was all ears, hoping he'd reveal more. But all I heard was a haunted lament.

"Aaaaaaaahhhh!!! The Eternal Flame! It's gone out!"

"Oh, my Gods! Someone's killed it!"

My heart jumped into my throat as I heard someone stumble over the paint.

"What's that?

"Ouch!" Alexander complained. "That glass is hot."

"Break it."

I heard a tiny, tinkling crash.

If he lights the Flame, he'll see where we're hiding!

A curious odor filled the Air, pungent, oily, and…

"Here," said Alexander, "I'll re-light it."

It was a mistake.

First, an explosion. Then a frightened scream. The Excelsior prince and his Leon cousin flew roughly to the ground. Their locks were aglow, the stench of burnt hair spoiling the night. Screaming like pigs, they sprinted to the fountain, dunking their heads into the Eternal Water.

The Twins squealed with laughter as I glanced upon the Flame. The Fire was reborn…not as a small and elegant Fire, but a huge, chaotic blaze. The entire shrine was pitted and scarred; the tablets of gold, cracked and ruined. Scorched, broken marble scattered the lawn.

We retreated to the shadows of Tauran Academy. Plastering ourselves against the wall, we watched Alexander and Corona streak back to the Red Square.

But what are they doing here, in the middle of the night?

In answer, we heard more voices.

"What happened?" asked a haughty girl. "Where's Alexander?"

"Dunno," said a lumbering boy. From the shadows, I saw Ophelia and Obsid peeking from the Tauran breezeway.

My mind was racing. *We need to get out of here!* Yet there was no way to sneak past.

Before I could think what to do, Casey threw a stone, smashing a window. Ophelia and Obsid dashed away, fleeing towards the Brown Gates.

"Come on," muttered Casey.

We crept through the Tauran breezeway, then ducked behind a crate. Brown soldiers hurried through the archway we'd just escaped. Keeping to the shadows, we reached the Water Quarter's wall.

I felt too sick to scale the wall, yet fear drove me mercilessly on. Inside the Aquarian stronghold, we scampered like rats, dodging squads of frantic Marines. Finally reaching Catagen Manor, we threw open the cellar door and tumbled down the stairs…

A porcelain sentinel towered above us, sneering at the scoundrels splayed upon her feet.

"My, my!" tittered Elena. "Pray, tell me, what have you darling cherubs been up to?"

"N...n...nothing."

"Lie to me, will you?" she snarled. "Just wait till I tell Grandfather!"

"Please," I pleaded. "Please, don't..."

"Don't 'please' me!" she roared. "The entire Quarter is up in arms, something dreadful has happened at University, and I find you skulking about like thieves?"

It's far worse than that! I thought as I tried on my puppy-dog eyes. They worked better with Elena than they did with the cat.

"Here," she huffed, tossing nightdresses at us. "Take off those filthy things and burn them."

"You brought pajamas?"

"I saw you leave and thought you might be up to something frightful. Though I had no idea you were off destroying things...again!"

I felt like a moron as I peeled off my things.

"In the furnace," Elena ordered, throwing our clothing pell-mell into the blaze, "and not a word to anyone...*anyone*! Do you hear?!?"

The Twins wordlessly escaped to the kitchen.

I hesitated, considering my benefactor. "Thanks."

"You are so *not* welcome!" she cried. Her pallid face looked lost and forlorn, as if I had personally wounded her. But then her voice grew spiteful. "Anyway, I'm not doing this for you."

"Who are you doing it for?"

"House Catagen. It'll be far worse for the family if anyone finds out *who* did it...whatever it is you did."

I managed a grim smile.

"Hurry," she spat, "before we're caught."

π

The manor was wild with excitement. Othello saw the Twins scamper off to bed. But his pupil's brief hesitation made her miss her chance. Instead, she followed Elena, who melted into the crowd.

Quite resourceful, admired the cat, slinking from the cellar into the kitchen. *The nightdresses were a stroke of brilliance. Everyone will assume the man-cub just came down from bed.*

He only hoped no one would notice her dirty hands.

Elena strolled confidently into the parlor. The cat continued to be impressed.

She lives for crisis, this Catagen jewel.

Mulling over rumors from the other Houses, the Old Man paced the oaken floor.

A major of the Marines walked in. "The reports are confirmed, Commodore. The shrine of that wretched Flame has been blown to smithereens."

The officers offered reluctant cheers, too feeble to be believed. Othello skulked into the parlor before launching into the man-cub's arms. His actress pretended innocence, but he could tell she was both guilty and terrified.

"Who did it?" asked the Commodore. "Any ideas?"

"Princes Alexander and Corona were caught in the blast," said the lieutenant. "Some sort of spell, they claimed. But...that doesn't explain the blue paint."

The officers issued a collective groan.

Othello winced. *Please! Tell me you didn't.*

A Marine knocked at the doorway, rendering a sharp salute. "Commodore, Sir."

"What is it, Sergeant?"

"The Lady Uncial has arrived, unannounced. She's in the foyer."

"Triton's Waves!" said the Commodore, springing out the door. Elena and the officers followed.

The man-cub huddled alone on the couch.

The Lady Uncial, thought Othello, *unannounced. There's a bold play.* "What have you done *this* time?"

"You don't want to know," she said.

"Please," he sniped. "Tell me you had nothing to do with that infernal Flame."

"Shut up."

"I might have known," he groused. "It wasn't enough to joust about like medieval knights through the halls of University. It wasn't enough to slap the Excelsior Crown Prince in front of his friends. You had to up the ante, didn't you? Make things absolutely impossible for everyone?"

"Shut up!"

"Neolithic stupidity. Reckless, thoughtless, hysterical – any number of adjectives come to mind. Oh…and did I forget…irresponsible?"

"Blah – blah – blah. I'm not listening. Dya hear?"

"So…you're just going to sit here and mope?"

"Yes…I…am!"

Ugh! he thought with distaste. *Why does she have to be so dreadfully brainless?* "We might discover something important."

"Elena will find out for us."

"Elena won't know what she's looking for. Though she did have that old fool eating out the palm of her hand last night."

"Like that, did you?"

"You could learn from her. She has a real gift. Reminds me of…well…"

"Reminds you of whom?"

"She who loved me best," he said with a sad, longsuffering meow.

The man-cub swore with frustration. "Oh, all right." She stood, cradling the cat in her arms.

"That's my girl," he cooed. *Works every time!*

π

Troubled voices trembled down the hall. I was wracked with fright and guilt.

I didn't mean to blow it up! Honestly! Just blow it…out.

106

The guards were visibly on edge; the officers looked grave. The whole of House Catagen was awash with dread.

I swore at myself. The Commodore, Elena and the Twins...they all shared my twisted plight. *This is how I repay them? They've all been so patient, so very kind.*

I looked at my furry bundle.

Well...some of them.

"I want to see her, Lord Catagen," demanded the Chancellor. "And I want to see her now!"

She knows, I thought with horror. *She knows I did it!*

"Don't do anything rash," said Othello. "Our stratagem shall be a play of innocent denial..."

"I must protest," said the Old Man. "That..." he paused for a moment in a rare loss for words, "...whatever *that* is, has nothing to do with the Mistress."

She must have found something, some sort of evidence!

"It's very important that I speak to her," said the Chancellor. "Preferably alone."

She wants to interrogate me, cow me into a confession!

"Madam Chancellor," growled the Commodore, "I am the head of House Catagen. If you have anything to say to her, you shall do it in front of me."

Well, it's not going to work! I vowed, vengeful and mad. *She has no right to talk to the Old Man that way!*

"Remain completely silent," advised the cat. "Take your cue from me..."

π

"Show me what?" demanded the man-cub as she crashed into the room.

Othello rolled his emerald eyes, wishing it was Elena and not Pallas who had climbed into his raft.

The room was less crowded than the cat expected, the fools-the-Commodore-called-officers having all been sent away. Elena and the Healer stood to the right while Uncial and Lady Jingo were to the left.

…and I must say that outfit looks completely ridiculous, he thought as he surveyed the Lady Jingo. *Only a Tauran could be so droll.* Clad in armor festooned with orange and brown, the Marshal of the *Zoo* commanded the elite Corps. Her hair was cropped in a severe crew-cut, adding to the starkness of her martial attire. *No one wears orange on brown. It simply isn't done.*

Uncial studied the man-cub with a discerning glare, visibly taking in her soiled hands. Gracefully crossing the floor, she kissed the teenager's cheeks. "Pallas, my dear," she said in a motherly tone, "it's so good to see you again."

That was smooth. Othello expected an angry accusation. Instead, his pupil was greeted with softness and grace. *What is the Chancellor playing at?*

"Show me what?" said the man-cub.

Why do you have to be so ignorant? Look! You've embarrassed your Neanderthal friends. The Commodore was biting his lip. Elena hid her anguish with a smile. Hebe stared at his shuffling feet. Lady Jingo glared.

"My dear," said the Chancellor. "I am stunned and deeply upset about what happened tonight. Thank the Gods *you* were *not* involved."

That was a warning, he thought with alarm. Extending his claws into her chest he thought, *Please, for once in your life, stop and listen.*

But the cub continued her rebellious Air. "You don't care about me! All you care about is that stupid Fire thing."

Just kill me. Just let me die.

A quiet protest filled the room, all of them staring at the reckless cub. The Commodore grew ashen-faced. "What the Mistress means is…"

"I know what she means," said the Chancellor. She squeezed the man-cub's hands like a vice, domineering over her with a shrewd stare. "You must remember, Pallas, dear. We're all…on…the same side."

"What mustn't you show me, Lady Chancellor?" said the man-cub, a little more politely…

…though not much, thought the cat. *I never would have brought you if I knew you were going to continue this foul little tantrum.*

"I'd prefer to be alone," said the Chancellor.

"Whatever you have to show her," said the Commodore.

"Fine," she curtly replied. "We're all friends here." Reaching into her cloak, she revealed a role of parchment. Scratched in ink were a series of letters. Letters formed into words. Words formed into a message…

Black Bishop to Queen Knight Seven.

Kassan

"What's a Bishop?" asked the man-cub.

Othello broke into a pathetic meow, wailing a pitiful lament.

The Commodore gawked with surprise. Elena looked puzzled; Hebe, inquisitive. Jingo was horrified; Uncial, triumphant.

"It's true!" gasped the Chancellor, goose-bumps shivering down her arm. "I hardly dared believe it."

Jupiter's moons! thought Othello.

"What's true?" asked the cub. Othello felt fear ripple through her body.

Uncial smiled, looking upon the man-cub as if she'd just revealed a God in hiding. "Oh, I think you know the answer to *that* question." Then she rounded on the Commodore. "The Leos are in an uproar. There'll be trouble in the *Zoo*. Think about what I said..."

He bowed, confused. "Uh...yes, my Lady."

That's when the Chancellor noticed him, as if seeing him for the very first time. She stared at Othello with giddy delight. "Then this," she stroked his furry head, "this must be Iago!"

Don't say it! thought Othello, uttering a guttural growl.

"Othello," said the man-cub.

The Chancellor jumped back as if bitten by a snake.

No! thought Othello. *Don't make it worse...*

The Commodore steadied his stricken friend. "Lady Chancellor, are you...are you quite all right?"

But Uncial ignored him, gaping at the cub. Her heart was fast and pounding; her face was scared and pale. "Jupiter's Moons!"

Othello arched his back, caterwauling a vicious warning. *Shut up! Don't say another word!*

"My Lady?" said the Commodore, just as stupidly as he could.

Uncial closed her slack-jawed mouth, staring at the man-cub as if she were a spy. "Othello?" she muttered. "But…that would mean…"

Othello heightened his growl.

Comprehension flitted over the Chancellor's face, followed by a moment of profound regret. "I…I must be off," she said with a huff. "Tomorrow will be…well, tomorrow is already here, isn't it?"

The clock commenced its ominous peal, marking the hour as midnight. The Lady Uncial made her escape, followed quickly by the Lady Jingo.

Othello considered the woman as she ignobly fled the room.

I have to contact her. The message was clear…

"What was that about?" accused Elena.

But what if the note is actually a trap?

"No idea," said the man-cub.

I'll need to monitor her conversations, investigate her friends. Uncial must be my new focus. Pouncing upon the cold stone floor, he pursued the Chancellor's escape.

Elena followed a tentative step. "There's something odd about that cat!"

Chapter Nine

The *Zoo*

Poseida clapped her hands. "What did I tell you? Triumphant again! Look at the way I made a fool of that Excelsior brat!"

"Triumphant, or lucky?"

"Who cares? As long as she's besting Mulciber's Token."

"Yes," Cypris complained, "but…who is she?"

Elena followed me up the stairs to my bedroom. "What just happened?"

"I…I really don't know." *Who is Iago? And how did Uncial learn to read?*

But my thin denial couldn't placate my sister. "What was that parchment thing about? What was she saying about that cat?"

"I'm telling you. I don't know."

Elena brandished a wicked sneer. "Uncle William was right about you! You and your confounded secrets! Grandfather *should* keep you in irons until you tell us the entire lot!"

I blanched a silent apology before retreating to my room.

Othello was on my bed, dismembering my favorite pillow. Feathers bled from its silken corpse.

"That couldn't have gone much worse!"

"What was *that* about?" I accused. "Why did you bolt away like that?"

"Me? That is so deliciously rich. The more obvious question would be: why did *you* read that letter?"

I winced.

"What's a Bishop?" he said with disgust. "Haven't you ever played chess?"

What's chess? I thought as I bit my tongue, feeling stupid and guilty and small.

Othello sprang upon the bureau. "Fetch me a RADIO out of the harness."

"A what?"

"RADIO. You remember."

Vaguely. "Wasn't that one of those black boxes you said you didn't know how to work?"

"Yes, well...I've had a sudden inspiration."

"Yeah, right; more like you've been lying to me all this time..." Opening the lid of the trunk, I fumbled to the bottom to find the harness. I tried four different pockets before finding the device he was looking for.

"Yes, yes, that's it. Now, remove the receiver."

"The what?"

"Open the little compartment on the bottom."

I obeyed. A tiny clip fell into my hand.

"Turn this dial to REMOTE."

I turned the dial from OFF to GUARD.

Beep!

"No, no," he said. "All the way to REMOTE."

I twisted the knob from GUARD past BOTH and FREQ to REMOTE. A hiss of static crackled through the Air as the RADIO sought the solace of a paired transmission.

"Speak into the microphone."

"What?"

"That little clip."

I held the clip to my mouth. "What do I say?"

"What do I say?" the RADIO magically repeated.

"Good. Now, attach the RADIO to my collar. There's a Velcro strip..."

I knew about Velcro, the cloth that was clingy yet easy to pull apart. Another enchantment created by the Gods, the harness was full of it.

"You'll look ridiculous..."

"This from the queen of fools?" he snarled. "Just do it."

I did what I was told. It took a little adjusting, but the RADIO was tiny and fit on his collar. He grabbed the receiver in his mouth and dashed out the door.

"Wait…"

"Wake up, my love," Elena cooed. "It's time to go to school."

I felt awful after my sleepless night. "Do I…do I have to?"

"Don't you want to see the *Zoo* today?"

"That's today?"

As Fate would have it, the sophomores were making our very first pilgrimage to the *Zoo*. Lord Duma had been loads of times, of course, using his special privilege to cut class – usually math. But neither I nor Elena had ever entered its hallowed walls.

"Of course, it's today. I'm ever so excited. Aren't you?"

I huffed. *Last night you wanted me chained to my bed. Now you want to play nice?*

"They'll be talking about the Eternal Flame," said the princess, a note of desperation in her lilting voice. "Think what people will say if you're…if you're absent?"

The worry in her voice shook the cobwebs from my head. *She's right! If I don't show up, people will know I had something to do with it!* Jumping from my bed, I threw on my freshly ironed uniform.

"I brought some muffins and a spot of tea. Here, let me help you with your hair."

I felt a stab of guilt. *She's trying, really trying, to be sweet. Why do we always end up fighting?*

"I'm really sorry, Elena…about last night."

The beauty managed a sympathetic frown. "I know you are. It's just…things are getting very complicated, and…"

"And it's all because of me, isn't it?"

She softened into a melancholy smile.

The colored columns brimmed with excitement as we entered the Center Lawn.

All eyes were on the Leon shrine. Metallic molasses oozed from the marble, slopping out like a bombed-out goblet. Once a small, elegant token, the Fire was now a devouring blaze – devouring the golden walls into puddles of molten wealth.

The four columns reached the center, whispers leaping to and fro. Bald heads topping red, raw faces, Alexander and Corona scowled at the others.

Oh my! Won't he be angry?

Cringing as I passed the wreck that used to be Miss Polish's ballroom, I followed Elena to Herodotus' classroom. Classmates instantly surrounded me.

"What happened?" asked a Tauran.

"How did you do it?" said a Gemini.

"Any more spells you'd like to cast?" alleged Ophelia.

For a frantic moment, I thought she must have seen me last night. Then I realized the reason for her wild (yet accurate) accusations…

"I know it was you!" seethed Alexander. Gone was his hair; gone were his eyebrows. His eyelashes were singed to little black nubs. A shiny sheen of ointment covered his furious face. "You cast a spell of Fire, just like you did on Isolaverde."

My guilt almost betrayed me. Instead, I brandished a rash reply. "Look, boys and girls; it's the hairless wonder!"

My classmates roared with laughter, adding to Alexander's shame.

"You'll pay," he warned, "filthy Witch."

Oliver muscled his way to the front of the group. His teeth were ground into a murderous glare. "Never…ever…say that again!"

Alexander considered his new opponent. Then he glanced at the watching Taurans.

"You've been spending too much time at Sea," said Ophelia. "Too much slimy Water beneath your feet, instead of Terra's Good Earth. Best watch yourself, Oliver, allying your fate with those Catagens…"

A gesture from Ophelia brought Obsid to the fore. Standing chest to chest to Oliver, he was almost a head taller and twice as burly.

Oliver glowered at the giant. "I *am* a Catagen!"

The Taurans gasped as if viciously betrayed. Obsid took a startled step backwards, glancing stupidly at Ophelia.

"Then you'll suffer the same as that filthy Witch," said Ophelia. Then she nodded.

Obsid launched himself upon Oliver. But the mariner was quicker, diving at his legs.

The children of the nobility cheered and clapped as the two Taurans toppled to the ground.

I was aghast. Fighting was strictly forbidden at University. *If Oliver's caught, he'll be expelled!*

"Elena! Do something!"

But the tall beauty raised her chin in an Air of cool divinity.

Oliver was on top, raining blows upon Obsid, when Atlanta inexplicably joined the fray. Grabbing Oliver's crimson fist, she pulled him from his foe.

"Get off!" spat Oliver, shoving around her to get at Obsid.

But Atlanta tripped him against her leg, throwing him to the floor.

The crowd cheered.

"A fight between opposites!"

"Air against Earth!"

"Teach her a lesson!"

"Make the Gemini pay!"

Obsid crawled away like a beaten dog.

Furious and embarrassed, Oliver rose to face his new quarry. A minute ago, the Taurans were cursing him for his lack of loyalty. Now they sang his praises as he faced the unpopular Gemini. The Geminis who rarely talked to Atlanta were cheering her name…when she unexpectedly lowered her guard.

"Get her!" yelled the Taurans.

"You…will…not!" roared Elena. Returned from her moment of reverie, she strode between the combatants with an imperious glare. "That's quite enough, Oliver."

"Come on!" chided a longing voice.

"Don't listen to her," begged another.

"Do it for the Good Earth."

"Do it for Gauntle."

But Elena held her ground. "That's enough, Oliver. I won't have you fighting like...like a common street urchin."

Oliver swallowed a wicked snarl. Merciless classmates egged him on.

Just then, Professor Herodotus sauntered through the door.

Everyone scampered to their desks. Oliver took a seat in the rear, wiping blood from his hands with a handkerchief. Obsid was long gone.

Probably escaped to fix that nose, I thought.

The professor seemed oblivious to the fight. "Everyone to your places, please. I've a few things to say before we go. Now...who can tell me the origin of the name...*Zoo?*"

"It was name given to us by the Gods," said a Gemini. "As a token of respect for our ability to rule ourselves."

"Quite right," said the professor. "For it is in the *Zoo* that government is formed, that laws are passed, that men..."

I could care less. *All this fighting. It's all because of me!* Besides, given last night's disaster, I was sure our visit to the *Zoo* would be cancelled.

Yet Herodotus lectured on as if nothing had occurred.

"See what I told you?" whispered Elena. "He's no idea about anything unless it happened a hundred years ago."

I attempted a tepid smile, nervously glancing around. *I never meant to cause all of this trouble!*

Oliver was livid, shooting scowls about the room. Atlanta sat in a corner, abandoned yet again. Such was the fickleness of her Gemini friends.

I wondered why Atlanta stopped the fight. *But at least Oliver wasn't expelled...because he didn't get caught, did he? Atlanta stopped him before the professor arrived. The Gemini actually did him a favor. Though I'm sure Oliver wouldn't see it that way.*

An hour later Herodotus led us to the *Zoo*. Tiny beneath its massive pyre, I marveled at its sheer size. Moss-covered stones adorned the "A" shaped frame, surrounding two massive, wooden doors. A company of orange and brown soldiers, part of the Marshal's elite Corps under the command of Lady Jingo, guarded the hall. After speaking with the aged professor, the captain of the Corps admitted us into an elaborate foyer.

"Listen and learn," said Herodotus, "for this is the culmination of what is best in men. All five elements – twenty-five great Houses – sitting in perfect peace and harmony. Making decisions with words, not swords..."

"I will not stand here and be accused!" bellowed a voice from the hall. "I object in the strongest terms to your poorly-disguised innuendo!"

We silently seated ourselves in the upstairs balcony.

Below us was the *Zoo*. Four corners of the cathedral-sized chamber were tiled in the familiar colors of blue, red, brown, and yellow. Throne-like chairs surrounded a railing of gold, which, in turn, encircled a round platform. Inside the doughnut-shaped platform, half buried in the ground, was a huge, luminescent, green boulder: The Green Stone – the sacred bolt from heaven.

Lady Uncial was seated among the Aquarians. Standing on the platform was a man wearing velvet crimson robes, lined with a mantle of black mink.

"Who's he?" I whispered.

"Excelsior," spat Elena. "Lord Defender of the Titan."

A thrill of hatred raced down my spine. "But...he doesn't look a thing like Alexander."

"Doesn't he?" she quipped. The princess looked completely engrossed. It was obvious she didn't want to be bothered by my foolish questions.

Yet I couldn't help but wonder. Alexander had jet black hair, striking dark eyes, and features that were admittedly handsome. *Before he blew up that stupid Flame, that is.* The man below me wore a washed-out face with balding, wispy hair. Tall and frail, his belly was so fat he looked nine-months pregnant.

"No one is accusing you of anything, Lord Excelsior," said Lady Uncial. "An attack has been made upon University, in the very shadow of the *Zoo*. There must be an investigation."

Excelsior toured the room with his greedy eyes. "There was never an investigation of Lord Catagen's raid on Capro Bay."

"We have discussed that issue at length. Lord Catagen issued a statement of contrition for the alleged offense."

"A statement of contrition is not the same as an investigation, and you know it. Lord Catagen is guilty of piracy, kidnapping, and..."

"I object," stood Lord Joculo. "Piracy is too strong a word to be uttered before this august body. Without proof, such an accusation can not be tolerated."

"Very good," whispered Elena. "See how Grandfather sits back and lets Joculo do the talking?"

"Uh…yeah," I agreed, having no idea what she meant. *How can being called a pirate be a good thing?*

"The point is well taken," Uncial said. "Lord Excelsior, will you withdraw your hasty words?"

Excelsior glared malevolently at the Commodore. And in that evil gaze, I saw the only thing that recommended that he was Alexander's father. Both were filled with an endless craving – hunger so terrible, it could never be sated.

The Commodore looked bored and unconcerned.

"He's trying to rile him," said Elena. "But Grandfather's too smart to take the bait."

"Do you withdraw?" said Uncial.

Excelsior's face changed into a sickly smile, his enormous belly contrasting weirdly with his wasted face, as if his willowy body was unable to contain such ravenous feedings. "My words were taken out of context," he declared. "I did not mean to say that Lord Catagen was a pirate."

"Thank you, Lord Excelsior. You may continue."

He prowled the floor like an arrogant lion, regaling his audience with theatrical flair. In the meantime, I took a moment to study the lords and ladies of my world.

First I looked at the Taurans. Oxymid and Rance supported Excelsior, nodding at his every word. Gauntle's great bulk, however, remained stone-faced and impassive. The one with the excellent physique must be Lord Zeliox, who was famous for his prowess in the Games. Lady Jingo, the Marshal, seemed strangely preoccupied.

I'd never seen any of the Leos before. If there was a pirate in the group, it had to be Corsair, who commanded the *Yamato*. The only other one I knew was the handsome Lord Quid, a Voting member and head of the Treasury.

I looked hopefully at the Geminis. Lady Gemello sat stiffly, difficult to read. Lady Miser, head of the Judiciary, was old and attentive. Another Voting member, she had a pleasant grandmotherly face.

A solitary green lord sat among the Taurans – Lord Tzu, the only Deme. As the ninth and often tie-breaking Voting member, he was allowed to sit wherever he pleased. He was healthy and strong, thick black hair topping a remarkably tan face.

"We Leos are not fooled by the Chancellor's demands," said Lord Excelsior. "When she sues for an investigation, she is looking for an excuse to search the Red Square…and our Manors."

"What a bunch of drivel," protested a Gemini lord.

"I have the floor, Lord Djincar."

"A brief repose, perhaps?" said Lord Djincar. "Madame Chancellor, I request to obtain the floor pro tem to issue an objection to consideration of the question."

"I just love the way Lord Djincar speaks." Elena wiggled in her seat. "He uses the most fascinating words."

"Uh, yeah…me too."

"By all means," said the Chancellor, tiredly waving her hand. "Pontificate to your heart's desire."

"I demand the floor when the Lord Djincar finishes pontifi…" Excelsior sulked. "After he's done."

"Very well, Lord Excelsior," Uncial said. "You will please yield the floor."

Excelsior skulked to his seat as Djincar entered the ring.

"Ladies and Lords," said Djincar, "a grave injustice should occur if this vile offense is not discovered and punished. Once every year, for the sake of peace and justice, each of us leads our Houses – indeed our very families – into the peril of Greenstone. Every one of us understands the dangers that await us, here in proximity with our rival clans. Yet we collectively conclude that any advantage won through an act of guile would be a tawdry bauble compared to the anarchy that would prevail if we, the great Houses, warred upon this hallowed ground."

"Here, here," chorused a smattering of voices.

"See how he draws attention back to the central issue," tittered Elena. "I know his speech *sounds* a bit flowery, but his point is dead on."

"Indeed, it is an offense to the holy Gods that such a vile act should occur to the sacred Flame."

"A great offense indeed," complained Lord Quid, in an effeminate voice I found surprising.

"Yet someone has thrown caution to the Wind. Someone has brought all our lives into jeopardy."

"Here, here," they agreed.

"If this villain is not caught, more occurrences of insurrection shall occur. Houses shall become bolder, more virulent…until this heinous deed consumes us all in rampant dissolution and wonton destruction."

"Here, here!"

I bowed my guilty head. *This is all my fault!*

Uncial stood. "Lord Djincar has spoken eloquently and to the point. Further discussion is unnecessary. Do I have a motion to…?"

"Point of order!" Excelsior shot to his feet. "I shall not rescind my position on the floor."

Uncial frowned, but the Fire lord was procedurally correct. "Very well, Lord Excelsior. You may continue."

Excelsior strode to the floor with relish. "This…investigation," he said indignantly, "is totally unprecedented."

"As is an attack inside the University," interrupted Lord Joculo.

"Once the Chancellor has searched the Red Square, the Lady will search each and every one of your Manors in turn."

"I have no intention of searching anyone's Manor," she protested.

"I contend it is impossible to give the Chancellor such unsurpassed authority. It would be an abuse of power, a dangerous infringement on the rights of the great Houses."

"Anarchy will follow if the villain of this deed is not apprehended!" Joculo declared.

"See how the Aquarians boast with anger?" he shrilled with patronizing contempt. "The lot of them – jealous, impotent and weak. They hide behind legislation, hoping to use this incident to gobble up just a little more power."

"You're one to talk about gobbling!" Elena angrily accused. "Fat ogre hasn't missed a meal in his entire life."

"Why doesn't he want an investigation?" I whispered.

"No idea. But if he doesn't want one, we should insist on it…just for spite. He must be hiding something."

"Lord Excelsior," Uncial said. "An attack has been made upon the Center Lawn. Unless you can give us a clear account – full of proofs, not conjecture – of how this unprecedented event occurred…"

"Isn't it obvious?" he smiled. "To all but the wet-ones. The Eternal Flame has been expanded by the grace of Vulcana, to burn with ever greater glory!"

"And did the Fire Goddess destroy the shrine as well?" snorted Djincar.

"The well-placed joke," said Elena. "Using ridicule to diffuse the enemy's argument."

But I couldn't find any humor in the situation. Excelsior might, at any moment, drop a bombshell, evidence that implicated me and the Twins.

Scorned by the chuckles the coursed about the room, Excelsior cursed at Djincar. "You are in danger of Hellfire, Sir! Dare you question the power of Vulcana?"

"Lord Excelsior," said Lady Uncial. "Never before has one of the Gods committed an act of divine intervention within the grounds of University."

"It could be nothing *other* than divine intervention!" he bellowed, spit flying from his fleshy jowls. "How *else* could a holy relic explode of its own accord?"

"That's why we desire an investigation. I cannot fathom why you are opposed to discovering the culprit who destroyed your sacred artifact."

"Isn't it obvious?" said Joculo with a lazy drawl. "I contend we are being entertained by a fiction, better played out in a theater than this, the site of the Green Stone. A fiction perpetrated to hide *your* son's culpability!"

"My son?!" Excelsior stammered. An actor would have been proud to give such a performance. "My sweet, innocent child has nothing to do with this!"

I stifled a laugh. Elena slapped my hand.

"Your son was caught in the blast," chortled the Lord of Kelly Tree. "Toasted to a crisp, from what I hear tell!"

A chorus of laughter searched around the room. I laughed loudest of all. My sovereign was witty and bold. *No wonder Daddy likes him so much.*

Excelsior surveyed the heckling lords. Gone was his theatrical Air, replaced with the anger of a proud man humbled by a disappointing son. "And does my son carry blue paint when he strolls through University?"

"Perhaps he wants to be an Aquarian!" laughed Lord Joculo.

The cavern howled with rapturous delight. Even the Taurans joined in.

"Of course he doesn't!" roared Excelsior. He stamped upon the floor, another shower flying from his lips. "That blue paint proves the perpetrator must have been an Aquarian!"

"There were no Aquarians discovered at the scene," Joculo argued. "Your son was caught out of bounds, in University, well after hours…"

"How dare you accuse my son?" shrieked Excelsior. "When everyone knows none of this would ever have happened if that Catagen Witch hadn't showed up, polluting our sacred *Zoo* with her scum and waste and filth!"

I reeled in my seat, my mirth – a distant memory.

He knows, I wheezed. *He knows!*

The Commodore suddenly rose to his feet. His eyes were a stormy tempest, his weathered countenance wild and torn. "That, Sir, is an insult I cannot bear!"

"That Witch," glared Excelsior, "has been nothing but trouble!"

A murmur of caution rifled through the cathedral. Even Elena looked worried.

"This isn't good."

"Why?" I fretted. "What's happening?"

"The fox is out of his hole. The lion will try to trap him."

I chewed my nails, thinking, *Who's the fox?*

Filled with new bravado, Excelsior donned a wicked smile. "Lord Catagen has brought a demon amongst us…an evil, loathsome hag. Indeed, the Lord God Mulciber has demanded she be sacrificed. Yet here she remains…spreading distrust…upsetting the status quo. And if I hear one more word about the Age of Aquarius…"

"Ye'll 'ave seen the last of this age if ye don't shut ye're hatch," menaced the Old Man, hammering his fists upon the golden rail.

"Commodore, please," Uncial pleaded, rubbing her forehead.

"Point of order," said Excelsior. "*I* have the floor."

122

"I will not yield!" barked the Commodore. "For the sake of the Mistress' honor, there will be blood feud between House Catagen and Turner Hill if there is not an immediate apology!"

"Honor?" laughed the Fire lord. "What honor is there amongst House Catagen, home of pirates and Witches alike?"

The Old Man vaulted over the rail. "To Davey Jones locker wit ye, ya filthy, lying landlubber."

Excelsior retreated a few frightened steps. "Infringement!" he said with twinge of panic. "I claim a violation of the code of standards!"

The Old Man continued his advance. "Who among you would suffer such unfounded accusations against one of your daughters?"

"She isn't one of your daughters," Oxymid spat.

"She's my daughter until Poseida takes her back to Atlantis!" he roared. "House Catagen stands ready to crush any man or woman that says otherwise. I should think you, of all people, should know that."

Oxymid opened and closed her mouth before slumping back into her chair.

My breathing was short and sporadic. *So much trouble! All because of a stupid prank!*

Elena gently took my hand. "Not to worry, darling. Not to worry. It's a bold play, but Grandfather knows exactly what he's doing."

"He does?"

Lady Uncial stood. "Lord Catagen, you are in violation of the code of standards. You must yield until Lord Excelsior's time has expired."

"I will not yield!" he said, openly defying his superior. "If Lord Excelsior will not withdraw, then I demand right to fair combat."

The cathedral sounded a collective gasp. My anguish instantly doubled.

Fair combat? What does that mean?

"You wouldn't dare," whined Excelsior.

"Jes try me."

"What's going on?" I pleaded.

Elena gave me a cross little look, a hint of frustration on her perfect face. "He's challenging Excelsior to a duel."

"Oh," I said, not sure what that meant. "That isn't…too bad…is it?"

"To the death."

Oh my Gods! It is that bad!

"This is highly irregular," pleaded Excelsior. "The floor is mine. He must withdraw."

"Don't needs a blade," threatened the Old Man, "I'll snuff ye out, wit' mi' own bare 'ands."

"There will be no combat in the *Zoo*," demanded the Chancellor. "Lord Catagen, you are in violation of the code of standards."

Lady Jingo abruptly stood. "I motion for a vote of censure."

"Yes!" whispered Elena, elation favoring her gorgeous smile.

"And who shall we censure, Lady Jingo?" Uncial growled, clearly annoyed with her life-long friend. She was obviously trying to diffuse the situation, not make it worse.

"Lord Excelsior," said the martial Tauran.

"Of course," Elena agreed, patting my hand.

Excelsior guffawed, his eyes ablaze with anger.

"Lord Excelsior has questioned the honor of a princess of House Catagen," said Jingo. "Such a charge can only be settled by fair combat."

"I second the motion," Lord Djincar announced. Surprised heads turned to the portly lord.

A Gemini supporting a Tauran? I thought. *Earth and Air are opposites. That would be like an Aquarian agreeing with a Leo!*

The Chancellor seized her chance to get the Old Man back in his chair. "A motion has been called for, Lord Catagen. You *will* withdraw."

"Will he sit down now?" I asked, marveling at the way Elena was one step ahead of the proceedings.

"Oh, yes."

Sure enough, the Commodore returned to his seat, though he still wore a malevolent glare.

Uncial breathed a sigh of relief. "There shall be a roll call vote to censure Lord Excelsior. If the resolution passes, Lord Catagen will have right to enter personal combat with Lord Excelsior."

Rance, Zeliox, and Oxymid huddled around Gauntle's girth, whispering frantic instructions. The Earth lord looked completely bewildered, looking back and forth between the Taurans and the Fire lord. He finally spoke in a morose voice, "I motion…that the *Zoo*…recess…until tomorrow. To, uh…discuss the matter."

But Djincar was way ahead of him. "The vote of censure is a privileged motion. Lord Catagen must have satisfaction before he leaves these halls."

"Thank you, Lord Djincar," said the Chancellor. "The alleged offense occurred here, in the *Zoo*, for all to see. There is no need for further discussion. We shall begin the vote."

I was sick with misery. "Can't we do anything to stop them?"

"Stop them?" Elena exclaimed, triumph painted on her porcelain face. "Grandfather has him right where he wants him."

"He does?"

"Of course. Listen and learn."

"Lady Miser," Uncial said with renewed authority. "How do you say in this vote of censure against Lord Excelsior?"

The Gemini grandmother looked very concerned. "Lord Excelsior has questioned the honor of Lord Catagen's daughter. That is a very serious offense."

"How do you vote?" asked Lady Uncial.

"Yea."

One for the Commodore.

"Lord Quid?"

"Nay," he said with a high-pitched voice. Young and wealthy, "dandy" was the word that came to mind for the world's most eligible bachelor.

"He's the Treasurer of the *Zoo*," said Elena. "He's been skimming money into his family's coffers for years."

Lady Uncial eyed her best friend with a quizzical look. "Lady Jingo?"

"Yea," she said without hesitation. The other Taurans glared at her.

"Lord Catagen?"

"Yea," hissed the Old Man.

"Lord Tzu?"

"Nay." The Deme Lord sided with the Leos, against Lord Catagen. The sweating Excelsior managed a thin smile. There were two votes for the Fire lord – three for the Old Man.

"Lady Gemello?"

Borelo's mother fidgeted uncomfortably in her chair. After considering the glares of the Leos, she gave the Commodore a "this will cost you" expression, pursed her lips, and said, "Yea."

"Lord Excelsior?"

He gulped a long swallow from a hip flask, slopping the drink down his robes. "Nay," he said in an embarrassed whisper.

"Lord Gauntle?"

The Old Man's son-in-law shuffled in his chair, bitter eyes frowning at Lady Jingo. There were now four votes for the Commodore and three for Excelsior. Since Uncial was sure to vote for Catagen, even if Gauntle voted for Excelsior, Catagen would win. He appeared to be mulling this over when he was unexpectedly interrupted.

Excelsior could add the votes just as well as the lumbering Gauntle – probably better. Quite suddenly he lost his nerve. "I misspoke! I...I did not mean to besmirch Lord Catagen's honor."

I stole a glance at Alexander. Humiliation was scorched upon his face.

But the Old Man pressed his advantage. "It's not my honor that's in question. It's the Mistress's honor you must avow."

"Very well," said Excelsior, derisively flipping his hand. "I apologize for anything I might have said about...the *girl*...in question." He said *girl* as if it were a dirty word.

"Not to me, Excelsior," he shrewdly declared. "You must apologize to the Mistress of the Sea."

"Alas, I would," he smiled, "but as Lord Djincar stated, the matter must be handled now, in the hallowed halls of the *Zoo*. Therefore, I don't see how that would be possible."

"Oh, but this is a happy day, for she's sitting right over there!" Pivoting smartly towards the balcony, he surprised me with an eloquent bow.

I was stunned he even knew I was there. Excelsior obviously hadn't seen us. My very first trip to the *Zoo,* and every eye was riveted on me.

"Stand up," Elena whispered, "and repeat after me."

126

I obeyed. I looked down upon the Fire lord and waited.

Excelsior quivered with epileptic rage. He glared at his son, curling his lips with dislike.

Alexander looked horrified. Anguished red drained from his face, into frightened, ashen embarrassment.

"Shall I continue the vote?" Uncial warned. "I believe Lord Gauntle is next."

Excelsior glanced at his fellow Leos, as if hoping for a miraculous reprieve. But none would help the Lord Defender salvage his wounded pride. Desperate, he looked pleadingly at Lord Gauntle.

The silent Tauran was as still as stone.

"Continue the vote," said Djincar.

"On with it!" Joculo retorted.

A grumble of annoyance swept through the nobility, punctuated with chuckles and edgy jeers.

"Lord Gauntle?" said Uncial.

Excelsior was red with fury. "I apologize, Mistress," he snarled, his voice aflame with venom, "I...misspoke."

"I accept your apology, Lord Excelsior," whispered Elena, "on behalf of Holy Poseida, Triton the Magnificent, and all the Gods of the Mighty Sea."

"I accept your apology, Lord Excelsior," I announced, "on behalf of Holy Poseida, Triton the Magnificent, and all the Gods of the Mighty Sea."

This was too much for the lord of Turner Hill. After shooting another glance at his son, he marched towards the towering doors. Six orange soldiers labored to open them. A blast of sunlight swallowed the bully as he vanished in the brilliance of the blinding glare.

"Now," said Lady Uncial, "to the investigation."

Chapter Ten

Whispers

There is no question when the Taurans made their treacherous pact. Catagen II's famous humiliation of Excelsior III was lauded round the world as one of his finest hours, but it was a Pyrrhic victory at best. For it marked a sharp reversal in Gauntle III's relationship with his erstwhile father-in-law...

"Rise and Fall of the Pentathanon Gods"

Herodotus III

"Wasn't that exciting!" Elena merrily exclaimed. "Did you see the way Grandfather out-maneuvered that camp-Fire fool?"

But I wasn't thinking about Excelsior. Instead, my mind tarried on the only Deme. "Wasn't it odd how Lord Tzu voted against the Commodore?"

"Rather," she said, her giddy joy diminished by a tiny jot. "Only, I must tell you plainly that Tzu often votes against us, especially of late."

"Why?"

"Oh, bother, probably just a nutter holed up on that ridiculous island of his. Gauntle is the one that makes me mad. Notice how the great lump refused to cast his vote?"

"Yeah."

"I know Excelsior interrupted him," she interrupted. "But in days of old he would have bullied ahead and voted anyway. He loved irritating Excelsior."

"Yeah, but..." I hesitated, not wanting to spoil her good mood. But as clumsy as I was – so ill at ease with the political tempests that tossed me – I ruined it without meaning to. "Isn't your cousin married to Gauntle? Aren't Oliver and Genevieve his children?"

"What rot?!" snarled the princess. "You are *so* unfair! How dare you blame Oliver and Genevieve when you know very well whose fault it was?"

"I...I didn't mean."

"You're the one who used the magic! You're the one who blew up the Flame! Now you want to pin it on Oliver?"

"No!"

But the beauty turned and huffed away, her happiness wasted on her troublesome sister.

The Aquarians talked of nothing but the Eternal Flame. Every House had been burned by Lord Excelsior at one time or another; the Fire lord had a healthy appetite for bullying.

The Geminis and Taurans joined in the fun, discussing the Leo's apology with eager delight. And when they weren't vilifying the father, they joked about his son, quieting the prince into a crushing repose.

The Water Jesters made it worse. Though they never actually used my name, their homilies spoke of a new beginning, a Dawning that would drown the hated Flame. Their sermons, laced with healthy doses of *ambrosian* ecstasy, started the other Water lords believing.

Hiding my face from my intoxicated admirers, I fled the Water Temple in a humble retreat. A trio of Aquarians followed in a daze. Their words were loud and ringing.

"What if the prophecy's true?" said Lord Cannes, his face, a paragon of contentment. "What if she really is a God?!"

Lord Ionian walked with his noble kin, his arm wrapped jovially around his middle. "A hallowed Atlantian! Born of the Seven Seas! Heralding a new and wondrous age!"

"This could be the Dawning of the Age of Aquarius!" sang Lord Duma.

Their words of praise should have made me proud, but they didn't. For they were bred...not by love...but a drug: a happy elixir both my father and Lord Catagen warned me of. Instead of boosting my ego, their flattery overwhelmed me, my notoriety eclipsing my ability to cope.

Worst of all was Othello...or rather, the lack of him. For once in my life, I actually wanted his company. Yet suddenly, he was nowhere to be found. He even skipped our nightly reading lessons, something he'd never done before...

His absence made me wary.

And what was that Uncial-thing about? Can she actually read? And why was my name written on that message?

The mysteries entangling me grew reckless and bold.

Why would he leave when I need him the most?

But as heavily as these questions burdened my soul, I had more pressing concerns. Chariot tryouts were tomorrow, and I was still quite worried about my chances.

∞

Casey and Phillip helped me harness Calypso and his three white mares. Thanks to Phillip, everything was ready, my Arabians glistening like fresh winter snow.

"Be careful," Casey muttered, "Dusan is a real idiot."

"I know."

"I'll be watching from the stands. Lucy and the Old Man…"

"Did Elena come?"

Casey rolled her eyes. "Come on. You know what she's like. Friend one minute, enemy the next. Anyway, she's in a real huff about…well, you know. Told us off yesterday…and again this morning, just for spite. I've never seen her so mad."

My face collapsed into a melancholy frown.

"It was worth it!" said Casey with a savage smile. "Seeing the hairless-wonder fly across the lawn! And the way you made a fool out of Lord Excelsior was absolutely brilliant."

"Me? I didn't do that. It was the Old Man…"

Casey huffed. "Don't be so bloody modest. You're the talk of the town…the world, rather. Come on! Lap it up. Live a little!"

"I…I don't know," I stammered. As far as I was concerned, my fame was a bane and not a boon.

Casey laughed. "You're a funny sort of God, ya know that? Do the all Atlantians worry so much?"

I grimaced a sigh. I knew she was trying to cheer me up. But I didn't have a clue what Atlantians worried about.

"Oh, bother," said Casey. "Don't think about it. Just concentrate on racing your very best race. And stay away from Dusan."

"I will."

Lord Duma held the pole position on the track. Urban was next, then young Joculo, and then me. I was so nervous, I dared not look in the stands.

"Five, four, three, two, one."

"Go!"

Dusan catapulted ahead, followed closely by Urban. I let Joculo pass, veering left towards the inside track. Dusan and Urban were nearly a dozen car lengths ahead when they rounded the first bend.

I wasn't worried.

"You don't win by finishing the first lap first!" I called to my milk-white team. "You win by finishing the last lap first!"

Joculo looked back to see me on his left. Expecting me on his right, he swerved left to slow me. I moved right to escape his dusty trail.

Coming to the first turn, Joculo pulled hard to the left. But he took the turn a little too quickly, skidding his chariot towards the right.

I was ready. I knew he was going too fast and slowed Calypso a moment before. As Joculo swerved wide right I leaned my team left, cutting neatly behind. A dust cloud rose to meet me as I shot the narrow gap, squeezing between his car and the stone center. When I cleared the turn, I was neatly ahead.

Dusan and Urban were battling it out, unmercifully whipping their horses. Clumsily taking the next turn wide, they tired their team with their reckless driving.

I kept an even pace, keeping care to stay ahead of Joculo.

The next turn completed Lap One. Six more to go. I watched Urban and Dusan squabble for the inner track. Urban was a rank amateur, but Dusan definitely knew what he was doing. Still, he beat his horses as if this was the last lap and not the second.

Lap Three. Dusan held the inside track. Urban foolishly tried to pass wide right.

Idiot! But I really didn't care. As long as they kept sparring, they'd be tired when I made my move.

Lap Four. Urban was now a car length behind Dusan when I slowly closed the distance. Looking back with startled fury, he saw me pacing on the left. Noting his surprise, I nudged my steeds right.

Urban looked right, swerving to stop me. Timing it perfectly, I leaned left. Urban looked right again, trying to locate me in the dust as I passed to his left.

Lap Five. Dusan was still well ahead. Urban charged right – then left, vainly trying to pass. I kept a careful vigil, watchfully cutting him off. Joculo seemed more patient. Still in fourth place, he waited for Urban to tire his horses.

Lap Six. Urban was falling behind. Joculo passed him in the turn; I didn't see how. But there was only one more lap to go. I was running out of time.

"Hiyaah!" I yelled at the top of my lungs. "Adrena! Aquata! Anona!"

The four responded with a burst of speed. Closing the distance, I planned my attack. Well before the next turn, I nudged right, and then made a move to the left.

But Dusan was clever and covered left. I ate a cloud of dust as I gently retreated right. Dusan moved to follow.

I could see flecks of blood oozing off Dusan's horses. Dirt and sweat caked my hair, painting my face like a savage barbarian. I urged my team left, flicking the reins. Then to the right. Dusan moved to stop me, his track getting wider and wider. I didn't understand the finer points of harmonic waves, but I knew his weaving was getting wilder and wilder.

I fainted right again, slowing my team as we approached the turn. As Dusan moved right I turned sharply left, skidding round the stone barrier. Dusan, his rampant course too reckless to master, couldn't match my turn. He wagged right as I surged left, hugging the inner track, half a car ahead.

But Lord Duma wasn't going to give up that easily. Yesterday, he'd said that I was the beginning of the Age of Aquarians. Now, he was so mad at me that he collided his horses into my car.

"Get off!" I shrieked.

"Out of my way!" he bellowed.

But there was nowhere for me to go. On one side was a wall of stone, on the other the lunatic lord. I snapped my reigns, screaming at the top of my lungs.

"Hiiyaaah! Calypso!"

My warhorse accelerated into a full gallop.

Dusan punished his horses with the brunt of his whip. His team responded with desperate courage, charging recklessly forward. I felt his horses' breath, hot upon my shoulder. I glanced back and gasped. Their trampling hooves were mere inches away.

"Slow down, you fool! You're going to kill them!"

"Never! You stupid, filthy Witch!"

"Uh!" I huffed, resentful and mad.

Calypso was paying more attention than I was. Automatically slowing the team, he swung round the coming turn.

The young lord thought he saw an opening. Whipping and cursing, he yanked his team to the left.

It was a mistake.

His horses were spent. They couldn't make the turn he demanded. Instead, his post collided into my chariot, thundering on top of my floorboard for a few hopeless strides. Inches from destruction, I flung forward against my hood. Heavy hooves obliterated the deck of my chariot.

"No!" I shrieked. I knew Dusan was an idiot, *But how could he be so reckless!?*

The poor beast couldn't continue. His forelegs stumbled upon the floorboard as his hind legs tried to push his body forward. The team careened madly to the right – around the gallant post who stumbled and tripped and fell. Panicked, the fallen gelding thrashed his legs in a valiant effort to stand, hobbling on wrecked knees and torn sinew. The car flipped over, rolling in blood, throwing House Duma brazenly to the ground.

I cringed at the carnage – said a prayer for the horses. A pang of guilt wished I could hope that Dusan was safe, but…I couldn't. Easily rounding the final turn, I slowed to a victorious finish. Joculo followed three cars behind. Urban brought up a miserable third.

Phillip was the first to greet me as I slowed to a halt. "Ya did it, miss! Ya did it! Bless your soul, ya beat the lot!"

I enjoyed an ecstatic grin as I descended from my battered car. Liam surprised me by catching me. "I knew you could do it!" he said, swallowing me with his strong embrace.

"Brilliant!" cried Lucy.

"The way you took that last turn!" Casey shouted.

133

I was too happy to speak. Liam set me down as a host of Aquarians surrounded me. Even the Commodore joined in, clapping me hard on my dusty back.

"You're a mess!"

"Thanks!" I brandished in mock surprise.

"Mistress of the Sea!" he said. "Covered in Earth! Aye, what would Poseida say?"

Everyone laughed. Clay was indeed caked in every crevice. Dirt in my hair, my eyes, my ears, my face…

But the Twins didn't care as they pressed close against me, sharing in the excitement of the dangerous race. It was a testament to their joy that they didn't bristle when Elena approached.

In the frantic haze of the many compliments, I winced at her sapphire eyes. Dazzlingly in their beauty – shrill as the winter Wind – they fell upon my dirty garb, my sandy hair, my filthy face.

There was a brief, tense reckoning, the two famous princesses…glaring at each other…

…when the beauty finally smiled, gracing me with a heart-felt embrace. "You were fabulous, Pallas! Really, I am ever so proud."

"Thanks." I didn't know why, but this was the hug I remembered most, the caress I cherished above all others.

"We'll spend time together this weekend…or this afternoon, rather," she promised. But when she pulled away, she let out a revolted gasp. A layer of dirt was caked upon her gown. "After I've given you a bath!"

I laughed.

Elena laughed.

We all laughed together.

Elena proceeded to the Manor to prepare our bath. I walked beside Calypso and the Twins, jabbering down the grassy path.

"I mean to say!" Casey exclaimed. "Neither Dusan nor Urban will be driving now. They've raced the last three years, and now they're out."

"Dusan's out altogether," said Lucy. "He didn't make the team at all!"

"Is he all right?" I asked.

"Broke his leg," said Casey, "useless git."

"Almost every event has new contestants!" said Lucy. "Pallas is driving in the Circus; the two of you will be riding in the Mounted Javelin…"

"And you're boxing," said Casey with a hint of resentment.

"Now don't start that again."

Joculo was already at the stables. Dusan's and Urban's teams were there as well, but the defeated boys were absent. Having lost the race, Urban didn't bother tending to his horses, leaving the chore to the livery boys. Dusan's leg, of course, was being healed by the magic Demes.

Joculo was rubbing down his anchor. He approached me with a warm smile. "Congratulations," he said, shaking my hand.

"You too."

"You know what this means, don't you?"

"You and I will be riding together."

"Yeah, but…now that you've won, you can have the pick of the lot." He waved at Dusan's geldings. "Any horse you want."

"You kidding?" I said, nuzzling my head into Calypso's face. "I wouldn't trade these for the world."

"Us girls" and Lord Catagen spent the next happy hours grooming my tired team. Poor Phillip didn't know what to think about having a Voting Member of the *Zoo* wash Anona, and kept begging to let him do it himself. But the Old Man took a liking to the boy, insisting *he* was going to brush the triumphant mare. Unfortunately, he sneezed a lot as he was allergic to horses. But Lord Catagen wouldn't stop until Anona was groomed to Phillip's exacting standards.

I wallowed in contentment as I listened to the banter. I was family now, an unlikely thread in the Catagen quilt.

I remembered what Oliver had said…

"I am a Catagen!"

Well, I thought, grateful belonging swelling in my chest, *I am too.*

But my reverie was hounded by complicated thoughts. What would Gauntle, Oliver's father, say about Oliver's loyalty to the Old Man? What would Uncial discover during her investigation? Was Djincar right; could my childish prank really destroy the *Zoo*?

And where is that stupid cat?

My happiness had already soured when I started on Calypso's back. I ran my hands along his many scars, reminded of the cruelty of the brutal lord.

"What happened to Dusan's post?"

Casey frowned. "He had to be put down."

"No!" I sighed, miserable and sad. *Is Dusan's broken leg payment enough for such savagery?* I didn't know. But before I could ponder this any further, a huge bear approached.

"Dad!" said young Joculo, embracing his father.

Large and burly, the Lord of Kelly Tree had thick, powerful arms. I, of course, had seen my sovereign plenty of times from a distance. Still, up close, his brawn was surprising.

Lord Joculo gave his son an earnest hug before turning to the girl who beat him.

I curtsied the best I could. "My Lord," I said submissively.

The great bear bowed, then smoothed my hands in his massive paws. "Mistress," he hushed, "a real pleasure it is for me."

"You're too kind, my Lord." I didn't know why, but he made me feel like a slave all over again. In the village of Kelly Tree, Lord Joculo was my master. He literally held the power of life or death. Deeply-rooted instincts obliged a loyalty all their own, making this lord more imposing than the others.

"You needn't 'my Lord' me," he laughed. "Not after that race! What a finish!"

"Prince Joculo beat Urban and Dusan."

"I'm very proud of my son."

His gaze was inquisitive, as if puzzling together a distant memory. Then, without warning, a dawn of comprehension blanketed his face. "You…you have gray eyes."

I drooped my face to hide from his stare. *Stupid twit! What if he recognizes me?* "Yes, my Lord…like my mother's."

"But…that would mean…"

Then he gasped.

I didn't dare look up. *What if he recognizes me?* But curiosity overcame my fear. I sneaked a peek through my dusty hair and saw a trembling wreck. His face had turned to wide-eyed horror, quaking from some unknown dread.

"Are you…all right, my Lord?"

"Yes, yes, indeed," he said, running a paw through his thick brown hair. Then, as if throwing a switch, he merrily addressed his son. "Come along, Team Captain!" he boomed too loudly. "Mother has a surprise waiting; of that you can be sure!"

With that, he hurriedly left.

What was that about? I thought, feeling inadequate and small. For seeing my master made me visit the same, old question: the question that plagued me ever since I climbed aboard that raft…

Am I really the Mistress of the Sea…or just a slave from Kelly Tree?

π

Elena had already sunk in the pool-like bath when the Goddess appeared.

Why a divine creature would allow herself to get so filthy I shall never understand, she thought as Abbey helped her out of her grubby gear. *Why would a God compete in the first place?* There were so many inconsistencies to this silly deity, so many things she didn't understand.

But she rode a dolphin…she bested the Lord God Mulciber…

…and yet.

"I'll just wash this," Abbey said before leaving.

The Goddess slipped into the bath.

She's not even beautiful enough to be a God. Elena hated herself for thinking this, but she simply couldn't help it. *Aren't the Gods supposed to be perfect? I mean…look at those mismatched ears!*

"I'm certainly glad you won," she said, "and I'm rather sorry I've been so…"

"Distant?"

Elena shrugged. *She can be perceptive. I'll give her that.*

137

The Goddess lazily closed her eyes. "That's all right, Elena. I'm just so glad you're my friend."

"Friend?" she lilted like a song. "We are sisters, you and I."

The Goddess opened her misty eyes – gratefulness quivering on her trembling lips. "Sister," she hushed. "You...you don't know how much that means to me."

Elena blushed. *Oh! But I think I do.* She reproached herself for her own impiety. But she salved her conceit with the thought that she wasn't doing this to hurt the Goddess...but to help her.

It isn't my fault she loves me so much.

"I have so much love for you," she said. "And I am...ever so proud."

"Thanks."

And that is why I must do this! she thought. *But I must do it carefully.*

"Won't you taste this lovely sherbet, Pallas? The cold drink in the hot bath gives me such a rush!" The fact that it was laced with ill-gotten *ambrosia* was a tawdry, but necessary sin. The Goddess was, after all, far too excitable *not* to take every conceivable precaution.

The Goddess took a deep, long drink. She shivered a moment in the steamy bath.

Smiling, Elena poured another. "You must be ever so parched."

"Yeah," said the Goddess, gulping more of the sherbet.

Pleased, Elena placed the silver pitcher back in the bowl of ice.

Then, taking a deep cleansing breath, she began...

"I wish I could make you better cheer, darling. I've been just beastly, I know I have. But...you've been really worrying me, and I won't deny it."

"Why?"

"Honestly, sister. Where do I begin?"

The Goddess' spirit seemed to slump.

Does a God even have emotions? Can they really feel depressed? "I love you darling...like a sister. You know that."

She narrowed her grey eyes. "You already said that."

"I did?" she said with hidden alarm. *Careful, Elena; you must be careful!* She thought for a moment to abandon her attempt. But brutal necessity made her carry on. "Have some more sherbet, before the ice melts away."

The Goddess dutifully drank.

Elena said a silent prayer. *Oh please, Poseida, help me do this!* Subtleties, she knew, were wasted on the child. She responded much better to bold dramatics. "You've been scaring me, Pallas. You've been scaring the lot of us."

"How?"

"Oh, bother. In Herodotus' class, you questioned the morality of the holy Gods. You tricked Pythagoras into claiming that mathematicians were on the same level as the Gods. And, in science, you actually added a sixth Pentathanon God!"

"No one cares about that."

"But they do, Pallas; they really do. Everyone cares. Everyone's watching."

The Goddess frowned.

"Then you make friends with Atlanta."

"What's wrong with Atlanta?"

What isn't *wrong with Atlanta?* she thought. "Please. You can hardly deny she's a very odd bird."

"You play love-bird with that despicable Bore-us-loads character."

"That's different. That's politics."

"Not everything in the world is about politics."

"Nearly. It isn't a dirty word, you know."

"It is to me."

"Look, I don't want to upset you." *Dare I upset an Atlantian? What if she rains lightning from the Sky...or...or turns me into a tree?* But, studied as she was with courtly intrigues, Elena could see the tiny, tell-tale widening of her sister's eyes. The *ambrosia* was having the desired effect. "I only say this because I love you, darling. You need to watch yourself."

"Why?"

"Because...you're collecting more enemies than friends."

This seemed to strike the Goddess quite hard. "Like who?"

"Please! Have you learned nothing from Herodotus' class? The day the Old Man rescued you, you gained Oxymid and Rance as enemies. Two months later, you beat up prince Borelo."

"He deserved it."

"I'm not saying he didn't. But then you humiliate House Excelsior, both the younger and the elder."

"I thought you were happy about the *Zoo*?"

"I am. I was. I hate the Excelsiors, more than I can tell. But the point is…you've managed to acquire, in very short order, a House in every corner that simply loathes you."

"The Aquarians like me."

"You just crippled Lord Duma. Urban and Anthony detest you, and…"

"And what?"

"Pallas, dear, I don't mean to pry. But you have been spending a great deal of time with Keleron."

"He's on my team!"

"Eunice has noticed. She's in a right state."

"Listen," she hissed, "I've never so much as…"

"Eunice thinks you have. She has the Aquarian girls in a tizzy."

"All of them?"

"Not all of them. Janice seems to like you. In fact, the entirety of House Joculo won't hear a word against you. But it's a frightfully trivial House, one of the smallest in the *Zoo*. Wherever is it that they come from?"

"Kelly Tree."

"Precisely. Half-way across the world, in the middle of nowhere. I mean to say, the smelly hovel hardly rates as a great House in the first place."

For some reason, this aroused the Atlantian's anger.

Gentle, Elena! Remember…she's a God. "Sister," she cooed, reaching out her delicate fingers to clasp the charioteer's calloused hands. "I only say this because I love you. You're a Catagen now, and Catagens stick together."

The Goddess grimaced.

What is she thinking? thought the princess. *Is she angry I call her a Catagen, that we've given her a mortal name?*

No. It couldn't be. *She's delighted we count her as family. I know it!*

"There's something else," Elena said with a shudder. "Something I...I need to know."

"What?"

"Late last summer, Oliver sailed with Captain Tiberius aboard *Enterprise*."

"Yeah, I know. The Twins were furious when you wouldn't let them go."

"Yes, well," she sported a naughty grin, "I was having a very bad hair day, and in a rather uncharitable tiff."

"Yeah."

"Tell me, darling, do you remember that sacred object you gave to Oliver? The one with the little arrow?"

"The compass?"

"Yes, yes, that's the one. Well, Captain Tiberius and Oliver used it to venture out into the Western Sea."

"So?"

Why won't you tell me plainly? Why do you make me drag it out of you? "They discovered something, something quite important."

"What?"

"A Continent."

"A what?"

You really don't know? "A Continent, an enormous land mass thousands of miles long."

"Thousands?"

Or are you just an incredible actress? That's what Lucy claims...that you pretend this childish lunacy to keep us guessing. "Why yes. At least...that's what the people who live there tell us."

"People?"

"Loads of people," she hushed with dread. "An entire city no one knows about."

"What *kind* of people?"

The princess trembled, haunted by the heresy...

141

Elena's world was changing, and it was changing far too fast. Before that summer, her entire universe was contained in fourteen small islands. News of a vast Continent, populated by an unknown people just beyond the Western Sea, was very troubling indeed.

But that wasn't the worst of it. *Dare I tell her? Will she turn me into stone...or burn me in a column of Fire...or...*

But the beauty mastered her fear. *I have to know!* "People who don't worship the Pentathanon Gods," she whispered. Elena didn't know the word infidel. But if she did, she would have used it.

"They don't worship the Gods?" asked the Goddess.

"They don't even *know* about the Gods," she said, bravely confronting that sacrilegious suggestion. "Beastly savages, you might suppose. Yet...they are very noble people according to Tiberius. Very noble people indeed. People like...Liam."

"Liam!" gasped the Goddess. "But...how could that be?"

"Tiberius brought him here from the Continent. We left Fletcher, Oliver's uncle, in his stead. Sort of an exchange program if you will. For us to learn their ways, and for them to learn ours."

The Goddess' eyes filled with wonder. "That's why he's allowed to attend University," she said, mulling through her transparent emotions, "but not allowed to compete in the University Games."

"That's why you must keep your distance, Sister. The man is a foreigner...an intelligent, beautiful heathen."

"I can't believe the other Houses allowed it," said Pallas.

"Many were indisposed," said Elena. "Yet Lady Uncial was quite firm, both with Liam and the Atlanta oddity."

"Don't call her that," said Pallas. "She's really sweet..."

"Sweet?" mocked Elena.

"Well," admitted the Goddess. "Maybe not...sweet. But she's my friend."

"Of course," said Elena, wisely deciding not to fight about it. "But there's something else I must tell you. Something really frightening."

"What?"

"The people on the Continent. They knew about *you*."

"Me?" she gasped.

"They knew about the Egg, the dolphins, Fort Isolaverde. They even knew…" she blanched…"they knew about the prophecy."

"That's impossible. How could they possibly know about that?"

"I was hoping…well," she shrugged. "I was hoping…*you* would tell me."

"I don't know anything about that stupid prophecy. Besides, no one believes that stuff."

"Not believe!?" she said, rolling her sapphire eyes. "Oh, what nonsense! Of course they believe."

Despite the *ambrosia*, the Goddess frowned. "But if Oliver was on the *Enterprise*, and we left Fletcher there as well, then Gauntle will know about the Continent."

"Indeed, it's making the other Houses quite jealous."

"Why?"

Why am I telling her things she should be explaining to me? "Because, love, Grandfather is making friends with people no one else has the slightest inkling about. The potential for profits are enormous."

"They are?"

Elena sighed. *She looks like an adult, yet her mind is like a child's. She must have hatched from that Egg…fully grown…like she is right now.* "Think about it. No one can get to the Continent except House Catagen. Tiberius has already formed a trade agreement. Before you know it, we'll have an alliance."

"An alliance?!" she gasped. "You mean…in case the Leos, Geminis, and Taurans make war against us Catagens?"

She said "us!" thought the princess, grateful beyond words. Whatever she thought of the ignorant God, whatever trouble she might be…

…*at least she's a Catagen.*

Perhaps it's my lot to tell her these things. Perhaps I've been chosen to teach her. Elena didn't know why Poseida gave her such a difficult task.

Perhaps it's penance for my unrivaled beauty…

But whatever the reason, no matter the cost, *I'll love her like my own – defend her like family.*

π

After our bath, Elena and I ate lunch in the glass-covered atrium. The winter days were cold and bleak, but the atrium was bright and warm in the light of the waning sun. We talked about ordinary things, the Ball, of course, being of peculiar interest.

She rattled off a dizzying number of boys who had asked her. She didn't say this to brag; to Elena it was just another political dilemma. Whom would she allow to escort her to the Ball?

The afternoon was spent shopping. Any excuse to go shopping was a good excuse to Elena.

"Now that you're going to drive in the Circus, you simply *must* look the part." To my surprise, Elena knew exactly what a charioteer should wear: "A bright silver breast plate with a floor-length cape, silver brassards for your arms, silver greaves for your legs. I don't fancy the ones that come up over your knees. They might be fine for racing, but they make your thighs look fat."

"People aren't going to be looking at my thighs," I huffed. Still, I posed sideways in the mirror, checking to see...

"You're a daughter of House Catagen, darling. I simply won't allow you to look anything short of fantastic." To Elena, how I looked at the race was far more important than the race itself.

We visited several different shops: one for the cape, one for the silver breastplate, another for the gauntlets and greaves. I tried on a hundred boots before Elena settled on a pair of white elephant hide that came just short of my knees.

"Elephant?" I asked. "What's an elephant?"

"A new creation, most hallowed princess," said the shopkeeper, "a rare and special gift from the bountiful Gods."

"An elephant is a creature from the Continent," hushed Elena. "Tiberius actually saw one. Absolutely huge! As big as a house!"

I gasped when I saw the price.

"See what I told you," smiled Elena, who wasn't bothered by the outrageous outlay. "Rare commodities demand enormous costs. House Catagen has made a small fortune on this shipment alone. Think of the profits!"

I didn't even try, thinking instead of my poor father. The price of the boots would feed him for a year.

How he must be missing me!

I absentmindedly picked up a helmet, but Elena would have none of it.

"I know just the place," she said as she led our retinue of Marines down another crowded street. "That last shop was fine for accessories. But you simply must have a helmet made by Franz. I get all my helmets there, though his prices are rather dear."

"You have a helmet?"

"Why certainly, darling. I have several."

"Have you ever worn one?"

"Honestly, no. They're simply torture on my hair."

I wanted something light and simple. But Elena insisted on a heavy silver creation, complete with a train of frilly blue feathers.

"I won't be able to see a thing!" I complained.

"It's not for *you* to see," she giggled; "it's for people to see *you*!"

A crowd had gathered as we left the expensive shop. Cold, drab peasants gawked at our boxes, our colorful wrappings, our frivolous bows. Gaunt eyes peered at my clothes, my hair, my makeup, my well-fed frame. Nuzzling my coat against the bitter Wind, I was painfully embarrassed by its sable lavishness.

A small girl gaped in silent wonder. Shivering in the thin gray tunic that marked her as a slave, she marveled at our many colors. Her eyes were wide and haunting, her lips, cold and blue.

I approached the girl and knelt to my knees. Her eyes reminded me of Cindy. "Where is your coat?" I asked with a smile.

"What are you doing?" said Elena.

I ignored the princess and focused on the slave. "Don't you have a coat, sweetheart?"

"Please, your worship," said the cowering mother. "It was stolen."

"Are you an angel?" said the awe-struck child.

"Hush, Polly," said the frightened mother. "You speak to royalty."

I avoided the eyes of the groveling mother, sad and ashamed at her gilded lie. "Polly," I said as I stroked the girl's hair. "I like that name, I like it a lot. A pretty name for a pretty girl."

The crowd strengthened at her innocent blush. The Marines grew edgy and tense. "Pallas, dear," cooed Elena, clandestinely giving me a cruel pinch. "We must be going."

"Pallas?" cried the stricken mother, falling to her humble knees. "Then you…you are the Mistress! The Dawning of the Aquarians!"

"Yes," I mumbled, both pleased and mortified. The brightness of the wide-eyed child filled my heart with joy. Yet the simpering worship of the slavish mother curdled my stomach.

The curious crowd pressed earnestly closer. The Marines pushed back with the blunt of their spears. "Pallas!" hushed Elena. "We really *must* be going."

I toured the eyes of the quizzical crowd, knowing she was right. But instead of obeying my prudent sister, I spoke instead to the innocent child. "May I give you gift, sweet Polly?"

"Oh my!" she gasped, lively and bright. "A gift from the Gods?"

"No…" I smiled, whipping off my sable coat and nuzzling it over the frozen child, "a gift…from me."

Her brilliant eyes were as wide as saucers. Far too large for the little child, the fur's luxuriousness scraped the squalor ground. Its arms hung limp over her dirty hands, its thick, dyed leather swallowing her whole. The colorful coat, so fine and odd upon the peasant, reminded me of another bittersweet garment; the multi-colored dress my father gave me. Succumbing to a morbid dose of pique, I wondered, *Will this coat doom her as well?*

Her mother nearly feinted. The crowd whispered its hushed approval.

"She gives the girl the cloak off her back…"

"She comforts the lowly child…"

Their praise somehow angered me. *This moment is between me and Polly, not some voyeuristic mob.* "We *must* suffer the little children," I blurted. "For theirs is the kingdom of God." The quote – unbidden, yet uttered from my lips – surprised me just as much as it did the watching crowd. Brutal silence, sweet yet mighty, quelled the chattering street.

The busy multitude watched and stared; dumb-struck, open-mouthed. Elena, slack-jawed like the rest of them, teetered on an irreverent glare. Then, suddenly remembering herself, she launched into a regal display. "Here…take mine too!" she flourished, adorning her coat upon another child. Its sleek mink lining and ivory leather was shocking against the peasant gray.

I recoiled for a moment into my solitary thoughts. *How on Earth did I say that? Where did I come up with such powerful words?* Then I remembered. *Father taught me that noble passage! The lowly blacksmith from Kelly Tree.*

Sensing that something special had occurred, I hugged Polly and gave her a kiss. This delighted her so much that I kissed the next child as well. Soon I was surrounded by a happy chorus, girls and boys with spirited voices.

I kissed the foreheads of the gathered children, smoothing their hands with Aquarian prayers. My sister tentatively patted their shoulders, as if bound by some disgusting dare. But soon our carriage ended the reverie, its silver sparkling in the sudden sun. The happy crowd cheered our farewell, merry tidings racing along.

Two Marines clothed us in their jackets as we climbed into the opulent coach. "How grand!" snorted Elena. "Why don't we all give our coats away?"

I smiled at my sister and gave her a hug. "Sorry. I know that was odd. I know the coats were expensive. But…we ought to help the poor, don't you think?"

"What I think," she pouted as she waved to the crowd, "is that little stunt of yours was fantastic publicity. Still! A slave is wearing my new Benici?"

The carriage clattered from the festive scene; the bitter Wind, chattering my teeth. Grateful for the woolen blankets that covered our laps, I gazed at my sister's frowning face. Her distant eyes made me wonder, as much as the eyes of the hungry child.

Who am I, but a crass pretender? What glory had I won that was not a lie? Why do I live in a mansion — why does Polly live in a shack — when I'm the one who's being dishonest?

"What's that?" I asked as we neared the Temple of Vulcana. A teenage girl was standing on a wooden platform.

"A hanging," said Elena with mild disgust.

"Oh!" I gasped. "What for?"

"It's rather moronic. The simpleton released a dozen rats in the Fire Temple."

"Uh!" I gasped again.

"There's been a spat of that lately. Alicante, Hadrianus, Capro Bay…even Turner Hill…though they say it began in Kelly Tree. Foolish, ignorant, disobedient slaves…trying to "change the world" with their bad behavior."

A stab of guilt sliced through my heart. "It, uh…began in Kelly Tree? In the Temple of Vulcana?"

"No," she mocked. "That's the stupidest thing about it. It started in a Temple of Poseida, about three years ago. But it has spread like wildFire these past few months, ever since…well…ever since you arrived."

My sordid soul was full of dread. *What have I done?!*

"The Jesters say the slave who did it drowned," said Elena. "And good riddance. Still, it's rather bad policy for anyone to desecrate any of the Pentathanon Temples."

We rumbled past the lonely gallows, miserable onlookers gathered at its feet. A stooped mother cried for her daughter.

"Stop it!" I shouted. "Turn around!"

"What?" glared the princess. "Are you mad?"

"We have to stop it! We have to save her!"

"Pallas! She's a heretic!"

I grabbed the arm of one of the Marines. "Stop! Turn around! We have to rescue her!"

"You'll do no such thing!" commanded Elena. "Gee up those horses and take us home!"

The lieutenant nodded to the baffled driver. The crack of the whip sped us swiftly along.

Haunted, paralyzed, I turned around and stared. The teenage girl was sad and solemn. The horrible hangman fitted his noose…

∞

I trudged to my room after a long, confusing day. Praying that Othello was back, I was elated to find him curled upon the dresser.

"What, no sarcastic remarks?" I joked. "Go ahead and say it, I'm late for my reading lesson."

"You're what?" whispered a girl's voice.

148

I jumped in surprise. The bundle wasn't Othello; it was Elena's white fox-fur mantle. Behind me, hidden in the shadows, was a dark cloaked figure. "Casey?"

"Not Casey." A diminutive figure stepped from the gloom.

"Genny! What are you doing here?"

"Sneaked in," said the Tauran, ashen and afraid.

"Why?"

"I've come to warn you." Gone was her unflappable poise. Gone was her graceful demeanor. What remained was a pensive, nervous child.

"Warn me?"

"They're plotting against you."

"Who?"

"Father and his new set of friends."

"Oxymid and Excelsior?"

"Certainly. But not just them..."

"Sit down." I motioned to a chair.

"I can't," she said, retreating back to the shadows.

"What's wrong?"

"Pallas, darling. I can't be seen. You mustn't tell anyone I came, not even Elena or the Twins."

"Why?"

"Because...my father is Gauntle, Lord Protector of the Pass. If he learns I'm here..."

"But why?"

"It's going to happen very soon."

"What's going to happen?"

She shook her head in frustration. "I didn't catch it all. There's a traitor close to you. One of the Aquarian Lords. They want you...and...and someone else."

"Who?"

"That's the part I didn't understand. There was a strange word they used. You said it too...when you first came in the room."

"What kind of word?"

"Reading!" she whispered with a shock of dread.

I stifled an incriminating gasp.

"That's right, isn't it?" she said, excited...yet troubled.

I nodded my guilty head.

"Well," she said. "I don't know what reading is, but I can tell you someone does. And they're not happy about it."

I placed a hand over my throbbing heart. *They know! They know about my sacrilege!*

"Pallas, darling, you mustn't trust my father. You mustn't trust any of the Taurans."

"But you're a Tauran. Why are you telling me this?"

She swallowed a mournful frown. "From days of old, the Good Earth has always been a friend to the Water. But now..." she hushed, penitent tears streaming down her face, "we've lost our way, dear Pallas. Father has sold us to the Flame."

A cold shiver rifled down my spine. Oliver. Liam. Elena. Genevieve. All with the same message, the same dire warning. The age-old alliance of Water and Earth was torn asunder.

All because of me!

Chapter Eleven

Strangers from a Strange Land

Many the wonders, but none walks stranger than man.

Antigone
Sophocles, Greek playwright
circa 450BC: Earth Standard

Lovingly cradled in tender arms, she looked up at the beautiful woman. Her caring eyes were soft and wise, emblazoned with a steely sheen of grey. The woman was singing a lullaby, a song the babe had never heard before.

Holding out her chubby hand, she struggled to snatch the shiny strand that gathered around the woman's neck. But her tiny fingers, velveted by the softness of her newborn skin, were strangely uncoordinated.

The woman smiled, beaming with pride, a charm hidden beneath her blouse.

The baby made a clumsy grasp, clutching the silver cube...

...I woke with a sudden start, clinging to my own silver totem.

∞

The investigation discovered nothing. It was said this greatly annoyed the Chancellor, but I wondered if that was true. Not only was I convinced that Lady Uncial could read, but I was sure she knew a great deal more than she was letting on.

As for Othello, he was ever present, yet horribly absent. He was alive and near, for Abbey fed him every day. But he made it a point to be gone when I was home and present when I was away.

It felt like a game of cat-and-mouse...with me as the helpless prey. From that time onward, I always felt pity for the mice I saw.

151

His departure affected me more than I liked to admit. For as annoying as he was, his absence was even worse. Again the word "spy" came to my mind.

There was also my growing renown, the prophecy that added to my unwanted mystique.

Innocent slaves were following my footsteps – innocent teens were being hanged.

Worst of all was the Aquarian traitor, *a friend who'd sell me to the Flame!*

On the eighth week of University, a green appendage joined the four columns on the Center Lawn.

The Sagittarians had arrived.

There was no pathway for the reclusive Demes. Instead, they walked on the dormant grass – forbidden to the Taurans, Leos, Geminis and Aquarians. In the Center stood five professors, the fifth being a tall, well-proportioned woman.

Indeed, every Sagittarian was a fine specimen; there were none too fat or small or weak. Yet they all looked incredibly different. Some were fair-haired with sharp blue eyes. Others had narrow eyes and raven hair. Still others had olive complexions, wide mouths and chestnut curls. They were all beautiful and strong, with calm, serene faces.

The odd dissymmetry made me wonder. Normally, there were four academies, four paths, four corners. Now, stuck between the red and the brown, was an extra appendage – a fifth wheel.

I fingered the silver cube, thinking about the sixth column.

What is opposite Life?

The arrival of the Demes meant the University Games were close at hand. But before the Games could be played, there was a week-long Festival, culminating in the University Ball. Though I couldn't wait for the Games, I rued the coming Ball, for that meant getting a date.

Normally, this wouldn't be such a problem as I was very well-known.

But being well-known was not the same as being popular. Most boys found me daunting, to say the least. Who dare court the Mistress of the Sea?

Liam found me in the stables. He'd been strangely aloof these days. Perhaps it was due to the rigors of training. But perhaps it was because…

Don't even think about it! Elena told me to avoid him; the heathen foreigner from the dreaded Continent. The Aquarian girls didn't like him either, mostly because he seemed to like me.

Liam called to Joculo. "Ho, Captain! How goes the Circus?"

"Great," he said, slapping Liam on the shoulder. "How didya like those Wind sprints?"

"Ya kidding? You're an absolute lunatic." He did a hoarse imitation of the Aquarian prince. "Ya sissies 'll win the Gold or die trying!"

"That's the spirit!" Joculo laughed. "We'll beat those Leos yet."

"Yeah," Liam sighed, "I guess. Only…do you really think you can actually win the Gold? I mean, really?"

"Sure we can!"

But his eyes weren't as confident.

The Leos were perennial favorites. They'd won five years in a row. On the other hand, the Taurans had Clovis, who was a shoe-in for the Wrestling and the Boxing and a heavy favorite for the Javelin and Mounted Javelin. If he placed in the Pentathlon and the Circus, it was hard to see how anyone could beat the Good Earth. Still, hope springs eternal. No one has more faith than a sports fan.

"Yeah," Liam agreed, looking at me and not at Joculo. I felt a strange tension between the two young men.

"Listen, I'm done here," said Joculo. "Wanna walk back to the Quarter with me?"

"No, uh…I'll help Pallas get her horses brushed."

"OK," Joculo said with forced restraint. "I'll help too."

"No, really," Liam answered. "I can do it."

Joculo glared. Weighty moments passed as they continued to stare at each other. "Fine," said Joculo with a huff of impatience, leaving the two of us alone with each other.

They've been fighting about something. Could it be me?

The familiar stranger approached. My heart pitter-pattered in a nervous trance. Without a word the handsome senior started to brush Adrena. I donned a weak smile, flush with an emotion I'd been fighting for weeks.

"So, how's it going?" Liam asked.

"Great. Really great."

"What do you think of those Sagittarians?"

"Creepy, I guess."

"Creepy?"

"Yeah, well," I said, not sure how to convey my sense of strangeness, "they all seem to look the same, don't they?"

"They all looked different to me."

"Their faces do, sure…but not their eyes. They all have the same…I dunno…peaceful look about them."

"You're right," he admitted. "That's very insightful."

A long silence ensued. Dreading the next words that followed, I desperately hoped they'd come…

"Next Friday there's going to be a Ball," he said.

"Yeah, I know."

"Has, uh, anyone…"

"No," I said with hopeful eyes.

He garlanded a furtive smile, nervously glancing over Adrena's withers. "Well, I…I wanted to ask you…"

I held my breath. *Elena would be absolutely furious! The Uncial girls would be worse!* But none of that mattered right now. His eyes were an adorable sparkle. His face was humble and yearning. Spirited butterflies danced in my chest, catching my breath in delicate spasms.

"What I wanted to ask you was…" he repeated, when he suddenly stopped short. Menace marred his gorgeous brow as he stared, not at me, but someone right behind me.

I whirled around to see…

Borelo. "Hello," he cooed in his silkiest voice.

"What do you want?" snarled Liam.

"Nothing from you," said the Gemelleon prince. His face was brash and annoyed. "I wanted to speak to Pallas."

I was annoyed too, come to think of it. But it was Liam who spoke first. "Come to spy on her?" he accused.

That was weird... I thought. But then I remembered. The pretty-boy girl-chaser was riding in the Circus for the Geminis.

"Of course not," said Borelo. "Just wanted to ask her something."

"So ask."

"Alone, if you don't mind."

"I don't think so," said Liam, aggressively stalking forward.

The Gemini retreated outside the stable.

Elena rounded the corner. "There you are, Pallas. I've been looking everywhere..."

The glances exchanged were brief and venomous. Elena scalded red. I swore bitterly at Borelo who was annoyed with Liam who frowned at Elena. The brutal silence finally ended when Elena gestured to the stranger from the Continent. "Come," she scowled at Liam. "Lord Catagen wishes to see you."

Liam gave me a furtive look before leaving with the tall beauty.

Borelo huffed importantly. "I'm certainly glad *they're* gone."

"I bet you are!" I savagely replied. Whether or not I'd accept the invitation was irrelevant. Whether or not I wanted to start a feud with Elena was beside the point.

"Pallas," said Borelo, "I've come to deliver the most fantastic offer! You. Me. The Ball. Together."

I stared at the pretty-boy Gemini, anger curdling into rampant dislike. The dream I'd dreamed for over a month – the hope that, somehow, it could all come true – washed away by a stupid clod.

For more than anything else in the whole-wide-world, I wanted Liam to ask that question...

In the cold of the wintry eve – warm beneath my silken blankets – I spent another Othello-less night thinking about the day's events. The dreamlike-promise of a date with Liam made me miserable. Yet I feared the hatred that would follow me if he *did* ask me.

Don't I have enough trouble for one sixteen-year-old girl?

∞

The Demes were famous for their secrecy, jealously guarding their healing ways. Because of this, I was intrigued about meeting the Sagittarians.

I was alone. My classmates were far more interested in the Sagittarian's team than their splendid isolation.

"They're all so odd," Elena complained as we walked to Etiquette.

"What do you mean?"

"The way they talk. The things they say. You'll see."

"Worse than Atlanta?"

"Rather," she huffed as she opened the wooden door. The priceless crystal doorway could never be replaced, as Miss Polish reminded me each and every day.

Five Sagittarians, dressed in green, were huddled in a corner. They hushed themselves to silence as we walked through the door. Abruptly – as if assigned this task ages ago – one of them separated from the wary pack.

She walked straight at me with bold intent, a look of serenity in her narrow eyes. "I am Deirdre," she said. Jet black hair, dark tan skin; her eyes were wise and narrow. "You are Pallas, Mistress of the Sea."

"Pallas will do," I carefully replied. "How do you know my name?"

"The dragon is known by all. One cannot soar amongst the heavens and hope to remain unseen."

I scrunched my nose in a puzzled look, wondering what a 'dragon' was.

Elena gave me an "I told you so" look.

"We've heard so much about you. Your birth from the Egg is legend."

I was about to say I wasn't "born" from the Egg, but for once, kept my mouth shut.

I'm learning, I thought. *Othello would be proud.* But thinking about my missing mentor made me lonely and out of place.

"She's not a bird," quipped Elena. "She's a girl! Don't you people know the difference?"

"Ah," said Deirdre, a peaceful smile upon her face. "Men differ from animals only by a little, and most people throw that away."

Elena furrowed her brow. Grasping my hand, she led me away. "I told you they were odd."

But I was stunned. *Animals and people aren't that different? What did she mean by that?* Would the stranger be comfortable with a talking cat?

π

"What did that odd Sagittarian want?" said Eunice during lunch.

"Dunno," the Goddess blandly replied. "Curious about the Egg, I guess."

Pretending her sister had told a joke, Elena feigned a tittering giggle. Yet, inside, she was seething. *I told her not to talk to those Demes! And the first thing she does...*

"Everyone's curious about that Egg," scolded Uncial. "You told your secret to a stranger, and not to one of your friends?"

"Didn't tell her anything," muttered the lonely God.

"Speaking of strangers," said Eunice, "I still can't understand why Liam's allowed to attend University."

"Or Atlanta, for that matter," added Uncial IV.

"At least Atlanta is good for a laugh," snickered Eunice. "Watching her stumble around Etiquette is always such sport!"

Pallas raised her sullen head to glare at the obnoxious girl. "I think she's great."

"Yes," smarmed Eunice. "I imagine you would."

Elena drew a patient breath, managing to keep her cool. But inside, she was absolutely furious. "I believe it was your mother, Uncial III, who decided that both Liam and Atlanta should attend University."

"Only after *your* grandfather insisted he come," moped Uncial IV.

"Where did he come from anyway?" asked Eunice. "It's so...unseemly, children of the nobility attending classes with...rabble."

Miffed as she was by her obnoxious companions, Elena pretended a delightful smile. "We're so glad you've joined us, Janice dear!"

"Me too!" she briskly replied. Rewarding the Queen Bee with puppy-dog eyes, she added, "I've been like...dying to hang out with you girls forever!"

Elena knew this, of course. She'd known it for years. But she prided herself in gathering sycophants who were older, not younger than she. The

157

simpering affections of the insignificant princess were hardly worth her cherished attentions…

…until the advent of the bewildering God.

She glanced at her silent, sulking sister. She'd tried; yes, she'd really tried, over and over again, to engage her in conversation. But the orphaned Goddess was far too busy mutilating her Cornish hen. She turned and smiled at the Uncials. Their escalating boorishness had become quite impossible, necessitating the addition of another participant…

"Janice," she sang in her sweet soprano. "You were always welcome. Besides, ever since Maureen and Amelia graduated, we've been too few in number."

Eunice brooded over her beef stroganoff. "I never liked them much."

Which is precisely why I insisted on their company, thought Elena. The compliant girls had been easy to manipulate, providing perfect, if unaware, foils to the Uncials.

"I just adore Amelia," said Janice. "She's so sweet."

"I heard she's *finally* getting married," smirked Eunice. "To Vigo of House Virgon, of all people."

"Why anyone would want to live in Anatolia is beyond comprehension," said Uncial.

"I heard she's in love," said Janice.

"I think it's splendid," said Elena. "An Aquarian-Tauran marriage is precisely what is needed." She'd hoped the Uncials would've agreed. Just to be polite, if nothing else.

Instead, the banter came to an awkward halt.

Elena silently swore to herself. These uncomfortable impasses were alarming in their rapidity. "Who's taking you to the Ball, Janice?"

"Djincar IV!" she said excitedly. "Asked me…like two weeks ago."

"He's ever so handsome," said Eunice. "Though not as handsome as Keleron."

"Yeah," the Goddess miserably agreed.

Eunice and Uncial gasped in feigned outrage. Elena stared at her sullen sister. *You haven't said a peep all day! Now you walk right into Eunice's pathetic trap?*

"So, like Pallas," said Janice, "who's taking you to the Ball?"

"No one," she mumbled.

"What?" said merry Eunice. "No one's asked you?"

"No."

"Why, that's terrible!" said Uncial with a fresh dose of pettiness. Then she smiled at Eunice. "I would have thought lots of boys…"

How dare you! thought Elena. *How dare you treat her that away!* Of course the Goddess is sad. Of course she feels out of place. *What makes it your business to be cruel to the child!*

She vividly remembered her very first meeting with the Uncials. How excited she had been! She'd dressed in her prettiest dress. She'd arranged a bouquet of flowers. She'd presented them gifts of finest chocolate, graced in boxes of delicate lace.

Eunice had frowned. "I don't like chocolate."

"Uncials prefer tarts and cakes," said young Uncial.

Armed with the wit of a rapier, Elena had longed to give the "tart-lovers" a piece of her mind. Yet even at the tender age of eight, she held her tongue, knowing how important it was to be friends with these girls. Duty dictated patient prudence. Intellect demanded shrewd diplomacy.

Still, the Uncialians' antics were testing her long-suffering fortitude.

She forced a smile and turned to Eunice. "I'm afraid, dear, that when you're as famous as my sister Pallas, men are quite afraid to vie for your favor. It's a burden I unfortunately share myself."

"Come off it," rasped Eunice. "Lots of boys have asked you."

"You've been greedily deliberating for over a month," griped Uncial.

"When Borelo asked you this morning," said Eunice.

"You finally said yes," said Uncial.

The torpid Goddess gasped in surprise.

Again, Elena frowned at her sister. *I know what you're thinking! Of course, he's a ridiculous lout. Of course he's a pompous clod. But whereas you have the privilege to say or do the first thing that pops into your head, I have House Catagen to think of!*

The tall beauty sparkled her eyes, shrewdly considering the Uncial pair. Their oafish attack was surprising, both in its directness and its venom. She thought for a moment for an artful reply when Janice came to her unexpected defense.

"Do be kind! It's not Elena's fault she's so beautiful, nor Pallas's that she's a dolphin rider!"

The Uncials raised their eyebrows in silent answer.

"I think it's fabulous," said Janice, "all the attention House Catagen is getting. A rising tide lifts all boats. Catagen's fortunes are Aquarian fortunes."

"What a lovely sentiment," said Elena, patting Janice's hand. "Honestly! You're too adorable to be allowed."

Janice blushed. "Of course…it's natural to be jealous. But Aquarians flow together. Don't you think?"

"Absolutely," beamed Elena, re-evaluating her opinion of the Joculo princess. *To be quite honest, I wanted to include her the entire year. She's a perfect vehicle for my many gambits.* But Pallas, who never cared one way or another about any of her other friends, wouldn't hear of it. Puzzled for a moment, Elena wondered why.

"Elena?" said Eunice, rudely pointing at Pallas. "Why haven't you…?"

Begged every eligible Aquarian to keep her from going dateless! Sorted through the Geminis and Taurans as well. Elena crafted her face into a threatening smile, demanding – without words – an end to the topic.

But the Uncials refused to comply. "I'm surprised," jibed Uncial. "With all the boys you have at your disposal? You couldn't spare just one…"

"Not losing our touch, are we?" sneered Eunice.

She glanced again at her gloomy sister, wondering how the Goddess could be so naïve. *Do you have any idea, the vicious jibes being heaped upon you?*

But the disinterested deity seemed completely unaware, staring morosely out a random window.

Again, Janice came to her unasked-for defense. "Of course Elena hasn't lost her touch. Of course she's working on our little problem. I think we all should."

π

Deities were my least favorite subject. I never liked the Gods before, and, after my near-death experience with Mulciber, I liked them even less.

Today, Professor Hesiod was lecturing about Deme's position as the central, yet least prominent God. "Whereas the Four Pillar Gods play influential parts in our history, Deme exhibits a practice of minimal action."

Whatever!

Instead, I thought about Borelo. As indignant as I was that he ruined my date with Liam, I was horrified to learn Borelo was going with Elena. *I don't dare tell her he asked me first!*

This "date" thing was now a real problem. I'd hoped Oliver would've asked me…just as a friend, of course. But the quiet boy rarely spoke to me, so what were the chances of his asking me to a dance? Lucy was going with Karl, Keleron's younger brother. Of course, what I really wanted was for Liam to ask. But that seemed impossible now.

"You have lovely hair," Deirdre whispered, running her hand through my tresses. "Was your mother blond as well?"

That's an odd question, I thought, frowning at the offending hand.

"You do not know your mother," said the girl.

"No," I said. Then I felt a prick.

"Sorry," said Deirdre. "Caught in my ring."

But I saw her conceal the hair in a clear little jar.

"Your eyes are gray, as were your mother's."

"How didya know that?"

"The wise man does not struggle against the stream. He lets it wash over him, bending to its will. Bend and you straighten, empty and you fill."

"Uh…" I said, stumbling on the cryptic riddle. *What on Earth is she talking about?* "How did you know my mother had gray eyes?"

"You just told me."

"I did not!"

But I realized I had.

"Didn't what, Miss Catagen?" asked Professor Hesiod.

The entire class turned to stare.

"Uh, nothing," I said, shrinking into my chair.

I left class in a ruffled huff, worried and oddly annoyed.

Liam's lost proposal made me furious. Lunch with the Uncials made it worse. The odd Sagittarian made me confused. Determined to get *something* right today, I cornered my biggest fan in the crowded hallway.

"Oliver!" I called above the chattering clatter. "C'm here. Need a favor."

The mariner nervously blanched. But obedient to his upbringing, he dutifully presented himself before me, stomping his foot in the traditional Tauran greeting. "Anything, my Mistress."

"Great," I flippantly replied, "'cause I need a date to this dance…thing. Wanna go?"

His coal black eyes bulged with shock. His dark complexion softened to pink. A bashful flamingo couldn't have blushed as much. "Nay, my Mistress. I…I can't. Ask me anything…but that."

"Just as friends, of course. I mean…what a pain? Right?"

"I…I can't," he stuttered. "Forgive me. In this request only, I must fail you."

"Fail me? Come on? It's just a stupid dance!"

The muscled boy looked miserable. "I'm…truly sorry, Mistress…"

"My name is Pallas!"

"I'm sorry…Pallas. I…cannot go. I have…prior obligations."

"Oh!" I gasped, mortified. "You're like, already going with somebody else…?"

He stared at the marbled floor, mumbling an incoherent reply.

"Damn it, Oliver! Why didn't you say so?" Absolutely humiliated, I tore away.

∞

I was desperate now to find Othello. For things were happening all around me that I didn't understand.

Fresh from these embarrassing episodes, I decided to play hooky the next day, both to catch my furry mentor and to avoid the Uncials. Sneaking down to the kitchen, I hid in a china cabinet to spy on his favorite bowl, the pretty one with the cherry-blossom pattern.

He never came to eat his tuna.

After many long hours, I left my vigil to use the bathroom.

When I returned, the bowl was licked clean.

Angry and annoyed, I thought of another way to trap him.

Then I remembered. *Hebe once gave me a sleeping draft. I wonder if I could drug him?*

Flush with the idea, I hurried to his laboratory. *And, I can ask him about the tan Sagittarian.*

"Well, well," said Deme, "not feeling our best, I hear."

"Uh, yeah," I said, pretending to cough. "Think I've got a cold."

"Yes, yes. I came to your room this morning, but Abbey told me you were hiding in a cupboard."

I cringed. "She saw me?"

"Now, now," he said with a smile, "not much gets past that girl, especially in her own kitchen."

My face grew red with embarrassment.

"Open wide," he said as he peered down my throat.

"Ahhhhhh…"

"Hum…just as I suspected."

"What?"

"I'm afraid you have a very severe case of collegiatis."

"Is that bad?"

"Oh yes…quite serious. Strikes even the strongest constitutions. Rare, but not always fatal. The only cure," he said gravely, "is to take the weight of the world off your shoulders. Really, Mistress, you've been far too stressed these past few weeks."

"Ha, ha," I sarcastically replied. "Collegi… What did you call it?"

"Collegiatis, from the root word collegiate, a person who is enrolled in college, an ancient word meaning University."

"What does 'ancient' mean?"

"Ancient means something that is very, very old…over a thousand years old, perhaps."

"Nothing is a thousand years old. Our entire world has only been around about a hundred."

"So they say," he placidly agreed, his eyes alight with amusement.

I frowned, puzzled by the exchange. But I came to talk about Deirdre. "You're a Sagittarian, aren't you, Hebe?"

"I am the loyal servant of House Catagen."

"No, I don't mean that. I mean…you studied on the lonely Isle of Solüt, in the House of Wonders, right?"

"Long ago."

"One of them, a girl, asked me about my mother."

"Perhaps she was curious."

"Yeah, but…she seemed to know a lot about me."

"What exactly did she know?"

"Just things." Though I started the line of questioning, I didn't like where it was going. "Why do they talk so…I dunno…funny?"

"When the weak learn Truth, they laugh; yet he who laughs does not learn. Therefore it is said: he who understands seems foolish."

"Uh…yeah."

"Now, now…I know that sounded rather…complicated."

"Kinda." *Though 'complicated' isn't the word I'd use. More like weird.*

"You must remember, Mistress, I've been indentured to Lord Catagen for over forty years. One shouldn't wonder that I've learned to assimilate a bit more than your young friend."

"I guess," I said, wondering what 'assimilate' meant. "Hebe, I've a favor to ask."

"Anything."

"It's my cat. He's been running off lately, so… I wondered if you could give me a sleeping draft, so…you know, I can catch him."

"You want me to drug your cat?"

"Well, yes. He won't come when I call, and…I'm worried."

But the questioning eyes of the Healer told me I'd made a mistake. "Is this cat, is he somehow…more than a cat?"

"Of course not. I miss him, that's all, and…he won't come home."

"Where did you get this cat?"

"I've always had him," I lied. I hoped it was a good one.

"Before the Egg?"

Suddenly threatened by the sweet old man, his questions endangering my elaborate lie, I relied on my old standby…

"Hebe! You know I can't talk about the Egg. The Commodore said."

"No, no," said the Healer. "Of course not. I was only curious. An academic fascination…that's all."

"Well…see you later," I smiled, beating a hasty retreat.

∞

"Guess who Oliver asked to the Ball today?" said Uncial.

"I can't imagine!" crowed Eunice.

"Adrian!" snapped Uncial. "Oliver asked Adrian to the Ball!"

"What?!" gasped Eunice in mock surprise. "You're kidding!"

"I'm not!" said Uncial.

"Imagine!" boasted Eunice. "The crown prince of House Gauntle asked the princess of House Excelsior…"

"Do you know what that means?" asked Uncial.

The tall beauty smiled. "The two of you finally learned the great Houses?"

"Don't play coy with us," smarmed Eunice. "Everyone knows that Pallas asked Oliver first. She did it in the halls of University, for all the world to see."

"Well!" said Uncial. "After he turned her down, Oliver went and asked a Leo…"

"Not just any Leo!" sang Eunice. "The most eligible princess from the most powerful Fire House!"

"Can't you just see it?" scolded Uncial. "The Mistress of the Sea, upstaged by the Excelsior princess!"

I paused to look at my beautiful sister. She was silent and horribly sad. I bowed my head in shame. I hadn't thought twice about asking Oliver. But my heinous breach of protocol – witnessed in the halls of University – was now a wellspring of infamy. I wanted to say something...anything...to defend myself. Yet, I too was flabbergasted. *Oliver, who practically lives on the Sea, is going to the Ball with the daughter of the Fire lord?*

"While you're busy celebrating the torment of my dear sister Pallas," countered Elena, "did it ever occur to you what an epic disaster this is for House Uncial?"

"Yeah, right," said Eunice, just as stupidly as she could.

"Like, why should we care?" said Uncial.

"The most powerful Earth prince dating the most powerful Fire princess?" cooed Elena. "Why darlings, it's simply a catastrophe!"

"How?" said Eunice.

"Think of the marriage of Earth and Water. Think of the allies we stand to lose."

"What allies?" said Uncial.

"Glad to hear you've thought this out," said Elena. "Glad to hear you're on top of things. We'll need that sort of prophetic wisdom, when you're the Lady of House Uncial and we Aquarians are completely isolated."

Uncial stuttered, flushed and confused.

"Imagine if you can, my clever friend," said Elena, "the Geminis, Sagittarians, and the Taurans...all following Excelsior's lead. Because that is what would happen if House Gauntle married House Excelsior. Only we shan't be calling him Lord Defender of the Titan. No, indeed. Not at all. His title shall then be...Lord Chancellor of the *Zoo!*"

The tiny Uncial sat un-answering, pathetic astonishment on her pallid face. "But...where would that leave me? I'm supposed to be the next Chancellor."

"Then you might think about what's good for the Aquarians," smarmed Elena. "You might think about the Balance of Power."

"Well!" barked Eunice. "If the Aquarians are isolated – if the Balance of Power is wrecked – it's all Pallas' fault!"

We were practicing weekends now, Joculo becoming boorish with his ever-increasing standards. I always defended him against his detractors, Aquarians who were weary of his strenuous regime. But my loyalty was tested when we visited the weapons master.

Three-time Boxing champion in the Menagerie Games and retired sergeant major of the elite Old Guard, Dio was an expert in the Games. His face adorned with a long purple scar, it was he who was teaching Lucy how to box.

Now, he would teach me the finer points of the whip.

"The Leos 're anxious," he warned, "bad blood 'tween the Water and the Fire. So…ya needs to be ready for 'nything. Like how to use a knife to cut a cord thas binding ya. How to fight wit' a ruddy scourge."

I frowned. *They whip each other in University Games? This isn't going to be anything like Kelly Tree!*

"Tis not a nobleman's weapon," he scorned. "Still, ya got to know…"

"I will not use a whip," I said.

Joculo sighed. "I knew you'd be like this. It's unbelievable you won the qualifying race without a whip. But everyone carries one. Everyone."

"Not me. Calypso hates them."

Dio creased his scar into an ugly glare. "Ya's gonna learn how to defend yerself, wither ya likes it or no. It's up to ye whethers you use it."

I answered with a huff.

"Now. I's gonna learn ya how it's done. Joculo, take that whip, and strikes me."

Standing several paces away, Joculo swung the heavy whip.

I gasped at the violent crack.

Unfazed, Dio caught the tail around the steel brassard that protected his forearm. "Thas wha ya gotta do." He demonstrated several times, detailing the precise technique. Then he told me to scourge the prince.

"No. I won't do it."

"Fine," muttered Dio. I'll whip the young master, and then Joculo can have a go at you."

"Whatever."

I watched with a sense of growing disaster. Joculo winced at every blow, even the ones he caught. After fifteen harrowing minutes, it was my turn.

I timidly took my place, staring fitfully at the waiting python. The leather curled beside the prince's legs.

I don't know if I can do this!

Joculo reared his arm. The python leapt. Agony lanced my shoulder.

"Ooow!" I gasped, falling to the floor. "That hurt!"

"Ya need to catch it with the metal, not your skin," rasped Dio. "Here, 'ave 'nother go."

I stood, glaring at Joculo with utter loathing.

The scourge fell again, seeking blood for its many troubles.

I nervously stuck out my arm. But I missed, the cord biting into my leathered palm.

Painfully jerking away, I nursed my soul with silent tears.

Joculo flung the snake to the ground. "I've changed my mind! This isn't necessary."

"Do ya think no one's gonna try it?" growled Dio. "That Alexander...he's a real soft spot for the lass, 'as he?"

"He wouldn't dare use a whip."

"Ya didn't watch lass year race, did ya, lad? R'member how 'e took the whip to Clovis?"

"Yes," said the prince, "I remember."

Dio took my wounded hand, applying a soothing ointment. "Ye thinks Lucy never gots hit, when I learnt her how to box?"

"How should I know!?" I savagely replied. "You keep it such a wretched secret!"

"It's no good 'oping fer the best. Ya gots to prepare for the worse."

I fiercely nodded, brushing away my tears. Trembling, enraged, I steeled myself for the coming blow. "Get on with it."

The scourge came crashing like a bolt of lightening. I stuck out my arm and felt the cord wrap around the steel brassard. Shrieking at the top of my lungs, I yanked the weapon from Joculo's grasp.

"Thas my girl!" cheered Dio. "Knews ya could do it!"

We practiced like this for hours. It was an extremely painful lesson. But eventually, I could catch the whip almost every time.

But whenever I missed, the leather reminded me, ravaging my arms and hands.

"Pallas!" Joculo called, hurrying to catch up.

"What?" I snapped. Bruised and furious, I'd left after practice without saying a word.

"Sorry about that."

"Yeah…right." Intellectually, I knew he was just trying to get me ready for the Circus. But emotionally, I held him responsible for every stroke.

"Listen. I've…I've something to ask you."

"So ask."

He hesitated, gracing me with an intimidated stare. Yet something emboldened him despite my rudeness. "Could you…I mean…would you…go to the Ball with me?"

"What!?" I mocked, just as meanly as I could.

"Would you, ya know, go to the Ball…with me?"

I suddenly went numb, racing through the many ironies…

I thought about the pretty girls in Kelly Tree. *They'd do anything to be invited to a Ball by Prince Joculo!*

I thought about our conversation at lunch. *Did Janice put him up to this, to keep me from going dateless?* I'd been avoiding Janice all term long, hoping she wouldn't remember me from Kelly Tree. Did the same, sweet girl fix me up with the prince of the town I was pretending not to be from?

I don't want a mercy date, I thought as I scowled at his somewhat handsome face. *Why couldn't he be his adorable cousin, the one with the glimmering eyes?*

Then again, who'd have thought a slave would attend the Ball with the prince of Kelly Tree?

I should say yes. I should say no.

"OK."

Chapter Twelve

Radio

It is difficult to overemphasize the importance of the new Continent. Up until the moment of its discovery, it was believed that the entire world was compassed of fourteen islands. The fact that there was another land mass — indeed, another world — just beyond the Western Sea was just as disturbing to the great Houses as if discovering that Mars was indeed inhabited by little green men. For House Catagen was the only one who had the navigational skill to sail beyond dawn's early morn, exploiting the treasures that lie there.

"Rise and Fall of the Pentathanon Gods"

Herodotus III

The Games approached with reckless abandon, making me excited, nervous and scared.

All term long I'd been neatly sheltered, completely isolated from the outside world. Quite suddenly, hundreds of visitors appeared, transforming stoic University into a carnival of commotion. Mushrooming with their eclectic sights and sounds, colorful pavilions sprouted on the grounds.

The great Houses garnered support amongst the Houses minor by rewarding them with aristocratic favors: tickets to choice events, posh seats, and invitations to various parties. As such, Lord Catagen and Captain Dewey were incredibly busy entertaining merchants, shipbuilders, guild masters…the list went on and on.

The newcomers were frankly frightening. For they made me realize how famous I'd become.

A jeweler from Acadia begged me to recount my dolphin ride. A landowner from Pyth asked about the Golden Egg. A guildsman from Misty Dale complimented me on my humiliation of the Excelsior lord.

They wanted to see me, hear me, get into my mind…

…I was a celebrity.

Elena tried to warn me. But I never listened. Instead, I'd spent that last few months hiding within my ignorance, hoping my legend would magically go away.

I could no longer pretend. The proof was undeniable. People everywhere stopped and stared.

Men pretended brash indifference, treating me to flattering sidelong glances. Women whispered in their jealous coveys, displaying a curiosity they couldn't conceal. Children ogled and pointed.

A wizened Water cleric begged me for a blessing. A straw-like man, his ancient eyes watering as he smoothed his trembling hands in mine, he said, "I came all the way from McFarland to see thy holy Mistress."

"I…" *What am I supposed to say?*

The Eternal Flame added to my fame. The Holy Fire had scorched the marble, replacing the tablets with scars of soot. The puddle of gold coagulated and hardened into a priceless pool of wealth and muck.

The disaster had become a favorite attraction. Tourists bribed University professors to enter the Center Lawn.

Leos boasted about the epic change, from a simple Fire to a psychotic torrent. To me, it showed how desperate they'd become.

Even the weather conspired against me. The winter was the warmest on record. No one could remember a better harvest. All the granaries were full to the brim.

Worse, the pixies from the fairy tree migrated, from the Isle of Catagen to the clock tower of the Water Quarter. The haunted belfry whispered at night, of marvelous deeds and prophetic delights.

Crowds of spectators gathered at dusk, marveling at the miracle of the angelic chorus. Though their voices were legion, sweet and varied, they sang these verses anon and again…

She is the Dawning,
of the Age of Aquarius.

Sensing the need for added security, the Commodore assigned Lieutenant O'Brien as my personal bodyguard. Trying to avoid the many stares, I was walking towards the stables when Janice spotted me. The princess was escorting a merchant and his family.

"Oh! And there's Pallas," she said. "You simply *must* meet her."

"Pallas?" said Derrick IX. "That's funny. I once knew a slave named Pallas. The stupid wench drowned."

Terrified, I turned and sprinted through the crowd. O'Brien dashed after me, a squad of Marines in desperate pursuit. I knew I looked like an idiot. But I simply didn't care.

I can't be seen…not by Derrick!

Darting between the folds of two closely cropped tents, I stopped to catch my breath.

O'Brien caught up. His Marines set up a grim perimeter, swords drawn and ready. "What was that about?" he demanded.

"I, uh…thought I saw something."

He bent over to catch his breath. "What did ye see?"

"I, uh…dunno."

He gave a great huff. "Back to that, are we?"

"Yeah, uh…let's go home."

The mariner was clearly not happy. But he shelved his misgivings and did what he was told. "Aye, all right. Back to the manor, boys. Our fair lassie's changed her mind."

"Thanks," I said, precocious and shy.

"Aye," he grinned. "Anything fer you, my Mistress. Still like to know why. Ah! But, that'd take the fun out of it, wouldn't it?"

I shrugged my impish shoulders.

I couldn't sleep that night. Instead, I thought about the morning procession upon the Center Lawn. There were five columns now, not four – the pillar of green pioneering an odd dissymmetry to my symmetrical world.

Pythagoras adored symmetry, transfixed by the "perfect" cube. Part of me hated the egotistical mathematician. But another part admired him. For he was the only professor who dared compare his knowledge to the Gods.

'For the cube transforms the square into a three dimensional form," he'd said, *"the classic culmination of the number of the universe."*

I dangled the silver cube in the candle light. The five jeweled columns cast colors about the room. Yet they spoiled the symmetry of the perfect cube.

The black column is missing...hidden...aloof.

The clock struck twelve.

Beep!

Panicked by the alien sound, I dropped the silver charm.

But the cube just sat there, quiet as a mouse.

That's odd, I smirked, amused by my skittishness. *You've never done that before!* Picking up the cube, I dangled it over the flickering candle.

Why won't you tell me what you are? Why won't you show me your magic secrets?

But the tiny cube was silent, twirling in the dancing Flame.

"Oh my Gods! The RADIO!" *It made that same little chirp, just before Othello stole it!* Running my fingers through my frantic hair, I tried to remember that confusing night. *That darned cat! He must have stolen the RADIO so I couldn't hear what the cube was saying!*

But no, that wasn't right. The cube didn't *say* anything. It just made a noise: vague, unintelligible.

Then it hit me.

The cat told me to speak into the little clip. When I did, the RADIO mimicked what I said.

Is that your magic secret? You repeat what that clip-thingy hears?

Again, I studied the cube, begging it to perform its sorcery.

Then another thought struck me. *Isn't there another RADIO in the harness?*

Flinging out of my bed, I scoured the pockets of the magic harness. Holding the second RADIO in my hands, I turned the dial from OFF to GUARD.

Beep!

"That's right, isn't it?" I said with delight. Excitedly, I turned the knob from GUARD past BOTH and FREQ to REMOTE.

Instantly, I heard voices...

"I received a package from the Continent today."

"Is it about the man-cub?"

Othello!

"Yes…it contains a message, telling us where to take her, once we've…"

"…kidnapped the petulant cub?"

They're going to kidnap me?

"Yes, yes," said Uncial. "But…it must be *after* the Hunt."

"Why?" scolded the cat.

"It has to be carefully planned. Lord Catagen has too much security around the girl. It would be impossible to arrange till after the Hunt."

"Isn't there some sort of pathetic ritual the night of the Hunt, a pagan rite of some kind?"

"The Consecration of the Golden Stag. The ceremony where we dedicate the holy hide."

"How perfectly primeval. Tell me; do you bathe in the blood of the murdered beast…or just drink it?"

"We do nothing of the sort. We offer it up to the Gods as a holy sacrifice, then celebrate with *ambrosia.*"

"Will all the nobility be present?"

"Of course. It's a required event."

"That's when we'll do it."

"We can't!" she shrilled. "It would be the most heinous sacrilege."

"Control yourself!" said the cat. "We'll do it at the Consecration of the Golden Stag."

"Please!" she pleaded. "No!"

"It's decided. And no more of your pathetic whining."

There was a brief moment of tense silence. I was certain the lady would tell him off. Unbelievably, she acquiesced. "As you wish."

I gaped with surprise. *The most powerful person in the world, taking orders from a cat?*

"I want to study the message," said the cat. "Leave it out, so I can…"

"What if it's seen? Someone might recognize it for what it is."

"A heresy?" he laughed. "Really, you're more superstitious than the cub."

"We need to be careful," she warned. "I've heard disturbing reports. About a plot about a monster."

"Beware the Jabberwock!" he chortled

"The what?" said Uncial, annoyed.

"A monster?" he laughed. "Really! You humans are so neurotic. Leave the message out where I can see it. I'll come to your office around two in the morning."

"Fine," she huffed, "I'll leave the window cracked."

I was now completely unnerved.

Heresy? Inside a package? What kind of package could contain both a message and a heresy?

Then I realized.

It had to be full of letters. It had to be full of words.

It has to be reading!

The cat's betrayal was thick in my thoughts, poisoned by familiarity and bitter longing. *He's been playing me for a fool all this time! He and that two-faced Uncial!* With powerful enemies like the two of these, how could I possibly survive?

Loneliness made me desperate. Unable to bear my solitary burden, I decided, spur of the moment, to share it with the two people I trusted most.

"Lucy?" I whispered as I skulked into their room. "Casey?"

"What is it?" Lucy yawned.

"There's something…something I have to tell you."

"What?"

I cringed. *I shouldn't reveal too much.* But before I could help myself, I'd gushed out everything I knew about the plot.

The Twins were stunned.

"I can't believe Uncial would team up with the Leos," Casey said.

"Me neither," I replied. I didn't tell them about reading, of course…or the silver cube. *Never tell anyone, at any time, for any reason!* It was the one thing Othello took seriously: the one commandment I felt compelled to obey.

"But, how did you hear it?" asked Lucy.

"I, uh…" *What should I tell them? How much is too much?* "I, uh…heard it…on…on the RADIO."

"What's…radio?"

"Sometimes I can hear what people are saying, people who are far away." Even if I'd wanted to, I couldn't explain the sorcery any better than that.

"How?"

"What people?"

"It's…difficult to explain," I said, unnerved by my own inadequacies.

But the Twins didn't think I was inadequate. They found me amazing.

"I think it's great!" Casey said.

"Maybe we can use the radio to spy on Elena!" said Lucy.

"But why?" I said, willing them to concentrate. "Why would Uncial be after me?"

"She's afraid of you," said Casey.

"Shut up."

"She's afraid of this 'Age of Aquarius' everyone's talking about. She's worried you'll supplant her."

"That's dumb," I huffed. "She can't possibly think…"

"Of course, she can," said Lucy. "Everyone thinks it."

"But what's in the package?" wondered Casey.

"A message…I think."

"A message?" asked Lucy. "But…how can a message be inside a package?"

"I don't know," I lied.

"Well," Casey decided, "we'll just have to find out."

"How?"

"By sneaking in to Uncial's office," said Lucy.

"What?"

"She said she'd leave the window open, right?"

"We'll climb right in!" said Casey.

I paused, feeling snake-bit after our debacle with the Eternal Fire. *The last thing I need is another midnight escapade!*

But the Twins' enthusiasm was infectious. Far from being worried, they were eager for another bold adventure.

Besides…this is important. I have to intercept that message, before that little spy!

We exchanged merry grins as we stealthily approached Uncial Manor. An ugly, block-like, monolithic fortress, the Manor dominated the Water Square with its gargantuan size. We crept behind a row of bushes, hiding from the bitter Wind. A blue-cloaked soldier, one of the elite Old Guard, paced along the wall.

"What now?" I asked through chattering teeth. The winter Wind splayed my hair into my eyes. I tied it in a quick pony tail.

"I thought you had a plan," whispered Lucy.

"Maybe this is a bad idea," I winced.

"Leave it to me," hissed Casey.

"Wait…"

But Casey didn't wait. Instead, she crept along the bushes. Suddenly, silently, she threw something at the guard. He slumped upon the frozen ground.

Lucy and I raced forward. "What was that?"

"Sleeping dart. Stole it from Hebe a week ago."

"Honestly," said Lucy, "you might have told me."

"I'm still waiting to hear what you're doing with Dio."

"Shh!" I said. "We're trying to get into the Manor. Remember?"

"Right," they giggled.

"Here," I said. "The two of you stand guard."

"But," said Casey, "how will you scale that wall?"

"Just watch."

I'd never used the grappling hook before. Bathed in pallid moonlight, I squinted my eyes to read the instructions. Finding the magic words, I considered the paradox of the situation.

Just think! I'm using the sorcery of reading…in order to foil my reading professor!

I blessed the cat for teaching me how to read…

…before cursing the cat for teaching me how to read.

I focused on the placard of the gun. "COCK THE GRAPPLING GUN IN THE LOADED POSITION," I said, muttering the mysterious words. "POSITION THE GUN IN THE DESIRED DIRECTION OF ASCENT. RANGE OF THIRTY METERS VERTICAL, FORTY METERS DIAGONAL. TRIGGER FIRES THE GRAPPLER. RED RELEASES THE LINE. YELLOW RELEASES GRAPPLING ARM. GREEN RECOILS THE LINE."

The gun was connected to the belt of the harness. Cocking the gun, I pointed it at the roof and pulled the trigger.

Wumpff!

The grappler streaked silently Skyward, my sisters marveling in animated delight. I heard a tiny clatter as the hook found purchase on the roof.

"I'll go," I mouthed, "I'll know what I'm looking for."

They gave me an eager thumbs-up.

I pressed the green button. It aggressively pulled me towards the wall. Surprised, I released the button. The pulling stopped. I pushed the button again. The grappler pulled me up the vertical wall.

I was shocked. I expected to have to climb the rope. But the enchanted harness did it for me.

I stopped my assent at the open window. Quietly, I crawled in.

The office was dark and cold, the howl of the Wind sweeping through the room. There were oddities everywhere: enormous peacock feathers, a wall-full of portraits, a cabinet of porcelain curios…even a telescope.

An army of soldiers on a checkerboard battlefield caught my attention. I marveled at the figures, eternally poised for war, when I found myself drawn to a shield-like object. It was a huge, leathery scale, belonging to what had to be a monstrous lizard. As tall as a man, it was tinged in red and smelled of sulfur.

I shuddered. *The creature must be nothing short of colossal!*

Then I heard a creak at the door…

Chapter Thirteen

Lord Joculo

The Gods were greatly dismayed when the mortals discovered the forbidden Continent. For each divine Element, secure in their comfortable ante bellum, found themselves irrevocably thrust forward into a state of upheaval. They knew full-well what the mortals would find, and they were afraid.

Yet one God stood above the fray: Poseida, Queen of the Unquenchable Sea. She knew it was inevitable that mortals would eventually discover the forbidden Continent. Secure in the knowledge that She controlled Catagen, just as Catagen controlled the Mistress, She welcomed his discovery as a way to increase Her own personal power.

But fortune sometimes harbors unexpected consequences. Ideas were exchanged: tales of a New and wondrous Age. At first, Poseida welcomed the Age of the Aquarians, as She seemed to be the direct beneficiary.

That would change.

"Compendium, Chronicles of the Pentathanon Gods"

Ovid XII

I dove behind the wooden desk, praying I hadn't been seen. But the rope connected to my harness was hanging out the window.

How could I be so stupid? The Chancellor will see me for sure!

Hidden, I spied the silhouette of a short, thin woman. Rifling through the many objects, she carried no candle or lantern.

Why would she be looking for something in the dark?

Before I could answer, the winter Wind blustered through the room. The woman shivered with alarm, dashing past the feathers to close the open window.

My heart pounded as the woman spotted the rope. *What will she do to me? Kidnap me? Kill me? Call her guards to carry me away?*

Slowly, the woman turned, following the rope to where I was hiding…

"Genny!" I gasped.

"Pallas! What are you doing here?" But before I could tell her, she shrewdly answered her question. "You came for the package!"

"You know about the package?"

"I heard father talking about it."

"Gauntle knows too?"

"We heard it was about you. Oliver and I decided to steal it, and bring it to you at once."

"Oliver?"

"He's downstairs with father. The Chancellor called him here on urgent business."

"At this hour? Why?"

"Father wouldn't say. I'm surprised he let us come, but…he said we'd improve her mood. I don't know what he meant by that."

I was incredulous. "How?"

She fended off my question. "Hurry, love. I'm pretending to be in the ladies room." And with that, she quickly turned away, rummaging through the cabinet.

I stood there, puzzled, not knowing what to think, when I spied some parchment sitting on the desk. Two black knights and an ebony queen guarded the traitorous scroll.

That's it! That's the package!

Genevieve gawked. "You…know what it says, don't you?"

"Yeah," I muttered. With trepidation, I read…

Subject: Pallas

Othello: Code Green, Volcano operative
Pallas: return to Continent, Priority ONE

Kassan

"Volcano. That's where Vulcana lives," said the Tauran. "The Continent is where *Enterprise* has been sailing."

"You know about the Continent?"

Again, Genevieve ignored my question. "I don't know the other names except for Uncial's. Do you?"

"Yes," I sighed, every shred of love I ever had for that cat, mocking me. "The first one is a spy – a spy that used to be a friend."

Her eyes grew wide with wonder. "And Kassan?"

"No idea."

Another blast of winter rustled round the room. Genevieve shivered. "Oh, how I hate the Wind!"

I marveled at the tiny Tauran. *She's brave enough to sneak into the Chancellor's office, yet frightened by a breeze?*

"We have to get you out of here," said Genevieve, "take the…" But she paused, having no words in her vocabulary to describe what she was looking at.

"The letter."

"Yes, love, the letter," she said while kissing my cheek. "Hurry, Pallas. Take it and go!"

Safely back in the Twins bedroom, we stared at the cryptic scroll.

"There are words on this parchment?" said Lucy. Like Genevieve, she didn't understand how a message could be ciphered amongst the scrawls that littered the page.

"Yes. I can…read…this."

They answered me with dumbfounded stares.

I scolded myself for my indiscretion. *I wasn't going to tell them about reading! I've said too much already!* "It's a way the Gods communicate with each other." I didn't add that it was a sacrilege, an unholy magic forbidden by the Gods.

Their eyes grew wider and wider. "Then you…you know what this says?" said Casey.

"It's addressed to a person named Oscar," I lied.

"Who's that?"

I shrugged. Despite the betrayal, despite my anger, I still didn't tell them about the four-legged beast.

Why? I thought to myself. *Why am I protecting him?*

Yet something stayed my hand. Something instinctual, primitive.

"It says his name, then…I don't understand this word: Kô-d," I said, sounding it out. Luckily, Othello taught me phonics.

"Code is used by spies…in case they're intercepted by an enemy," said Casey.

"Yeah," I said, my temper rising. "Code Green: Volcano operative."

"Volcano is where Mulciber lives," said Lucy.

"An operative is a spy," said Casey.

I was so angry, I could spit. Here it was – in black and white – proof that Othello was indeed a spy for Vulcana. "Then my name, return to Continent," I said. "The Continent is…"

"We know about the Continent," said Lucy.

"You do?"

"*Everyone* knows about the Continent," said Casey. "Just like everyone knows about the prophecy."

"Honestly," Lucy laughed. "You Gods have a lot to learn about keeping secrets."

"Yeah," I sighed, feeling lost without my malevolent mentor. *Why does everyone know everything except for me?* I hid my concern and continued to read. "Priority ONE. Then another name, Kassan."

Lucy let out a low whistle.

"Why would they take you to the Continent?" asked Casey.

"How would they get you there?" said Lucy.

"No idea," I admitted. "But there's more. About three weeks ago Uncial showed me a letter from this same Kassan person. That message said something like, 'Black Bishop to Queen Knight Seven.'"

Casey sat in thought. "That's chess, that is. Uncle Tiberius taught me. He's a rather brilliant player."

"What rot," said Lucy. "What does chess have to do with anything?"

"I bet that was code as well," said Casey. "Secret orders to do something."

"Yeah," I sighed. "Like kidnap me."

"Right," said Lucy. "And Uncial knew what that letter said, right?"

"I think she can read."

This, in the Twin's opinion, sealed the case. Uncial was taking orders from Kassan to kidnap me. But they would wait till the night of the Hunt, during the Consecration of the Golden Stag.

"You'll be safe till the Consecration," said Casey. "In the meantime, we can whisk you back to the Isle."

"You might miss final exams!" Lucy said.

"Excellent!" said Casey, giving Lucy a happy high-five. "I bet we'll miss them too!"

"Maybe we'll have to fight our way out of the city!" said Lucy.

"Or…maybe you *will* get kidnapped," said Casey. "And then we'll rescue you!"

"Capital idea!" said Lucy.

But I fidgeted from the dangerous talk. Far from being excited, my soul was worn with dread.

Jittery with nervousness, I swore them both to secrecy. They mustn't tell anyone about reading or the message. Reading was sacred; Othello pounded that into my head. It had to be kept a secret.

Finally, the night everyone had been waiting for arrived. The Ball was not only a celebration of spectacle and pomp, it also marked the beginning of the University Games.

As "matron" of House Catagen, Elena selected dresses for her sisters weeks ago. Casey was resplendent in a gown of aqua-blue chiffon. Lucy wore a strapless, turquoise sheath with a delicate train of tulle in Sea-foam green.

I wore a sleeveless ice-blue, silk gown. It featured a plunging neckline with an elegant flare just below my ankles. Blue, it seemed, was Elena's favorite color for the Mistress of the Sea. My hair was up in a carefree bun, my eyes alight with purples and blues.

Elena wore an exquisite creation in pale pink. Featuring an elegant train, it fit perfectly in all the right places. A tiny tiara, gathered in a flowing arrangement, graced her dazzling hair. The teardrop open-back was highlighted by an enormous diamond which lay enticingly at the nape of her neck.

I remembered my first day in Castle Mare when Elena "dressed and painted" my hell-bent sisters. Tonight, they were patient and still, chatting happily as servants did their nails and hair.

We entered the hall fashionably late. This was not to the Commodore's liking, but Elena insisted. As strict as the Old Man thought he was, Elena figured out long ago how to get what she wanted.

The Commodore entered the hall first, Captain Dewey close behind. Both widowers were dateless. I found this odd. The Old Man was too old to get married again, but Captain Dewey was a very young man when his wife died. *Why had he never chosen another?* He was quite eligible, strong and handsome with a gentle Air. Yet neither Elena nor the Twins ever mentioned his courting again.

"I present to you," the crier called, "Princess Lucy of House of Catagen, escorted by Prince Karl of House Keleron!"

Karl was dressed in the traditional black tunic with a turquoise high-collared shirt. Lucy descended the stairs, carrying herself like a perfect lady.

"I present to you…Princess Casey of House of Catagen, escorted by crown Prince Telmar of House Tel!"

The fact that the Tel prince was going with the Catagen princess was another bit of shrewd diplomacy.

During Catagen's brief war with Lord Gemello, Lord Tel sailed *Argo* to guard the port of Geminus. Tel had no reason to fight the Catagens, but he was intimidated into helping his fellow Gemini by the boorish antics of the Lord Gemello, Lord Defender of the Twins.

Argo made a spirited display of defying the Seafaring Catagens. Her boisterous crew boasted loud and strong, itching for a fight. But their rampant boasts turned to feeble groans when *Hornet* entered the narrow sound. Sprinting neatly into the harbor, Dewey caught *Argo* weak and napping. A tense, short skirmish ensued, followed by *Argo's* ignoble retreat. Dewey quickly tacked into the port, scuttled Gemello's merchant ships, and torched her granaries.

The expensive affair spelled the mysterious end of the ill-mannered Lord Gemello. Quite coincidentally, it also precipitated the swift rise of his ambitious daughter. Shrewd and prudent, she sued for peace, ending the costly catastrophe.

But House Tel was deeply ashamed, humbled by *Argo's* spineless flight. Sailors and troubadours spread the tale – mocking chanteys about the one-sided fight.

Yet now that Catagen needed Gemini allies, that particular feud must be muted. Elena encouraged young Telmar to ask Casey, while making him think it was his idea. Such was the prowess of the Catagen jewel: to make men believe the thoughts she sowed.

Telmar's violet shirt and black tunic looked perfect with Casey's aqua-blue. The princess descended the noble stairs with a grace and poise I hardly believed.

She looks so elegant, I thought to myself, until I realized I was next in line. Fidgeting nervously at the marbled entrance, I prayed to Poseida that I could gracefully descend the stairs.

"You look really beautiful," Joculo said. He was dressed exactly like Karl, except with a royal blue collar.

"Yeah, well. I clean up good," I said. "You look good too, without that whip in your hand."

"Yeah," he mumbled. "Listen…I'm really sorry about that."

"Forget it. It's training, right?"

"Yeah," he agreed, "you, uh…don't hold it against me, do you?"

"Well, I did…" I toyed, seeing his face drop in alarm, "until you asked me to the dance!"

Joculo laughed at my stupid joke, and some of my nervousness washed away.

This is going to be fun!

"I present to you…the hallowed Atlantian…Princess Pallas, Mistress of the Sea! Escorted by crown Prince Joculo of House Joculo!"

Uh! I swore. *Who came up with that?* I wanted to be introduced as a Catagen, not as a God. The casual glances at the teenage Twins morphed into prying, probing stares. An eager hush, swift and curious, conquered the lively room.

I'd have thought I'd gotten used to this. But I was wrong. So I faked a smile and raised my chin, remembering Elena's many lessons.

I don't care what that crier says. I'm a Catagen! I successfully descended the marbled stairs before melting into the waiting crowd.

"I present to you…Princess Elena of House Catagen, escorted by crown Prince Borelo of House Gemello!"

Gasps of shock filled the Air. Instead of the traditional black tunic and trousers, Borelo wore white on white.

Elena, I knew, was absolutely furious. But she graced the crowd with a captivating smile, deciding that his flamboyant attire would make an even more stunning entrance. She could always ditch him later. *In fact, I bet she means to.*

The knight in white satin was certainly a surprise. But after the initial shock, all eyes fell on the tall beauty. For any man seeing Elena that night could not honestly say he'd ever seen a woman more beautiful.

Stunning failed as an adjective. Her dazzling eyes danced upon the crowd, preying upon the souls of each and every bachelor.

The princes were enraptured, the princesses enraged. For there was not a single man, eligible or not, who didn't want Elena on his arm.

The music started. The couples danced. Joculo was a fun date. Not too serious, not too coy. I laughed and chatted with the somewhat handsome boy as we twirled to the music on the ballroom floor.

I saw Keleron and Eunice. She looked sulky. He looked bored. Lord Duma was off his crutches now. Lady Uncial danced with the Commodore. She was a widow, I'd heard. Captain Dewey stood alone, refusing the advances of many a lady.

Why does he spurn them? Normally a jolly host, *Hornet's* captain looked coldly aloof.

I looked over at the Taurans. Oliver was a surprise. Instead of wearing charcoal and brown, he was dressed in a formal midshipman uniform. His camp-Fire date looked sour and annoyed. Oliver was obviously ignoring her.

I saw the Old Man give his great-grandson a heartfelt nod. I knew it meant so much to him that Oliver, who loved the Sea as much as he did, wasn't wearing the Tauran brown – but the navy blue of a sailor of the Three.

Lord Gauntle, however, was not amused. Heaving his girth into a waddling stance, he pointed at the delicate Fire princess and then to the dance floor.

The midshipman reluctantly obeyed…giving his father a vitriolic stare.

"Oh, look," said Joculo. "There's my sister."

Janice graced Djincar IV with a happy smile, gliding along with obvious delight. "They make such a cute couple," I said, "We ought to say hello." I was feeling much fonder of Janice after she'd kept me from going dateless.

"She'd like that," said Joculo. "In fact, she wanted to ask you something. One of the merchants from Kelly Tree said he knew a slave named Pallas."

Ice plummeted down my spine.

"Isn't that strange?" he added. "It certainly isn't a common name."

"No," I hushed. "Not a common name at all."

Joculo seemed to sense my displeasure. "I think it's a lie. I can't believe the Jesters let the Derricks buy their freedom in the first place."

"Me neither."

Janice and Djincar were dancing closer. I was desperate to get away.

"Oh, look! There's Genny."

The Gauntle princess looked happy and at ease, but her muscled date seemed oddly out of place. I frantically dragged Joculo to the Tauran couple.

Genevieve smoothed my hands in the Aquarian fashion before kissing both my cheeks. "Pallas, love. You look so lovely!"

"You too." *It's so hard to look good in brown,* I thought, so I was happy Genevieve was in a delicate lilac.

"Have you met Clovis, darling?"

"No."

So this is Clovis, I thought, *the guy who won four events last year and placed second in the Circus. If that isn't a record, it ought to be.* The athletic senior was a perfect specimen, broad shoulders and trunk-like legs. He was handsome too, reddish hair topping a likeable face.

"You are Pallas," said the chiseled jaw.

"Yeah," I answered, frankly staring.

"I am Clovis, son of Zeliox."

"Clovis, dear," said Genevieve, petting his muscled arm, "do take Joculo and get us some punch, won't you, darling?"

"Of course," he said with a curt bow.

I shrugged my shoulders at Joculo in a "please" sort of way.

Joculo frowned. Clovis was the single biggest obstacle the Aquarians had to winning a medal. But he did as he was told, leaving us girls alone.

"He looks really nervous," I said.

"He's under a great deal of stress," said Genevieve. "Everyone expects him to win the Gold all by himself. And his father makes it worse."

"Oh?"

"You know, Lord Zeliox won the Wrestling five times in a row in the Menagerie Games."

"Yeah, but the Taurans never won the Menagerie Games with Zeliox on the team. Not once. Sounds like he wants his son to win the Gold he never could."

"You're right, of course," said Genevieve. "He expects Clovis to live up to his own, impossible standards. Oh, look. Elena's gotten rid of Borelo."

Elena was dancing with Michael, eldest son of Lady Miser, the other Gemini Voting member.

"It's about time she lost that loser," I said.

"Darling, what a thing to say! Personally, I can't see the difference between one Gemini and another."

"Trust me. She can't do much worse than 'Bore-us-loads.'"

"I'll keep that in mind," she said, gazing at Borelo. The pretty boy was sulking in a corner, angry and alone.

"Oliver told me about your invitation," said Genevieve. "He's rather embarrassed."

"Sorry if I hurt his granite feelings."

Genevieve's response was surprising and bitter. "A rock has no feelings. Haven't you heard?"

"Uh…wow," I mumbled. "Sorry. I didn't mean."

She placed her gentle hands in mine. "Don't be sorry," she hushed. "It's father's fault, not yours. Stealing the best of my brother's love, cynically hardening his wounded heart."

"Uh…yeah. Like…I had no idea."

"Of course not, love. How could you? It's just…when we were both young, and life was still mellow, father and Lord Catagen were like brothers. Now…" she blanched, "everything's…changed."

"Because of me," I said.

"Yes," she admitted. "Because of you."

"I never thought. I didn't know."

"That's why Oliver's so conflicted. Whom does he obey? His overbearing father or his famous great-grandfather? The Good Earth or the Unquenchable Sea? His Tauran duty or his Aquarian…" But she stopped herself before saying.

"Aquarian what?" I asked.

"Oh, Pallas! Isn't it obvious?"

"What's obvious?"

Just then, the boys returned.

I frowned at Clovis, wanting Genny to tell me more about Oliver. I sighed at Joculo, wanting to talk to Genny about the message in Uncial's office. *Oh, well!* I thought. *We can talk about it later.*

I was having too much fun to discuss my doom.

We laughed. We talked. Joculo and I danced several times before Casey cut in, insisting she dance with "the team captain."

This left me unwillingly alone. I glanced around, searching for a friendly face, when my solitude was interrupted by the white peacock.

"Alone at last," he cooed in my ear, sneaking up from behind me. Nimbly taking my hand, he wrapped the other around my waist.

I pivoted sharply, ready to slap him, when a brawny chest appeared. "I'm afraid this dance is mine," said Oliver. "You've had one too many capers with the Mistress already."

Borelo bristled. "Stay away, you monolithic moron!"

"Forgetting that black eye I gave you on the Isle?"

"Forgetting my promise to pay you back?"

"Bring it," snared Oliver.

I bit my lip, wanting to re-connect my fist with the pompous Gemini. Instead, I smiled with petty delight as I placed my hand in Oliver's. "About time you asked. Sure keep a girl waiting!"

"My apologies, Mistress," he said with a bow. "I shall attempt to do better in the future."

"You do that," I said with an impish grin.

"This isn't over," said Borelo.

"Yeah," I flashed before dragging Oliver to the dance floor. "It is."

Oliver was a good dancer, better than Joculo, in fact.

"Genevieve taught me," he humbly explained. "Otherwise, I'd be quite a wreck. You know how clumsy I am. Every courtesy I attempt to employ, you can safely attribute to my sister."

"Genny's just awesome. I love her."

He smiled a pensive, hopeful smile before turning his bashful gaze away.

I enjoyed dancing with Oliver, but didn't think he felt the same. He was always careful to avoid my eyes, as if he were afraid of me somehow. He spoke very little, and, when he did, it was always about the Games. "The Circus will be down to Clovis, Alexander, and you," he said.

"Ya think so?"

"I've seen you drive. You can win."

I blushed, catching his dark, sparkling eyes in a longing stare. But the moment was gone as he quickly turned away.

"Oliver," I said. "We've been friends for almost a year now. Why don't you call me...why do you *still* call me...Mistress?"

"Because," he said. "You are the Dawning."

"Is that all I am to you? A mythic princess? A daughter of Atlantis?"

His gaze was wide and wondering. "What more is there?"

I blanched, feeling an eager yearning die within my chest. I sought a companion in the husky mariner. Perhaps, something even more. Yet all he could see was the Mistress of the Sea.

I want a friend, not a disciple.

Oliver seemed to sense my sadness. "I'm sorry. I...I never know what to say to you."

I carelessly caressed an impish smile. "What do you want to say?"

He opened his mouth and drew in a sigh, heaving his chest in a "Bull" sort of way. Holding me tight with his muscular arms, he rounded me with the rhythm of the romancing ballet. His coal black eyes were soft and knowing. For once, he held my penetrating gaze...

And in that moment, that particular moment – with the orchestra playing and the bright gowns swaying, and the light in my eyes, a pool of gray – in that one, infinitesimally brief moment...he would tell me.

But the orchestra ceased its melodic playing, the colors stopped their graceful swaying...

...and my one brief moment was shorn away.

The colors divided into their many corners, leaving us exposed on the empty dance floor. Imperiled by his father's stern disapproval, Oliver stamped his foot before turning away.

What was that about? I wondered, scampering alone to the opposite wall. Free from the spectacle of that lonely isolation, I came face to face with Lady Jingo.

"Mistress," she said, her military attire looking odd amongst the flowing gowns. "I'm so glad you're competing in the Games. You and your sisters. It's such an important step, having so many girls compete."

"Uh...yeah," I stuttered, having no idea why the martial Tauran was speaking to me.

"I'm disappointed the Taurans aren't sporting any girls. I noticed Atlanta's competing for the Geminis."

"I've heard she's really fast."

"Yes," said the Marshal, pursing her lips. "Well...good luck in the Games."

"Thanks," I said, completely forgetting to curtsy.

The lady offered a furtive smile before melting into the crowd.

That was nice, I thought, scanning the hall to find that Keleron and Eunice had left. *Thank goodness for small favors!* Janice was busy with Djincar, so no worries there. Elena was dancing with another Gemini I didn't know. I let out a saucy giggle. A sort of queue had formed, anxious suitors waiting for a brief opportunity with the tall beauty.

Cast aside were the disgruntled remains of their suitors' desire. The disappointed girls, forgotten by their dates, were huddled around the punch bowl. They glared at Elena with deepest loathing.

I giggled. Joculo was still dancing with Casey, so I took a moment to sit at a vacant table. I took my shoes off and rubbed my feet. I was having a wonderful time. *But why can't they make women's shoes more comfortable?*

"She can run ten miles across the wilds of the hinterland, but place her in a ballroom and watch her tire."

I angrily looked up, straight into the gorgeous face of Liam. Armored in a breastplate of silver and bronze, his robes were a graceful metallic gray. "Hypocrite," I brandished. "You wouldn't last five minutes in high heels."

"No," he laughed, "I'm sure I wouldn't. So why, then, do you wear them? Aren't you grateful for the height the Maker gave you? Why, indeed, should you pine for more?"

"Maker?" I huffed. "Don't you mean the Pentathanon Gods?"

He smiled that irresistible smile, mesmerizing me with those deep orbs. "As you like it...though I'm confident only one deity dare manufacture a soul as vibrant as yours."

For a moment I pondered this weird remark, unsure whether it was a compliment or not. "Ya hear to dance, or talk?"

"Both, I hope."

"Then let's do it," I said, taking his hand and leading him to the floor.

The music was slow and warmly inviting, pressing our hearts close upon each other. I gazed, intrigued, into his hazel eyes, into the vast mysteries that he hid behind them.

"You're beautiful," he whispered. "So beautiful. Far more than I could have imagined. Strong, smart, bold..."

"Strong?" I teased. "Bold? Sounds like you're wooing a soldier, not a girl."

"We're all soldiers in the service of the Maker. There is neither noble or peasant, servant or free..."

"Maker?" I asked. "Who is this Maker you keep talking about?"

"Someone very close," he hushed, a solemn expression on his handsome face.

I was about to ask him what he meant when Elena appeared. A line of princes trailed behind her, grousing rudely at my dancing partner. "Liam," she sang in her smooth contralto, "pray, let me cut in."

Liam's face was stern. "Is that really necessary, Princess?"

Elena raised her chin so slightly, assuming her trademark Air of superiority. "Yes, my guest, I'm afraid it is. And I'm quite confident you know why."

Liam looked guilty, as if wounded somehow. But then he posed in an elegant bow. "Very well. May I have the high honor and distinct privilege of this dance?"

"Yes," she glared, "you may."

Annoyed, I let go of the mysterious boy to face the group of her following fans. They scattered like flies under the weight of my stare. Again, I retreated the safety of the wall, far away from the many faces.

"Good evening, Mistress," said a deep, rumbling voice.

I twirled around to see Lord Joculo. Startled, I performed a perfect curtsy. "My Lord."

"I wondered," he whispered, "could I have a private word?"

Is this about Derrick?! I thought with alarm. But I pretended a smile and said, "Of course, my Lord."

"Not here. There's a room just behind that door."

"Yes, my Lord." I blindly followed my sovereign to the open door. The room was completely empty except for a stone table. Without a word, he closed the only door.

All the slaves in Kelly Tree loved Lord Joculo. Indeed, it was commonly said far and wide, that no one cared for his subjects the way he did. He was a fount of philanthropy, a shrewd debater, a towering intellect.

Yet the bear seemed humble and sad. This surprised me. Every time I'd ever seen him before, he seemed confident, joyful, full of life.

"Pallas," he said kindly. "I have something for you." From within his cloak, he produced a silver cylinder. It was a beautiful thing, playful nymphs embossed upon its polished sides.

I recognized the workmanship at once. Squealing inside, not daring to hope, I asked, "Who is it from, my Lord?"

He considered his answer for a very long time. Finally, with difficulty, he emoted a cheerless sigh. "Your father."

My heart leapt! I was so excited, I actually giggled. Only, I realized, he hadn't actually given me the cylinder.

"May I have it, please, my Lord?" I said as sweetly as I could.

The bear simply stared at me, spellbound, paralyzed. He seemed both awed and horrified by the girl who stood before him.

I stood there…waiting…giddy with anticipation.

I waited…and I waited…

After what seemed like a very long time, he finally wakened from his hibernation. "Forgive me. Yes, yes…of course."

I opened the proffered cylinder, fidgeting with surprise. Inside was a parchment of paper. On the parchment were letters, formed into words. Not the crude scrawl I inexpertly labored with, but beautifully crafted prose, fashioned by someone who had written for years, and was good at it.

My dearest baby girl…

Happy tears streamed down grateful cheeks. Here was a message from my beloved father! The old man I loved the best.

But before I could read the next line, the realization of what I held astounded me. Remembering my mistake with Lady Uncial, I was determined not to repeat it.

"What is it?" I lied. I hoped it was a good one.

But Lord Joculo seemed to see right through me. "It's a letter, Pallas. A letter from your learned father, Gerard; the very best blacksmith in the tiny fiefdom of Kelly Tree."

Suspicion filled my wary mind. Of all the bizarre things I had seen this year, the simple parchment with its flowing words, written by my illiterate father, was the most bizarre of all. But before I could stop to ponder this paradox, before I could think at all, I devoured the words, feeding on them like a starving man set before a feast…

My dearest baby girl,

I hope this letter finds you well. Lord Joculo told me when he realized who you were. I pray for a day when I can see you again, but know it must wait for another time.

You must be brave, Pallas, as I know you are. But you also must be strong. I yearn to hear your voice again, but know that the Gods would destroy us both should we ever be seen together. Perhaps there will come a time when this danger will pass. I will tell you if it does. But know this: your Safety is more important than anything in the world.

Do not come home.

I must tell you the thing which I have longed to tell you, yet dreaded all these long years. I wished to do it face to face. But alas, the Fates have not been kind.

Your mother is the daughter of Poseida, and she is very much alive.

My dearest baby girl, I pray you can forgive me. Only know that I kept this from you to keep you from harm. Even now I cannot tell you all that I know, only this: Mulciber is your mortal enemy and the reason for all our woes.

Let the Gods fight the Gods. It is not for you to wage the wars of heaven. Speak of this to no one except Lord Joculo, not even to Lord Catagen. He would not understand. Keep this secret deep in your heart, as your mother and I keep our love for you deep in our hearts.

I love you more than life itself,

Your Father

I plastered the parchment against my chest. My stricken soul rejoiced and wept.

Yet my startled skepticism scoffed. "You wrote this!" I accused. "You wrote this to hurt me."

But I could see in the sadness of his eyes that I was wrong, as wrong as I could be. His gentle face was etched with sorrow, a gloomy portrait of a morose giant.

"Your father wrote it," said the bear. "Gerard, the very best blacksmith in Kelly Tree."

The mention of his name struck an emotional chord. Clutching the letter to my beating bosom, prompted by a misery I'd harbored for years, I fell upon the hulk and cried.

Burying my head into his burly chest, I cried about the raft, the wicked raft that plucked me from home. I cried about my father, the father I'd never see again.

But most of all, I cried about my mother – the mother I'd never known.

Grateful tears bathed me in their purity. Though intellectually irrelevant, the Water healed me…in a soulful way I couldn't explain.

Finally, slowly, I pulled myself together. Disentangling myself from my noble peer, I said, "I…I'm very sorry, my Lord."

"You needn't call me Lord," he mewled, "I should be calling you, your…your Holiness."

His haunted words stunned me.

He's right! If my mother is a God, and my grandmother is Poseida, that means…

…I'm a God!

Unable to fathom this revelation, another reached out and stung me.

Othello! I gasped. *He was right! I am an Atlantian!*

But my mind didn't tarry on titles. "Who wrote this?" I demanded, still not certain of anything.

Pensive, as if walking on eggshells, the great bear said, "You're father."

"My father can't write. No mortals can."

"There are some who can. Lady Uncial for one. I, for another…though only poorly."

"And my father?"

"Gerard VII can read and write. The proof is in your hands."

I knew he spoke truth. The words were exactly what my father would have said. *My dearest baby girl…* He used to call me that all the time.

"But why?"

"It's a very long story," he morbidly replied. "A difficult story, I'm afraid."

I would not be deterred. My stare demanded an answer.

"When your mother arrived in Kelly Tree, I was a young man. I...noticed her. *Everyone* noticed her. She was lovely and kind and generous and smart. A rose amongst the many thorns, a fragrant bloom amongst the smelly quay."

"No one knew, not even I, that she wasn't a slave at all, but a Goddess in hiding, the eldest daughter of Poseida herself."

"I was in love," he admitted. "She helped me with the sewer project, and...I was smitten. We spent hours and hours together, philosophizing about the plight of man, the heavens above, the Gods among us. She even taught me to read," he said in a pathetic chortle. "I'm afraid she thought I was a very slow learner. But...I still read, and write. I hope she'd be proud of me for that."

I looked into his doleful eyes, mesmerized by the tear trickling down his face.

"Soon after, she met your father, and...the two got married. Their union was...flabbergasting...a scandal, the talk of our tiny town. Why would a fantastic young woman marry a poor old blacksmith?"

He took a deep, solemn breath, looking far, far away. "I acted badly. She never loved me. She never wronged me. Yet I was mad with envy, wracked with spite! *I* was the Lord of Kelly Tree! She rejected me for an old blacksmith!?"

His voice was building to a frightening crescendo, his eyes, wild and cagey. "Every young man in Kelly Tree was angry, angry that *they* were not the one she'd chosen! But alas, whereas other men could do no more than nurse their egos, *I* held the power of life and death! I was obsessed with your mother and your father, and so I waited...and I waited. And then...I took my revenge."

His face was white now, pale as death. His eyes never blinked as his voice became a howl. "I told the Captain of the Guard to frame your father, plant one of my golden cups in his workshop. The penalty, of course, was death."

I shuddered. Shock, mingled with unbearable curiosity, formed an elixir I could barely stomach.

"The trial was rigged. I bribed the judge. Gerard was sentenced to hang. Your mother," he winced, "She begged me, begged me to spare his life. But I was too mad to hear the pleas of the only woman I truly loved."

"What did you do?" I asked, not daring to know, desperate to find out.

His growls softened to a somber whisper. "I sent her away."

"You sent her away? But then…"

"She left the castle and ran to the shore. Crazed by jealousy, I followed. Followed…from…from a safe distance. Followed her…followed her…to the wide and gentle shore."

His huge voice broke, in a high-pitched shrill that was ignoble and small. "There she stood, grieving to the Ocean, crying out to the mighty Sea! She begged her Mother…pleading forgiveness…yearning to go back home!"

His eyes were wet and reverent, his face a mournful scowl. "Poseida heard her, and forgave her. Riding upon her clam-shaped shell, pulled along by gallant dolphins, surrounded by mermen and Orcas and whales – she came to bring her daughter, back to Her hallowed fold."

I cried a happy wave of tears, joy engulfing my vibrant soul. "Then…she's safe in Atlantis, living among immortals, watching me this very moment!"

"No!"

The wounded bear was suddenly a monster, raising his paws to crush me.

"Noo!!"

Towering to his gigantic height, he moaned with the violence of a wailing ghost.

"Nooo!!!"

Too shocked to run, too scared to flee, I cowered beneath the hulk.

CRACK!!!

I knew that I was dead; knew the bear had killed me. Yet the rending was not my flesh and bones, but the sudden sundering of marble and stone.

Befuddled, I opened my eyes…

The table lay broken, severed cleanly in two.

My lord lay prostrate, his noble face askew.

My heart started beating again. Recovering from my blind moment of terror, I discovered I was still on my feet.

If I'd had any sense, I'd have turned and run away. I'd seek the safety of the Commodore, or Elena, or the Twins...

But I remained, petrified, inconsolable. Hearing the rest of Lord Joculo's story was more important than living.

My burly sovereign lay weeping on the ground. His anguished sobs died to whimpers.

Against my better judgment...with a severe, imperial tone, I demanded, "Where is my Mother?"

The bear stared weakly at the scattered stone.

"Where...is...my...Mother!?!"

"I...I followed her to the shore. I saw her praying to Poseida. I ran to her, to beg forgiveness. I ran to her...I ran..."

But he couldn't finish. Tears baptized his ruddy face, opening that old and bitter wound.

"Where is my Mother!?!" My voice was now a threat, my face, an ugly frown. Something was wrong. Something was dreadfully wrong...

He swallowed hard, grinding his teeth. "*It* came down...down from Volcano. It grabbed your mother...and...and...and carried her away."

A bout of terror completely overwhelmed me. "What came down!?"

"A chariot," he hushed. "A chariot...of Fire."

"Fire?" I whimpered. "Volcano!?" I howled. My voice was suddenly pathetic – my face, a frightened scowl. Panic gripped me, its evil fingers prying into the chasms of my soul. "Poseida doesn't ride a chariot of Fire! She doesn't ride...not of Fire!"

For the very first time, he looked straight into my eyes. And in those fathomless windows I saw the horror of the man. "Don't you think I know that?" lilted his deep and powerful voice. "Don't you think I know? The love of my life was standing there, and then she was...then she was...gone."

Mulciber! I mouthed the name, yet dare not say it.

The wretched animal read my mind. "Mulciber! The Fire lord. He seized her and flew her away. I cursed him, begged him to come down and fight me! But he just laughed. Laughed at Joculo...Lord of Kelly Tree."

My labored breaths were desperate gasps.

"When Poseida reached the shore," he mewled, "she nearly killed me. I nearly killed myself. But the damage was done. Poseida left me to my misery, and her daughter…to the Flame."

I struggled to regain my composure by ruthlessly biting my lip. Woozy with emotion, steadying myself against the broken table, I lorded over the wounded bear.

"I hate you."

Chapter Fourteen

The Games

The cub, of course, would have been completely adrift had I not been there every step of the way, nurturing and guiding her through the treacherous waters in which she found herself.

"Memoirs of a Saint, the Cat Who Saved the Dawning"

Othello

Tomorrow came. I stayed in bed the entire day, reading the letter a hundred times and more. For the parchment contained the most wonderful and horrible news I'd ever heard.

Yet it also generated a myriad of questions.

Why didn't Father tell me? If I really am a Goddess, why didn't I grow up in Atlantis? Where is my mother? Why hasn't Father searched for her?

But as much as these questions engulfed me, one mystery dominated the others...

Does the cat have all the answers? Does he know I'm divine?

Othello was the key, I knew it. He was the architect of my destiny, the creator of my legend.

But where is he? Why is he absent when I need him the most?

"I don't care about that cat!" I swore to myself. Instead, I tarried on my mother.

I should leave this very moment! Run away to Kelly Tree. My father and I can search for my mother. We'll rescue her from Mulciber...

But my father told me *not* to come home.

"Let the Gods fight the Gods. It is not for you to wage the wars of heaven."

Yet how could I sit idly, enjoying the bounty of freedom, while my mother lay captive in the clutches of mine enemy?

∞

Monday morning came. And with it, the University Games. Even amidst my many troubles, I found the excitement infectious. It was a relief, really. It kept my mind off other things…

Despite the maddening revelations, despite my longing to run away, I forced myself to forget…if only for a week. Promising myself, *after the Games, after the Games,* I shut away my horrors to bask in the pleasantries of bread and circuses.

My heart fluttering with swift anticipation, I sat in the locker room with my Aquarian teammates. Joculo stood in front of his team, finishing a motivating speech.

"…we've worked harder than we ever have before. The hours of sweat and toil will finally be put to the test! We have a real shot for a medal this year – Silver, maybe even Gold. Our chance to atone for last year's dismal showing. We can do it! I know we can. This…is our year!"

The athletes stood and cheered, surrounding Joculo in a raucous huddle. All the Aquarians laughed and smiled, hoping he was right, hoping we could triumph over the hated Leos.

But when I looked at young Joculo, I couldn't help but think of the bear and the terrible curse he'd laid upon my family.

A herald blew a fancy fanfare. The appointed time had come. We lined ourselves into an eager column. Taking a deep breath, Joculo looked once again at his team.

"This is our year," he said. His defiance brought goose-bumps down my arms. "Go out there and prove it."

University Stadium was five times the size of the one in Kelly Tree. Different too, were the army of competitors. Back home, I competed against rival schools, not rival elements. Here, the shock of blue, red, brown, yellow and green electrified the sense of competition.

The Chancellor stood in the middle of the arena as the crowd roared its raucous approval. After walking a glorious ceremonial lap, the five columns converged on the center.

Another fanfare announced a runner carrying a Flaming torch. It was Alexander, crown prince of House Excelsior, winner of last year's Circus.

Celebrating their fourth championship in a row, the Leos rose their feet to the blast of trumpets. Alexander circled the Stadium in a lazy jog.

His hair's much better, I smirked, his little nubs passing for an extremely short haircut. After finishing his lap, he climbed the flight of stairs which led to a huge, golden cauldron. Turning to face the crowd, he held the torch high in the Air. With a rush of sound he lit the cauldron, a colossal Flame leaping from its chalice.

Lady Uncial raised her arms to silence the crowd. Without speeches or proclamations, she shouted, "Let the Games begin!"

But I watched in troubled silence, thinking it a bad omen that Fire was used to consecrate the Games.

∞

There were ten events in the Games, spread out over five days. Two athletes competed in each event from each Academy. Points were awarded for the top three competitors in each event, three points for first place; two points for second; and one for third. The team with the most points at the end of the ten events received the Gold Medal. Second and third place teams won Silver and Bronze.

The first event was a surprise. Atlanta, the only girl in the race, won the 24 Stad Run six strides in front of the Leo who placed second and Keleron who placed third. Urban came in a disappointing ninth place. Like everyone else, I was dumbfounded by the Gemini's success.

Atlanta didn't beat the other boys; she crushed them!

That afternoon came the Discus. I watched as young Joculo and Mark of House Ionian heaved the iron plates. Still struggling with my sordid feelings, I spotted Janice sitting with the bear. Did I welcome the news that my mother was alive, or did I loathe my team captain for the sins of his father?

But as I looked upon his somewhat handsome son, I felt sympathy for young Joculo and Janice.

They're my friends, after all, and have never done anything to harm me.

In the end, a Leon sophomore took the wreath, narrowly edging young Djincar, the Gemini Janice went to the Ball with; and Oliver, who took third. I wanted to congratulate the loyal mariner, but the Twins would have none of it.

"This is the Games." scolded Casey. "We don't laud a Tauran, cousin or no."

Overall, the first day was disappointing. Keleron had the only Aquarian point. The heavily favored Leos shared the lead with the surprising Geminis at five a piece.

∞

Next morning in the Long Jump, Joculo placed third behind two Leos. Lucy finished fifth. I hoped she wasn't too disappointed, as I knew she wouldn't get far in the Boxing that afternoon. She unfortunately drew a seed against Clovis her very first heat.

"You sure you want to go though with this?" I asked as we walked to the Coliseum.

"I should jolly well think so," she riled. For the very first time, I saw a hint of irritation on her eternally happy face. "Don't worry. I'll be all right. You've forgotten my little secret."

I shrugged, casting a doubtful eye at Casey. We both doubted Lucy's "little secret" could keep her alive for three rounds with Clovis.

Boxing and Wrestling were conducted on four successive days, so that no athlete had to fight in either sport more than once a day. Today was the round of eight, which would be whittled down to the final four.

I joined the Catagens in the crowded Coliseum. Much smaller than the Stadium, it was roofed, hot, and noisy. Casey, looking as nervous as I felt, kept biting her nails. The Old Man and Dewey spoke in short, tense sentences. Elena refused to come, saying she couldn't bear to watch.

204

Clovis entered the ring, greeted by a tumult of wild whooping. Lord Zeliox, Clovis' father, stood in his son's corner. Disdainful and impatient, he prowled the mat like an angry wolverine.

Lucy arrived, Dio by her side. Enduring nasty cat-calls and jeers, she stripped down to a simple tunic. Grim determination spoiled her cheerful face.

"In this corner," the crier announced, "weighing in at two hundred and twenty pounds, the undisputed University Boxing Champion of the World: Clovis, son...of...Zeliox!!!"

Smiling at the supportive crowd, Lord Zeliox raised his hands. From his proud reaction, one would have thought the Taurans were cheering for him, and not his son. Perhaps they were.

Clovis kept his hands at his side, ignoring the fans.

"And in this corner, weighing in at one hundred and five pounds, we have first-time contestant Lucy, daughter of Dewey!"

More cat-calls greeted Lucy as she shimmied out to meet Clovis, greeting him with the traditional stamping of the fists.

I flinched at the size difference. Lucy looked like a doll next to his fantastic physique. Standing a head shorter, she had thin, tiny arms. Clovis' arms were thick, stocky, chiseled.

The boxers returned to their corners.

Dio whispered encouragements.

Zeliox yelled at his son. "Knock her out the first round! No mercy!"

The bell rang.

The eagerness of the crowd reverberated though the Coliseum as the contestants pranced to the center of the ring. Lucy kept her arms flat in front of her face, swaying them loosely with her dancing hips. Confused by her strange posture, Clovis paced around her. They circled each other for a minute and a half.

"What's she doing?" I asked.

"No idea," said Casey.

"At least she hasn't been killed."

"Not yet."

The crowd started complaining.

"Get on with it!"

"Ya gonna dance or fight?"

But the crowd's dismay was nothing compared to Clovis' angry father. "Throw a punch, you idiot! Knock her out!"

Clovis reluctantly obeyed. Faking left, he crossed with a powerful right straight at Lucy's bobbing head.

But Lucy danced aside, nimbly circling the bewildered boy.

Boos abounded. Zeliox screamed.

Clovis kept his cool, cornering Lucy. Another jab, cross, jab, jab.

Lucy ducked them all, twirling away like a top.

The bell rang. The first of three rounds was over.

Lucy retreated to a smiling Dio.

Clovis faced a wrathful father. "Moron!" he cursed, slapping his son. "Get out there and kill her!"

Boos and cat-calls hounded the boy. Clovis stared blankly at his father.

"Go, I said! Get!"

The boy returned to the center of the ring, without so much as a swallow of water.

Dio rubbed Lucy's shoulders, whispering words of cheer.

The bell rang again. The same spectacle played before the crowd, Lucy avoiding his lightning jabs as Clovis tried to land a punch. Lucy threw no punches. It didn't look like she meant to. After another fruitless three minutes, the bell rang again.

Again, Zeliox chased his son away from his corner, spit flying everywhere. Gauntle was ringside, demanding he finish off his tiny niece. The Tauran crowd howled in dismay, throwing tomatoes at their vaunted hero.

The bell rang a third time.

Lucy danced forward, fleet and sprite and gay.

Clovis lunged with reckless abandon.

The crowd cheered their approval. He flailed away with a fury of blows, each punch just missing.

The princess danced sprightly away, using her forearms to parry his attacks.

The bell pealed its final chime. The match was over.

A cacophony of groans filled the hall: confusion and bitter disappointment. Fans demanded the referee add another round so a winner could be determined.

The referee consulted the judges table. Bewildered, he called the two combatants to the center of the ring, taking a hand of each. "By unanimous decision…I declare Lucy, daughter of Dewey…the winner!" he said, raising her arm into the Air.

The crowd was stunned. Silence blanketed the angry Taurans as Lucy bounded into her father's arms.

"What?" I gasped. "What happened?"

Casey slapped herself on the forehead. "Of course! How could I be so stupid?"

"What?"

"They deduct a point for every punch that misses."

"So?"

"Clovis never landed a punch, and Lucy never threw one. That means Lucy has zero points, and Clovis probably minus a hundred."

Negative seventy-seven, to be exact.

The silence subsided into shouts of anger as Clovis retreated from the ignoble ring.

Lord Gauntle demanded an investigation, but this was flatly denied. Rules were rules; Lucy beat him fair and square.

News of Clovis' defeat swept through University like wild Fire.

The hero of last year's Games…beaten by a girl?

∞

Early next morning, I went to the stables to be with Calypso. Phillip had him washed and ready, his white hair gleaming in the bright, cloudless day.

"You must have spent all night working on him," I admired.

"Nearly!" he replied. "Still, 'e don't mind. Thinks he likes it."

"Only from you," I teased. Calypso wouldn't let any other boys near him.

"'e's got good taste, that 'orse."

"I most certainly agree."

"I've got your saddle ready, Miss," he said as he produced the English creation from beneath an oil cloth. Its seat was so polished I could see my refection.

"You are a prize, little man," I said as I kissed his forehead. "Let's take him for a stroll. Stretch his legs a bit."

"Capital idea, miss. Capital idea!" Phillip heard the Commodore use the phrase last week. Now the boy said it every ten minutes.

I found Casey and Callisto on the Aquarian field. Competitors for the day in the Mounted Javelin, we forced false smiles and words of encouragement. It felt strange that she was my rival, yet that was the reality if we both made it to the medal round.

After several painfully slow hours, we headed for the Hippodrome.

Why the horse track was called the Hippodrome, no one seemed to know. Othello once told me if I didn't stop eating, I'd get as big as a hippopotamus, yet even he didn't know what the expression meant.

Besides, why would they name a racetrack after a fat horse?

Unlike the oval-shaped Stadium, the Hippodrome was long and narrow. With a capacity of sixty-thousand, it held twice the population of Kelly Tree.

"How did Keleron do in the Pentathlon?" I asked Lucy. Keleron had become something of an Aquarian star, as he'd won the 1 Stad Run and placed third in the 24 Stad Run. In fact, besides young Joculo, he had the only Aquarian points.

"It's not quite over yet. Only, he didn't get into the medal round."

"Darn." That meant he wouldn't win any points. "What about Clovis? He's supposed to compete in the Mounted Javelin in ten minutes."

"Well, he got into the medal round. Only he's in the loser bracket. Two Sagittarians are competing for first."

Another blow to the confident Taurans! If Clovis had gotten into the winners bracket, he would have easily won the wreath, as Wrestling was his strongest event. Now he had to settle for third at best.

The ten minutes passed. Sweating, dazed, and ruffled, Clovis charged into the Hippodrome as the judges made their last call.

News came soon after. He'd won third.

Mounted Javelin was unlike any other sport. It began with two riders facing each other on opposite ends of a pitch. In the middle was a target for each, connected by a long pivot arm. The target that was struck first made its opposite fall. First to hit their target got a point. Three points won the heat, advancing the athlete to the next round.

I sized up my competitors. I didn't worry too much about the Sagittarians or the Geminis. Casey was in the same bracket as Clovis, so I wouldn't have to deal with either unless they got into the medal round.

No, the opponent that concerned me was Alexander, riding tall upon a jet black thoroughbred.

I was pitted against Borelo my first heat. Relishing the opportunity to pay him back for ruining my date with Liam, I said a prayer to Poseida as I mounted Calypso.

"Good luck, miss," said Phillip, handing me a javelin.

I nodded, pursing my lips.

At the drop of the flag, Calypso charged in an explosive gallop. Rising and falling with his powerful back, breathing in rhythm with his churning legs, I kept my eyes on the tiny target. On the count of five, I flung my javelin…

Once the javelin was away, I gently reined Calypso in. My javelin struck first, causing Borelo's target to fall away. The deceleration of the horses carried both riders past each other. I smiled at the scowl that marred his pretty face.

Two more charges, two more hits. I easily advanced to the next round. And though I wanted to savor the sweet revenge of beating the crown prince of Geminus.

I've got other princes to worry about.

I studied Alexander as he trounced a Sagittarian, thrill and dread swimming in my gut. The next round would pit the Fire prince against the Mistress of the Sea.

Phillip produced a carrot for Calypso. I petted the stallion as I watched Casey eliminate Michael, son of Miser. The final four would be Clovis against Casey, and then me against Alexander.

The Taurans roared anew as Clovis took his place. But the boy looked exhausted, the Pentathlon having visibly sapped his strength. Casey was well-rested and confident, Callisto raring to go.

The first heat, Clovis threw from a distance I would never have tried. The crowd cheered his effort. But he missed badly while Casey scored from a much easier distance.

Clovis swore bitterly at himself; it was a stupid thing to do. Another howl of complaints persecuted the Tauran. But it was nothing compared to the withering condemnations from his father.

"What are you doing, moron!? Focus! Focus! Focus!"

I felt sorry for the quiet boy. *It's cruel for the Taurans to put so much pressure on him.* Still, I wanted Casey to win, and clapped enthusiastically as she returned for another javelin.

The crowd yelled their righteous disapproval. They evidently couldn't believe last year's champion was losing to a fourteen-year-old girl...again!

Clovis tried twice more. But the tired, desperate Tauran couldn't find his target. Angry boos hounded his retreat as he left the pitch in shame.

"It's sad, really," I said to Calypso.

The behemoth whinnied his sage agreement.

But I had my own problems to deal with. Across the field of dirt and clay was the hair-less wonder, mounted atop his magnificent steed.

I couldn't help but think about the first time I saw him. *It was a midsummer night on the Isle of Fort Isolaverde.* I bit my lip to focus on the "now" and not on the strangeness of that near-fatal night.

The crowd cheered as we took our places. Amid the shouts of "Leos again!" and "Alleexaaaander!" I heard "Aquarius!" and "Mistress of the Sea!"

Mounted Javelin was as much a psychological game as one of skill. The crucial decision was when to throw the javelin. Most athletes tried to keep an eye on their opponent, throwing just before he did. The problem with this strategy was that one had to pay a great deal of attention to the other rider instead of his own target. Instead, I watched the opponent ahead of time, timing in my head how long he took to throw.

Alexander took six counts with the Sagittarian. I normally threw on five.

I said a silent prayer as I took my place opposite Alexander. The crowd was yelling their incoherent din, silenced in my mind by grim determination.

The flag dropped.

Calypso rocketed forward. Gelled in our symbiotic relationship, I breathed with each step of his front left hoof. I counted aloud to the rhythm of his stride, "One, two, three, four, five!"

I threw the javelin just as his right rear hoof pushed my body forward. After months of training, Calypso knew to lower his head just as I released the javelin.

I looked up, trying to determine which javelin would hit first. They flew together on a collision course…

Thunk!

"Mistress…of…the Sea!!!" yelled the rabid mass of blue. A surge of pride thrilled my heart as Calypso carried me past the Excelsior prince.

"One," I said, holding up my index finger.

"One and only, Water Witch!"

Up close, I could see he'd penciled-in his eyebrows to hide the ones that'd been burned away.

The next go, however, was more to Alexander's liking. He threw ahead of me, and his aim was true.

Choruses of "Excelsior!" and "Leos again!" filled my ears as I conferred with Casey.

"He threw on four and a half," my sister told me.

"Any ideas?" I frowned.

"If he throws at four and a half, you'll have to throw at four."

"I might miss at four."

"You've no chance at five, unless you expect him to miss."

"Maybe I should throw on four and a half?"

"Calypso expects you to throw on the right rear hoof," Casey argued. "You've trained him to throw on the count."

"You're right," I said, wiping my brow.

"You've trained at four. Calypso is ready. Just give him the little kick on three. He knows what to do."

I took another javelin, concentrating on the heat.

Alexander cantered proudly, waving to the crowd.

"Alleexaaaander!"

"Leos again!"

The flag. The charge. Calypso was as steady as a metronome. I counted three, giving Calypso the little kick. I counted four. Calypso lowered his head, his powerful right rear hoof pushing my body forward. I swung my arm forward, keeping my eye on my target. The javelins flew...

Thunk!

Red groans drowned into blue ecstasy.

"Aquarius! Aquarius! Aquaaaaarius!"

"Two," I said with a haughty smile. The anguish in his face was sweet revenge.

But the horror in his eyes made me pause. It wasn't anger, and it wasn't loathing. The boy looked cornered, terrified.

"Whadya you think?" I said as Casey handed me another javelin.

"Just do what you're doing. Don't change a thing."

"Yeah," I smiled, returning to the line.

Alexander's face was a frightened scowl.

I steadied my courage, forcing myself to concentrate on the tiny target, and not my hated foe.

The multi-colored fans rose to their feet; clamoring, cheering, singing, and more. I couldn't understand most of the mad cacophony, but four words rang clear...

"MISTRESS...OF...THE SEA!!!"

Alexander cringed at the chanting crowd, as if cowered by mounting disaster. Troubled, he took a very long time before returning to the line. But when he did, he changed his expression to an evil smile.

I didn't like that smile.

The flag. The charge. The metronome. The count.

I reached four, hurling my javelin.

A nervous whinny. A wicked smile. Why was Alexander so close?

Thunk.

That was mine! But where was his?

I found the evil, errant javelin…a second from skewering my beating heart!

It was Calypso that saved me, veering sharply to the right. Pain lanced my wounded shoulder as I desperately arched away…

"AAAAAAHHHHHH!!!"

The crowd erupted with heat and noise, spangled with joy and wanton wishes. They howled as I fell, limp on my horse, lifeless upon his lathered withers. My body twisted like a thin, rag doll.

The prince passed the prostrate mannequin, sporting a malicious smile. "Sorry!"

I righted myself with a grunt of pain. Acting on instinct, not thinking at all, I turned my warhorse at my vile tormentor.

The stallion charged.

Alexander circled lazily round, jauntily waving to the crowd. He didn't see me until it was too late.

Standing aggressively in my stirrups, brandishing my arm like a dread avenger, I punched him ruthlessly in the nose. Calypso swerved into the hapless boy, adding his weight to the punishing blow. Blood spurted everywhere as Alexander flew off his horse.

"HURRRRRAAAAHHHH!!!" roared the crowd, pandemonium littered with ecstasy. Nothing delights a sports fan more than good old-fashioned violence.

I rounded Calypso, ready to charge again. But Casey, riding Callisto, corralled me before I could act.

"Stop!" she ordered. "You'll be disqualified!"

"Get off!" I raged. Adrenaline kept the pain at bay.

Philip was alongside me now, as well as young Joculo. Leon teammates surrounded the fallen, armed with javelins and teeming knives.

The crowd reached a frenzied pinnacle, praying we would fight. But young Joculo pulled me away before we turned into teenage gladiators.

"Really stupid, that was!"

"He tried to kill me!"

"Come on," he said, glancing at the blossoming patch of blood. "Let's get you to a Deme."

With difficulty, they helped me into the locker room. Hebe cut the remnants of my bloody tunic. Beneath the crimson tatters was an ugly, ochre wound.

"My goodness," he said. "Always an adventure, hmmm?"

"How bad is it?"

"The cut isn't too deep. You've been very lucky."

"Can I ride?" I asked, a single tear fleeing from my eye. "My right arm is fine. I don't throw with my left."

"You hold the reins with your left," mumbled Lucy.

"I can handle the pain!" I yelped, wincing at the fever.

The eyes of the Healer betrayed his alarm, but his voice was soft and smooth. "Now, now," he said, "just…drink this."

I soured my face after downing the liquid. "What is it?"

"A sedative, for the pain. Combined with a powerful anti-biotic."

"Will it put me to sleep?" I asked as I slumped upon the cot.

Chapter Fifteen

Chariot of Fire

Divine Intervention was an incredibly rare event until the advent of the New Age, when the impetuous Mistress of the Sea exploded upon the political landscape. Hitherto the Gods stayed aloof of the lives of mortals, save for the dalliances of a few love-sick individuals, protecting their divinity by the act of not acting at all.

Yet suddenly, the Pentathanon Gods tipped their hands to save their precious Tokens. Arguments have been made as to which Godhead was to blame, either Mulciber or Poseida. But the result was ultimately the same. It was the beginning of the end of the Pentathanon system, to the doom of them all.

"Compendium, Chronicles of the Pentathanon Gods"

Ovid XII

Thursday started with a win by Clovis in the Wrestling semi-final round. Confined to my bed per Hebe's orders, I unfortunately missed the match. But the Twins reported that Clovis was especially brutal to the Sagittarian he shared the ring with. Amazingly, Atlanta won as well. They'd face each other in the finals tomorrow.

My shoulder ached as I listened to the account. Then Casey gave me a blow-by-blow replay of Lucy's second match, where she won again without throwing a punch. "She's fighting Corona this afternoon for the wreath!"

Lucy blushed with proud delight.

I managed a furtive smile. I was happy for Lucy; I really was. But I couldn't hide my fury about my own match.

"You won second," said Lucy, picking up on my bad mood, "and Casey won first. Either way, the team gets a perfect five points. We can't do better than that!"

Lucy was right, of course. I won my heat, putting me into the winner's bracket of the medal round. So even though I didn't compete against Casey for first place, I still won second.

But after all those months of training, my sullen heart complained, *I should have had a shot at the wreath!*

Casey grimaced as if reading my mind. She too wanted to win fair and square, not by a technicality.

Hebe arrived. After giving me something for the pain, he gingerly re-dressed my shoulder.

"Will I be ready to race tomorrow?" I asked.

"Now, now...perhaps," he said. "Well...maybe. *If* you get some rest."

Later at noon, Joculo called a team meeting. Though I knew Hebe wouldn't approve, I sneaked out anyway.

Inside the Aquarian locker room, I felt extremely smug as I greeted Urban, Anthony, and Mark.

The Catagen sisters have won at least seven points, and you boys haven't won any!

The mood was giddy as we took our seats. But Joculo was serious and sober. "It's been nine years since we won the Gold. Yet here we are, tied with those camp-Fire fools, well ahead of everyone else."

It was true. With Casey and my five points, we were tied with the Leos at ten a piece. The Sagittarians were third with six, while the Taurans and Geminis each had five.

"Yes," Urban said, "but Clovis wrestles Atlanta tomorrow. The Taurans will catch up when he beats her. Plus, he's a shoe in for the Javelin and the Circus."

"What if Atlanta wins?" I asked.

"Clovis is going to kill her," said Keleron. "Poor girl doesn't stand a chance."

"Obsid will probably get third in the Boxing," said Mark. "I expect the Taurans to gain at least four, maybe five points today.

"But if Lucy wins the Boxing..." said Joculo,

"Come off it," said Anthony. "She's not going to..."

"Don't think Lucy can win!?" I snarled.

"Well," he drawled, "anything can happen. Only I don't think..."

"You don't think at all, ya big lump! Or practice, for that matter. If you'd spend half as much time training as you did whining..."

216

Anthony, Urban, and Mark rose angrily to their feet. So did Joculo and Keleron, placing themselves between the warring factions.

"Lucy's going to win first or second in the Boxing," said Joculo. "Which is more than I can say for most of us. If we place in the Javelin and in the Circus, we could actually win this thing!"

Half the team agreed. Urban's clan did not.

"The Taurans are going to get at least four, maybe six points today," said Urban. "Clovis will win the Wrestling. Then they're up to fourteen. Then Clovis wins the Circus and the Gold."

"Clovis, Clovis, Clovis!" I mocked. "I'm sick of hearing about him. He's not invincible, you know. Lucy beat him. Casey beat him."

"Have you ever seen Clovis drive a chariot?" said Urban.

"No."

"Well I have," he glowered, remembering his loss to the Mistress of the Sea. "He'll make mincemeat out of you...and Joculo for that matter," he said, sneering at his team captain. "The only one who stands a chance of beating him is Alexander."

The Javelin competition was later that afternoon. Unfortunately, Urban called this right. Clovis won easily, while Oliver took third. Four more points for the surging Taurans. The surprise again was Atlanta who took second.

But the Taurans were back in it, trailing the leaders by a mere point.

That evening, the long awaited Boxing final began. Just as Mark predicted, Obsid beat the Sagittarian in the loser's bracket, taking third and another point for the Taurans.

Now it was Lucy's turn.

Corona and Alexander were cousins and best friends. Last year Corona placed second in Boxing, but was badly mauled by Clovis in the final heat. Now that Clovis was gone, the Leos fully expected to win the event, pulling ahead of the Taurans for good.

The crowd, still not pleased with the pint-sized pummeler, clapped half-heartedly as the crier announced Lucy. Boxing fans want to watch people hit each other. Lucy hadn't even thrown a punch.

As Corona was the overwhelming favorite, the Leon red was well represented. Yet there were Taurans there as well, rooting for the tiny Aquarian. The Taurans, behind the Leos by a single point, needed Lucy to win to have any chance of catching up.

Such is the lot of the sports fan, cheering the rival he jeered just the other day...

Corona entered the ring, red fans rising in bullied applause. The senior was big and bulky with short, powerful arms. Lucy said that Dio considered this an advantage, as his strategy was designed to fool fighters who were all brawn and little brains. Corona met that profile perfectly.

Gold flags with red lions furled among the stands. Alexander was leading a pep rally, gleeful in his malice. If he was embarrassed by his loss to the Mistress of the Sea, he hid it well.

"Hit her again! Hit her again!" he cheered.

"Harder! Harder!" sang the Leon chorus.

Their warm-ups complete, the contestants stood sweating in the oppressive heat. Lucy wore grim determination. Corona sported wicked expectation.

After the fanfare of heralded introductions, the two stamped their leathered fists.

"I'm gonna hurt you," said Corona, "real bad."

Lucy snarled in reply. Prowling back to her corner, she steeled herself for battle.

The bell rang.

Corona strode purposefully to the middle of the ring. Lucy began her wary dance. The princess toyed with the Leon brute, a vixen eluding an eager hound.

"Luuuuuuucy!" sang Alexander. "Luuuuuuucy! Where are you?"

Lucy ignored him as the familiar pattern played itself out, Corona pressing her into a corner, Lucy ducking nimbly away.

But Corona had a plan. Huddling his body into a low crouch, he launched his mass upon her. Lucy leapt for the corner, but couldn't escape. The leviathan tackled her round the middle, pinning her against the post.

Dio jumped into the ring. Grabbing Corona with a single hand, he flung him viciously to the mat. The referee hounded Dio as Lucy, gasping for stolen breath, struggled to remain on her feet by tangling her arms in the ropes.

Corona peeled himself off the sweaty mat, grinning ear to ear. Ambling to the center of the ring, he raised his arms to a chorus of cheers.

The referee scolded Corona and then Dio before the bell announced the end of the round.

The scarlet hoard was on their feet, chanting with fiendish glee. "Leos! Leos! Leos! Leos! Coroooonaa!"

Lucy stumbled drunkenly to her corner before collapsing upon her three-legged stool. Dewey was there, speaking to his child in hushed, anxious tones. Dio placed something under Lucy's nose to shake the cobwebs away.

Tackling was illegal and didn't earn Corona any points. But it was clear to everyone that Corona would finish her the next round.

"Luuuuuuuuuucy! Where are you?"

Lucy fiercely shook her head, as if shaking herself back to life. Dewey, rabid with worry, demanded that Dio call off the fight. Lucy stood, pleading with her father, begging to continue. Dewey's hesitation was palpable, but, in the end, he relented to his daughter's wishes. The three conferred in restless whispers as the clamor reached a feverish howl.

"Leos! Leos! Leos! Leos! Coroooooonaa!!!"

The bell rang.

Taking a last, fleeting look at her father, Lucy slunk towards her doom.

The crowd was chanting, whistling, stomping.

Corona opened his arms wide, bending low to tackle her again.

Lucy faked right, crouching to escape.

Corona bent lower, ready to pounce.

Lucy stumbled to her knees, spinning wildly in a sick, desperate twirl. The Leos screeched in delight as Corona just missed with a wicked right cross. Beaten and beleaguered, she scampered to her feet...

"I can't watch!" shrieked Elena, digging her nails into my arms. I didn't feel a thing, terror numbing the pain.

The chanting reached a vile ferocity, unrivaled by anything I'd heard before. The wooden stands shook with violence as the eager crowd stomped and shouted.

"LEOS! LEOS! LEOS! LEOS! COROOOOOONAA!!!"

Corona paced forward. Lucy had real fear in her eyes. Her dance was rambling and sporadic, like a dying fish caught out of water. She wobbled on spindly, straw-like knees…

Corona pounced.

Quick as lightening, Lucy leapt towards him, swallowed aloft by his massive girth. Clenching her teeth, she pivoted into a punch…

Crunch!

Silence conquered the mad cacophony. The colossus teetered and tottered before toppling to the ground.

Trapped beneath the ruin, Lucy nimbly sprang away.

He hit the mat like a side of beef.

The referee, as stunned as everyone else, forgot to start the count.

Lucy pranced gazelle-like to her corner, an impish smile upon her angelic face. Dewey stole her in a rapturous hug, defying the will of the angry crowd.

A dawning of awareness spread through the Aquarians as they suddenly leapt to their feet.

Wakened by the joyful chorus, the crier took Lucy's hand. "I present to you!" he called above Leon groans, "by…a…knockout!!! Lucy, daughter of Dewey, princess of House Catagen! University Champion…of the World!"

The Aquarians rushed the ring. Joculo got there first, hoisting Lucy on his shoulders. Casey and I followed, screaming at the top of our lungs. Even Urban's friends were there, basking in the glory of the girl they ridiculed that very morn. The jubilee sallied from the Coliseum, lost in a pageant of praise and noise.

Lucy won the Boxing! The Aquarians shared the lead!

∞

"I simply can't believe it!" popped Lucy. The three of us were huddled on my bed, giddy with girlish excitement. "Can you ever remember a closer finish?"

"It's a three-way tie!" Casey agreed.

Joculo had been right. Assuming Clovis won the wrestling, the Taurans, Leos, and Aquarians would be tied at thirteen when we raced the Circus.

"It'll be down to you, Pallas," said Lucy.

"Yeah," I said with a sickly smile. As much as I'd prepared, as much as I *wanted* to race, the weight of my team's rising fortunes burdened my weary soul.

∞

I didn't watch the Wrestling next morning. Instead, Casey and I tended to my horses. The team was washed and ready, Calypso and his harem raring to go.

Phillip was beside himself with anticipation. "Today's the day, miss! The day ye show that Tauran lot!"

"I'm not worried about the Taurans," I mumbled, managing a thin smile.

The three of us spent the morning with the horses, stretching their legs on the dewy turf. It was nearly noon when Lucy ran to find us.

"You'll never believe what happened!"

"What?"

"Atlanta beat Clovis!"

"No way!" said Casey.

"You're kidding," I said.

"I'm not. Pinned him in the first few seconds. Quick as lightning. Never seen anything like it."

"How?"

"Honestly, I don't rightly know. He charged her and…she sort of flipped him over her back…used his strength against him. It happened so very fast."

"But…what does that mean?" I asked. "How did the Leo do?"

"Lost to Djincar!"

"The Geminis got four points in the wrestling?" gasped Casey. "That means we're in the lead!"

"By a single point!" said Lucy. "We have thirteen, the Taurans and Leos have twelve, and the Geminis are up to eleven."

I sat down on the cold grass, thinking. The news was startling, to say the least, but…it didn't really change a thing. I still needed to win the race in order to capture the Gold for my team.

"Oh no!" I gasped. "What time is it?"

"Noon."

"I've to go! Gotta date!"

"I hope he's tall and handsome," said Casey.

"You know she's not," I smirked.

"Oh bother," Lucy laughed. "Let's not fight about *her* today."

The matron of House Catagen insisted that she do my hair before the race. I could care less, of course. But it was important to Elena. So we scampered to the manor, happily jabbering about the surprising news.

I practically flew to my bedroom, taking the stairs two steps at a time.

Elena was patiently waiting…

…stroking a snow white cat.

"Meow."

I froze at the doorway, shocked with horror.

Piercing my soul with his evil eyes, he held his head in a regal pose. The noble display reminded me of the tall beauty.

"He's such a pretty puss," she said as she petted the spy. "Aren't you, my dear little sweetheart?"

I gave the cat a contemptuous glare. *What if I ring your furry little neck?*

But Abbey got to me first, planting me in a chair. "Dear, now, Miss. Give Abbey a moment or two wit' your lovely 'air."

"Let's ruffle the ends," said Elena, gently stroking the purring kitten.

But it was my nerves that were ruffled. *After six lonely weeks, after dozens of sleepless nights, why do you show up on this of all days?*

The shampooing. The conditioning. The combing. The brushing. I endured the feline's sinister stares for an entire grueling hour.

I need to talk to him, interrogate him, make him tell me what's going on.

But he'd never tell me! It was his signature strategy, *jealously hiding his many secrets.*

My emotions fled from hate to hope – from pride to humbling pleading. *Because I do need him! I can't do this by myself.*

I looked at him with wanting eyes, pathetically wishing for a friendly glimpse.

But if his carnivorous heart harbored even a shred of compassion, he hid it well.

He terrified me; I saw that now…far more than Alexander…even Mulciber. I'd bested the Excelsior several times, even outwitted the God.

But I've never gotten the better of Othello! Not once.

By the time my hair was finished, my nerves were taught and raw. Quivers of anxiousness shot through my limbs.

Elena rose to inspect the results. "You look absolutely ravishing!" she said as Abbey placed the silver helm on my head.

Othello, cuddled in her arms, mocked me with treacherous eyes.

"I must confess," said Elena. "I've never seen a lovelier charioteer."

Othello's face was only inches away as Elena applied a touch of blush.

"Don't race," whispered a feminine voice.

"Of course, my love," said Elena. "The loveliest in the race."

Confused at first, I realized the cat had actually spoken. Incredulous, I hissed, "Why not?"

"Danger!" he hushed, in a voice identical to my own.

I gasped, flabbergasted by his clandestine powers.

Elena pulled away, inspecting her handiwork. "Yes, darling, I absolutely agree. The silver helmet is ever so shiny, there is indeed a danger it will make your face look rather washed out." Turning brightly to the maid, she announced, "That's why you need mascara!"

I fidgeted with his warning as Abbey applied mascara. Elena hovered close, adding a few needless touches.

"Alexander!" whispered the cat.

"Oh pooh!" said Elena. "I wouldn't worry about him. He's always dressed in that gaudy red and black. Simply frightful. And that garish cape he wears!"

I was impressed by the cat's clever trick, I really was. But he wasn't going to scare me into missing the biggest event in my life. "I'm going to race."

"Of course you are," Elena airily replied.

"There's nothing anyone can say to stop me."

"Not at all," said Elena, confused. "Really, darling. What a thing to say?"

Othello answered with an angry moan.

"Look what you've done," scolded Elena. "You've upset poor little puss. Here." She brought the furry bundle right up to my face. "Kiss and make up."

Nose to nose with the malicious spy, I stared determinedly in his emerald eyes.

"Take heart of grace, dear Pallas! Give poor baby a kiss. It shall bring you good luck. I promise."

I reluctantly obeyed, kissing the furry mouth.

The cat whispered, "Wear the harness!"

"Is that what you call it, dear?" said Elena, depositing Othello on the bed before picking up the silver breastplate. "Oh, bother. Look at the time. You need to get dressed straightaway."

I made a move to grab the cat, but Abbey cornered me with lipstick.

Othello pounced away.

"There, there, my noble sister," said Elena. "Don't you look like an angel?"

But I didn't *feel* like an angel, hatred corroding my wounded heart. Far from feeling good and kind, I wanted to murder someone...

...or something.

I'm going to race! I have to! Still, it wouldn't hurt to take a safety precaution. So I took the cat's cryptic advice and wore the magic harness. Underneath my polished breastplate, no one would ever know...

Casey, Phillip, and I wordlessly rigged my snow-white team. Lucy was there as well, chatting about idle, silly things. I smiled, silently thanking her for keeping my mind off my nervousness. After re-inspecting the rigging for the hundredth time, we retired to the locker rooms.

Joculo fitted silver brassards on my arms. "Don't jump in the pack," he said. "Let the others have their wrecks." He bent down to tie the silver greaves around my legs. "And stay away from Alexander."

I attempted a weak smile, my stomach churning in a horrible morass. I'd no idea I'd be so nervous.

"Mighty fancy," he said, frowning at the feathery monstrosity. "That helmet will be the death of you."

"I'm not going to race in it!" I snapped. "Elena insists I wear it during the promenade."

"You have to wear something. Here, boy. Get a helmet for the Mistress."

"Got one already," said Phillip. "All shiny and clean."

"Thanks, Phillip," I said, managing a true smile. "You're such a prize."

Phillip beamed, tipped his hat, then left to mind the horses.

Joculo looked me square in the eyes. "Be careful out there. Don't do anything stupid."

I shrugged. "You know me…"

"Yeah," he grunted, looking coy and sheepish. Looking over his shoulder to see that no one was listening, he added, "I just wanted you to know how…how very proud I am to have you on my team." He smoothed his hands upon mine, an awkward smile upon his somewhat handsome face. "I'm honored. Really."

"Thanks," I smiled, returning the Aquarian greeting. I liked young Joculo, and his sister Janice…

…but I'll never forgive their wretched father! Never!

Elena returned to drape a floor-length royal-blue cape over my shoulders. This took ten minutes. "It has to look just right." Then, with the solemnity of crowning a heroic emperor, she placed the silver helmet over my head. Its weight was simply enormous.

"Oh, but it looks divine!" she said as she kissed my cheeks. But her practiced smile didn't mask her worry; her sapphire eyes couldn't contain her fear. "Good luck, little sister!"

"Thanks," I grimly replied.

Finally, mercifully…it was time. The anxious wait was over. I took a moment to nuzzle each Arabian before climbing into my chariot.

It was a beautiful thing, a bright blue car embossed with silver dolphins…

Ten cars and forty horses lined the starting block. A discordant chorus lauded their heroes.

Borelo and his dappled palominos were in the pole position. Next was Corona the Leo, then a Sagittarian, Oliver, and young Joculo. Alexander was on my left, looking resplendent in a chariot of red and gold, his slick, black leathers complementing his burnt, knobby hair. I was next, followed by Clovis with his magnificent chestnut thoroughbreds. Then came another Gemini with a team of paints and, finally, the other Sagittarian.

Despite his disappointing performance, Clovis could still win Gold if he won the race. In fact, the points were as close as anyone could remember. The only ones out of the medal chase were the odd Sagittarians.

I glared at Alexander with contemptuous delight. "I like what you've done with your hair."

"Just die," he maliciously replied.

"You're such a dreamer," I snarled. But his evil grin did plague me. Turning my head to avoid his gaze, I looked over at Clovis.

"Good luck," he said.

"Yeah," I offered. "You, too."

Trumpets blared their triumphant fanfare. Phillip stood ready in front of my chariot. He proudly carried the Catagen standard, a blue number three on a Sea of white. To my right was a brown flag bearing the symbol of a snake, while Alexander's groom flew a blood-red lion on a field of gold.

A single mounted knight, one of the Marshal's men, led the chariots into the cacophony. Decked in the ugly orange on brown, he carried no flag or banner, for there was no standard that brought the great Houses together as a nation. Indeed, the only identity the nobles knew was the unity of collective antagonism.

I didn't understand this. No one did. But one day…I would.

Tumultuous, ear-splitting applause greeted us as we entered the Hippodrome. The venue was filled to capacity, brown and red expanses dotted with blue, yellow, and a smattering of green.

I heard rampant calls of "Mistress of the Sea!" and "She is the Dawning!" But more often, "Aleexaaaander!" and "Clooooovis!" filled my anxious ears.

Slowly, the row of chariots circled the enormous Hippodrome. I held my head high, just like Elena taught me, the frilly feathers flowing gallantly in the Wind.

Finally, we returned to the starting line. Phillip produced a simple white helmet. I gratefully traded it for Elena's monstrosity. In a single motion, I gathered my hair in a pony tail before fitting on the helm.

"Good luck, miss," said Phillip, with the unquenchable confidence only a little boy can have.

"Thanks," I said, kissing his forehead.

Triumphantly, and with loud applause, the crier announced the names of the contestants. Staring at the narrow track, I completely tuned him out. Eight stads of tumultuous humanity, ending in a tight, treacherous turn.

Finally, after a long litany of eager introductions, it was time to begin. The white flag fell.

We were off!

Immediately, Alexander veered straight into me.

I fully expected it. I actually led my horses backwards at the start, watching with satisfaction as he collided into Clovis. Their chariots bounced off each other, Clovis cursing the malicious Leo.

Borelo took an early lead, followed closely by the Sagittarian and Oliver. Next came Corona, Clovis, and the other Sagittarian. Alexander kept his champion blacks well behind the leaders. Taking Joculo's advice, I held back too. Oddly, Corona, the second best spot at the start, immediately slowed down. He was looking towards the rear, not towards the front. Finding what he was looking for, he made a bee-line for Clovis, squeezing him into the second Sagittarian. I peeled to the right as they pinned Clovis in a jam. In a violent moment of leather and wood, Clovis's and the Sagittarian's cars disintegrated.

The Taurans screamed with apoplectic horror! The Sagittarian deliberately sacrificed himself to take Clovis out of the race, his last chance to win the University Games, squandered by an act of treachery.

Lap Two. Corona sprinted his horses forward, pulling even with Oliver on the outside. The remaining Tauran hadn't seen the accident behind him. Corona edged ever closer, pressing him against the wall. The Sagittarian in Oliver's front quarter swerved viciously in as well. Oliver, a cloud of dust in his eyes, didn't see him until it was too late.

The chariots collided, chewing angrily at each other's wheels. Timbers erupted as Oliver grinded to a screeching halt, his car in useless tatters.

Wailing and gnashing consumed the rabid Taurans. *So much expectation! So much hope for victory.*

But then I thought a more troubling thought. *What did the Leos offer the Sagittarians to treacherously foil the Good Earth?*

I raced my team round the middle of the next turn. Careful to keep the second Gemini behind me, I also stayed away from Alexander who was now in fourth. Joculo held a wary third behind Corona and Borelo, who still led.

Lap Three. Corona pulled abeam Borelo, yelling obscenities at the pretty-boy girl-chaser. Borelo pulled well behind, tepidly letting him pass. Joculo surged ahead, taking second.

I edged closer. But Alexander kept pacing me, expertly keeping me behind.

Lap Four. Borelo fell behind Alexander on his left side. Though I didn't plan on passing Alexander this early in the race, I welcomed the opportunity to put Borelo between Alexander and myself. Making a split-second decision, I took a daring stab, leaning left to move behind Borelo.

It worked! Alexander couldn't stop my sudden move and found himself outside a slowing Borelo. He cursed as I raced by the Gemini, temporarily out of reach.

Corona, having just acquired the lead, starting slowing again. With all the violent maneuvers, his team was too exhausted to keep up. Soon, the crowd was lauding a new champion, erupting in pleasure as Joculo passed the Leo.

"Aquaaaaaarius!" they shouted. "Aquarians for the Gold!" The Taurans, treacherously out of the race, were now praying for an Aquarian victory. Anything to keep the hated Leos from winning.

Lap Five. Corona slowed even further, positioning himself in front of me and to the left.

They're marking me! I thought as Alexander move behind me and to the right. Grim determination steeled my brow as Corona and Alexander communicated with hand signals.

I'm next!

Startled, I tried to keep my cool. *Joculo's still in the lead,* I thought. As the two red chariots slowed to trap me, I slowed even more, planting myself firmly in front of Alexander.

Meanwhile, Joculo's lead was growing.

As much as I want to wear the wreath, I thought, *if those idiots want to chase after me and let Joculo win Aquarian Gold, that's fine by me!*

The Leos seemed to realize their dilemma. Alexander signaled to Corona, then pointed at me. Corona nodded his head, swerving left to cover.

Corona marked me with his tall blacks, pushing me roughly towards the outside. Alexander, letting Corona fend me off, swerved neatly in front of Borelo. Though Borelo was in a good position to pass all three, he immediately pulled back.

I cursed Corona as Alexander moved ahead, my hard-won pass, spoiled by the Leos' double-teaming. Furrowing my brow, I planned my next move.

First, I had to pass Corona. Another turn was coming. I had to time it just right. As Corona turned to the left, I made a move to the right. Corona moved right to cover when I gently nudged left, swerving inside his tired team. I felt the pleasure of the crowd as Calypso charged with vigor.

"MISTRESS...OF...THE SEA!!!" rang in my ears as I led my team past the exhausted geldings. Alexander, who was still ahead of me, was catching up to Joculo.

Lap Six. Alexander mercilessly beat his magnificent blacks until they pulled slightly ahead of Joculo. I was third, working my way forward. Amid the roar of the horse's hooves, I remembered what Joculo told me before the race.

"Remember...we're one point ahead of the Leos and the Taurans. So if we finish second and third, we'll still win the Gold even if someone else wins the race."

Alexander seemed to realize this as well. He was leading by a hair, but still needed to eliminate one of the Aquarians. As I raced closer, I saw him lob something at Joculo's team.

"Watch out!" I screamed. But my shout didn't even reach my ears in the din of the rolling thunder.

A second later, a fireball erupted in front of Joculo's horses. Terrorized by the sudden blaze, his Arabians swerved recklessly to the right, careening pell-mell towards the outside wall.

"HURRRRAHHH!!!" erupted the Leos.

Scalded by the searing heat, I glimpsed back at poor Joculo. Somehow, he stopped his team before they crashed into the wall. But he was out of it now as Borelo, the second Gemini, and Corona sped ruthlessly past.

It's me against Alexander...for the wreath, and the Gold!

Alexander looked back to admire his handiwork. He paid for it dearly as I accelerated into the coming turn.

"Hiyyaah, Calypso!" I screamed. A Banshee couldn't have produced a more ear-splitting wail. The stallion responded brilliantly, aggressively swerving his harem through the narrow gap. By the time we were out of the turn, I had the lead on the inside track.

"MISTRESS...OF...THE SEA!!!" A typhoon of supporters screamed my name. Ears ringing from the dissonant cheers, I savored my narrow lead.

But Alexander refused to be beaten. Whipping his horses even harder, he pulled closer and closer.

We entered the seventh and final lap, the drumming of the thunderous hooves deafening me into a noiseless reality. Orange clay swallowed my entire horizon as I struggled to stay ahead of my nemesis.

Alexander tried squeezing me into the wall, but I urged my team forward to place my car next to his blacks. He whipped his horses over and over, dollops of blood flying from their backs.

My horses were bronze, not white; orange dust gathered on their lathered hides.

The blacks inched ever closer and closer when I felt a sudden stab of pain.

I nearly jumped out of my skin. The agony had a familiar feel. Remembering Joculo's lashings, I looked furiously behind me.

The whip thrashed again.

"Ayeeeeee!" I screamed, instinctively sticking my arm out to catch the leathered lightening. The snake wrapped savagely around my arm, biting hard upon my silver greaves. Grinding my jaw, I yanked it from his grasp.

Alexander stared blankly at his empty hands.

Without knowing it, we'd reached the next to the last turn. Leaning left with the motion of my horses, I glanced again at the Excelsior prince. He was pulling something out of his black leather jerkin.

I looked forward again, then back at Alexander. His smile was wicked as he brandished a copper ball.

My panic turned to fury. Without a second thought, I swung the whip back at Alexander. The scourge hit his hands, causing him to bobble his precious bauble. Horror screwed up his reddened face as it clattered to the floor of his chariot. Helplessly flailing his legs, he frantically kicked the dangerous device. But the copper assassin would not leave him, ricocheting recklessly around his hood.

Alexander flung to his knees, grabbing the deadly trinket…

I held my breath, mesmerized by the macabre theater played before this mass of tens of thousands. A furious explosion overwhelmed the cacophony, then…the agony of lost chances as a column of Fire erupted behind Alexander's chariot. His flaccid body was tossed against his hood; burnt, broken and bleeding.

"HUUUURRRRAAHHHHH!!!" screamed the Taurans and Aquarians.

I tasted the heat of the torrid blast as I barely escaped the holy hand grenade.

I reached the final turn two cars ahead of Alexander's blacks. A delighted grin graced my face, caked with dust and toil and clay. The din of victory rose higher and higher as I glanced back to see Alexander, then Borelo, then Joculo.

The wreath is mine! Nothing can stop me!

As my car rounded the final turn, I watched with distracted interest as my wheel broke free of its iron axel. Time stood still as it left the chariot, bouncing carelessly towards the opposite wall.

"Nooooo!" I cried for what seemed like an eternity.

But my distant voice was drowned by cheers. Everything I'd worked for, all the sacrifices I'd made, mocked me as the wheel rolled heedlessly away.

Am I not a God? Am I not the granddaughter of Poseida? In a moment of righteous fury, I used every bit of my divine power to command the wheel to return to its axel…

…but the wheel would not obey. It bounced – and bounced – and bounced away.

The cacophony of the crowd became a calm, surreal silence. I saw my mother's face, my father, the raft, the silver cube, Othello, The Commodore, the Twins, Elena, Liam…

...when, suddenly; the earsplitting resonance of sixty-thousand fans crashed over me like an avalanche. The floor of my chariot heaved violently to the right, digging an ugly scar upon the field of clay.

Calypso and his harem whinnied in anger, alarmed at the sudden stop.

Climbing over me like a ruthless tsunami, the car engulfed me, swallowing me in the crest of its violent wave.

I looked behind and saw four black horses, charging directly at me. Leaning against the char-grilled hood was Alexander's blood-stained face...mad, maniacal, and grim. "Yes!" he shouted as he swerved to run me down.

I leapt as the bright blue car, embossed with silver dolphins, came crashing down upon me.

It tumbled over and over and over again...

Chapter Sixteen

Who Mourns for House Duma?

Men ought to be indulged, or utterly destroyed...

The Prince
Niccolo Machiavelli, Italian author
circa 1500: Earth Standard

The young lord stood at the precipice of Fire, anguish riddling his Aquarian soul.

The God stood in his golden chariot, magically hovering over the fey, holy Flame. Beside him was a handsome boy, perhaps six years old. He had flowing blond hair and striking black brows. Though his face was tender with his few short years, his eyes were vicious and hungry.

The child was obviously a monster.

The only person who could make the situation worse was the young lord's brother. Cowed by the presence of the fearsome God, his younger sibling wept with fear.

Duma III laughed at the irony. The thing his mother had teased him about...it had finally come true.

His brother, Dusan, had betrayed him.

But to turn me over to the Fire God! Dusan had always been a lazy lay-about, cruel to his servants and manipulative to his peers. But to betray his womb mate to the Lord God Mulciber?

Why did Mulciber want to kill me? The Gods never interfered with mortals. *What did I do to deserve such punishment?*

But young Lord Duma knew exactly what he'd done. Once, many years ago, he'd lain with a Goddess. Whom, he didn't even know. He only knew that today, here upon the rim of Volcano, that afternoon would destroy him.

But how did Mulciber find out? I never told anyone!

But he knew the answer to this riddle as well. He'd guarded the secret all his life. But once – when the wine was flowing and he was in the company of friends – he had foolishly boasted how an Atlantian came upon a golden chariot. How wolves and doves had clung to her side, how he'd joined her on skins of deep-roaring lions.

"You know why you are here," said the fearsome God. "You know the sin you committed."

"I know it," said Duma.

"Then you know your punishment as well?"

He tore his gaze from the Fire God, fashioning it upon his treacherous brother. "I will die. Here, amongst the Flames of Volcano, while my younger brother assumes my throne."

The fierce God chuckled. Turning to the boy, he said, "You must admire his courage. Strange valor can sometimes be found, even in the heart of animals. Remember that, my son."

The divine boy did not speak, but nodded his head in answer. His eyes were piercing with vivid intent, cataloguing the details of the macabre event.

The God turned back to the condemned. "What you do not know, drone, is that your un-holy liaison produced a bastard son, a son who's been sheltered by Shiva the Destroyer."

A son?! gasped Lord Duma. His wife had given him three loving daughters, but…he'd always prayed for a son.

Duma smiled, despite his doom; straightening into a tall, proud stance. *Thank you, Poseida, for your generous bounty! Thank you for giving me a son! Bless his deeds and his many heirs. Guide him as he grows in wisdom and stature…*

The stab of pain was a mind-numbing surprise. Agony swept down his burning spine. Every fiber trembled with rage – torture flew through his limbs and face. The spasms of his heart raced and sputtered.

He welcomed the vicious, Fiery Hell…

…as his limp body collapsed and fell.

Chapter Seventeen

Final Exams

It is not the critic who counts — The credit belongs to the man who is actually in the arena; whose face is marred by the dust and sweat and blood; who, at the best, knows in the end the triumph of high achievement, and who, at the worst, if he fails, at least fails while daring greatly.

Theodore Roosevelt
American President
circa: 1900: Earth Standard

I woke a day later, my head painfully throbbing.

Lucy sat on my bed, gently stroking Othello. Lounging luxuriously in her gentle lap, he greeted me with a sarcastic scowl.

"Meow."

Startled, Lucy jumped up and grasped my hand. "Pallas, Pallas! Are you quite all right?"

I tried to lift my head, but nausea overpowered me. I settled back on my pillow.

"Can you hear me?" she said in a trembling voice, an anxious tear streaking down her cheek.

Othello seemed interested as well, his emerald eyes, wide with curiosity.

"Come to gloat?" I said to the cat. "Come to say you told me so?"

"Pallas," said Lucy, "I…"

Othello snorted with a disgusted huff, waving his tail into a marshmallow fluff.

Casey bolted through the door. "Is she all right? What did she say?"

Lucy stroked my fevered brow. "She's delirious, poor dear! Hot as an oven."

"I'll get Hebe! He wanted to know when she woke up." With that, Casey flew down the stairs.

"Pallas," pleaded Lucy. "Can you...can you hear me?"

"Yes, Lucy. I can hear you."

"My goodness!" she sighed. "You gave me such a fright!"

"Sorry," I whispered.

Othello nuzzled the princess with a purr before alighting upon the dresser. Adorning himself with an imperious Air, he peered down upon me like a pitiless judge.

"What happened?" I asked.

"I...I don't really know if I should be the one to tell you."

"The race?"

"Alexander won...the wreath and the Gold. Joculo came in third behind Borelo."

"Borelo?" I gasped. "No!"

"Forget Borelo...what about Alexander? It was just awful, watching him parade around the city, when you...when you..." But she couldn't go on.

Hebe rushed through the door, followed by Casey, Elena, and the Commodore.

I felt a sudden wave of love, of kindred spirits and shared experiences. For a single, precious moment I felt like truly belonged, as if these people were family.

But, then I remembered. *I already have a family. An impoverished father and an imprisoned mother.*

The Catagens offered me well-meaning sympathies. Their gentle words were sweet music; their touching voices, tokens of belonging.

Hurt and sad, I completely ignored them. Instead, I focused on the leering cat. His furry brow was curt and annoyed, as if I'd disappointed him.

Quite suddenly, like the bitter shrill of a winter Wind, realization cut my soul. *He knew! He knew all along!*

Hebe took my temperature. He had my drink some of this and swallow some of that. The Catagens kept saying things to cheer me up.

But my mind was glazed in a daze of sorrow.

He knew! He knew all along!

I closed my eyes and cried. I loved that cat. I saw that now. It was he who gave me a home with the Catagens. It was he who made me a mythic princess. Shepherding me past Lady Oxymid, it was he who taught me how to read. Ever since I swam out to that stupid raft, Othello was the only one I could really trust, the only one with whom I could share my deepest, darkest secrets.

Yet he betrayed me! The letter was clear.

Opening my bleary eyes, I frowned at that cat with a grimaced plea; hoping he'd give me a sign, a token, even a nod. Anything to salve my suffering soul.

But Othello wouldn't ease my burden, nor soothe my aching heart. Instead, he cast a poisonous sheen, jaded spheres of evil green.

"Don't cry," Lucy whimpered. "You're safe now."

"It'll be all right, Mistress," said the Old Man, his iron voice rusty with emotion.

I couldn't help it. The enormity of my woes completely overwhelmed me. I was broken, defeated, lost on an Ocean of cruel despair. Surrounded by a family who loved me, I felt utterly alone.

"I think we should give her some time," said Elena.

"Right," hushed the Commodore. "Come along, the lot of you."

But before Elena could leave, I wordlessly grasped her hand.

"I think I'll stay," Elena whispered.

Seeing our clasped hands, he nodded, wordlessly ushering the Twins from the room. After a minute or so, Hebe left as well.

Why I wanted Elena to stay, even I didn't know. I liked and trusted the Twins far more than the tall beauty. But in my mounting misery, in my crushing despair, I craved the affection of the complicated diva more than the easy friendship of the Twins.

Elena understood pain and loss. She knew the brutal cost of lofty goals. In a convoluted way the Twins couldn't fathom, she knew the hurt and wretchedness that bled from my soul.

She stayed for a long time, silently holding my hand.

I tried not to feel sorry for myself, *but it's so hard!* And I couldn't help feel sorry about the stupidest things. The real tragedy in my life was caused by

Lord Joculo and his misguided infatuation with a Goddess. My mother was imprisoned and suffering, and I was irreparably separated from my father. These were things worth crying about.

Instead, I mourned my loss in the Games. *If Alexander hadn't thrown that javelin at me, I could have won the wreath. If that wheel hadn't...*

"What happened to my chariot?"

Elena sighed. "Someone tampered with the axel. Replaced the bolts with rods of wax."

My eyes grew wide with disbelief.

"Joculo's surprised the wheel didn't come off sooner."

"Who?"

"No idea," she said with a frown. "Only grandfather's mad as a hornet."

"Then the Leos won the Gold." I repeated, the idea of Alexander leading a triumphant parade making me ill.

"But you won the Silver!" she said with a smile. She floated to the dresser to retrieve a silver medallion attached to a blue ribbon. "It's the best finish the Aquarians have had in ages!"

I frowned in stoic answer, finding no pleasure in Silver knowing that Gold should have been mine. *Besides...for some idiotic reason, it reminds me of that silver cube.* "So...the Taurans got the Bronze?"

"No!" Elena smiled, a genuine one this time. "The Geminis won Bronze! Borelo finished second, remember? And Atlanta won the wrestling and all."

My head fell back on my pillow. *The Taurans finished a lowly fourth place! How they must be hating that!* Still, I loathed the idea of Borelo placing second in the chariot race.

"I know what you're thinking," said Elena, "and I haven't spoken a word to the git since the night of the Ball. On my honor," she added with a precocious laugh, "I'll never forgive him for wearing that ridiculous outfit! And why should I? When I have an entire world of men to choose from?"

I laughed. It was good to laugh, no matter the reason.

Othello disappeared during one of my many naps. It was just as well. I didn't have the strength to get out of bed, much less catch the illusive spy.

But in my mournful convalescence, love congealed into bitter hatred.

He isn't a friend! He's a spiteful little monster, manipulating me all along.

∞

I stayed in bed two whole days…brooding.

I promised I'd wait till after the Games. Well, the Games were over. The decision I evaded for nearly a year could no longer be avoided.

I thought about my loving father. *How he must be missing me!* His only joy was my fawning love, his only friend, his devoted daughter.

I thought about the many-colored dress, it's impossibly smooth texture and amazing sheen. *He hid it in our hovel all those years! How on Earth did he do that?*

I thought about the garish kite, the one with my mother's face upon it.

"She's looking down on us," my father had said, *"from way up high. Just like…just like your mother's love. Though you may not always see her, Pallas, she's always watching over you. Always."*

Since my earliest childhood, I always thought of my mother's face nestled in the heavens.

Now I knew why.

"Only, like the string, you must hold on tight," Daddy told me. *"Hold on tight and never let go. Never let go of your mother's love."*

"It's time," I told myself. "It's time to find my mother."

But the more I thought about my mother, the more I thought about that horrible cat. For if he really did live with Mulciber, and Mulciber captured my mother…

…then Othello must know my mother!

Again, I felt betrayed. Ever since I climbed into that raft, through all my trials and tribulations…

…Othello knew my mother!

I kept reliving that night aboard *Yorktown*, how he tricked me into revealing my deepest, most shameful secrets. I remembered how I cried and cried.

He knew my father was innocent! He knew my mother was alive! And yet, he told me nothing! Nothing to ease my pain.

∞

The next day, Elena returned from school with startling news. "The Marshal's men discovered who sabotaged your chariot. It was Eunice! Can you believe it?"

I couldn't believe it. I knew Eunice didn't like me, but didn't think she'd resort to murder.

"One of House Uncial's soldiers confessed to the whole thing. It seems Eunice IV, you know, the one in our class…"

"I know."

"…ordered him to do it. Jealous, I shouldn't wonder. Mad, though, don't you think?"

"What's Eunice saying?"

"She denies it, of course, the two-faced brat."

"She denies it?"

"There'll be a trial, of course. Only Lady Miser wants it short and secret. Can't let the slaves find out," she winced. "It's rather bad policy."

"Yeah," I agreed, wondering what she meant.

"And to think, I've been pretending to be nice to her all these years!"

"Yeah."

"Pallas, love," she said, contorting her radiance into a frightened frown. "There's something else I must tell you."

"What?" I said, sitting up in my bed.

"This is going to be difficult, so I pray you'll steel your courage."

"What is it?"

"We've word that someone is trying to kidnap you."

A sudden shudder tingled down my spine. "What makes you think that?"

Elena sighed. "Captain Tiberius heard it. From the Continent, of all places."

"The Continent?" I said. "How do they even know about me?"

"I told you, darling, we haven't the foggiest idea. But they *do* know about you. Tiberius learned that someone wants to kidnap you and bring you back to the Continent."

"Why?"

"Never mind *why*. The crucial point is *when*. The, uh…event…is to take place during the Consecration of the Golden Stag."

"During the Consecration," I repeated. *That's what Uncial had said, the night I listened on the Radio!*

"Grandfather's decided we shall return to the Isle an hour after sunset. The Consecration begins at midnight, so we can sail away under the cover of darkness before anybody notices."

"Won't that look odd?"

"Of course it will. Uncial will be furious. Excelsior and Gauntle will be worse. We'll miss our exams, the Consecration, and the final session of the *Zoo*. But *our* priority is *your* safety."

I huddled my knees, sick with guilt. "I have to tell *you* something."

"What?" frowned Elena, wary of yet another unwelcome surprise.

I quickly recounted what I heard on the Radio and the message in Uncial's office.

"And you didn't tell me?" she scolded. "Or Grandfather, for that matter?"

"I didn't want to worry you…and I wanted to compete in the Games."

"You were nearly killed in the Games!"

"But they said they'd wait till after the Consecration. I thought I'd be safe."

"You thought?!" she cried. "When have you ever *thought* about anything?"

It was uncanny how she resembled Othello. For though the fury in the sapphire didn't rival the wickedness of the emerald, there was just as much rage in those blazing orbs.

"But the Twins…"

"The Twins?!" she snarled. She closed her eyes and drew her breath, somehow regaining her composure. Gathering her hands in mine, she knelt at the side of my bed. "Pallas. Sister. You need to *tell* me these things. Please…trust me enough to share the truth."

But that's the problem! I can't! The cat had planned his lies so well, the truth would literally destroy me. *And which truth do I tell her? That I'm a Goddess, a slave, or a sacrilegious Witch?*

Elena, of course, went straight to the Old Man. How he received the news that Uncial, his most trusted ally, was in league with his enemies, I never knew. But he visibly stiffened whenever the lady's name was used.

Armed with this new knowledge, it was confirmed that we'd escape the evening of the Hunt. The trick was to pretend that everything was normal until the moment we actually took flight. As two different sources said the kidnapping would occur during the Consecration of the Golden Stag, the safest course was to go through the motions of enjoying the Hunt and leaving early that evening. House Catagen would slip away aboard *Yorktown* after dusk, with *Hornet* and *Enterprise* in close support.

I woke early the very next morn, resigned to go back to school. Breakfast was a sullen affair, the worries of House Catagen weighing heavily on the family. The Twins tried to liven the mood by bragging about the Isle, about the snow that would greet us when we reached her chilly shores.

I longed for the pleasantly mild winters of Kelly Tree…

"Commodore," I said when the glum conversation sagged to another depressing halt, "did you ever find out anything about those – I don't even know what to call them – balls of Fire Alexander used?"

The Old Man huffed with deep frown. "Nuthin' in the rule book 'bout magic, mi' lass. Nuthin' at all."

"It's a wonder Poseida allowed it!" said Casey. "Right in the middle of the Games!"

The Old Man furrowed his brow. "Hush, child. It's not for mortals to question the Gods."

Dewey pursed his lips, as if ready to add something. But he kept his stoic silence. Silverware clattered as we wordlessly ate.

Casey broke the sad stillness. "What I want to know, Pallas, is how you jumped clear of the chariot? I mean to say, you flew through the Air like a javelin, must have gone thirty feet!"

"Casey," scolded Elena.

Dewey cast a reproachful frown.

I hesitated, considering my answer. *I know very well how I escaped; it was the magic harness Othello made me wear.* But I couldn't tell my sister that. Nor could I tell her that my cat insisted I wear it...or even why.

Yet why did he give me that cryptic warning? Did he know about the wheel? As usual, I was at a complete loss to explain his many mysteries.

Instead, I catalogued it in his list of good deeds...

...weighing them against his mountain of crimes.

"Just lucky, I guess."

Scarlet banners adorned University, another Gold Medal for the triumphant Leos. Since they'd won the last five University Games and the last Menagerie Games as well, they were heavily favored to win this summer's Menagerie Games. If they did, they'd complete a coveted Dynasty – an Element that won every Game in a four year cycle. A Dynasty had only been won once before, long ago by the tenacious Taurans.

The Sagittarians had left for their House of Wonders on the lonely island of Solüt, their duplicity gaining them a place in infamy. The Taurans grumbled about their vile treachery, unsuccessfully salving their wounded pride. Even Oliver walked around in a permanent bad mood, snapping at everyone...except for me.

Surprisingly, the Tauran who took it best was Clovis. The stoic prince shook the whole thing off, promising to redeem himself by killing the Golden Stag. For whoever killed the Stag would have the unrivaled honor of wearing its pelt during the opening ceremony of the Menagerie Games.

The Hunt was now the topic at school. This year, the sacrificial animal would be provided by Vulcana, the Fire Goddess.

"They say it brings good luck," Casey said. "Eighteen out of twenty-five times the team that killed the Stag won the Games."

"And the Hunt is so much fun," said Lucy. "At least, that's what everyone says." Her delightful eagerness was the only source of joy in the otherwise beleaguered family.

I could care less about the stupid hunt. I needed to escape to Kelly Tree, not chase a deer through some God-forsaken forest.

I know Daddy told me not to return. I know he told me to stay safe. But homesickness pulled at my heartstrings, tempting me against his will.

Othello warned me as well. *But he's such a liar. Why should I listen to him?*

But how? The Quartz Mountains were quite impassable. Nor could I follow the circuitous shore. There were no roads to Kelly Tree; the only way to get there was by boat.

The obvious solution was to leave with House Joculo. *Maybe I could sneak aboard his ship?* But ships were too small to stow away and not get caught.

I could tell the Twins. They'd help me escape. But then they'd face the wrath of the Commodore. I didn't dream of telling Elena, as I knew where her loyalties lay. I could ask the Old Man directly. *But he'd never let me leave.*

The next few days were tense and secretive. Only the immediate family knew our clandestine plans. In the meantime, security was doubled; Lord Catagen's Marines in a continuous heightened state of alert.

As for me, my every moment was spent on thinking of a way back home. *And I've got to do it quickly, before the Catagens sail for the Isle.*

But the Goddess in hiding was completely bereft of divine revelations. Dollops of time wasted away, forcing dangerous ideas into my troubled head.

Such was my state when I entered my very last class. Professor Archimedes was touching on a new subject, Aerodynamics.

"Much like a fish swimming through the Water," he said as he held up a falcon, "the wings of a bird propel it through the Air."

So what?! I need a way back home.

Perhaps I should tell Elena? Perhaps I should burden the Twins? Anything to get me away from here; anything to return me to my father.

"It is Bernoulli's principle that allows an airfoil to achieve lift. By splitting the Air, we increase the velocity of Air over the wing, which corresponds to a decrease in pressure."

Maybe I could ride away on Calypso? But then I'd have to travel past Turner Hill and Misty Dale. I was sure to be captured, by the Commodore...*or someone much worse!*

"A unique animal that can provide us with a better example is the penguin," he said, pointing to a tiny penguin swimming in an enormous glass aquarium. "The penguin cannot fly. Yet using its wings, it moves through the Water, much like a bird flies through the Sky."

I could care less. *Isn't this supposed to be a class about Aero-whatsit? Why is he talking about a swimming bird?*

"The penguin's wings are essentially fins. Fish move through the Water by flexing their fins, arriving with the principle stated by Bernoulli...though I rather doubt a fish would know to call it that," he chuckled, amused by his stupid joke.

He chuckled alone. The class was restless and bored, eager for the end of term.

"Another phenomenon is the soaring of an eagle. Remember that heat makes things float, light things, creatures with aerodynamic wings."

Maybe I could sneak over the walls. Maybe I could pretend I'm a sailor. Maybe I could...

I hurried from class an hour later, obsessed with escaping my gilded cage. Unexpectedly, I ran into Genevieve.

"Pallas!" she said, kissing both my cheeks. "Fancy a visit after school?"

"OK."

We had tea in the glass-covered atrium. It was one of my favorite places, as the sunlight warmed the room to near-tropical proportions. Being from the north, I was sick of the cold. The idea of wintering on the Isle made me shiver.

We talked about the weather, the Hunt for the Golden Stag, and our many returns. Genevieve would travel to Quartz by carriage. Lord Gauntle didn't like boats. She planned to accompany Oliver when he returned to the Isle, and wouldn't it be nice to spend some time together in Castle Mare?

I hungrily stared in the lithe girl's eyes.

"What's wrong, dear Pallas? You seem...distracted."

She'd be perfect! I thought. *And she wouldn't have to lie because the Commodore would never think to ask her.*

"I need your help," I blurted. "To escape…back home. Back…where I belong."

As soon as the words left my mouth, I knew I'd been stupid. *What are you trying to do, scare her out of her wits?*

But the tiny Tauran didn't bat an eye. "Of course, love. What do you need me to do?"

Her quiet acceptance surprised me. "Don't you want to know, I mean…aren't you going to ask?"

"Would you like me to?"

"Well…no, only…"

"Pallas, love. I know you don't belong in the world of men. I've always known."

"You have?"

"Of course. You're blood is not of a nobleman. It can only be divine. You're the daughter of a God, a God who must have abandoned you."

"She didn't abandon me!" I foolishly denied.

"Sorry," she apologized. "But…this God didn't raise you. Of that, I'm quite certain. You grew up among slaves…in a fishing village, up north."

I was stunned by the accuracy of her guess. "What makes you think that?"

"Isn't it obvious, dear? You walk and talk like a fisherman, yet you have the undaunted courage of an epic hero."

I frowned.

"No offense. But your mannerisms are that of a pauper, not a princess."

"How did you know I came from the north?"

"You made your appearance in Capro Bay, didn't you? I'd guess you were raised in Misty Dale or Acadia, perhaps even Kelly Tree."

I tried to make my face inscrutable, but it was no good.

"Don't worry, love," said Genevieve, "your secret's safe with me."

I marveled at the tiny Tauran. I didn't think to lie. *That would be stupid!* Instead, I sought for refuge in my clever, loyal friend.

Genevieve was amazingly cool as I divulged my desperate plan. But then she pointed out several problems, things I'd never considered.

"You're a celebrity now. Even if you escaped outside the walls, you'd be recognized at once. You'd never make it past Turner Hill. No, no, I have a better idea. Come to our stables and I'll put you in a light wooden box. Then I'll have the box delivered to a private cabin on a merchant ship bound for Kelly Tree. Once you're in your cabin, you can pop out and wait to you arrive. I can provide you with tickets, money, and a clever disguise. You'll need clothes, baggage, a false identity…"

Genevieve's knowledge of clandestine operations was impressive. I listened with rapt attention, realizing my own disjointed plan would have gotten me caught for sure. We decided to do it the morning of the Hunt. Everything was set…

"Only, Genny, please don't tell Oliver."

"Why not?" she demanded, hesitant for the very first time.

"You know how loyal he is to the Old Man. If he knows what we're doing, he'll feel duty-bound to tell him."

Genevieve gave me a discerning look. "We have eyes like twins, my brother and I. We never keep secrets from each other. Never."

"But you can't," I begged. "Don't you see? He'd be miserable if he knew."

We argued like this for half an hour. But in the end, Genevieve agreed.

"Only I want you to think about what you're doing. Lord Catagen will keep you safe. If you go into the world alone…"

But I was determined. Nothing could sway me from my chosen path.

π

Leaving? thought the shrewd little spy. *No…I really don't think so.*

Chapter Eighteen

The Hunt

*Very few things happen at the right time, and the rest do not happen at all.
The conscientious historian will correct these defects.*

The Histories of Herodotus
Herodotus, Greek historian
circa 450BC: Earth Standard

I could care less about the stupid stag, my escape occupying my every thought. But the Twins were delighted about the coming adventure.

"It shall be ever so exciting," said Lucy.

"We'll really take the Wind out of those camp-Fire fools if we get the pelt!" said Casey.

"And Uncial when we steal to the Isle!" said Lucy.

Normally, the Hunt for the Golden Stag was like a carnival, an opportunity for the great Houses to bond together in a last bit of fun. But given the recent disasters, the Commodore was anxious and wary.

"We'll stay towards the rear," he told the Twins, "and not put ourselves in the thick of things. Liam will be with us as well, as an added precaution. You'll stay close to our Marines and obey their every order."

"But Grandfather!" said Casey.

"We want to kill the Golden Stag!"

"Swear it, the lot of you, or ye shan't go at all."

"Oh, bother," Lucy complained.

They begged me, of course, to come as well. But I forcefully declined, pretending to be ill. Covered in shawls, I soaked up the eagerness of the chatting Twins, imprinting memories that would never fade away.

After dinner, the Catagens got ready to go to bed. A lonely tear streaked down my face.

"Don't cry, Pallas, dear," said Lucy. "Everything will be all right."

"I know," I whispered. Then I gazed at the ancient mariner.

"Not to worry, Mistress. We shall get you safely to the Isle. Triton's Waves, I swear it."

Neither the slave nor the Goddess knew what to say. I bit my lip and hugged the man, frail in his iron embrace.

My last night as a princess was blissful and sad. The Twins camped out on my bed, chatting happily about our summer upon the Isle. Things were simple then, uncomplicated. I knew my enemies, and I knew my friends. The cat was a friend...

No! I rued. *Don't think about him!*

Instead, I cherished my time with the Twins, knowing I'd never see them again.

∞

I woke early next morning and quietly dressed. I only packed a few essentials, warm clothes and my father's letter. I wore the harness under my garments, regretting the theft of the other RADIO.

I wanted to peek in on Elena, but didn't dare. *What if she corrals me into shopping, or another three-hour bath?* Besides, I knew I didn't have the strength to face the tall beauty.

I stopped by the stables to see Calypso. Gazing into his large, liquid eyes was wonderfully melancholy and sad. What I wouldn't give to take my magnificent friend! *Only I don't think you'd fit in a box!* Instead, I kissed his whiskery nose, whispering a cheerless farewell.

Hiding in a shed until the hunting party was away, I disguised myself with a wig and a fake scar, both provided by Genevieve. Anyone seeing me now would remember the jet-black hair and jagged wound instead of my long blond strands. At the appointed hour, I snuck into Gauntle's stables. Genevieve was waiting...

...as was that horrible cat.

Stunned, I stared at the prowling monster. *Come to haunt me, you wicked thing?*

Yet something wasn't right. My nemesis was pacing, worried and afraid. His churlish calm was completely gone, his sneer replaced with a nervous frown.

"Isn't this your cat, Pallas, love?" asked Genevieve.

"Not exactly," I huffed. "You might as well say I'm *his* human."

"If…you…say so, dear," she said, confused. "Do you want him in the box, then?"

I peered inside. The crate was layered with thick, orange material. There was a crowbar, a satchel of food, skins of water, a purse of money…

"Sorry about that dreadful orange. Mother received a bolt of it as a gift from Lord Rance. She absolutely hates it, so I know it won't be missed. Besides," she smiled, "it reminds me of the Golden Egg you drove into Capro Bay."

I wasn't listening, focused on those evil eyes.

"I tried to make it as comfortable as I could. I'll nail the top on very lightly, and you can use this crowbar to…"

"I know you're angry," said a tinny voice. "But there's something you must know."

"Love," said Genevieve, confused again. "I'm not angry. Why…?"

But I was through playing his stupid little game. *If you're going to talk in front of my friend, so am I!* "You've got a lot of nerve!"

"Pallas?" said Genevieve, hurt. "I don't understand."

"Shut up!" ordered Othello. There was no camouflage in his rapt little voice; rather, fear and nervous alarm. "The Hunt is a trap! The Marshal's men are in the forest. They've orders to kill you, Uncial, and the Commodore."

Genevieve clamped her hands over her mouth, silencing a startled scream. Evidently, the idea of a talking cat arguing with a bastard Goddess was more than she could handle.

I turned to her and scowled. "Cute, eh? A gift from the Gods…*if* you can call him that."

"I'm not a gift from anyone, you brainless cub!" hissed Othello. "Listen, I'm not kidding. You must come with me this very instant. There's a ship that will transport us to the Continent."

"I'm not going to fall for that, you filthy little liar!"

"I have never lied to you," he said. "Well...not really...not about anything important. Not unless I absolutely had to."

"You're lying right now! Why would the Marshal kill the Chancellor? Everyone knows they're best friends."

"Please!" he viciously replied, wiggling his whiskers to mock me. "What do you know of such things?"

"Enough to know that Jingo would never betray the Lady Uncial."

He waved his tail with mounting dislike. "Ah! But that was before Jingo saw Uncial commit sacrilege...when you foolishly read that note in front of the Chancellor!"

"Read!" whispered Genevieve, horror marring her pretty face.

I sighed. The princess couldn't know its meaning, only that it must be a truly deplorable word to harvest such treachery.

"We planned to collect you at the Consecration," said Othello.

"You mean kidnap," I accused.

"But there was a...miscalculation. Something we didn't account for. And if we don't escape this very instant you'll be captured...and everything I've worked for shall be for naught!"

The direness of his warning should have frightened me. But I was too angry to think. Instead, I clenched my jaw and shrieked, "You know my Mother!"

Othello stopped his pacing, surprised. He thought for a moment as if to fabricate another lie. Yet he seemed to realize that another lie, however clever, was *not* what was needed.

"Yes...I do."

"Why didn't you tell me?"

"I wasn't sure. I *had* to be sure."

"Sure about what?"

"You have no idea how difficult it was for me," he complained. "My only clue was the color of your eyes."

"What about my eyes?"

"Drones don't have gray eyes. It's a very recessive trait. They haven't worked themselves into the genetic pattern."

"Stop talking rubbish! You've been spying on me all along."

"Back to that, are we…you ungrateful pest? Yes, I've been spying on you! In order to keep you alive!"

"That's a lie!" Lunging forward, I reached out to ring his neck.

But Othello was quicker, springing onto a crate. In the brief scramble, something clattered to the floor. It was the tiny microphone from the stolen RADIO.

Beep!

"Uh!" I gasped, a wave of awareness flittering up my spine. If my soul had shared its most cherished secret, my mind would have known this truth long ago. But as distracted as I was, frenzied by the life of a mythic princess, I needed this token to finally understand.

I grasped the cube around my neck, remembering the night it made its magic sound. Unbidden, the six jeweled columns popped into my mind.

Water is opposite Fire. Air is opposite Earth. But what is opposite Life? The obvious answer was Death, but I knew that wasn't right.

I twirled the tiny charm, willing it to reveal its many secrets. A black column was hiding in the silver cube. Could it be the symbol of a sixth Pentathanon God?

Suddenly, frightfully, I finally understood. *The black column…the sixth column…it's a totem of those who read!*

"That's it!" I said, excited. "You've been spying on me all along…because…because my mother is part of this sixth column!"

Othello looked me square in the eyes. "No," he whispered, just above a purr, "I took protected you because your mother *is* the Sixth Column."

Placing a hand over my heart, I retreated a horrified step.

The cat spoke again, with a quiet veneration I would never have believed from the demonic beast. "Ever since our leader, your mother, was captured by Mulciber, we've been tirelessly working to free her. When I discovered you…"

"…you realized I was her daughter."

"Yes," he answered, as if grudgingly impressed. "I took you in. I had to. You're the flesh and blood of my creator."

"She taught you how to read!" I shouted, gifted with yet another revelation. "She taught Daddy, and Uncial, and Joculo, and…"

"Shh!" he hissed. "Of course she did."

"Huh!" I gasped. "That's why you taught me."

He closed his emerald eyes and whispered. "That's why I taught you."

His humility surprised me, causing me to pause. For a moment, we shared an extraordinary bond...

But then I remembered my pain. "Where is she?" I demanded. "Where is my mother?"

"I don't know," he said, much too shrill for my frazzled nerves.

It was a mistake. For once, he miscalculated the savagery of my teenage emotions. A malicious mania completely overwhelmed me, such as I'd never ever known before. I seized the iron crowbar and swung it upon the cat.

He catapulted into the rafters with a frightened screech. I obliterated the crate he was standing on...and then another, and then another, wielding the crowbar like a two-handed axe.

Hissing with anger, he clawed up a post. "Stupid child! Ignorant drone! And you call yourself..."

"I don't care! I don't care! I don't care what you say!" I chopped the post as if felling a tree, ripping out a gash of wood. "I hate you! I hate you! I hate you, I do!'"

"Hate me, love me; it's all the same to me! Only do as I say, or you'll be utterly destroyed!"

But my maddened frenzy could not be contained as I tore and mutilated the tortured wood. For, in my mind, the wooden pillar was the Black Column...the wicked Sixth Column. "I hate you! I hate you! I hate you..."

"Pallas," whispered a loving voice.

I jumped at the hand that graced my shoulder, turning to strike a killing blow.

It was Genevieve, her face as white as a ghost.

I raised my club with reckless fury, letting out a guttural growl.

But she firmly held her ground. "What if he's telling the truth? What if there *is* a trap?"

My mind was wild and cagey. My spirit, a tempest I could not tame. "You're going to take his side over mine!?!"

"No, love," she soothed...though she, herself, was trembling. "But...remember what I told you...the plot of the Leos and the Taurans? What if *this* is it?"

253

"But Uncial and Gauntle were going to kidnap me…at the Consecration of the Golden Stag."

"Uncial is part of the Sixth Column," hissed Othello. "She isn't working with Gauntle."

"But Eunice, her niece, tried to kill me in the Circus."

"What if Eunice was just a rogue act of jealousy?" said Genevieve.

"But what about the Consecration? That's when it's supposed to happen."

Genevieve nervously wrung her hands, fretting through the logic I could not master. "I don't know anything about the Consecration. But if Excelsior and my father are working against the Aquarians, the Hunt would be a perfect way to kill them…make it look like an accident. The Chancellor and the Commodore…out in the open…in one fell swoop."

"But what about Uncial? That letter *proves* she was trying to kidnap me."

"The letter was from the Sixth Column!" rasped the cat. "Kassan ordered Uncial to bring you to the Continent. Uncial has nothing to do with Gauntle and Excelsior."

I glanced at the box, its orange blankets reminding me of the wretched raft. More than anything I wanted to climb into that box, hide from all my problems, and simply go home.

My chance might never come again!

But Casey and Lucy were walking into a trap. So was the Old Man. *How can I run away? Burden them with the weight of my many transgressions?*

"I'll ride to the Hunt," I decided. "Warn the Catagens before it's too late."

"You will not!" said the cat. "You're coming with me!"

"Oh, no, Pallas," gasped Genevieve. "It's far too dangerous. Surely we can find someone…"

"Who? Everyone who can ride faster than me is already at the Hunt. We can scurry around looking for help, but that could take forever."

"Shut up!" hissed the cat. "Stop talking nonsense! You're life is far more important than those moronic sailors. Even Uncial's, for that matter."

"Because of my mother," I accused. "*She's* the reason you've kept me alive!"

"Yes, yes, yes! Why else would I put up with your lunacy?"

Clutching the crowbar like a deadly mace, I fought the desire to murder him…

…but anger turned to longing pain, as my soul lay naked beneath his pitiless gaze.

"Where is she?" I pleaded. "Where is my Mother?"

"I'll tell you when we get on the ship."

"Please," I whimpered, falling to my knees. "Tell me now."

"No."

I sobbed, bowing my head to cry. Then, with a gasp of rage, I hurled the crowbar into the box. It stuck, upright, in the orange wooden slats…

…just like the arrows that pin-cushioned the raft.

"Pallas," said Genevieve, "I…"

"I'm going," I brusquely announced, brushing away my tears. "Send the Commodore's Marines and the Old Guard if you can find them. Tell Elena; she'll know what to do."

"Yes, yes. I will," she hushed.

"Stop!" ordered Othello. "You don't know what's out there. There's a monster!"

"Really?!" I spat, mounting a thoroughbred before dashing away.

I lost the scar and wig before reaching the Catagen stables. Phillip appeared as I leapt from the chestnut mare.

"Lord Catagen is in danger! The Marshal's men are after him!"

"What?" said the startled boy.

"At the Hunt! I'm riding off to warn him! Tell Mister Rees. Have him send the Marines!"

"Yes, miss, but…"

"Just do it!" I said as I mounted Calypso, galloping away on bareback.

π

Elena sat in bed, thinking.

255

Tonight's clandestine gambit plagued her, as did the political catastrophes that would follow. Instead of being the center of attention of the grandest, most festive party of the year, she and the whole of House Catagen would steal away like a band of thieves.

Another disaster for House Catagen.

It wasn't the danger that annoyed her. Catagens were courageous, fearless, and true. The duty of protecting her adopted sister was nothing, nothing she wouldn't do for Lucy or Casey. The Goddess was family. Grandfather said so. No peril, warranted or not, could cower her into anything less than undying loyalty.

But misgivings grated her gifted mind. Doubt haunted her heroic thoughts.

The Goddess lost the race, not won it. She wasn't divinely beautiful; she wasn't omnipotent. Far from being omniscient, she was grossly naïve.

What if there's been a mistake?

She hated herself for thinking these thoughts, but she simply couldn't help it. She was too keen, too practical *not* to think.

But that wasn't the worst of it. For Elena knew a horrible secret, a monstrous mystery, both proud...and profane.

Her father was always a pillar of strength; a solemn pool of boundless affection. Even during her stormiest days, the years that followed the loss of her mother, Dewey was always warm and kind; quiet, wise and empathetic.

But once, when the wine was flowing and he was alone, a little girl, no older than six, had wanted a new pony. Staying up past bedtime during a huge House party, she stole into his office during the jovial night.

Plotting to catch him in a generous mood, she found her father busy at his desk. Surrounded by rolls of scattered parchment, he passionately scratched on the creamy white.

The child peeked over her father's shoulders. She expected rows of countless numbers, or perhaps a map of one of his journeys. Instead, strange symbols littered the page.

The child let out a girlish giggle, a delightful melody that never failed to please. "Father!" she laughed. "Why are you drawing all those funny pictures?"

Slowly, deliberately, he turned his head. His solemn gaze was bleary and doleful.

The little girl paused. His breath was heavy with wine. His eyes were shorn and red. "Father," she cooed. "Aren't you well?"

He poured out a sorrowful smile.

The wine is definitely an advantage! she thought, reading the tenderness written on his face. *With any luck…I'll get a new saddle along with that pony!* Looking at the parchment, she fondly said, "These drawings are ever so interesting. Won't you tell your dear daughter what they mean?"

"It's a poem," he whispered. "A sonnet, of sorts."

The little girl blushed. She, herself, would never stop pining over her mother. But Father was too handsome, too eligible to stay a widower. Besides, she adored gossip, especially about romances. "Do be kind, noble Sire, and tell your daughter who this lady is!"

His smile softened to a crinkled grimace. "Your mother, of course."

The child donned a cherubic pout. "You are ever so chivalrous, my dutiful lord!" Indeed, she adored the man who was her father. "But really! My beloved mother, may she rest in peace, is happy with the hallowed Gods. You must steel your courage and gird your heart."

"I love her," he mewled through shining eyes. "I'll never stop loving her…"

"I loved her as well, loyal Father. Those who knew her could not *help* but love her."

He lovingly stroked her silver hair. "You're so alike," he said to the child. "She would be…*should* be…ever so proud."

"I'm sure she is. When she's looking down at us from heaven."

He barked a contemptuous laugh. His eyes were suddenly sour.

This surprised the child. Scorn was an emotion he never allowed himself. Guarded, she said, "You jest with me, Sire. Do be kind and tell me plainly."

That's when he told her his terrible secret, amongst the stupor of sorrow and wine. The wonderful, odious, tremulous secret…that wrecked her world and bolstered her pride.

Elena sat in bed, thinking.

Am I the only one who sees it? Or…has my own, selfish jealousy brought me to this unholy place?

A knock at the door summoned her to the present. "Enter," she said.

Abbey bustled through the door. "Please it to pardon me, miss. But the Gauntle princess, Miss Genevieve, she wants to speak to you, urgent like. And the stable boy, Phillip's his name, he's as bothersome as a cat to do the same."

The fluffy white cat vaulted onto her bed. His paws were oddly muddy, his fur strangely ruffled. A look of urgency was splayed upon his face.

Elena swore. *What has she done this time?!*

She immediately rose from her bed. Wrapping a shawl around her shoulders, she hurried down the marble stairs.

The conversations were short and frantic. Elena needed very few words to recognize her own mortal peril. Coming to an instant decision, she ordered the few remaining Marines to saddle their horses.

"Where shall we go?" demanded Lieutenant Rees, the most senior officer left at the house.

"The Hunt, of course," said Elena. "We *must* save our Mistress."

"But Princess," he said. "My orders are to protect you."

"The Mistress is your only priority," she ordered. "We must find her, rescue her, or die trying. Is that clear?"

π

I rode north, escaping the familiar walls that cocooned me these past few months. The Water Quarter guards tried to stop me, but Calypso rushed easily past them. Some of them followed on horses. That was fine with me.

The more Aquarians, the better.

Calypso soon outpaced them, leaving them trailing his frothy wake. Aquarian cavalry quickly followed. These too fell behind.

Greenstone became less populated the further inland I went. The city streets morphed into middle class neighborhoods before growing into wealthy estates. People recognized me everywhere. Many of them pointed and stared.

Entering the fertile countryside, I thought about slowing to let the soldiers catch up. But the fear of arriving too late kept me speeding ahead. Instead, I rode my stallion hard, pressing him to the end of his endurance.

He's trained to pull a chariot eighteen miles. He'd covered twice that distance already. Yet his pace never wavered, like a giant, four-legged metronome.

An hour later, I heard a merry horn. Calypso answered by racing across a meadow and plunging into the forest.

"That's the one!" cried a hiding horseman. He wore the ugly orange on brown.

"Get her!" called another, spurring his steed to the chase.

The Marshal's men! I spurred Calypso into a desperate race.

My steed was spent; the Marshal's horses, fresh and strong. I looked back, shocked by how close they were. One of them brandished a sword, swinging it at my head. I ducked with alarm, digging my heels into the Arabian's flanks.

Calypso responded with a daring bolt of speed. For a few, fleeting strides he outpaced them.

But it was no use. Again, the horsemen closed the distance, raising their swords to strike...

...when we came upon a girl, alone in a clearing.

It was Atlanta.

"Help me!"

Without a moment's hesitation, the huntress raised her bow and shot two arrows straight at me!

The Geminis are after me too!?! I gasped.

Missed!!! I wheezed as they whistled by my ear. Still, hopelessness overwhelmed me. Atlanta wouldn't miss again.

But the arrows were not meant for me. A pair of grunts and heavy falls told me my pursuers were dead. Halting my huffing charger, I paused to thank my friend.

"Nice shot," I panted. "Why are you all alone?"

Atlanta frowned. "I was put on the far right flank. No one wants to hunt with a girl." Surveying her deed with a quizzical stare, she said, "The Marshal's men?"

"Yeah! They're here to kill the Chancellor!"

For once, the huntress looked horrified. "The lady is in that direction," she pointed. "There, near the center."

"Listen, thanks for saving my life." I said, deciding there wasn't another person alive I'd rather hunt with than Atlanta.

Anguish erased her stoic face. "I know you are grateful. Be gone!"

"Uh, yeah," I said, perpetually puzzled by her strange reactions.

"Hurry!" she shouted. "Save the Chancellor!" Then she slapped the stallion's rump.

Calypso was off, charging in the direction Atlanta pointed. I marveled at his machine-like pace; worried how much more he could take.

He'd run himself to death if I asked him to.

I heard Aquarian horns and bore left to find them. "Just a little bit farther," I told Calypso, stroking his hot, slick back.

But I didn't find Uncial or Catagen…but Lord Joculo. I cursed my bad luck as I charged upon the bear. *At least he's an Aquarian! At least he's on a horse.*

"My Lord," I rasped, "where's Uncial? Where's the Commodore?"

"Mistress," he said, looking uncomfortably at Calypso's heaving chest. "You're horse is spent. You ride him too hard."

"Where's the Commodore!?" I demanded, frantic at his delay.

Joculo heard the desperation in my voice and answered. "Lady Uncial's off to my left. The Commodore's that way, to the right. We're in a huge semicircle, in order to trap…"

"Fly, my Lord, fly!" I shouted. "The Marshal's men are trying to kill the Chancellor!"

"Are you sure?"

"Seen them with my own eyes. There're two dead," I pointed behind me, "half a mile or so."

"My word. Ride with me, Mistress, and we'll warn the Chancellor."

"No!" I cried, turning my exhausted steed around. "I've got to find the Commodore!" With nothing but a few seconds respite, I urged Calypso into a galloping sprint.

I followed the path my sovereign showed me, cursing every fleeting moment. *What if I'm too late? What if I don't make it in time?*

Calypso charged along a swollen brook that led into a willowy bog. Then, for the very first time, he slowed his pace, pinning his ears in the face of danger…

The willows erupted in heat and hair!

Swift came a boar, as big as a house, crashing through the hapless trees. The juggernaut crushed a flurry of men, violently trampling the tortured wood. The monster engulfed my entire horizon…

I froze in terror. Pandemonium filled my ears. For the second time in a week, my entire life flashed before me.

But Calypso wasn't ready to die. With a last bit of energy, he sprinted past the golden leviathan, saving me from a grisly end.

The beast was an abomination, a mockery of the beautiful, Golden Stag. Vulcana didn't indulge the nobility with a gentle giant, but a perilous engine of death and despair.

Hunters whimpered and scurried about, making mice of the miserable men. Borelo scrambled up a tree. Obsid and Mark both threw spears. They glanced away, unable to pierce the golden hide. Clovis and Atlanta, a long way off, sprinted towards the rout.

Zeliox charged the beast. But he tripped and fell, falling to the ground. Clovis yelled in anguish as his father was treated to certain death.

Only Atlanta kept her cool. Barely in range, halting to aim, she let a single arrow fly. The missile dug deep behind the monster's ear.

Roaring with agony, the behemoth veered away from the fallen lord, tearing an ugly scar in the frozen turf. Missing Zeliox by inches, it crashed into a stand of willows, making matchwood of the luckless trees.

Lord Duma waddled into battle. "That's no way to hunt!" he mocked. "Watch me!"

The colossus erupted from the watching willows, surprising the fat little lord. Crushing his bones with ivory tusks, it tossed House Duma high into the Air.

Zeliox was on his feet now. Spear in hand, he threw hastily, and off balance. The missile sailed behind the swine...straight into Lady Jingo. The martial lady grasped at the skewer, gazing at the colleague who killed her.

The Hunt was now a rout; the hunters were now the hunted. The braying beast trampled away; spreading cowardice, death and dismay.

Apart from the savage carnage, I dismounted Calypso and grabbed a bow. Atlanta shot another arrow, this one lodging in its shoulder. I fired as well, aiming at its face. My arrow found purchase in its crimson eye, launching the fiend into a frenzied rage.

Keleron threw a spear and missed. Djincar cast one into its flank. The monster belched snorts of pain as he gored a fleeing Gemini. Children cowered in its brutal path when Clovis reached the frantic fray.

He charged with reckless, savage career. Storming beneath the creature's jowls, he plunged his spear into the leviathan's chest.

The fey monster stamped and spewed, shaking the Earth with its thunderous feet. But Clovis would not yield. He thrust his weapon further and further, cleaving its massive, murderous heart.

With a deafening roar and whoosh of blood, the villain finally collapsed, trapping the Tauran beneath an avalanche of flesh.

Clovis struggled to free himself, valiantly heaving against the enormous weight. But the proud nobility, cowered by the monster, could not muster the courage to save him. Instead, they watched in strangled silence as their buried hero smothered and died.

Only one would come to his rescue, only one could quell his fear. Atlanta climbed the mountain of hair, reaching boldly into the quivering mass. Shoving past a yard-long tusk, she pulled at a cloven foot.

A head emerged, gasping for Air. Crimson with blood, covered in hair, he unearthed himself from the grime and gore. Panting for breath, he gazed at his savior, marveling that it was a Gemini girl.

Exhausted and beaten, the nobility crumpled to the ground.

Borelo climbed out of his tree.

A dozen were dead, including Lord Duma and Lady Jingo. All were mourned by some, but Lady Jingo was mourned by all. For the Marshal was well respected, especially by the Taurans and the Aquarians.

None knew the treachery she committed, the plot to kill her best friend. But by a strange twist of Fate, the Marshal was dead…and her treasonous sedition with her.

If Zeliox was sorry that he killed his friend, he hid it well. He laughed as he prowled the grisly field, reliving House Zeliox's victory with surviving friends. For, by a unanimous decision, his son was given the coveted honor of flaying the Golden hide.

But after completing this Herculean task, Clovis did something that changed his life forever…

…he gave the bloody burden to Atlanta.

The proud nobility was outraged as she accepted the precious hide.

"The Golden Pelt is an enormous honor!"

"A tribute to eclipse his disappointing Games."

"Why give it to a title-less freak?

Zeliox's rage was worst of all, shrill against the hallowed wood. "What?!? You're giving the Pelt to a stupid tramp?"

"It is mine to give, my Lord," said Clovis. "She drew first blood and saved my father's life."

Lord Zeliox slapped his son. "Don't talk nonsense! If you don't want the Pelt, then it is mine by virtue that I'm your Lord and father!"

"The prize goes to Atlanta."

Zeliox struck his son again. Clovis caught the blow in his hand.

I did not witness this paternal spectacle. For in the cacophony of the horrid fray, two men, clothed in black, snuck up behind me. A prick in my arm was my only warning, blurring my vision into a dizzy reality. But before the drug could steal me, I got a glimpse of their faces.

I've seen these two before, in the woods of Isolaverde! I remembered the tree branch that felled the one, the God who cowered the other.

Lady Jingo was dead, her destiny cut short by the justice of an errant spear.

Still, these vile assassins, servants of House Excelsior, collected what they came for. Careful to remain unseen, they carried their prize away…

…a long awaited gift for the Volcano God.

Chapter Nineteen

The Death of Pallas

My own captivity, I count as nothing,
compared to the death of my sister, Pallas.

"My Life, Reflections of Elena Catagen"

I woke to the sounds of heavy feet and grunting men. Straining against the ropes that bound me, I looked into the cold, cruel eyes of Alexander.

"Glad you've joined us, Water Weird."

I did not answer. Instead, I drew an empty breath, gasping to quench my aching lungs. The Air was thin, the Sky resting on a blanket of clouds.

"My, my," said Alexander. "You have had a rough semester. First, my javelin; then, the Circus, and now…"

"Have you forgotten about the Eternal Flame?" I offered. "You looked a real idiot, running around the Center Lawn with your hair on Fire."

"Aha!" he exclaimed. "I *knew* it was you!" He admired me for a moment, a hunter glorying in the majesty of a trapped lion. "My, my…but you *have* been busy."

"Busier than you think," I said, pressing my brief advantage.

"But that does make this all *so* sweet," he shivered. Or perhaps it was the Wind. I was absolutely freezing. He wore a heavy coat, while nothing but a thin tunic covered my trembling frame. "It's been such a joy planning your destruction. Ever since that night upon Isolaverde…"

For a moment, he donned a haunted face, involuntarily placing a hand over his heart. It was surprisingly eerie and almost sad, his vile conceit softened by anguish. But then he recoiled the guilty hand. "But you mustn't think I deserve *all* the credit. Oh, no. I've had loads of help. Dusan for one," he said with eager eyes, lapping up my astonishment like a cat over spilt milk. "It was he who sabotaged your chariot, not Eunice."

Dusan?

"Not that I'm not grateful. Wouldn't have won the Circus without him. But that wasn't part of the plan, and Uncial nearly discovered…"

"But why frame Eunice?"

The mirthless Wind stole his laughter. "To let you think the danger had passed! To protect our traitor, moron that he was. Dusan nearly ruined everything. But it's just as well. The worthless slime-ball died during the Hunt, and good riddance."

I turned my eyes and looked away, far away from that evil face. Then I surveyed my jailers. I was tied to a litter carried by soldiers.

How could I have been so stupid? All this time I've been worried about Uncial and Othello, when it was the Leos and Taurans who've been after me! And the Aquarian traitor was Lord Duma, not Uncial!

"But…why did the Marshal betray the Chancellor?" I said.

"It was you, really, who turned her to our side. You, and that bit of 'reading' you did for Lady Uncial."

Again, my jaw dropped.

"Oh, yes, Pallas. We know about that too."

"But how?"

"Pallas, dear, I can't give away all my secrets. I have spies as well as you, though none as efficient as yours, I dare say."

He paused a moment with this bold announcement, hoping for another reckless response.

For once, I didn't answer, biting my lip instead.

"Anyways, Jingo didn't like this reading nonsense. No, not at all. Called it…a sacrilege!"

Again, I held my feeble tongue, a flurry of doubts whirling through my head. It carried so many daring burdens, so many gifts of wanton pain. Yet none of my miseries had ever destroyed me, not till I learned how to…

…*read!* I hissed the deplorable word. *Reading has destroyed me.*

Whatever his true intentions, whether it was for good or for ill, Othello had doomed me by teaching me how to read.

"We were ever so disappointed when you didn't ride to the Hunt this morning. But you never fail to please. I simply *love* that about you, Pallas, darling."

I gnashed my teeth, but did not speak.

He enjoyed another pitiless laugh, one the Wind was powerless to steal. "Imagine my surprise when the Marshal seized Elena as well!"

No!

"Yes!" He brandished a triumphant fist. "The Marshal's men caught her, trying to rescue the Mistress of the Sea! Now she's locked in a dark dungeon, deep within the bowels of Turner Hill!"

I collapsed my head upon the loathsome litter, unable to support its heavy weight. Too stunned to move, too sick to breath, I quaked with mounting agony.

"How else did you ride to the Hunt so easily? How else did you elude the entire Corps? The Catagen jewel eased your escape with her own foolish sacrifice!"

No!

"What made you flee from your hiding place? What made you race to your doom? Was it Fate that sent you? Divine intervention, perhaps?"

I ignored his horrid questions. Instead, I wrestled with my own. *How could I have let this have happened? If I really am a God, why did everything go wrong? Did my father's blood spoil the divine?*

"Or…was it someone else? Do tell, Pallas, dear; was it your wicked little spy?

That cat! I whimpered. *That darned cat! He tricked me into coming, just like he did on Isolaverde!*

"Treachery!" he recited with theatrical flair. "It's such a melancholy word. Do tell us who she is, won't you, Pallas, dear?"

But something in his words didn't ring true. Something in his query told a lie. He was fishing for an answer.

I steadied my intellect, biting back my fear. "Where am I?"

"You don't know?" he howled with idiotic glee. "You're at the mouth of Volcano. Behold your funeral pyre!"

I looked up and saw the rounded crest of a gigantic ring. Black rubble littered the landscape, lava vomited from ages passed. A sickly cloud billowed from the maw, white ash and the stench of rotten eggs.

Too frightened to watch, I gazed at the caravan of Excelsior soldiers. Lady Oxymid was at its bitter end, her wheezing betraying a woman too old to climb mountains such as these.

The grunting men reached the crest. Heat engulfed my freezing frame. Though my body welcomed the warmth, my spirit loathed it, fearing the Fire like a mortal enemy. The soldiers roughly loosened my bonds, forcing me to stand upon the jagged rim.

Flames burned with ceaseless anguish, tempests of angry, liquid steel. The heat soared my hair over my shoulders, as I stared wide-eyed at the molten ferocity. The Wind corralled the clouds around me, blanketing me in a cellar of impenetrable doom.

"I'm not going to die!" I boldly announced. "Poseida will rescue me!" That was the last hope I'd enjoy as I stood upon my ruin.

"What?!?" jeered the prince, maniac with relish. "Do you think you're going to be rescued, here in the mouth of Volcano? You stand in the Realm of the Indomitable Flame. Neither Poseida, nor her minions, dare tread *these* hallowed halls!"

For once in his life, the boy spoke true. Just like that, my hope faded.

I'm truly alone.

Just then, a whiff of sun disturbed the darkness. On the edge of Fire and death, a breeze cleaved a window into my horrid perdition. There, in the light that shone through the chasm, I saw the mouth of a dancing river; a tiny fishing village, nestled upon a gentle shore.

I cried a single tear. *What cruel Fate shows me my heart's desire, just as it's taken away?* I cherished the tear as it pressed upon my lips, a gift of precious Water, given up by my thin, frail body.

But if the light meant to comfort me, it could not combat the power of dread. Clouds of cinder bellowed from the maw, as if angry at the light…determined to keep it from me.

Just like that, my vision was gone.

"We have visitors!" Alexander proclaimed.

Awakened from my loathsome nightmare, six chariots rose from the blaze. Black leather glistened in the glow, adorning the God in a snake-like embrace. His long, blond hair billowed in the Air, lifted by the heat from the abyss below.

"Is this her?" asked the God, confident of Alexander's reply.

"Yes, my Lord God Mulciber," bowed the submissive boy, as if eager to make amends for his failure on Isolaverde.

"I have come too," gasped Lady Oxymid.

"You are not the Lady Jingo. Where is the Marshal?"

"She has died, my Lord God...in the Hunt."

Mulciber snorted. "I see. Such is the lot of mortal man."

"My Lord God," whimpered Oxymid, "what of the forces of Poseida? Uncial and Catagen escaped from the Hunt."

I breathed a sigh of rapturous relief. *My sacrifice was not in vain! Lord Catagen escaped!*

But the God's reprisal filled me with terror. "*Never* mention that name in my presence!!!" he riled, pointing his finger at the lady of Capro Bay.

Oxymid shrieked for mercy, sharing the pain that Alexander suffered on Isolaverde.

The Excelsior prince clutched at his heart.

"You tread upon the holiest of holy grounds!" bellowed the God. "What do I care for your pitiful lives?"

Oxymid writhed on the rocks. The leathered men chuckled. An albatross flew amongst the putrid clouds, its caw a whisper amongst the roaring Flame.

The beautiful God set his eyes upon me. "So, Water Witch...we finally meet. Pallas, I've heard mortals call you. Yet I call you another name...Pyrrha."

He said the name as if it were important, as if he had chosen it with care. I was too terrified to ask what it meant, too petrified to even speak.

"Look upon your doom, Pyrrha, and despair. For such is the fate of any mortal, God, or drone, that dares to defy my omnipotent will. Look, fair princess, into the Indomitable Flame!"

He gestured to the boiling lava. As if on cue, a tongue of Fire leapt from the abyss. The great God laughed, an echoing jeer that lilted into a cruel contralto.

I blinked my eyes at the stinging ash that rose around me and floated away...

And floated away!

What did Archimedes say? I gasped, racing back to my science class. *Heat makes things rise, light things. Things with feathers. Things with wings!*

I felt the harness on my back, grasping the handles of the AERO-FOIL. *I always thought they were fins, like that of a manta ray. But what if they're not? Didn't Archimedes talk about Aero-whatsit? Didn't he talk about flying?*

I looked across the crest of Volcano. The albatross circled over the broken mantle. "Why are you here?" I murmured aloud. "Shouldn't you be near the salty Sea?"

"Now, princess, kindred though you be, I give you choice. The choice I gave your mother. To serve me forever. Or suffer the fabled fury...of the Lord God Mulciber!"

I stared, confused, at the gleeful God. *What is he saying? Is he offering me a way out?*

But then I remembered my years of pain. Reckless hate emboldened me.

"What have you done with my Mother?!?"

The God smiled. "She's alive...and suffering. Imprisoned for all time in a cell of my own choosing."

I frowned, the corners of my mouth tugging at my chin.

"What say you, princess of the Sea? Shall Poseida's granddaughter share her daughter's bane? Shall I have a new trophy? Or...shall you taste the Indomitable Flame?"

The leathered men laughed at the stupid riddle.

I scoured madly for the answer to my own.

A breath of Wind rustled through my hair as I ripped off my tunic.

It took a fantastic leap of faith to think that bit of canvas could make me fly.

I made that leap...

I fell...like a limp, rag doll...

...into the hell below.

Hot gas choked me, stung my feeble eyes. The heat was now an inferno. I reached for the magic handles and pulled...hard.

The fins unfurled, then…

Nothing!

Head and arms pointing downwards, I plummeted to my Fiery doom. *I'm not a God! I'm not immortal! I'm going to die…here, in the mouth of Volcano!* I raised my hands in a pathetic attempt to reach the Sky…

Wumpfh! jolted the wings.

"Caw!" shouted the bird.

"Huh!" I cried, my horrid descent coming to a miraculous end. "I'm flying!" I rasped, raising my arms to the salvation of the Sky.

But the putrid gas was killing me, scorching my lungs with its poisonous soot. I stared at Volcano's rim, bulging my eyes with despair.

I waited too long! I'm not going to make it!

But the albatross darted into the violent mist. I followed, expecting to crash into solid rock.

The wall of obsidian glass gave way to hot, scalding mist – wet, not acrid; warm, not steaming; cool, then cold.

"Woohoo!" I laughed, surveying the mirth of sun-lit clouds! I was flying…soaring…in footless halls of sacred Air!

Thousands of feet above the planet, vibrant colors decorated my birth: the green of the pinewood forest, the blue of the gurgling river, the endless strand of sugar-white sand.

"I'm free!" I cried, lungs feasting upon the cold, clean Air. "I'm going home!"

The albatross stayed right beside me, banking into a nearby cloud. Instinctively I followed as a bolt of steel zoomed past my head.

The chariots!

Panicked, I strayed inside the misty refuge. The blinding white surprised me, the freezing fog clinging to my body.

How long I hung there, held aloft by the magic of the Gods, I could not tell. Shivering with cold, Wind blasting my naked frame, I squinted against the brutal glare.

Yet I thanked Poseida for creating these clouds, this Water in the Air to hide me.

Slowly, eventually, I broke into the clear. By some outrageous stroke of chance, or perhaps the magic bird, I was directly over the Titan River. Kelly Tree was just a few miles ahead. So was the gentle Eastern shore.

But angry chariots swarmed around me, cannons blazing as they came.

I shrieked. The speed of the chariots was unbelievable. Desperate, I pulled the handles, retracting the wings back into the divine harness. Falling irreverently to the ground, I offered yet another prayer.

Please, Grandmother! Help me!

The plummet bought me a few seconds of life. The fey chariots missed their target, firing wildly as they whisked past. But then they circled round and round me, rocketing towards their fallen angel.

Cold Wind iced my joints, causing me to wince.

The cannons spoke again, missing left, then the right. One caught my windblown hair.

Hopelessness overwhelmed me as I fell towards my doom. *Even if I make it to the ground, how will I escape? I can't outrun those chariots.* Still, I had to try.

The magical cars buzzed around me in a blazing ring of death and despair. Yet this time, they did not Fire. Instead they circled patiently, as if hoping to see me splat.

But I wasn't in an entertaining mood. Screaming like a Banshee, I pulled the handles…hard.

The savage jolt rankled my limbs…

The engineer who designed the harness would have been quite proud. For he developed the AERO-FOIL to open in a free fall, insisting on using a slightly heavier canvas to withstand such brutal abuse. The arguments he made in committee, a few hundred years ago, bought me a few more seconds of life. The wings held, the canvas filled, as I gently floated towards the rushing river.

The ice-cold wetness was a shock. I gasped aloud and retracted my wings, treading mournfully in the welcome Water. I'd made it farther than I'd thought possible. Yet…in the end, I failed. Knowing what was coming next, I resolved myself to die.

I cried no tears of sorrow or regret. Instead, I glared at the ring of cannons, and the beautiful, victorious, magnificent God.

"A clever trick," he told me, lowering his chariot to the level of my head. The other chariots followed the God, hovering inches over the bristling river. "Witch, they call you...a caster of spells. I see the name suits you."

"You'll find I'm full of surprises!"

"I underestimated you, Pyrrha. I shan't do that again. Still, you are beaten...broken...down to your very last breath. Pray to me now, and breathe yet again."

I gasped a mouthful of Air, savoring the sweetness of the towering pines. Each breath was precious now, each a hope of yet another. I breathed in and out, in and out, over and over, faster and faster...

"I'll never bow to you!!!"

The handsome God frowned. This wasn't what he expected. "I gave you the choice of life, yet you have chosen death." Looking dramatically into the bright blue Sky, he tossed his mane with triumph.

"Let the heavens witness my victory in this blood feud! Let the depths of Erebus bury her soul. Let the Sirocco Winds of Aeolia tell my glorious tale! Let the halls of Volcano sing my praises! Let the slime of Atlantis gnash their teeth and wail. I...the Lord God Mulciber...Prince of the Eternal Fire...Bearer of the Sacred Flame! Victorious...yet...again!"

He garbed a smile and pointed his finger.

I frowned my face as I chose to die.

Yet the ray did not reach me, nor did I feel its agonizing pain.

Instead, an owl-like creature buzzed amongst the towering pines. Instead, my swimming legs collided into something quite hard. Instead, a chariot surfaced beneath me, encrusted with coral and silver and pearls.

The owl-like creature ceased its dancing, gazing at me with mechanical eyes.

Men with savage good looks gathered around me – impossibly blond with ice-blue eyes.

Bewilderment marred Mulciber's face. For the Volcano God suddenly realized...he was no longer in the realm of Fire...

...but that of Water!

"You're victory is gone, fell foe!" boomed a commanding voice. From somewhere beside me, a muscled arm wrapped around my shoulders. "The Lord God Poseida, Queen of the Unquenchable Sea, claims this child...as...is...her...right."

Mulciber brandished a dangerous sneer. "You have no right, Triton! *I* claim her as blood feud!"

"Blood is the Realm of all," said the burly God. His hair was a tangle of platinum blond, his face, a portrait of conviction. A golden crown graced his brow with sapphires and emeralds too numerous to count. "Yet you tread in the Realm of Water. Here, Mighty Poseida shall have her way."

"Back, you fool, or I'll destroy you all," came Mulciber's simpering reply. His once-proud voice was rattled with fear.

"Look around you and see," said Triton.

Mulciber surveyed the frightening scene. The Prince of Fire was surrounded by mermen, riding dolphins and Orcas and whales.

"None can die, or many," said Triton, in a rich baritone that warmed me to my toes. "Now...I give *you* choice."

The Volcano God was hot with rage, ugly veins popping out of his neck. He donned a hateful glowering scowl, as if steeling himself to battle...

...when his sense of preservation seemed to hold sway. Garlanding a winning smile, he feigned an Air of casual indifference. "I bid you adieu," he jauntily replied. "Until we meet again."

"Till that unhappy day," said the Prince of the Sea.

"As for you, young Witch," sneered the Fire God. "I'll send your regards, to dear mother!"

I was too astonished to speak.

The chariots of Fire jetted away, retreating to the safety of Volcano.

Triton turned his chariot downstream, following the flow to the vastness of the Sea.

Too shocked to form words, too grateful to do anything, I silently watched the Godly parade.

Summoned by mermen and their conch-shell horns, the inhabitants of Kelly Tree gathered by the river. Children laughing, parents singing, they bustled to watch the divine array.

I marveled at the merry crowd, certain that no one would recognize me as the slave from Kelly Tree, when I met eyes with a certain old blacksmith: the old man I truly loved the best...

My father wore a grateful sigh, tears splashing down his ancient face.

My teenage heart tore asunder, tears glistening my youthful face. *I'm going to be with Father again! Together, we'll find my mother! Everything's going to be all right!*

But the chariot didn't stop in Kelly Tree. Instead, it waded into the churning waves.

I looked up at the handsome God. "Please, Sir. May I…may I get out?"

"No," said Triton. "You may not."

"But why?" I gasped, startled at yet another change in my fortunes. "Where are you taking me?"

"I'm taking you home, Diandre."

"My name is Pallas."

"No longer," he pleasantly replied. "That name is dead. For it was born of a mortal, not fitting for one who abides in Heaven…or the Deep."

He plunged the chariot beneath the billowing brine.

I jumped with shock, sure the Water would drown me. Yet the sacred car stayed completely dry.

Inky darkness completely engulfed us. Powerful lights beamed into the blackness.

Dolphins and whales – in a carnival of shapes and sizes – escorted us down, down into the crushing Deep. How far down, I could not guess.

Far below me was a city of glass, dazzling in its jeweled extravagance. The Ocean floor was littered with lights – its myriad of colors, a sparkling enchantress.

"Behold your home!" said Triton, his majestic baritone rumbling through my soul. "Behold, the Glory…of Atlantis!!!"

…to be continued in "The City of God"

Appendix

AEOLIA: Home of the Air Gods.

ARCHIPELAGO: Fourteen islands, arranged along an "S" shaped pattern, which make up the known world.

ARGO: Warship commissioned to House Tel (Air).

ARIEN IV: Fire Lady.

ATLANTA: Winner of the Hide of the Golden Boar. An Aeolian Token.

ATLANTIS: Home of the Water Gods.

BLAINE, KENDAL: *see Vulcana.*

BISMARCK: Warship commissioned to House Rance (Earth).

BONNIE: Water Goddess. Daughter of Poseida.

BULL, THE: *see William Catagen.*

CANNES III: Water Lord.

CAPRO BAY: Capital of House Oxymid. The city where Pallas made her appearance upon the Golden Egg.

CATAGEN I: Water Lord. Massacred during the Rape of Piraeus.

CATAGEN II: Water Voting Member. Won Voting Chair from House Duma. Commodore of the Three. An Atlantian Token.

CATAGEN, CASEY: Twin daughter of Dewey.

CATAGEN, DEWEY: Captain of *Hornet.* Second son of Catagen II. Father of Elena, Casey, and Lucy. An Atlantian Token.

CATAGEN, ELENA: Daughter of Dewey. Kidnapped by Excelsior II.

CATAGEN, LUCY: Twin daughter of Dewey.

CATAGEN, TIBERIUS: Captain of *Enterprise.* Third son of Catagen II. Discovered the Continent.

CATAGEN, WILLIAM: (The Bull) Captain of *Yorktown.* Eldest son of Catagen II. Father of Clyme. Grandfather of Oliver and Genevieve.

CENTER LAWN: The lawn in the middle of the circle-shaped University. Second holiest spot on the planet.

CINDY: Childhood friend of Pallas. A drone.

CIRCUS: Last and most popular event of the Games. The winner has the honor of driving the Golden Chariot during the post-Games parade.

CONTINENT: Vast, unexplored landmass across the Western Sea.

CORPS, THE: Army sworn to protect the *Zoo.*

CORSAIR III: Fire Lord. Warden of the Southern Sea *(Yamato).*

CYPRIS: Water Goddess. A genetic creation.

DEME (YINGQUI VITALIS): Queen of the House of Wonders.

DEMES: Healers. Followers of Deme.

DIO: A University professor. Coach of the Water team.

DJINCAR III: Air Lord.

DRONE: A slave.

DUMA III: An Atlantian Token. A lover of Cypris. Killed by Mulciber II on Volcano.

DUSAN I: A Water Lord (third to House Duma) who succeeded Duma II. Warden of the Northern Sea *(Hood)*. Betrayed his brother (Duma III) to Mulciber I. Lost his Voting Chair to Catagen II.

DUSAN II (DUMA IV): Teenage Water Lord (fourth to House Duma) who succeeded Dusan I. Warden of the Northern Sea *(Hood)*. Killed in the Hunt for the Golden Boar.

DUSANA: Child Water Lady (fifth to House Duma) who succeeded her brother, Duma IV. Warden of the Northern Sea *(Hood)*.

ENTERPRISE: Warship commissioned to House Catagen. One of the Three. Captained by William Catagen.

EREBUS: Home of the Earth Gods.

EXCELSIOR II: Fire Voting Member. Lord Defender of the Titan. Grandfather of Alexander. Made Turner Hill the wealthiest city in the world. Responsible for the Rape of Piraeus. A Volcano Token.

EXCELSIOR III: Fire Voting Member. Lord Defender of the Titan. Father of Alexander. Started the War of the *Zoo*.

EXCELSIOR, ALEXANDER: Son of Excelsior II. Won the University Circus twice. A Volcano Token.

EUNICE: A minor princess of House Uncial. Teen friend of Uncial IV.

FLETCHER: Brother to Gauntle III. An officer aboard *Yorktown*.

GAMES, MENAGERIE: Played once every four years by any drone. Includes 10 events.

GAMES, UNIVERSITY: Played once a year by the children of the nobility. Includes 10 events.

GANYME III: Air Lady.

GANYMII: Capital of House Ganyme. Smaller of the twin cities.

GAUNTLE III: Earth Voting Member. Lord Master of the Pass. Father of Oliver and Genevieve.

GAUNTLE, CLYME: Wife of Gauntle III. Daughter of William Catagen. Mother of Oliver and Genevieve.

GAUNTLE, GENEVIEVE: Teenage daughter of Gauntle III. Great-granddaughter of Catagen II.

GAUNTLE, OLIVER: Teenage son of Gauntle III. Great-grandson of Catagen II.

GEMELLO III: Air Voting Member. Lord Defender of the Twins. Mother of Borelo.

GEMELLO, BORELO: Teenage son of Gemello III.

GEMINUS: Capital of House Gemello. Larger of the twin cities.

GERARD VII: Father of Pallas.

GOLDEN EGG: Raft on which Pallas, pushed by a pod of dolphins, first appeared in Capro Bay as the Mistress of the Sea. Historians mark the event as the advent of the Great Catastrophe.

GREENSTONE: Capital of the nobility. Seat of University and the *Zoo*.

HEALERS (DEMES): Followers of Deme.

HOOD: Warship commissioned to House Duma (Water).

HOUSE OF WONDERS: School of the Healers on the island of Solüt.

HORNET: Warship commissioned to House Catagen. One of the Three. Captained by Dewey Catagen.

HYPERIUS III: Fire Lord.

ISOLAVERDE: A tiny island situated in the southern loop of the "S" shaped archipelago. The site where Pallas first escaped Mulciber II.

JESTERS: Clerics of the Gods

JINGO III: Earth Voting Member. Marshall of the Corps. Betrayed Uncial III. Died during the Hunt for the Golden Boar.

JOCULO III: Water Lord.

KASSAN: A member of the Sixth Column. Sent written messages to Uncial III from the Continent.

KELERON IV: A minor prince of House Joculo.

KELLY TREE: Capital of House Joculo. Birthplace of Pallas.

LIBERION III: Air Lady.

LILY TIDEWATER: *see Poseida*

MARSHAL: Commander of the Corps.

MED III: Water Lady.

MENAGERIE: *see Games*

MISER II: Air Voting Member. Chief Justice of the *Zoo*.

MULCIBER I: Fire God. Son of Vulcana. Father of Mulciber II.

MULCIBER II: Fire God. Son of Mulciber I.

OPHELIA: Teenage daughter of Oxymid III.

OTHELLO: Cat who mentored Pallas. Part of the Sixth Column.

OXYMID III: Earth Lady.

PALLAS (DIANDRE): Harbinger of the Great Catastrophe. Mistress of the Sea.

PENTATHANONS: The Five Gods who defeated the Tighs and populated the world with drones. Poseida (Water), Vulcana (Fire), Terra (Earth), and Zephyr (Air) brought together by Deme (Life). Water and Fire were opposites, as well as Earth and Air.

POSEIDA (LILY TIDEWATER): Queen of the Sea. Mother of Teresa, Rhodes, Bonnie, and Triton. Grandmother of Pallas.

QUID IV: Fire Voting Member. Treasurer of the *Zoo*

RANCE II: Earth Lord. Warden of the Western Sea *(Bismarck)*.

RHODES: Water Goddess. Daughter of Poseida.

SALAMADRO III: Fire Lord.

SHIVA: *see Teresa.*

STROMBOLI, AQUILO: *see Zephyr.*

TARTARUS: Spaceship that transported humans to this planet. It crash-landed on the Continent after being hit by a meteor.

TEL III: Air Lord. Warden of the Eastern Sea *(Argo).*

TERESA (SHIVA): Won the War against the Tighs. Imprisoned for defying the Pentathanons.

TERRA I (FERRIS TERRASPOL): King of the Earth.

TERRA II: King of the Earth (second).

TERRASPOL, FERRIS: *see TERRA I*

TESS: Water Goddess. A genetic creation.

THREE, THE: The fleet of warships commissioned to the Commodore. *Yorktown, Hornet,* and *Enterprise.*

TRITON: Water God. Son of Poseida.

TURNER HILL: Capital of House Excelsior. Largest city in the world.

TZU: Deme Voting Member. Master of the Lone One.

UNCIAL I: Water Lady. Founder of the first Great House. First Chancellor of the *Zoo.* An Atlantian Token.

UNCIAL II: Water Lady. Second Chancellor of the *Zoo.* An Atlantian Token.

UNCIAL III: Water Lady. Third Chancellor of the *Zoo.* Member of the Sixth Column.

UNCIAL IV: Teenage crown princess of House Uncial.

UNIVERSITY: School of the nobility. Located in Greenstone.

VIRGON III: Earth Lady.

VITALIS, YINGQUI: *see Deme*

VOLCANO: Home of the Fire Gods.

VULCANA (KENDAL BLAINE): Queen of Fire.

VULCIANA: Fire Goddess. Young daughter of Mulciber II. She was killed when her hover plane fell into the sea.

WARDEN OF THE EASTERN SEA: (Lord Tel) Owner of the *Argo*.

WARDEN OF THE SOUTHERN SEA: (Lord Corsair) Owner of the *Yamato*.

WARDEN OF THE NORTHERN SEA: (Lord Duma) Owner of the *Hood*.

WARDEN OF THE WESTERN SEA: (Lord Rance) Owner of the *Bismarck*.

YAMATO: Warship commissioned to House Corsair (Fire).

YORKTOWN: Warship commissioned to House Catagen. Flagship of the Three. Captained by William Catagen.

ZELIOX III: Earth Lord. Lost Earth Voting Chair to House Jingo. Famous wrestler. Accidentally killed Lady Jingo during the Hunt for the Golden Boar. An Erebus Token.

ZELIOX, CLOVIS: Famous University athlete. Killed the Golden Boar. An Erebus Token.

ZEPHYR (AQUILO STROMBOLI): King of the Air.

ZOO: The parliamentary chamber that governs the world. Holiest spot on the planet.

ABOUT THE AUTHOR

D.C. Belton works internationally and is an elected School Board member from Buckhead, Georgia. When a constituent's son accidentally killed himself texting-while-driving, Belton spearheaded the successful passage of two safety laws to prevent future tragedies. Belton has a passion for literacy and female empowerment.

Learn more about Pallas at dcbelton.com.

Quantity discounts are available on bulk purchases of this book for educational purposes. Please contact Flying Lion Press, P.O. Box 36, Buckhead, Georgia, 30625.

Made in the USA
Charleston, SC
16 February 2015